Blood & Honor, a novel about Bleeding Kansas

By Andy May

Dedicated to
Caleb & Maggie May

A novel about Bleeding Kansas

Blood & Honor

By Andy May

© 2024 Andy May

All rights reserved. No part of this book may be reproduced or utilized in any form or by any means, electronic or mechanical, including photocopying, recording or by any information storage retrieval system without permission in writing from the publisher, except for a reviewer who may quote brief passages in a review to be printed in a newspaper, magazine or electronic publication.

This book is historical fiction. References to historical events, real people, or real places are used fictitiously. Many events described occurred, but they are usually changed to fit the narrative. Some of the characters lived during this period, but their individual stories have been changed in the book, sometimes a lot.

Hardback Version: 979-8-89619-703-4
Paperback Version: 979-8-89619-700-3
eBook Version: 979-8-89619-701-0

Cover art: Maarten Bosch, The Little Shop of Graphics, Almelo, The Netherlands
The cover drawing is from *Beyond the Mississippi; from the great river to the great ocean*, by Albert Richardson, 1867.
The cover map is from the National Archives and Records Administration, item number (NAID) 25464312, circa 1850.

First Edition-

Published by Andy May Petrophysicist LLC, The Woodlands, Texas USA.

Acknowledgements

To my wife Aurelia for her help on the sewing bee and with Maggie's character. I also acknowledge the help on early Kansas food from my sister Melissa May-Uhey, and my cousin Jeremy Pine for his help on our family history. I also acknowledge the help and excellent advice I received from Professor Blake Watson, University of Dayton Law School.

Aurelia, Melissa, my brother Jeff, my cousin Jeff Pine, and Blake all read the book and provided many helpful comments that were nearly all incorporated into the final draft. I also acknowledge my brother for putting up with me when I visited him while researching this book and my previous book on Kansas, and for the frequent loan of his truck that I used to explore northeastern Kansas. I owe them all a great debt.

Other Works by The Author

Climate Catastrophe! Science or Science Fiction?
Blood and Honor: The People of Bleeding Kansas
Politics and Climate Change: A History
The Great Climate Change Debate, Karoly v Happer
The Frozen Climate Views of the IPCC (co-edited with Marcel Crok)

Table of Contents

Acknowledgements   v

Other Works by The Author   vi

Preface   **xi**

Chapter 1: The Move to Kansas   **1**
   Caleb Returns   4
   Caleb and Maggie May   8
   Preparing to move   12
   Staking the claim   16
   Building the cabin   22
   Moving the family   26

Chapter 2: Charley Dunn   **37**
   Billy Cody   37
   Dunn's new job   41

Chapter 3: Atchison   **45**
   Reverend Starr   47
   November 1854   49
   The vote   50

Chapter 4: **Pardee Butler**   **53**
    The Squatter Sovereign   54
    Meeting Pardee Butler   55
    Crossing Missouri   59
    March 1855   62
    June 1855   64
    Pardee's Sermon   66
    Governor Andrew Reeder   68
    The election aftermath   69
    Charles Robinson   71
    A Special Election   76
    President Pierce   78
    One man can do little   79
    Sam and Caroline Moore   82

Chapter 5: **Pardee's trip**   **89**
    This is a memorable day   96
    Big Springs   98
    The Topeka Convention   103
    Jim   105
    Pardee's family   113
    Judge Tutt presiding   115
    The Quilting Bee   118
    A Cold Winter   120
    The Topeka Constitution   122
    Easton   127
    Dunn investigates   137
    January 1856   140
    Blockade!   148
    Retribution   150
    Dr. Stringfellow   156

Chapter 6: **Prepare for War**   **159**
    Atchison   163
    Pardee   165

The Ladies	168
Bitter cold	174

Chapter 7: **Walker**   **179**
The Battle	181
Blue Tail	186
Governor Shannon	190
An impasse	197
Shannon acts	199
Jefferson Davis	200
Colonel Sumner	203

Chapter 8: **Spring, 1856**   **205**
Sam Wood, Esq.	208
The legal case	211
Justice Lecompte	217
Jail	219
Slaves in jail	223
Lecompte's Plan	226
Escape!	231
A feast in Easton	238
Dunn's posse	240
Bill Phillips	248

Chapter 9: **War**   **253**
Dunn and Atchison Plan	255
Old Sacramento	261
The attack	265
Maggie	274

Afterword   **285**
Pardee Butler's Obituary	290
A Testimonial to Caleb May	294

Bibliography   297

About the Author   301

Preface

This book is a work of fiction. Many of the events described did occur in Kansas between 1854 and 1859. However, I've moved most of the events in time and place and nearly all the characters in the book are composites of multiple real people from the time. Some of the characters are entirely fictional, and still others, like Pardee Butler and David Atchison, are real people and portrayed much like they were in real life. Caleb May is a complex composite of himself and others.

Footnotes are provided to identify the source of often heavily paraphrased quotes and to help the reader find additional historical information on some of the interesting events described. Another source of the true events is my second book, Blood and Honor: The People of Bleeding Kansas. It was written more as a literal history, and less a story. The bibliography contains many of the original sources for those interested.

This book tries to explain the confusing, turbulent, and violent times right after the territory of Kansas was formed in an interesting way. It is based on reality, and I have tried to transport the reader into the times described. It is not exactly what happened then, but if I have done my job well, it will give the reader an accurate feel for how and why the events happened.

Andy May, October 18, 2024

Author of Climate Catastrophe! Science or Science Fiction?
Blood and Honor: The People of Bleeding Kansas
Politics and Climate Change: A History
The Great Climate Change Debate, Karoly v Happer
Co-editor of: The Frozen Climate Views of the IPCC

Chapter 1
The Move to Kansas

Above all else Caleb May loved his wife and family, but the bane of his existence was that he could not express his love. He brought his family to a small 40-acre farm in Buchannan County Missouri, near the small town of De Kalb in 1844. The land was rich, the climate was good, but with only 40 acres they barely got by. Caleb wanted more land and a better future for his family and himself.

Caleb was over six feet tall, a striking, muscular, rawboned, and angular man, with skin darkened by working in the sun every day. He had large hands and feet, piercing gray-blue eyes, and wavy dark hair. He was well-known in Buchannan County as a temperance man, even though he had always lived on the heavy-drinking frontier. He was a stern, hard, but soft-spoken man of firm principles, very religious, and fearless. He was known as a dead shot with both a rifle and pistol.

Caleb was not afraid of hard work, in fact he thrived on it. He was on Earth, in his view, to work, provide, and protect. To Caleb, his measure was in the quality and quantity of his work, and how well he provided for, and protected his family.

Many members of Caleb's extended family were already in Buchannan County when he and his family arrived. His older brother Isaac, Isaac's wife Jane, and their children Polly, David, and Elizabeth had moved there in 1839 from Indiana.

In 1854, ten years after they moved to De Kalb Caleb was 38, his wife Maggie was 31, and they already had seven children. The oldest, William was 15, Mary 10, the twins Enoch and Priscila were 8, Sam 5, Catherine 3, and little Isaac had just been born. Caleb and his brother

Isaac's families were a large presence in their small village in western Missouri.

Caleb was sometimes called a "dangerous" man and a man to be feared. However, he was religious and a member of the Disciples of Christ Church. No one wanted to be his enemy, but he was respected and loved by his friends and family. Caleb was a good man, and liked to say, "Whatever I do, I want to do it so well that the world will be none the worse for my having lived in it."

He was usually soft-spoken, but his visage could be intimidating. He was a serious man, not a jovial one. Comedy and small talk were not a part of him.

Maggie was only 15 when she and Caleb married; and only 16 when William was born. Life on the frontier was tough, especially for women. Caleb intimidated nearly everyone, but not Maggie. She knew her own mind and could be just as tough as Caleb when necessary. However, Maggie had a warm and fun side; she was an outstanding hostess, welcomed visitors, and always had time for everyone, especially her children.

Maggie had had seven children in only sixteen years, but she was still an attractive woman. She did not have the time, or the means, to dress well or fix her hair. She wore plain dresses and usually pulled her hair back in a tight bun under a bonnet. She had little jewelry, but she did have a silver hat pin that she wore on nice occasions. She loved that hat pin; it was the nicest thing she owned and a wedding gift from her father. She polished it often, so it shined in the sunlight. The end of the hat pin was decorated with bits of colored glass that gave off a multicolored glow. When she took it out of her hair, she carefully placed it in her pin cushion, with her sewing needles. Her pin cushion was nearly always in use, since she was constantly mending clothes.

When working outside, she usually wore a straw hat that she tied under her chin with a strip of cloth that matched her dress. She was careful to color-coordinate her clothing.

During their time in Missouri, they called themselves Democrats, but they were free-soil Democrats and opposed to slavery. Caleb and Maggie did not drink liquor or beer and did not like those around them to drink. Caleb was well known in Buchannan County for a fierce temperance speech he gave in De Kalb in January of 1854. It was after this speech on the evils of liquor that trouble began.

After giving his temperance speech, and in the dead of the 1853-54 winter when not much work could be done on the farm, Caleb left town to purchase some sorely needed farm implements and to have his plow repaired. There was no blacksmith in De Kalb, and Caleb needed one to fix his plow. He generally traveled to either St. Joseph or Kansas City most winters to buy supplies not available locally and to visit a blacksmith. This year, everything he needed was in St. Joseph, only 16 miles away, so he went there to save time. Kansas City would probably have been a three- or four-day trip because it was 47 miles from De Kalb. A trip to St. Joseph was usually just an overnight trip.

William, Caleb's 15-year-old son, was a handsome young man, with light brown hair and blue eyes like his parents. He was tall and just beginning to grow some muscle on his lanky frame. He will be muscular someday, but not yet. William had never tasted whiskey.

On the day Caleb left, Maggie sent William into De Kalb to purchase a few things they needed. Maggie had the new-born Isaac to care for and could not leave him. She relied on William a lot because Caleb was always working. William was totally devoted to his mother and always ready to help her with anything she needed. Like nearly everyone else, William was intimidated by his father. He idolized his father and loved him, but didn't feel close to him.

As he walked to the store, he passed the local saloon, where three loafers were drinking. They recognized William and knew he was Caleb's son. Charles (aka Charley) Dunn, a big Irish immigrant, turned to his two friends and said, "You know old Caleb is out of town, we should have a little fun with his boy."

Dunn shouted, "William May, come over here."

When William was close enough, they grabbed him and pinned him to the ground. Over the objections of Jacob the bartender, they poured some of their whiskey into his mouth. William was taken by surprise and before he knew what was going on, he had swallowed a lot of it, to avoid choking. The whiskey burned his throat and tasted awful, but he had swallowed enough to get drunk. Laughing hilariously, they let him go. William was humiliated and never made it to the store. He wandered home in an alcohol-fueled fog, without the goods he was supposed to buy for his mother.

Caleb Returns

When Caleb returned home the next evening, Maggie and William told him what had happened. He was furious! He told his friend and neighbor, Pardee Butler, years later, *"you bet I was wrathy!"*

William told his father, "Charley Dunn called me over to the saloon, he was with two men I don't know. That was when they grabbed me, pinned me to the ground, and forced me to drink their whiskey. I still have a headache and feel poorly."

Maggie confirmed it all and added, "The men are still in town and probably still in the saloon. I don't think any of them live in De Kalb."

Caleb said, "I know Charley Dunn, he is always trouble. He is a notorious drunk, a troublemaker, and proslavery. Everything I hate. I especially hate lazy men. Men should always work. Men don't lay about drinking all day in this world! Sloth is a sin; Satan will always find mischief for idle hands."

After a bit of soul searching, Caleb made his decision silently and grabbed a new hickory ax handle from his St. Joseph purchases and said, "I'll take care of it."

Maggie was not afraid for Caleb; she knew he would be fine. But experience had taught her that all actions, no matter how noble and just, had consequences. She said firmly, "Cale, don't kill them."

Caleb paused, then replied quietly and respectfully in an even voice, "I won't."

He saddled one of his horses and rode directly to the saloon. He threw open the door and turned to his friend and fellow Disciple of Christ, Jacob the bartender and asked, "Brother Jacob, who forced my boy to drink?"

Jacob, a small bald man with a full beard, nodded toward Charley Dunn and two other men in the far corner of the saloon. All three of the men then looked up at Caleb, Charley Dunn said nothing, but his face was twisted into a contemptuous smirk. Caleb told them, "You three are about to get a beating, everyone else get out now."

It was a small, rough bar with a dirt floor. The few other customers wanted nothing to do with either Charley Dunn or Caleb May and hurried outside. Jacob stood behind the bar and watched carefully. His hands below the bar held a double-barreled shotgun.

Dunn said nothing, and immediately pulled a large bowie knife out of a leather sheath on his belt and lunged at Caleb, knife hand fully extended. Charley was a big burley man, unkempt with greasy light-colored long hair. He was nearly as tall as Caleb and outweighed Caleb by at least fifty flabby pounds from too much drink and too little work. He knew how to handle a knife and had stabbed people before. He was as rough as they come. His two friends stood back; they were confident that Charley could take care of this farmer by himself.

Caleb saw the attack coming as if in slow motion. This was far from his first fight. He dispassionately analyzed Charley's lunge with the knife in his right hand. Dunn's furious lunge forced him off balance, he had too much forward motion and no control over it. His whole body was fully exposed on his left side. Caleb easily sidestepped to his right, avoiding the knife. Charley tried, but had no way to correct for this, he was too off balance and had foolishly 100% committed himself to attacking where Caleb had been. Caleb bent his knees, lowered the ax handle nearly to the floor, and drove it, two-handed, deep into Charley's gut at a slight upward angle and from Charley's left to his right. This had the intended effect of adding the force of Caleb's ax handle to Charley's motion and threw the knife wielding Charley well away from Caleb. The knife was now too far from Caleb to be a threat. Charley attempted to swing it around toward Caleb, but that only made him lose more of his balance and made it easier for Caleb to drive the ax handle deeper into him.

Caleb was a bit lucky or, maybe skillful, and struck him just under the rib cage in Charley's ample gut. The narrow end of the ax handle went deep into Charley's core. Charley was moving quickly, and Caleb was strong, so the blow lifted Charley off his feet slightly causing excruciating pain. Charley's forward motion, accelerated by the blow, threw his 250 pounds across the room where he landed hard on the dirt floor.

The thrust of the ax handle into his solar plexus was so painful that Charley couldn't even scream, he only managed a grunt. He was immobilized by the pain and his face was twisted in terrible agony. Caleb used his ax handle to pin Charley's arm to the dirt and took the knife from the now paralyzed and newly harmless Charley.

Caleb told him, "You depend on that knife too much, and don't know how to fight." Caleb tossed the knife toward the end of the bar and Jacob picked it up and placed it on the shelf behind the bar, next to his shotgun.

He turned from the retching and collapsed Charley to face the other two. Without any hesitation he swung at the nearest man, who was still shocked that Charley was down. The man managed to get his left arm up which took most of the powerful blow, but the ax handle continued its arc and connected with the side of the man's head, causing his ear to bleed. The blow was hard enough that he raised both of his hands to his head as if to see if it was still on his shoulders.

The third man came out of his shock at the events and lunged at Caleb before Caleb had fully turned to face him. He sent two mostly ineffectual blows with his fists to Caleb's head and shoulder. Caleb ignored the blows, completed his turn, and since the man's arms were still raised, he used both of his long arms to drive his ax handle into the man's midsection. The man brought his arms down and he tried to grab the ax handle, but Caleb's brute strength was such that he knocked the man to the floor.

Charley revived and started a move toward Caleb and in return received the small of the ax handle full in the face, breaking his nose. The blow was hard enough to send Charley's head to the hard dirt floor, where he lay in a pool of his own blood. Then Caleb landed another blow on the helpless Charley's side, near the kidneys. Charley wasn't going to get up soon.

Caleb turned toward the other two, who were helpless and in pain on the floor, and dealt two more blows to each of them, one to the head and one to their midsections, near the kidneys.

Caleb stood back and took a minute to admire his work, then cracked a rare smile. He had only been struck twice in the whole fight and didn't even have a bruise. He turned to Jacob and said, "With any luck, they'll be pissing blood for a week. They won't forget today."

Jacob was wide-eyed and startled, he had never seen Caleb fight before. He'd heard stories from Caleb's brother Isaac but had never seen anything like what he witnessed today. He did manage to say, "No sir, Brother Caleb, they won't forget. What should I do with Charley's knife?"

The men were all down, in severe pain, and couldn't move. Caleb replied, "Give it back to him when he can get up. Let the Sheriff know what happened next time he is in town. If he wants to talk to me, I'll be at my place."

Turning to the three men on the floor, he warned them, "You will all be OK eventually, but don't forget this beating. If you ever force another boy to drink your spirits again, and I hear about it, you won't get off so lucky next time."

Jacob managed a weak smile toward Caleb, then quickly resumed his normal stoic face. He said, more to himself than Caleb, "It can be difficult to be a bartender when you don't drink."

Jacob then asked, "Are you OK Brother Caleb? I'm sorry I could not stop them from forcing young William to drink."

Caleb nodded and said, "I'm fine Brother Jacob, and that's OK. Just protect your family. You were not the problem, these lazy bums on the floor were the problem."

Caleb felt better and his anger left him. The other bar patrons had returned, and Caleb turned to face them.

He announced in a firm, but calm tone, "Missouri has an optional township temperance law, and you had better find another place to drink liquor because I am going to make sure that De Kalb township becomes dry."

Caleb returned home late that night and told his family what had happened. The younger children were excited and proud of their father for defending William. William felt guilty for not being able to take care of the issue himself and leaving it to his father. Maggie, Isaac, and Isaac's wife Jane were concerned about retaliation. Isaac told Caleb that "You did what you had to do, but Charley Dunn has a bad reputation, and he will not let this go."

Caleb replied, "If Charley is ever sober, he might be a threat, but drunk, as he normally is, he will be no trouble for me to handle."

Isaac replied, "I hope so. Just remember little brother, I have your back. Ask me to help next time, you don't have to do everything yourself."

Caleb just smiled and was grateful for his brother and his whole family. Maggie was glad the saloons would close, she said, "With the saloons closed our town will be safer."

Everyone in De Kalb, especially Charley Dunn, remembered that day. The story spread far and wide that, "You don't mess with Caleb May or his kin."

The Buchanan County Sheriff visited Caleb and William to hear the details of what had happened. Charley and his two friends filed complaints against Caleb for the beating. The event was even written up in the *St. Joseph Gazette*, so the sheriff already knew the whole story, but thought he should talk to Caleb and write a report anyway.

After listening to William, Maggie, and Caleb's stories of the incident, the Sheriff said, "Well, Caleb, that matches up with what Jacob said happened. You did what was needed. We'll let this one go. You watch out for Charley Dunn. I let this go, he will not."

Caleb simply replied, "Yes sir."

Caleb and Maggie May

Caleb met Maggie at church when she was only 15 years old in Decatur County, Indiana. They were married January 4, 1838, just 6 months shy of Maggie's 16th birthday, and just before Caleb turned 22. Caleb had been a frequent guest at their house while he and Maggie were courting, and they all attended the Disciples of Christ Church together every Sunday.

Maggie was slender and much shorter than Caleb. She had long curly brown hair, large bright blue eyes, and just a few freckles across her small nose. She was a beautiful fun-loving young girl, quite the opposite of the serious Caleb. Caleb was entranced with her and wanted to marry her at first sight. Maggie was attracted to Caleb, but cautious at first. She liked that Caleb was serious and stable. He was much more mature and self-confident than her other suitors.

Caleb was entranced with her and enjoyed watching Maggie have fun with her family and friends, although he only occasionally participated, preferring to stand back and watch quietly. There were some problems in their small Indiana community with ruffians and thieves, but they avoided Caleb. Both Maggie and her family felt safer when Caleb was around. After six months of courtship, she found she adored him, felt very safe with him, and with her parents' enthusiastic blessing she agreed to marry him.

Indiana was admitted to the Union as the 19th state in 1816 as a free state and their constitution banned slavery. Slaves could not be bought and sold in Indiana, however there were many slaves and slave owners in the state and the slave state of Kentucky was on Indiana's southern border.

Caleb was born in Kentucky and one of the reasons his family moved to Indiana in 1832 was to get away from slavery. But it didn't work. In Kentucky slaves did all the menial work and if you were a poor white man with only a small plot of land, or no land at all, you had no work, no income, and no future. In a slave state, you could not work your way to the top, you were always poor, your kids were always poor, and you were "poor white trash" forever. In slave states the social classes were immovable and fixed. There was no upward mobility and no opportunity.

The move to Indiana didn't help, although Caleb's family moved from a slave state to a free state, the conflict was the same. The Fugitive Slave Act of 1793, which allowed slave owners to take slaves to non-slave states and to recover escaped slaves from non-slave states, essentially exported the problems poor white men had to non-slave states.

The only difference was that slaves in Indiana were bought in Kentucky or other slave states. Further, some people in Indiana did not agree slavery should be illegal, while others worked actively to help runaway slaves get away from their owners. This caused endless conflict in the state.

Just as he did later in life, after moving to Missouri and Kansas, Caleb helped runaway slaves reach freedom. There were some rough people in Indiana, who were always on the lookout for runaway slaves and those helping them. Runaways were worth one hundred dollars each if they were caught and returned to their owners, more if they were simply kidnapped and taken to Kentucky to be sold. No one could prove it, but slave catchers in Decatur County Indiana suspected Caleb was helping runaways. They confronted him, but he admitted nothing.

In one incident, before Maggie and Caleb were married, but after he began courting her, three bounty hunters confronted Caleb because they had been told he had helped a slave, named Paul, escape from his master. The leader said, "You are Caleb May. You are a slave-stealer, and we think you helped Paul escape. We are here to return him to his owner; you must help us as required by law or receive a beating!"

Caleb simply replied, "I've stolen nothing and no one, and I do not know Paul."

The men then rushed him. Caleb struck the lead man so hard he broke the man's nose and sent him writhing to ground. Caleb next kicked the second man in the groin incapacitating him. Finally, when the third man tried to strike Caleb in the face, Caleb dodged his fist, grabbed it, and twisted it with both hands so hard he dislocated the man's shoulder. Although the three men had simultaneously attacked Caleb, they landed no blows, and all three were incapacitated in a few seconds and required a doctor's care.

This occurred in town, in front of a crowd. When the Town Marshal arrived, everyone's story was the same and Caleb was exonerated. The Marshal immediately demanded the men provide some proof that Caleb had stolen Paul, but the witness they provided would not confirm their story. The Marshal then told the three men they had to leave town.

Word spread like wildfire and afterward few people, proslavery or not, ever confronted Caleb again. Caleb never told Maggie about the fight, but of course she and her family quickly found out about it and discussed it. Maggie's parents wanted to know what she thought about Caleb, would the fight end his courtship?

Maggie thought for a minute, then said, "I love Caleb, and he is in the right in this case. I'm proud of what he did and proud to be his friend. The fight does not matter to me."

Maggie's father said, "OK Maggie, we will allow the courtship to continue but carefully consider Caleb May's actions. Although we consider him to be in the right, and God may consider him to be in the right, this will have repercussions in the future. I predict that you will face hardships due to Caleb's views on slavery, his work to free slaves, and his fighting."

Maggie with the confidence and courage of youth simply said, "That may be true, but so be it."

Maggie and Caleb were married on January 4, 1838, by the Reverend Mathew Elder in their church in Decatur Indiana. Maggie wore a white dress that she had made with her mother's help and a white hat held to her head with the silver hat pin that her father had just given her as a wedding present. Caleb wore his nicest pants and shirt and a dress jacket he had bought for the wedding. He also had a new pair of boots that he shined to perfection.

After Caleb and Maggie married, their years in Indiana were not easy. Five years later, in 1843, things were not going well; and they had a young family to think about. When Caleb and Maggie discussed the issue, Caleb said, "Our problems are not just from the fighting, we are barely getting by. We have little money, and our prospects for a good future here just do not exist. Land is too expensive and all the jobs that I can do are done by slaves."

"Caleb, I agree, we cannot build a good life for us and the children here, we must move."

Caleb replied, "My older brother, Isaac, is doing well in Missouri. I'll ride out there and talk to him about moving and see what we can do."

It took Caleb 15 days to ride from his farm to De Kalb, Missouri. But when he got there, he was pleased. Isaac had a nice farm and quickly found a small farm that Caleb could afford to buy after he sold his farm in Indiana. Isaac told him, "Caleb, the land is rich and besides the 40 acres you can buy, I will let you farm 40 more of my land for a 10% share of your crops. That's 80 acres, twice what you have now. You'll make a good living. Plus, Kansas will be open for settlement soon and it is only seven miles west of here. In Kansas, once it is opened for settlement, you will be able to claim 160 acres and double your land again!"

This was January of 1844, little William was only 5 years old, and Mary had just been born. Caleb had just turned 28, and Maggie was 21. Missouri was a slave state, but to Caleb, Indiana was no different, even though technically it was a free state.

From the time he was born in Kentucky, in 1816, Caleb had always been on the frontier. He had ambition and wanderlust. Even though living on the frontier was hard, the people were rough, and lawmen were rare, it was Caleb's world, it was where he belonged. He often said he was born for the frontier.

The frontier offered hope for prosperity and a better life through hard work. Once he returned to Indiana, Caleb told his wife, "We are poor, but we want better, and we are not afraid to work hard to get it."

Maggie replied, "Yes Cale, we will!"

In the end, Caleb and Maggie moved to Missouri in the spring of 1844, not out of fear, but with hope for a better future. Caleb wanted and needed more land, and he was not going to get it in Indiana. He wasn't afraid of the men he had fought to protect his small Indiana farm for himself, but he did fear for his family's future. If Missouri did not work out, it was inevitable that Kansas and Nebraska would be opened for settlement someday.

Preparing to move

In the winter of 1853 and 1854, De Kalb township had many saloons, but the law allowed the saloons to be closed as a public nuisance if a majority of the men living in the township signed a petition directed to the local court. True to his words in the De Kalb saloon after he beat up Charlie Dunn and his friends, Caleb jumped on his horse and with fierce determination rode the township up and down until he had enough signatures to close the saloons. Caleb was normally a kind and quiet man, but few could face his determination and, undoubtedly, many men signed the petition because they dare not refuse. Besides, the populace was disgusted at how poor William May had been treated, it was long past time to close the saloons. As Jacob explained to his patrons before he shut down his saloon for good, "We don't need riff-raff like Charley Dunn loitering about the town and causing trouble."

After the last De Kalb township saloon was shuttered that winter, Caleb began to plan the move to the Kansas Territory. After negotiating a deal with the Indians living in Kansas, the Kansas-Nebraska Act passed the Senate on March 3rd, 1854, and the House of Representatives on May 22nd. The act formally opened the Kansas Territory for white settlement when it was signed by President Pierce on May 30th, making it the law of the land.

Caleb spent a lot of time in Kansas during the winter of 1853-54 looking for the perfect homestead claim for his family. He wanted the full 160 acres that he could claim in Kansas. He explained what he was feeling to Maggie, "We have outgrown this tiny 40-acre farm, and the additional 40 acres Isaac lets me farm. We need more. In Kansas, according to the new homesteading laws, we can claim an additional 160 acres for a future town. That is a total of 320 acres, larger than anything we could imagine anywhere else!"

Maggie wholeheartedly agreed and said, "Sounds grand! I'm with you, we should do it."

Caleb conducted his searches of eastern Kansas alone or with his son William. There were informal ferries available to cross the Missouri River near Rushville and Iatan, Missouri and Caleb also made a small boat that he kept near Rushville so he could cross even when ferries were not available. The area he explored was small enough that he usually had no need to get his horse across the river.

Caleb eventually chose a location near Stranger Creek, about three miles northwest of present-day Cummings, Kansas, and 10 miles from the Missouri River. It was perfect, he found some high ground south of Stranger Creek and between the head waters of two small tributaries. After carefully studying the land and drainage, he was pretty sure that Stranger Creek would never go dry. He also suspected that the two tributaries would nearly always have water in them. This suggested that he would not have to dig very far to find water next to his planned cabin.

Importantly, the claim was far enough inland from the Missouri River that few other settlers would be interested in it in the early days. The early settlers would all try to get land close to the Missouri River, this would give Caleb time to improve his claim and firmly define its boundaries, he did not want to contend with claim jumpers and cross-claims, if he could avoid it.

In March, right after the Kansas-Nebraska Act passed the U.S. Senate, Caleb and William went to the area Caleb had selected. He explained to William, "We want to stake two adjoining 160-acre squares, one for our farm and one for a future town."

Standing on the top of the gentle hill between the two tributaries, Caleb told William, "Our cabin must be on high ground, but as close to water as possible. We also want trees close by for wood and access to these limestone blocks." As he said this, he pointed to a block of limestone jutting out of the ground nearby.

The tributaries were lined with oak, walnut, and cottonwood trees on either side. Caleb judged that they would reach water after digging a 30- or 40-foot well.

Caleb explained, "Our cabin will be on our claim, but on the southern border of the town. The well will be in front of our cabin, but inside the town. A good, high quality accessible well will attract settlers to the town and sell town lots."

Preparing to move

"If there is trouble, we will have the high ground when defending the house. Also, the high ground protects us from flooding during heavy storms."

With the homesite selected, Caleb told William, "Both the claim and the town will be one-half mile on a side. A half mile is about 1000 paces."

Caleb pulled his old, decrepit, but working Dutch compass from his pocket and, standing on the site, found due west. He told William, "That is west, pointing to the compass and the direction. Our home will be south of where we are standing, and the well will be north."

He continued, "William, take the compass and pace off 500 steps west and keep on as straight a line as possible. I will watch and warn you if you change direction."

William took the compass and oriented himself, so he was facing west. Then he said, "Father, I'll walk toward that tall tree in the distance, it is due west."

Caleb replied, "Good idea son, 500 steps, a quarter of a mile."

William set off counting each step and keeping lined up with the tree he had selected. Caleb stood on the home site and made sure that William stayed on a straight line. At 500 steps, William placed a pile of rocks and a stake. Then he returned and guided his father as he did the same thing moving east. In this way they defined the line between the 160-acre townsite to the north and their future farm to the south. From each end of the line, they repeated the process, both north and south, until they had defined two square 160-acre claims oriented to the compass points. They closed each square by counting the steps between the far north and far south stakes. Each time they needed to make a small adjustment to the staked positions. When they were happy with the squares, they made sure each corner was well marked.

When the government surveyors came through, Caleb knew his lines would not line up perfectly with theirs, but he wanted to have the orientation as close to theirs as possible, it would minimize any lost land due to the official survey. Caleb knew that the official government surveyors would take a year, at least, to reach his claim and "perfect" it, that is officially document it and give him his legal deed. Until then, it was up to him to protect it.

Trees and limestone blocks were abundant on the land. Caleb pointed to these a second time and said, "Son, we will make a kiln and fire the limestone with dry oak. Dry oak makes a fire hot enough to burn this limestone, which looks very pure. We'll mix the burnt lime powder with sand from the creek bed and the light gray clay from that whitish layer in the creek bank to make cement. The cement will hold these limestone blocks together to build a firm foundation, chimney, fireplace and stove for the house. We'll sell the left-over cement and crushed limestone for money."

William asked, "How much can we get for the cement Pa?"

Caleb said, "I've seen a wagon load sold for five dollars son, but it will depend upon the buyer. He may not have money and might want to trade."

William was happy with that, "Gosh Pa, five dollars is a lot of money." Caleb replied, "It is indeed son."

Caleb added, "I don't see any sign that anyone else has been here. This is good, I want no competition or claim jumpers. We need time to build our cabin, get the farm going, lay out and clean up lots in the town. Then we need to register the town with the Territorial government."

He added, "We will officially arrive back here as soon as possible after the Kansas-Nebraska Act becomes law to officially stake our claim and build the cabin."

"Sounds great Pa."

Most prospective Kansas settlers in the DeKalb area of Missouri were planning on settling near Fort Leavenworth, across the river from Weston or farther north in the fertile Salt Creek Valley around the Kickapoo village and Rively's Indian Trading Post. Few early settlers planned on going as far west as Caleb's planned claim, they wanted to stay close to the established towns along the Missouri River for safety and convenience.

Caleb was not part of one of the large groups of settlers, usually called "Squatter's Associations," where the members agreed to support every other member's claim in disputes. Two U.S. Army Majors in Ft. Leavenworth had formed the Leavenworth Association to lay claim to valuable land next to the Fort. David Atchison, for whom Atchison, Kansas is named, formed the Salt Creek Squatter's Association, to lay claim to land near present day Atchison and Kickapoo, Kansas.

Caleb felt no such need for security and struck out on his own to lay claim to an isolated 160 acres, far from anyone else. Caleb's family would have the only claim in the whole 36 square mile Center Township, within the future Atchison County in early 1855. The extra 160 acres he claimed for a town was initially named Ocena, which he sometimes spelled Osena. While Caleb could read, he had great difficulty writing and spelling. He only received about six months of formal schooling before he had to leave school to work on his mother's farm after his father passed away.

Their work was done for now, so Caleb and William returned to De Kalb. William was so excited he could barely contain himself. Not only did he have a great adventure in the vast Kansas wilderness, he had the adventure with his father!

As usual, his father said little and showed little emotion, but he patiently listened as William talked excitedly about the move and their new house and farm. William wanted to be closer to his father and win his approval, but Caleb was a quiet man of few words. Caleb didn't say anything to William, but he was enjoying their time together as well. At home with the pressures of work he didn't get this sort of time with William. It did not escape his notice that William was growing into a man and his time with him was short.

Staking the claim

Before the Sun was up, on May 29, 1854, William and Caleb boarded their wagon filled with the supplies they would need to stake their claim and prepare a cabin for the family, dig a well, and build pens for their stock. President Pierce had not signed the Kansas-Nebraska bill yet but was expected to sign it in the next couple of days. Caleb was tired of waiting, he wanted to be on the land, and have it formally staked when the bill was signed and became law.

They had six oxen pulling the wagon and two spare oxen. They needed the oxen not only to pull the wagon, but also to help clear the fields they wanted to plant. They hoped for a crop of corn before the summer was over and to plant the new Russian Red winter wheat seeds that Caleb had purchased from a Russian immigrant in St. Joseph. Eventually Caleb wanted to grow fruit trees, and he had several seedlings to plant, but it would be years before they produced much fruit. They were also bringing one of their milk cows, a horse, several pigs, and chickens in crude wooden crates. Once they had a cabin built, a well dug, and were well established they would return for the rest of the family. Little Isaac had just been born and he and Maggie were in no shape to move to the frontier.

William loved and respected his father, as did nearly everyone he knew, but he hated leaving his mother behind. His father said it might take them all summer to prepare the homestead for the winter. His mother was still weak from giving birth, and he worried about her. He knew his cousins and Aunt Jane and Uncle Isaac would look after her and his brothers and sisters, but he would still miss them.

Once they were underway, he asked his father, "Pa will everyone be OK while we are gone?"

Caleb thought for a moment, then replied, "I have faith in my brother Isaac, your mother, your aunt Jane, and God son. It is good to worry but you must have confidence in your family and God as well."

Caleb was a stern and demanding father, he expected a lot from himself, and from William. William was strong and capable, but only 15-years-old. He didn't fully realize that to his father he was nearly a man now. William often felt more like a boy, than a man. He was in that cloudy, never-never land between a boy and a man. The boy in him wanted his mother, but he knew he couldn't say that to his father. William knew that his Pa would just tell him to "man up" and quit whining. His thoughts were too confusing and emotional, he decided he should just say as little as possible. He sometimes felt like whatever he said, he would look bad. He sure didn't want that.

William and Caleb rode in silence for a while. Originally, Caleb had expected to travel all the way to Yunt's Ferry, near present-day Port Williams, Kansas and Iatan, Missouri,[1] to catch a ferry that could get his wagon and oxen over the Missouri River, but one of the ferrymen from Yunt's Ferry had brought his ferry north to a point near present-day Rushville, only seven miles west of his farm and near where Caleb kept a small boat. The trip to Yunt's Ferry was farther than the trip to Rushville, but once across the Missouri River, he was much clos-

---

[1] Jake Yunt established a hand ferry near Port Williams, Kansas in 1854.
https://www.kshs.org/p/ferries-in-kansas-part-i-missouri-river-continued/12579

er to his planned claim. This had to be considered in light of the better roads in Missouri. What roads existed in Kansas were crude and stream crossings in Kansas were often not marked and hard to find.

Caleb understood the charge for his loaded wagon and oxen would only be two dollars at the new Rushville ferry, versus three at Yunt's Ferry, so that was where they headed. Besides, Caleb thought there would be many more people crossing the Missouri River at Yunt's Ferry than in Rushville, which might lead to a big delay. The road to Rushville was in good shape, and they made the trip to the improvised ferry landing in less than two hours, arriving before 8AM. Caleb knew there was a new steam ferry that crossed from Weston, Missouri to Fort Leavenworth, but it was too far from De Kalb and too expensive for him to consider using it.

The ferry was just returning from the Kansas side when they arrived. It was a large flatboat with two enormous oars, that were mostly used for steering. Smaller oars were used by the passengers and crew for propulsion, although the boat captain was skilled at using the currents to do most of the work. Eighteen-foot-long poles were used near the shore for propulsion and more precise steering. The wooden boat had a small, covered cabin in the middle, but most of the boat was flat and meant for wagons, teams, and goods. It had raisable ramps front and back for loading and unloading people, wagons, and livestock.

The ferry captain helped Caleb and William arrange their oxen, pigs, horse, and wagon on the boat, then they loaded the cow and chickens. It was done skillfully and there was still room left over. The fee was two dollars as Caleb expected, Caleb paid with two silver dollar coins.

Once everything was loaded, Caleb asked, "Can we leave now?"

The ferryman responded, "We still have some room, I'd like to wait and see if more travelers are coming."

They waited until around 9:30, and no new passengers arrived, so the ferryman set off. He and his crew carefully and expertly guided the ferry through the currents, avoiding sand bars. Only minimal paddling was needed due to good weather and quiet water. They reached the other shore less than half an hour later and sheltered by a large sand bar they were able to easily ground the ferry. They tied up to a large tree and unloaded William, Caleb, and their goods quickly. There was no road, but the ground was flat and firm.

The ferryman and his crew wished them well, and they immediately gathered their team of horses to help pull the flatboat upstream to the western launch point, a makeshift ferry landing. The horses helped, but most of the work was in the poling. The captain coordinated the process by regularly shouting "pole!" Ropes were strategically placed along the shore and on the sand bars to help in the process of moving the clumsy and heavy boat northward against the current. This was a tiring process they would repeat many times that day.

Caleb had tied his small boat to the ferry, so he now pulled it onto the shore and tied it to a large tree to keep it from washing away. He and William would probably need it to return to Missouri at some point. William and Caleb watched the ferry crew work their boat northward for a while and then secured their load and animals, mounted the wagon, and lightly whipped the oxen until they moved toward a barely perceptible path westward. Caleb and William had been here many times and knew the way to their claim.

William asked, "Pa, how are we going to get this heavy wagon over all the creeks? They were easy on horseback or walking, but this wagon could get stuck."

Caleb replied, "The creeks tend to run northwest to southeast in this area and we are moving southwest, so we will cross a lot of them. We need to find places in each creek where the creek bed is firm, and the water is shallow enough for the oxen. They can't swim like a horse can. We must be careful; we can't afford to lose any oxen."

As they set off, William said, "OK, we will be very careful." Then he asked, "Pa, can you teach me to fight?"

Caleb thought for a minute, then said, "William, fighting is sometimes necessary, but always to be avoided, if possible. I'll show you how to fight well, show you how to avoid a fight, and how to decide whether a fight should be avoided or fought. We live in a rough part of the world, I can't always be home, and you are a man now. You will need to protect the family. Fight and shoot, we'll work on both."

Caleb was normally a quiet man, but that day, spurred by William's question, he became animated and discussed fighting and avoiding fighting. He told William what he knew about muskets, rifles, pistols, knives, and hunting. He said, "William, watch your opponent's every move, watch his hands. Try and wait until he attacks, that will be when he is most off balance. Balance and control are everything in a fight. Keep *your* balance, make him lose his. Avoid the attack, strike hard and fast when he has missed and is confused. Think ahead."

He continued, "Most men will not be stopped with one blow, keep hitting them until you know they will not move. When you fight, it is all out. Fight to win. Keep at him until he stops. The most vulnerable places on a man are his nose, eyes, mouth, ears, groin, and kidneys, go for those. Face him sideways, with your right hand furthest from him, keep your arms up, ..."

Caleb shared his experience with his son, and over the next few weeks, they practiced all of it, over and over. William asked lots of questions and Caleb explained everything he knew.

They made plans to go hunting the next morning. Caleb had brought his single shot, muzzle-loaded, flintlock "common rifle" with him, but had left his shotgun and single shot muzzle-loaded flintlock pistol in De Kalb with his brother. Caleb loved hunting and guns; it was his weakness and his skill. He was a crack shot with a shotgun, rifle, or pistol.

William said, "Uncle Isaac said you never miss a shot with a pistol or rifle Pa."

Caleb said, "Your uncle exaggerates a bit son. I have missed before, just not often."

Their hunting would be for deer which were plentiful, and both Caleb and William were excited and looking forward to it. Caleb felt a little guilty since they had so much work to do but wanted to spend some quality time hunting with his son. Besides, they needed the meat, they could not afford to eat their cow, pigs, or chickens, they would need them.

They had set off around 11 o'clock and the claim was roughly fifteen miles from where the ferry landed, but they were in a loaded wagon, traveling over rough country, and progress was slow. The first seven miles west were not bad, the creeks and obstructions they encountered were easily crossed, but when they got to Deer Creek, they had to spend a lot of time searching for a good, safe place to cross. This task and getting across the creek took the rest of the day. It was an unexpected delay and there was no way to move safely at night, so they made camp while there was still light. They were still eight miles from the claim.

This was a huge disappointment, but not long after making camp, Caleb spotted a deer. It was only thirty or forty yards away and he was able to grab his old flintlock. He signaled to William to be quiet and handed him the old gun. Then he whispered, "Hit where the neck meets the body, in the center. Center the hindsight with the foresight, mind the hindsight. Nearly everyone forgets the hindsight in their excitement and shoot high."

William hit the deer perfectly and it dropped right away. Caleb breathed a sigh of relief, and said "Well done, son. Excellent shot!"

He went on to say, "If you strike right where the neck hits the body, and in the center of body, above the fore legs, the deer dies quickly. That way you don't have to chase a wounded deer all over the countryside. We never kill for fun, always for food. Never leave a wounded deer to suffer."

William let out a long breath; he was overjoyed that he hit the deer and was happy to gain his father's approval and praise. "Thanks Pa" was all he could think to say.

Caleb and William quickly gutted the deer and carved out the tenderloins for dinner. They cooked the tenderloins with wild onions, wild oregano, salt, and chopped wild dandelions. They finished off the meal with a dandelion and wild strawberry salad. The wild strawberries seemed to be everywhere. Their dinner was so good, and they were so hungry, they quickly forgot their disappointment at not reaching the claim that day.

After the meal, they used some of their salt to preserve and dry the rest of the prime meat to eat over the next few days and then let the pigs have the rest of the deer. It was a good day, the weather was nice, and they slept well.

They were within eight miles of the claim, and the rest of the trip should not be too rough. Except for crossing Stranger Creek, the worst was behind them. Caleb regretted going to the Rushville Ferry, he saved a dollar but was sure they would already be on the claim if he had spent the three dollars to use Yunt's Ferry.

At first light on May 30th, they set out. As expected, they made good time. Stranger Creek was down, and they found a broad, shallow crossing quickly and crossed it easily even with their fully loaded wagon. They arrived at the hill in the center of the planned claim by early afternoon. Caleb and William excitedly placed their permanent stakes on the markers they had left.

They saw no one, but Caleb expected this. The furious activity was not inland where they were but on the banks of the Missouri River near Fort Leavenworth and opposite Westport, Kansas City, and Weston. These were the areas settlers fought over, Caleb's chosen claim was seven miles west of the river, too far to be considered by anyone else that day.

William and Caleb immediately raised a tent for shelter and began building a chicken coop and a small, fenced area for the pigs. All the farm animals would have to live outside for the time being. Both Caleb and William needed to be on the watch for bobcats, cougars, wolves, and coyotes. They had some milled lumber and a small barrel of metal nails but needed to fell trees for more wood. They quickly got to work.

They did manage to find some time for wrestling and boxing training, as well. All the hard work and training made William much stronger, and he was beginning to fill out, losing his skinny teenage frame. Caleb was a good cook and an amateur nutritionist, he tried to prepare healthy meals every day and had a lot of help from the milk cow, the chickens, and the wildlife. Besides dandelions, strawberries, blackberries, oregano, sage, mint, and onions, they also found plenty of other fruits and vegetables all around them.

Caleb was pleased with William's work and thought the training in fighting and shooting was going well. The time alone helped their relationship. Caleb was so stern and hard, and worked so hard, they had never really bonded during the first fifteen years of William's life. William had always been close to his mother, but until this trip his relationship with his father had been distant, it was respectful, but not close. Now they were becoming close, it felt good.

Building the cabin

Using the oxen and sturdy, thick, and strong hemp ropes, Caleb and William cleared the trees and limestone blocks from a large area needed for the house and garden. Then they built a crude kiln open at the top and on one side. Caleb wanted to make a batch of cement that they could use as mortar around the limestone blocks that would form the cabin foundation.

First, they collected small irregular limestone blocks that were not good for building and crushed them with a sledgehammer. Then they built a hot fire in the kiln. On the fire they placed an iron grate, and on the grate a large metal pot filled with crushed limestone.

Caleb told William, "We must stir the crushed limestone and limestone dust every half hour or so while keeping the fire very hot. This will take six or seven hours, but by then most of the fragments will turn to dust. We'll let the batch cool, fish out any leftover fragments, then add white clay from the bentonite[2] bed in the creek bank, and then thoroughly stir the mixture over the fire."

Caleb insisted, "We must wear gloves when working with the quicklime since it can burn our skin."

While the cement was "cooking" they laid out shaped limestone blocks on the ground to form the lower layer of the foundation. The foundation was a rectangle of about 19 feet × 17 feet. They used string stretched tight that they had "leveled" using a plumb bob to make sure that the top surface of all the lower foundation blocks was flat. Sometimes they had to dig a bit into the ground to set some of the blocks deeper so the tops of all the blocks formed a level and flat surface.

Once the cement was made, they poured some of it into a wooden trough, mixed in washed fine sand and more dried clay to get the concrete to the right consistency.

They used the cement to fill the cracks between the blocks with the cement and put a layer of cement on top of the lower blocks as they added a second layer of blocks. This process continued until the full foundation for the house, a chimney, and a combination stove and fireplace of Caleb's own design were built.

Then they shaped the felled trees they had collected into logs that they used to build the cabin walls and the frame for the roof. Finally, they made split wood shingles to finish the roof. It was hard work, but it was a process they knew well. They had done it before for themselves and for their neighbors.

---

2 Fossilized volcanic ash.

Cracks in the log cabin walls were filled with cement. They had some lumber they had brought from Missouri so they were able to make a wooden floor for most of the cabin, the rest would remain dirt until they could buy more milled lumber.

They did not own any glass windows, so Caleb cut a narrow window on one wall and covered it with oiled paper so that some light would come into the cabin even with the door closed. He also cut another window, opposite the door, for ventilation. This one was uncovered. He made shutters for both windows that could be closed during storms. The cabin door was made with some of the milled lumber they had brought with them.

All-in-all, for their first Kansas cabin, it was nice and sturdy, the interior was 18 feet × 16 feet, which was plenty of room for the eight of them. Eventually, Caleb and Maggie wanted a proper two-story clapboard house made of milled lumber, but that would have to wait a few years.

The final big job was digging a water well. They had been walking to the creeks on either side of their hill for water, but that would not do for Maggie and the others. Besides they needed a well for the town they had planned.

They dug the well in front of the cabin on the town claim, Caleb considered it an improvement to the townsite, to help justify his townsite claim to the territorial government and to make purchasing lots in the town more attractive. The prospective residents would all have access to the well.

It was a two-man operation, one did the digging and the other hauled up the dirt and disposed of it. They worked hard, with a pick and shovel, switching places frequently, but eventually reached water at about 25 feet. It was messy and dirty, but they deepened the well another five feet below the water line.

To help with the process, they used a hand pump to pump water from the bottom of the well. This was the same hand pump that would eventually be used to bring water to the surface after the well was finished.

The final step was to lower shaped limestone blocks into the well to line the sides. This would prevent contaminated water from seeping into the well from the shallow depths. All the blocks were carefully cemented into place.

Caleb made a custom cement for the well. As he carefully explained to William, "We need to make the cement differently for the well because we want it to set and cure underwater. We will fire some of the bentonite clay from the bed in the creek until it is very dry, then mix it with the burned limestone, then fire them together and only add fine sand to the final mixture."

Once the mixture was made, he added wood ash from his oak fire. They lined the well from the bottom to the top, then extended the walls above the surface to protect the water from contamination.

This process took them more than a full week since they had to build the well walls in sections. Each section had to be braced firmly with timber until it hardened before the next section could be built. They couldn't risk having the walls collapse on them. Once the walls were in place and built to three feet above the surface, and well braced, they waited two full days for all the cement to harden properly.

Then they removed all the braces and Caleb lowered William into the well so he could inspect every block and all the mortar looking for cracks and imperfections. He applied more mortar or dug out the bad mortar around each imperfection and reapplied it.

Once they were comfortable with the walls, they filled the bottom three feet of the well with washed fine sand from the creek and lowered the pipe for their hand pump into the sand about a foot. The bottom of the pipe had a steel grid across it and was covered with a very strong, but permeable hemp fabric that would keep sand out of the pipe, but allow water in.

Finally, they covered the well with a sturdy cap made from milled lumber and a tarp and let it sit for a week longer before a final inspection. When it looked like the cement was fully cured, they built the final housing across the top of the well to keep animals and dirt out of it. The final step was to install the hand pump on the exposed pipe coming out of the well.

Caleb was pleased with their work and said, "We did a good job, this well looks perfect. It looks professional and modern. It should supply the whole town with good water for years. We may need to pull the pipe occasionally to replace the cloth filter at the bottom, but other than that it will work fine for a long time."

A pleased and proud William agreed, "Pa, it was a lot of work, but that is the best well we've ever built!"

"William, besides making and selling cement, we are going to have a good business digging and building wells."

"How much can we charge for making a well like this Pa?"

"I don't know son, maybe $50, maybe more, it depends on how deep the well must be. To do this kind of work we would have to charge at least three dollars a day each, plus the cost of the limestone and cement."

"Wow Pa, that is a lot of money. But it sure is a lot of work."

With the well in place, Caleb and William dug a latrine, downhill from the well and only six feet deep. They built an outhouse on top of it and used some of their precious lumber to make two nice seats for the inside, one seat was large for the adults, and one was smaller for children. They built a privacy wall between them. They now had a prestigious "two-holer" and were quite proud of it.

Every week they would lift each seat and shovel in dirt combined with crushed lime to reduce the smell and the fly population. Once the latrine was nearly full, they would dig a new one and move the privy to the new location. The key was to make sure the latrine was downhill and away from the well.

Moving the family

By the time the cabin, corral, pig pen, hen house, a rudimentary barn, smokehouse, and well were finished it was late August. Caleb and William were finally ready for the rest of the family. Caleb would go collect them and bring them to their new home and William would stay behind to care for and protect the livestock from the coyotes and bobcats. They had mostly worked that summer, but William's self-defense training continued. They hunted almost weekly, and Caleb was confident that William could take care of himself.

As he prepared to leave, Caleb said, "William, you've done well since we've been here and I'm proud of you. We've not seen anybody these past few months, but there may be Indians and others around so keep your rifle close. You are a very good shot, but if you have a problem, you must be close to your gun. Keep your knife with you always. Remember all I've taught you."

William replied, "Don't worry Pa, I'll be fine. Just bring Ma and the others here as soon as you can." At that, Caleb took their wagon, four oxen, and his horse and set out for De Kalb.

Since Caleb was alone, he needed to avoid the difficult stream crossings he and William had endured to save a dollar crossing the Missouri River, so he headed southeast to the new town of Port Williams, where Yunt's Ferry was located. It always had two or more ferry boats running. The route from his claim to the new town of Port Williams, was about 13 miles southeast, parallel to the direction of most of the major streams and rivers in the area which made the trip out easier than the trip in. The Rushville ferry was about the same distance, but northeast, which meant crossing more streams and rivers. In addition, the roads to Port Williams were better. Caleb had learned his lesson.

Settlers mostly had not ventured this far from the river yet, and the Indians had mostly moved south to the Delaware land or to Kickapoo or Horton. The Indians were happy with the deal they had made and peaceful. Caleb wanted William to be careful, but he had turned into a good fighter, was an excellent shot, and knew how to handle a knife. Caleb looked back on the past few months with pleasure, he was proud of his son, and happy with their time together.

The trip to Yunt's Ferry was not difficult for Caleb and he made it in less than a day. There were several ferries operating, so he got on board one quickly and only paid two dollars since he had an empty wagon, and only four oxen and one horse. Caleb was pleased, he had expected to pay three dollars. The ferry was over half empty, since most of the traffic was to Kansas, not back to Missouri. With the competition, Caleb figured the ferryman gave him a discount because he did not want to lose a rare customer that was going to the Missouri side.

Once back in Missouri, Caleb was able to use proper roads to make his way to De Kalb, a trip of eight miles, as the crow flies, but it took him most of the rest of the day. He reached his farm after dark, about 9PM, tired but happy to be home. He found his family at his brother Isaac's cabin and had a grand reunion with everyone. Caleb told them all about the new claim, the new cabin, teaching William to fight and shoot, how beautiful and how bountiful everything was.

Caleb was delighted to see Maggie and they hugged and kissed and told each other how much they missed each other. Maggie said, "I feel good Cale, and little Isaac is doing very well, look at him, how healthy and fat he is!"

Caleb also admired his wife and said, "My God Maggie you look wonderful!"

And she did, even after bearing seven children, Maggie was still slender and beautiful. A little gray was showing in her hair, but her blue eyes were as bright as ever. Maggie could be stern, just like her husband, but tonight she was effervescent, full of love, and fun.

Caleb held his new son and said, "He does look beautiful and healthy! Maggie, you are a wonderful mother. Isaac will do fine in Kansas."

Maggie said, "I'm feeling good, and ready to go to Kansas, my goodness Cale, 320 acres! Everyone who moves into our area is going to need your cement, we'll be rich."

Caleb said, "We will! Once we get settled, I will file the paper to incorporate the townsite I staked, which I named Ocena. Our house is on the south end of the townsite and on the north end of our claim. Nothing is final yet, but that is the plan. We can sell the early lots, then incorporate and the early settlers will be officers and share in the profit from the lots and in the expenses preparing lots for sale. William and I dug a nice water well for the town."

They had been cramped on their small 40-acre farm and needed more space and income. They were very poor here, and both Caleb and Maggie wanted better. Caleb had already sold their small Missouri farm to his brother, Isaac, who needed more land, and fortunately had the cash to pay Caleb. Isaac would give Caleb the rest of the money he owed him the next day. Caleb would take some of the payment in goods he needed for the claim, but the remainder would be paid in cash. They were both satisfied with their deal. Caleb had put a lot of work into that small Missouri farm but made a tidy profit when he sold it to Isaac.

Caleb explained to Isaac, "Mostly what I need is milled lumber, another barrel of nails, gunpowder, lead, rope, salt, coffee, and canning jars. Isaac, you wouldn't believe the game on the claim! Deer and rabbits walk right up to you. William or I shoot something for dinner almost every day, right on our claim. We have berries, cattails, onions, garlic, Kiss-me-quick,[3] plums, nuts, mint, sunflowers, dandelions, and other herbs all over the claim. The water from Stranger Creek is crystal clear, pure, and tastes wonderful."

Isaac saw their excitement and said, "I'm happy for both of you. I'm sure it will go well."

Caleb's description was reasonably accurate, if a bit embellished. While 1854 was dry over most of the Territory, the area around Caleb's claim received a lot of rain that year. Portions of Stranger Creek did sometimes go dry, but only downstream and south of Caleb's claim. Areas nearer the Missouri River were more thickly wooded, but Caleb's claim still had a rich forest, with abundant hardwoods like oak, walnut, pecan, and hickory. The advantage of Caleb's location was it was flatter, and more easily farmed than the land nearer the Missouri River.

While Caleb was seeing how Enoch, Priscila, Samuel, Catharine and Mary were doing, Isaac and Jane discussed the move. Jane said, "I'm glad to see them so happy, but I don't think we need to move. Our farm is big enough to support us well, and we are happy here in De Kalb. Caleb and Maggie need more land than they could possibly buy here. This is good move for them, and they will not be too far away."

Isaac agreed, "You are right Jane, but the adventure of it is enticing."

Jane saw the wistfulness in his eyes but knew staying put was the best thing for them.

Isaac added, to her relief, "I'll help my brother but will not follow him to Kansas."

Caleb told everyone, "The cabin is solid, made of good oak and walnut, all the cracks are sealed with concrete. We made a good solid door and two windows. The fireplace and stove are solid limestone, the fireplace opening is big and easy to cook in. I floored part of the cabin already. William and I dug a well and built good limestone walls for it that go down five feet into the water. Everything is rough right now, but ready to go."

Caleb continued, "In a few years we can build a two-story proper frame house and have glass windows, but for now we are good."

Maggie said, "I'm sure it is wonderful Cale, I'm happy we are moving."

---

3 Purslane

Jane said, "I'm so happy for you, but we will miss you. I'm especially going miss our little Isaac, he is such a happy little bundle of joy!"

It was late before Caleb and his family went to bed, but he planned on getting up and loading the wagon as soon as the sun came up. He knew they would not finish early enough to leave for the claim the next day but was hopeful that they could leave the following morning.

The next day was hectic. They had to select what to take on the wagon, what to leave with Isaac to be picked up later, what to sell, and what to purchase. They did find some good, milled lumber for sale in the town, as well as another barrel of nails. They also found a crate of Mason jars, with corks and wax. Caleb was very interested in using the new "canning" process to preserve the abundance of berries and fruits available on his claim for the cold winter months. Scurvy was always a problem in the winter, but if they canned the fruit and berries on their claim, they would have fruit all winter. In addition, they would make apple cider vinegar.[4]

Caleb also bought some new woodworking tools, a new ax, and a wood splitting wedge. He also bought a rock splitting sledgehammer and rock wedge. While they had no neighbors yet, Caleb knew they would come, and they would need split wood, nails, building stones, and cement. He meant to have these items for sale in his new town. They loaded their goods, and their remaining chickens on the wagon, Caleb got the final payment from his brother for their 40-acre farm, and they were prepared to go. They slept one last night in their old house and early the next morning they set out for Iatan and Yunt's Ferry. It was late August 1854.

Caleb drove the team of oxen and walked alongside them. Maggie, Catharine, and the infant Isaac rode in the wagon most of the time. Ten-year-old Mary, the eight-year-old twins, Enoch and Priscila, and five-year-old Sam generally walked, but occasionally one or the other would mount the wagon and ride with their mother. Everyone was excited and loved the chance to see new things. They rarely had the chance to leave their little farm community and any chance to travel was a huge adventure. They talked endlessly about everything they saw. Maggie and Caleb did their best to answer the endless stream of questions.

---

4   Apple cider vinegar contains vitamin C, unlike normal vinegar.

In no time at all, they arrived at Iatan, and then crossed three miles to Yunt's Ferry and found that three ferry boats were operating, so the wait was short. The wagon was fully loaded and there were seven of them, plus Caleb's horse, so the fee was three dollars and seventy cents. Caleb was upset at the charge, but people were waiting, and he had little choice.

By the time they crossed to Port Williams, it was noon, so they ate a snack that Maggie had prepared, watered the oxen, and horse, and took off for the claim. They still had nearly 15 miles to go, but the weather was nice, and it hadn't rained in a while, so the ground was dry. Caleb kept to the higher ground and the stream crossings were easy since west of where they were it was quite dry that year.

As Caleb and the rest of the family were slowly making their way to the claim, some rough looking men approached William. They all had pistols and knives on their belts and flintlock rifles. They wore high-topped boots, with their pants tucked into them and usually with a knife sticking out of one. All the men were bearded and unkempt. William gripped his rifle and greeted them, and one of the men said, "Hi there, young man, where are your kin?"

William told them, "They are returning soon. How are you doing? Can I help you?"

William was nervous but he had his bowie knife in his belt should he need it. Then the man speaking for the group said, "No, we are just looking for claims and stopped to say hello. Your claim looks nice, you picked a good location. You've done a nice job here."

William answered, "Thank you, we are pleased with it. Will you be making a claim nearby? We are founding a town here soon."

The man answered, "Perhaps, this is good land and that is a nice looking well you have there. We are all from Platte City and Weston, Missouri, and may very well move here. Are you sound on the goose?"

William was confused by the question, and asked, "Sound on the goose? What goose? We have no geese here, only chickens."

The men laughed and said, "We are members of the Platte County Self-Defensive Association and that is our way of asking if you support making Kansas a slave state, like Missouri. If you say you are 'sound on the goose,' it means you will vote for Kansas to enter the Union as a slave state."

Moving the family

William replied, "I'm not sure, I haven't thought about it and I'm too young to vote anyway."

The spokesman then said, "That is fine young man, just mention all this to your Pa when he returns. Let him know that there will be a vote on making Kansas a slave state in November and we prefer he vote Democrat. The Democrats are proslavery here in the Kansas Territory."

William replied, "My Pa is a Democrat."

The men all smiled and their leader said, "Good to hear! Do you mind if we fill our canteens with water from your well?"

"Sure, take all you need."

They filled their canteens, and the leader said, "Thank you, young man. You stay safe and have a good day, sir!"

William was still nervous and apprehensive about the men and kept his flintlock close by and the bowie knife in his belt. When Caleb, Maggie, and William's siblings got to the claim it was late and almost dark, they were worn out. William greeted them enthusiastically and it was a great homecoming. Maggie was delighted to see her first-born son after such a long time and commented on how healthy and strong he looked. She was amazed, because when she had last seen him, he was a string bean, and now he was filling out. Maggie hugged William to her and beamed at him.

Willam had shot a deer earlier in the day and had it hanging from a tree, and it was already dressed for them. Maggie and Mary were delighted and started a fire in their new fireplace and set about fixing a meal. Everyone was hungry. William said, "Ma, you don't know how grateful I am to have you cooking instead of Pa."

Caleb said, "Now son, you told me my cooking was good."

William said, "Pa, I had to say that if I wanted to eat."

Everyone laughed, and Caleb said, "Even I know your Ma is the best cook west of the Mississippi. There is no doubt she is a much better cook than I am."

Maggie said, "And you had to say that to keep on my good side!"

At that, everyone laughed again, then started talking nonstop as the meal was prepared.

William told Maggie, "I missed you Ma, it is so wonderful to have you here. But Pa and I really enjoyed building the cabin and digging the well together. Look at all we have done!"

Maggie made a show of looking around, and replied, "It is a wonderful cabin William, I am so proud of you! It is a blessing that you and your Pa had this adventure together."

Caleb added, "Maggie, William did a fine job, worked hard, never slacked off, we have a good boy."

Maggie said, "Good man, Cale, he is a good man. He is about the age I was when we got married."

She then put her arm around Caleb and hugged him from the side, as they both looked at William together

Caleb quickly corrected himself, "Yes, a very good man."

William said, "Thank you, I love what we built, and I love that I built it with you, father. This experience has changed my life."

Maggie looked carefully at her boy. She saw that he truly had changed, she saw more confidence, more poise, she liked it. She stepped over to him, hugged him again, and told him again how proud of him she was, and how much she loved the new farm. William greeted all his siblings, Enoch, Priscila, Sam, Mary, Catharine, and little Isaac. Isaac was growing quickly and was now a plump, healthy-looking baby. William smiled and said, "A new little brother!"

Once all the hellos and excitement subsided, he told them about the men who arrived earlier in the day and what transpired. Caleb said, "Sound on the goose? I've not heard that before, and I'm not sure where it comes from. But I've heard about the Platte County Self-Defensives, they are a rough bunch from Weston and Platte City."

William said, "Father, what did they mean about Democrats and slavery? I told them you were a Democrat, but you've always said you are against slavery."

Caleb replied, "I have always voted Democrat, but I am against slavery. Slavery is wrong, people can't be bought and sold like that. Slavery cheapens hard work for poor people, like us. I don't think we can outlaw slavery, that means taking property away from slave-owners, but I sure don't want it to spread to new territories like Kansas. Keep it where it exists, but don't make it worse."

William asked, "When you were young, you saw a slave auction in Kentucky, right?"

Caleb replied, "Yes. I saw a woman's children sold to one man and the woman to another. It was heartbreaking, she knew she would never see her children again and she wailed and wailed. I'll never forget that day and I will be against slavery until I die. Now that President Pierce and the Democratic Party have become the party of slavery, I'm not sure I can stay a Democrat."

They put politics aside, since they had more urgent concerns. But Caleb thought trouble was coming. The slave-owners in Missouri were worried about their property. If Kansas was admitted as a free state, Missouri would be surrounded by free states on three sides and in an untenable position. Caleb did not think this would end well.

It was a nice late summer evening with clear skies and a breeze. Most of the family decided to sleep outdoors, but Maggie and the baby set up a nice bed in the almost finished cabin. Everyone was exhausted and they slept well.

For the next several days Caleb and William, with help from Enoch and Sam, worked on the cabin. They floored over the rest of the cabin and for the first time they had a house with a raised wooden floor. Then Caleb and William built a loft on each side of the cabin with enough space for two to sleep in either loft. Maggie was very happy with the fireplace and stove. She thought, "Everything is just fine."

Maggie missed Jane May and her other friends in De Kalb, but thought this claim would provide them with a better future. She was glad they had moved.

Caleb and William continued to pull limestone from the fields as they cleared them for planting and kept all the blocks next to the house. Any they didn't use they would sell or use to make cement which they knew every new settler would want. They improved and enlarged the primitive kiln they had made and crushed a ready supply of ground limestone so it could easily be made into cement and concrete as needed. Their motto, often repeated by Maggie, was "be prepared."

They also stockpiled wood, the smaller pieces were for firewood and the longer pieces were for sale when more settlers arrived. They stored the wood off the ground, on limestone blocks, so the termites wouldn't get to it. If rule #1 was to be prepared, rule #2 was never throw anything away, store it, and store it properly.

No new settlers had arrived yet, but it was only September, Caleb figured a lot of people would arrive in the spring, since by then all the choice lots and farm claims near the Missouri River would be gone.

The winter of 1854-1855 was mild, and it was seventy degrees Fahrenheit on Christmas day. Caleb and William took advantage of the good weather and enlarged and improved their barn for the oxen, horse, mule, and cows before Christmas. With a mild winter they had a good corn crop, and planting the winter wheat went well. The land clearing progressed, and they had cleared over four acres by Christmas. Land clearing was brutal and difficult work, but William and Caleb were hard workers, Sam and Enoch helped when they could.

Caleb and his family were delighted to find wild ripe pawpaws in the fall on their property and enjoyed eating them straight from the tree. Maggie found a way to make a very pleasing pudding from them. Unfortunately, ripe pawpaws do not store well, so they were no help in feeding the family in the winter. They fed the overripe pawpaws to the pigs, they loved them.

They canned a lot of wild strawberries, sand hill plums, blackberries, and elderberries that they found in abundance. They also collected a lot of pecans, garlic, and walnuts.

Enoch was assigned the job of collecting the animal "chips" or poop and taking it to a clearing near the garden to dry. After it was thoroughly dry, it was mixed with soil in a ratio of two parts soil and one part animal manure, then it was spread on the garden and fields. He collected manure from all the animals, the chickens, the pigs, cows, oxen, and the horse. Sam often helped him with this smelly job.

By the spring of 1855, Caleb had big plans for the farm. The soil was a rich deep brown and sandy, perfect for the orchards he was planning. He had already planted apple and peach trees which were developing well but would not bear fruit for three to five years. His grape vines were also growing well. This spring they were going to plant at least two acres of corn. They would also grow potatoes, carrots, beets, turnips, beans, and peas. They didn't plant any lettuce since they had abundant wild dandelions, curly dock, sheep sorrel, wild asparagus, wild onions, purslane, and cattails on their farm. They also had wild sage, basil, mint, ginger, dill, and summer savory growing wild on the claim. Priscila, Mary, and Maggie collected these and often transplanted them to the garden, so they always had them close at hand. Maggie hung many of the spices on string to dry so she could keep them through the winter months.

Winter wheat was a new crop in Kansas and Missouri and Caleb was a bit skeptical of it but always ready to try something new. The stories he had heard suggested that these new seeds might be a good idea in Kansas where most of the precipitation was in the winter and spring.

Caleb rode to Ft. Leavenworth in October and hunted down the government claims official and secretary of the Kansas Territory, Daniel Woodson. There was no claims office yet, but President Franklin Pierce had appointed Woodson as secretary of the Territory and charged him with keeping the records. Caleb explained that he would like to officially file a claim for his farm and the new townsite. Caleb admitted that he could not write very well, but he described the property to Woodson's satisfaction. Woodson wrote Caleb's description up as a sworn affidavit and had Caleb sign it, then he made a copy for Caleb to take with him. Woodson told Caleb, "You are doing the right thing, get everything down on paper and filed with me. That will help you if there is a dispute."

Caleb did know how to sign his name and could read well. He signed both copies and had Woodson put his stamp on them, then left, happy to have that done. Claim jumping was common, and Caleb did not want to lose his claim that way. This paperwork cost him a valuable three days, but he felt it was well worth it.

Chapter 2
Charley Dunn

It was 1852 and Caleb and his family were still in De Kalb, when Isaac Cody, his six-year-old son Billy, and their family arrived in Weston, Missouri, just across the river from Fort Leavenworth. Young Billy would later be known as Buffalo Bill.[5] In Weston, his family initially stayed with Isaac's brother Elijah and his family.

Billy Cody

Elijah Cody was wealthy and owned several farms. When Isaac and his family arrived, he moved them into one of his farms for a 20% share of the crops. It was well-known that Kansas would be open for settlement soon, and Isaac planned on claiming his own land there. In the meantime, he was pleased that his brother gave him a place to stay and a way to earn some income. Congress had already begun the process of creating the Kansas territory and Ft. Riley was already established deep in the Territory to help protect the numerous wagon trains that crossed Kansas on their way to California and Oregon. Negotiations with the Delaware, Otoe, Kickapoo, Kaskaskia, Sac, and Fox Indians were well underway.

At this time Missouri Senator David Atchison was about to become President pro tempore of the Senate for the second time. Atchison was fervently proslavery. His fellow Missouri Senator, Thomas Hart Ben-

---

5 (Cody, 1879)

ton, was just as fervently anti-slavery. This reflected the population in Missouri, which was very divided on the issue.

Initially Kansas was supposed to be admitted to the Union as a free state, with no slavery allowed. But Atchison successfully negotiated a deal with Senator Stephen Douglas of Illinois, that allowed the people of the new state to vote on the issue of slavery and decide for themselves.

His longer-term plan, which he kept to himself, was to organize proslavery activists in Missouri to travel to Kansas, which would have a small voting population initially, and vote to make Kansas a slave state. Atchison lived in Platte City, Missouri, which is just five miles east of the border, when he was not in Washington DC, and he knew many men he could count on to help him. Foremost among them was Charley Dunn, one of the leaders of the Platte County Self-Defensive Association.

Isaac Cody was fervently against slavery and made no secret of it. This was even though his brother, Elijah, was proslavery and owned slaves. This was not a topic they discussed, and they had a good relationship despite their difference of opinion on the subject.

Full-time farming was not something the energetic and ambitious Isaac had in his plans. The day after they arrived in Weston, Isaac crossed the Missouri River on the Rialto Ferry and visited the Kickapoo Village Indian Agency, about three miles northwest of Fort Leavenworth and registered as an Indian trader.

After his family was settled on the farm, Isaac opened an Indian Trading Post in the Salt Creek Valley, about halfway between Fort Leavenworth and Kickapoo Village, and directly across the river from Weston, Missouri. Isaac was away from home a lot in that period, but he did visit frequently, and on one visit home he told six-year-old Billy, "I've bought you two excellent Indian ponies, and I'll take you straight to them tomorrow!"

Billy was speechless and excited about the ponies and didn't sleep a wink that night.

The next morning, after crossing the river on the Rialto Ferry, Isaac and Billy passed through Fort Leavenworth and watched a dress parade of soldiers. Billy was thrilled at the sight. Afterward they headed northwest to the top of Salt Creek Hill which gave them a magnificent view of the beautiful Salt Creek Valley.

Billy was not only impressed with the beauty of the valley, but also by the hundreds of white domed "prairie schooners" camped there. The valley was always a stop for wagon trains headed to California, Oregon, or the Mormon Country, which is now the state of Utah. In addition, at that time, several trains of Russell and Waddell freighter wagons were camped in the valley. William Russell and William Waddell were freighters that competed with the Kansas City freight company owned by Alexander Majors. Both shipped goods to and from Fort Riley, Kansas and Fort Union, New Mexico for the government and individuals.

Isaac Cody's trading post was on a hill, near Salt Creek and only two miles from the M. P. Rively trading post store. Isaac took his son to the Rively store where he saw Indians and frontiersmen for the first time. All the men, Indians, and Caucasian alike, had pistols and/or knives on their belts, their pants were tucked into their boots, and they wore large broad-brimmed hats. Billy was amazed at the sight.

When Isaac and Billy reached Cody's trading post, or more accurately a "trading tent" camp, Billy immediately saw the two ponies that Isaac had bought for him. Billy ran over them and was disappointed that they snorted and jumped away. His father told him that the ponies were not broken yet and Billy was disappointed.

One of the men who worked for Isaac at the post caught one of the ponies, put a bridle on it, put Billy on her back and led her around the pasture. Billy loved her immediately and petted her so much that eventually she allowed him to approach her. He named her Dolly. Billy named the other pony Prince, and he remained wild.

Isaac and his men were working hard on building more permanent houses and a store but were still living in tents. Billy thought that was wonderful and the best thing ever. Isaac's business was mostly trading clothing, sugar, and tobacco to the Indians in exchange for furs. Isaac did not know their language yet, so he traded using sign language.

Since Isaac was a registered Indian trader, he was allowed to build on the Kickapoo land. He fully expected that the Kansas-Nebraska Act would be approved by Congress soon and built a large stockpile of logs (for building houses) and fence rails in preparation for the event, as he planned to formally claim the land he was on as soon as it was allowed.

Once the act was finally passed and signed by the President on May 30, 1854, Isaac immediately and formally staked his claim. This was the most popular area to stake claims, it was near the fort and beautiful, fertile ground.

Nearly all the early settlers, especially in the Fort Leavenworth area, were proslavery Democrats. They loudly announced their intention to make Kansas a slave state, just like Missouri. Rively's Trading Post became the headquarters for these men and where they held their meetings.

At one meeting, not long after Kansas was opened, Isaac was present. Since his brother Elijah was a slave-owner and a Missourian, the others at the meeting assumed that Isaac supported their proslavery position and asked him to speak. Isaac was reluctant, but they insisted. The crowd outside Rively's store was large and rough looking, but they supplied a freight box for Isaac to stand on for his speech.

Isaac said he would speak, but reluctantly, he said, as recalled by Billy,

"My remarks, at this time, will be brief and to the point. The question before us today is, shall the territory of Kansas be a free or a slave state? The question of slavery in itself is a broad one, and one which I do not care at this time and place to discuss at length. I apprehend that your motive in calling upon me is to have me express my sentiments in regard to the introduction of slavery into Kansas. I shall gratify your wishes in that respect. I was one of the pioneers of the State of Iowa and aided in its settlement when it was a territory and helped to organize it as a state.

Gentlemen, I voted that it should be a white state, and slaves should never be allowed to locate within its limits; and, gentlemen, I say to you now, and I say it boldly, that I propose to exert all my power in making Kansas the same kind of a state as Iowa. I believe in letting slavery remain as it now exists, and I shall always oppose its further extension. These are my sentiments ..."[6]

The crowd loudly objected to what Isaac was saying, the heckling grew so loud Isaac could not be heard and stopped speaking. Charley Dunn was in the crowd and yelled, "You black abolitionist, shut up! Get down from that box! Get off that box, or I'll pull you off."

---

6 Modified from (Cody, 1879, pp. 40-42)

Isaac tried to ignore Dunn and the hecklers in the crowd, and to continue his speech, but Dunn suddenly jumped on the box and stabbed Isaac with his large bowie knife. It was the same bowie knife that he had attempted to stab Caleb May with several months earlier. Dunn still showed some of the injuries from the fight, a doctor had tried to straighten his nose, but it was still noticeably crooked. The beating obviously had no effect on Dunn's behavior.

Dunn moved to stab Isaac again but was pulled away by others in the crowd. Mr. Rively, the store owner, rushed Cody to Weston and to Doctor Hathaway and he lived, but he never completely recovered from the stab wound. Isaac had to remain in Weston, with his brother, for several weeks before he could get around on his own.

Dunn's new job

At the time of the stabbing, Charley Dunn was employed by Elijah Cody, who immediately fired him. Senator David Atchison heard about the stabbing and the speech almost immediately. He summoned both Charley and Elijah to his office. He told them, "Elijah, I'm very sorry your brother was hurt, hopefully he will recover. But Charley was justified, this sort of anti-slavery speech cannot be allowed. We must keep the Free-Soil Party out of Kansas! We must ensure that no Free-Soilers settle in Kansas! We cannot allow our great state of Missouri to become surrounded on three sides with free states. If that happens, we will not be able to keep our slaves, they will all run away!"

Elijah said nothing, he was too angry and too shocked to hear this crazy talk. Charley said, "What will happen to me? Mr. Cody just fired me, and I'll probably be arrested and tried. I don't have any money for a lawyer."

Atchison replied, "Of course Elijah fired you, you idiot, what do you expect? You stabbed his brother. But you can come to work for me, I'll need you in Kansas to drive out the Free-Soilers. Eli Thayer has just formed an emigrant aid society in Boston. The bastard plans on recruiting and moving hundreds of Free-Soilers to Kansas to turn it into a free state. We cannot let that happen! I need men like you to help me drive them away."

Elijah said, "I plan on having Charley arrested for attempted murder! My brother was not even armed when Charley stabbed him."

Atchison interjected, "You will not! I will not allow it. I need Charley."

Elijah was furious but held his tongue. He was afraid of Atchison and what he could do to him, his family, and his businesses. Also, he understood the importance of keeping Free-Soilers out of Kansas and how important it was to make sure Kansas was a slave state. Missouri's whole economy was based on slavery. Elijah silently called himself a coward but didn't think he could do anything. He remained silent.

Charley Dunn had just found a new career and a new employer. Atchison was true to his word, he made sure that Charley was not charged for any crime related to stabbing Isaac Cody, and he hired Charley. On paper Charley was to be a farm worker, but in reality, his job was to gather up proslavery gangs of men to harass Free-Soilers in Kansas. This was a job that Dunn was well suited for.

After Elijah left, Atchison said to Dunn, "Charley now that you work for me and represent me, you must control your drinking. I don't ever want to hear that you are drunk in public again. If I do, I'll fire you. Understand me?"

"Yes sir. I'm grateful for what you've done. I will do my job and I will not dishonor you."

Charley Dunn reformed. He didn't quit drinking all together, but he did stop going to bars and drinking in public. He liked working for Atchison and admired him.

Atchison replied, "I know you will do a good job Charley. You are just the man I need for this job."

Kickapoo City, Fort Leavenworth, and the future city of Atchison were the center of the Kansas proslavery community. This was a dangerous area for anyone opposed to slavery. Nationally, the Free-Soil Party was growing rapidly and was very influential. Later that same year, parts of the Free-Soil Party agreed to merge with the new Republican Party, a merger that was not fully complete until 1856.

The Kansas Free-Soilers were often called Free-State people, the terms were used interchangeably. When Isaac had recovered enough to get around, he headed back to his family home near Kickapoo City.

Upon his return, he was notified that he must leave the territory and if he didn't, he would be hung or shot.

A few nights later a gang of armed men, mounted on horses, surrounded the Cody home. Isaac saw what was happening from inside the house and disguised himself in his wife's bonnet and shawl and boldly walked out of the house and proceeded into his corn field. It was dark and the disguise worked, the men neither stopped him nor followed him. He continued into the corn field and hid.

The men dismounted and went to the door demanding Isaac, but Mary Ann, Isaac's wife, told them he was away. They were not satisfied and searched the house, when they didn't find him, they swore and threatened to kill him if he should ever appear again. Then they stole everything of value in the house and drove off all the horses. Thankfully, Billy's pony Prince was able to get away and make it back to the house. Isaac hid for three days, but the men watching the house did not give up. Finally, Isaac fled to Fort Leavenworth, where he had friends who would hide and protect him. Still later Isaac moved to a small Free-Soil community called Grasshopper Falls[7] about 30 miles west of Leavenworth. There he began building a sawmill.

Isaac eventually finished his sawmill but could not entice Mary Ann to join him there. She said the proslavery men had taken everything they had except the land and home, and she would remain there as long as she lived. She would not allow them to drive her off her land. Isaac did sneak back as often as he could, but he had to be careful.

The men of the town continued their harassment of the family for their free-state beliefs. They repeatedly came to the house looking for Isaac and Mary Ann always told them he was away. They inevitably carried off everything of value that they could find. Eventually, they even took Billy's horse Prince. Billy never saw the horse again.

Eight-year-old Billy, said, "I wish I were a man; I would love to kill all of those bad men that want to kill my father, and I will when I get big!"

---

7 it is called Valley Falls today

Chapter 3
Atchison

Although Caleb May formally staked his claim in the Kansas interior on the very first day settlement was allowed, there were not that many that moved so quickly, outside of the immediate Fort Leavenworth and Weston area. Final plans for founding Atchison, Kansas were not developed and agreed until Dr. John Stringfellow and his friends moved there late in July of 1854 from Platte City, Missouri. Caleb and William literally walked and rode right through present day Atchison on their way from the improvised Rushville ferry landing to the claim and saw no one late on May 29th.

Atchison was a good location for a town, but the most desirable locations in the new Kansas Territory were around Ft. Leavenworth. Settling there provided military protection in case of Indian troubles and provided business opportunities with the military.

Complicating the situation at Leavenworth, the Delaware Indians had not yet agreed to sell their land to the U.S. Government. As a result, many settlements next to the Fort were on Delaware land and the claims were not legal and could not be perfected. Under U.S. law Indian Treaties superseded the Homestead Act. The two army Majors that headed the Leavenworth Association said this was not a problem, as did the four members of the Association who were lawyers. In their view, the Delawares would eventually have to sell the land. The worst-case scenario for the settlers is they would have to pay twice for the land they settled on, once to the Leavenworth Association and a second time to the Delaware Indians.

The Delawares did complain about the Leavenworth Association claims and filed a petition to the U.S. government. However, the Association met with the Delaware Indians and set a minimum price for the land with them, whenever the sale should occur. The Delawares agreed to this arrangement and thereafter supported the settlers. They planned to sell their land but wanted a separate agreement from the other tribes in the hope they would get a higher price.

The Leavenworth Association officers, and the lawyers suspected, correctly it turned out, that the Delawares allowed settlers on their land, because the improvements the settlers made would only increase the ultimate sale price and they would have captive buyers already on the land. The Delawares were nobody's fools. Indeed, their plan worked, and the settlers had to pay twice for their claims. First, they paid the Leavenworth Association, which paid the Delawares most of the money they received. Then the settlers had to pay the Delawares directly a second time. But after paying the Delaware Indians, the settlers were rewarded with perfected claims. The second sale was an auction that occurred late in 1856 and in early 1857.

David Atchison felt betrayed, he had thought the land around the fort was off-limits and now there was a rival settler's association dividing some of the best land up among themselves. Atchison strongly suspected that the Leavenworth Association was led by abolitionists, who intended to ban slavery in the new Kansas Territory, and this further infuriated him. His association did not allow abolitionists or Free-Soilers to join and wanted none of them in the Salt Creek Valley. In fact, he wanted only proslavery settlers in the whole of Kansas Territory.

Two friends and colleagues of Atchison were Dr. John Stringfellow and Robert Kelley. They were strong proslavery Democrats and with encouragement and funding from Atchison, they founded the town of Atchison, Kansas and moved there, only nine miles northeast of Caleb May's claim. Robert Kelley was a newspaper man, and while building a house and print shop in Atchison, he continued publishing the *Democratic Platform* newspaper in Liberty, Missouri. Kelley wrote the following in that newspaper about the stabbing of Isaac Cody in Weston:

"A Mr. Cody, a noisy abolitionist, living near Salt Creek in Kansas Territory, was severely stabbed, while in a dispute about a claim with Mr. Dunn, on Monday week last. Cody is severely hurt, but not enough it is feared to cause his death. The settlers on Salt Creek regret that his wound is not more dangerous, and all sustain Mr. Dunn in the course he took. Abolitionists will yet find 'Jordan a hard road to travel.'"[8]

"Jordan is a hard road to travel" is a reference to a popular song of the time. The most interesting part of this newspaper story is that it openly acknowledges the stabbing and yet no one in authority arrested Dunn for his attempted murder of Isaac Cody. The second interesting thing is they say the dispute was about a claim, which was clearly not true. Dunn stabbed Isaac Cody because he was giving a speech supporting making Kansas a free state, this was attested to by all who witnessed the event. David Atchison's evil influence was very strong.

Reverend Starr

Benjamin Franklin Stringfellow, Dr. John Stringfellow's older brother, was also an ardent supporter of slavery. He moved to Weston, Missouri in Platte County in 1853 and set up a law practice. He also led the most famous of the proslavery "secret societies," the Platte County Self-Defensive Association with the enthusiastic support, both financial and political, of David Atchison. The Association, which Charley Dunn belonged to, and helped lead, resolved to drive all abolitionists out of Kansas and extend slavery from Missouri into the territory. Ben Stringfellow was described as a good-natured gentleman, but due to his politics, he had many enemies.

The Reverend Frederick Starr also lived in Weston, Missouri. He was a graduate of Yale College in 1846 and studied to become a Presbyterian minister. Once he graduated and was accepted by the church, he was given a church in Weston. Many anti-slavery people were simply anti-black. These were people who didn't want blacks in Kansas at all, either as slaves or free men. These were the views of both Isaac Cody and Caleb May. Frederick Starr was in the minority of anti-slavery people who thought all slavery was morally wrong. He welcomed black people and wanted to help them succeed as free men.

---

8 (Bisel, 2012, p. 27) and Gray, "Fact versus Fiction in the Kansas Boyhood of Buffalo Bill," Kansas History 8 (Spring, 1985).

Starr and Ben Stringfellow were acquainted since they both lived in Weston. Stringfellow suspected that the Leavenworth Association and the new town they had started to build south of the Fort, was a "front" being used to bring abolitionists into the territory. Starr's participation in the Leavenworth Association was all the proof Ben Stringfellow needed.

The "Self-Defensives" terrorized anyone they suspected of anti-slavery sentiments and often ran them out of town. They also made membership in their organization a test of allegiance. Many joined out of fear.

Starr was invited to a meeting with Benjamin Stringfellow and the Self-Defensives led by Dr. Bayless and John Vineyard to explain his views on slavery. The invitation was undoubtably because Starr had recently told Vineyard that he believed "slavery is a political and moral evil."

The meeting occurred Saturday October 28, 1854. It began at 3PM and when Starr entered the room, he estimated that 300 people were there. Prior to going to the meeting Starr promised his wife, Helen, that he would not call General Benjamin Stringfellow names.

General Stringfellow rose when Starr arrived and listed four accusations against him, "Reverend Starr taught a school of black children two years ago. Second, he suggested that Mrs. Bland free her slave, Henry, because Henry was too smart to be a slave. Third he repeated this suggestion to another slave owner and asked that he free all his slaves. Fourth, he was seen driving his buggy with a black man who carried his umbrella on the 4th of July, an insult to the ladies and gentlemen of Weston."

The Reverend Starr defended himself well and kept his temper in check, as he had promised his wife he would do. He said, "I only taught blacks to read with the explicit permission of their owners. My school only had six students and continued for about six months. It was ended when the Weston city leaders objected to it. Most of the students wanted to read so they could read the Bible themselves."

Starr never encouraged black resistance to slavery and pointed out that all slave owners rode alongside their servants. But, when asked his opinion of slavery, he simply said, "It is wrong."

Benjamin Stringfellow and the Self-Defensives then told Starr he must leave Weston. The following May, Reverend Starr sold his Leavenworth claim and left with his family to return to New York. Unfortunately, this sort of thing occurred regularly.[9]

Certainly, not everyone in Weston agreed with Stringfellow and many were opposed to the Self-Defensives. On September 1, 1854, the citizens met and condemned "mob law." One hundred and seventy-four people signed a resolution at the meeting rejecting the Self-Defensives' call to block northern immigration to Kansas. The citizens of Weston then affirmed the equal rights of all men in the territories according to the Kansas-Nebraska Act. They also affirmed their dislike of the Self-Defensives, who had disrupted their peace, quiet, good order, and business.

The leaders of the Self-Defensives were concerned about the New England abolitionists settling in communities like Lawrence, Kansas in 1854. Frederick Starr wrote, to his father, complaining that the local newspaper was demonizing the New England Emigrant Aid Society, the organization that supported the Lawrence settlement and sent over 700 immigrants, with supplies and weapons, to Kansas in 1854 and early 1855.

November 1854

The New England Emigrant Aid Society sent hundreds of armed Free-Soilers to Kansas, which was exactly what David Atchison feared would happen. Atchison was determined to fight back. He hosted a meeting in his office with the Stringfellow brothers, Charley Dunn, and Robert Kelly. He wanted them to step up the fight against the abolitionists and the immigration of abolitionists from the northern states. Atchison announced, "We will use rifles, revolvers, and bayonets to check northern immigration into Kansas. We will tar and feather all abolitionists we find and run them out of town on a rail."

He turned to Robert Kelley and said, "I will offer a $200 reward for the capture of Eli Thayer, dead or alive! Announce that in your newspaper!" Thayer was the Boston leader of the New England Immigration Society.

---

9 Frederick Starr's full story, only summarized here, can be read at: https://digital.shsmo.org/digital/collection/frontier/id/302

Kelly replied, "Gladly."

Then to the whole group, Atchison announced, "The first territorial election is to be held on November 29, 1854. It will elect a delegate to Congress for the Territory. There will be two Free-Soil Party candidates and one Democratic proslavery candidate, John Whitfield.

Whitfield must win that election. Kansas Governor Andrew Reeder has said that only Kansas residents can vote and has done a census, so he thinks he knows who is in the territory and who is not. But most people have not been in Kansas long, so how does he really know? Here is a list of the planned voting locations. I've marked which are likely to vote for Whitfield and which are not. I want you to organize groups of men to take to those districts unlikely to vote for Whitfield, and make sure enough of our people vote to elect him."

The men stood and began to leave to enthusiastically follow Atchison's orders. Charley Dunn turned to Atchison and said, "I expect no trouble gathering the men needed for this task. All I need is whiskey and a little money and I can gather as many men as I want."

Atchison replied, "You will have all you need."

The vote

Caleb made the trip to his voting district's polling place in Ozawkie, a small village about 20 miles south of his house. There were a few proslavery hecklers in the small village, but Caleb ignored them, voted for John Wakefield, an anti-slavery Whig Party member, and listed his address as Ocena, the name he had chosen for the town he founded. His district (the 13th) was overwhelmingly proslavery, and Caleb cast the only vote for John Wakefield. There were 69 votes for the proslavery candidate John Whitfield, and one vote for the other antislavery candidate Robert Flenneken.

There were few problems in Ozawkie because Atchison knew that nearly everyone in that district was proslavery, so it was not on his list. As Caleb later learned, other districts, with more anti-slavery voters had huge numbers of illegal votes. In the districts targeted by Atchison, legitimate voters suspected of being anti-slavery were often turned away from the polls or threatened with violence if they tried to vote.

One district, the 7th, where the census showed only 53 voters, had 584 illegal votes. Several hundred men arrived at the polling location the night before the election and camped nearby. On the day of the election, they took over the polling location, voted, and then boarded their wagons and returned to Missouri. The same thing took place in all seven districts where a majority of the settlers were anti-slavery.

The election was a disaster, thousands (perhaps 3,000 to 5,000 total) of Missouri ruffians, hired by Charley Dunn or volunteers for the Platte County Self-Defensive Association, showed up armed and even with cannons, to take over the polling places. They often installed their own district judges, and they elected Whitfield to the U. S. House of Representatives.

The number of votes exceeded the number of eligible voters in the territory and the number of illegal votes exceeded the number of legal votes. Whitfield received 2,258 votes and the Free-State candidates John Wakefield and Robert Flenneken received 248 and 305 votes respectively. Of the 2,833 votes later counted by a Congressional committee, 1,729 were found to be illegal, but even after the recount, Whitfield still won the election.

The territorial Governor Andrew Reeder reluctantly approved the election results. Whitfield was eventually seated in Congress, as a non-voting member, on December 20, 1854. Governor Reeder's proclamation before the election was that the voters must reside in Kansas and intend to stay in the territory. Enforcement of this rule was uneven, to say the least, and Caleb was completely unaware of all these problems until well after the election. The Missouri voters declared they had just as much right to vote as anyone from any other state.

Caleb's family heard many stories about the election disaster and the stories upset them, but they went on with their lives. They enjoyed the mild winter of 1854-1855 and spent their time improving the farm and their farm buildings, taking good care of their animals, and hunting for game and deer. Caleb improved their primitive smoke house and bought more salt in Atchison. The game was so abundant that they enjoyed smoked meat almost every day.

He and William also added a covered and raised sleeping porch to the cabin. It was ventilated from below and on all sides so the family could sleep more comfortably during warm evenings. They also expanded and strengthened the barn, the chicken coop, and the pig pen.

Daily tasks and their farm were much more important to them than politics. The farm and Caleb's family were doing well, they were all busy and happy.

Chapter 4
Pardee Butler

The winter had been productive and lucrative. When newcomers found out Caleb and William made cement, they quickly came to purchase it and the prepared limestone blocks that they had for sale. The money Caleb and William made was mostly used to buy milled lumber, tools, and nails that they used to make furniture, storage sheds on their land, expand their crowded cabin, and improve and expand the barn. But they also bought food and spices they couldn't grow themselves and clothes that Maggie and Mary couldn't make or didn't have time to make.

By spring Caleb and Maggie had a nice house with a bed for everyone. Although Maggie and Caleb made spending decisions jointly, Maggie controlled their budget, and she kept all their money in a lockbox that Caleb had made for her years earlier.

At first, they had to travel to Atchison to buy supplies, but a newcomer to the area, Elijah Smith, opened a store in Ocena, and soon they did nearly all their shopping in his store.

They felt like they had everything they needed. They also had money saved for emergencies, plans for more additions to the cabin, and were even planning to buy glass windows!

It was a beautiful spring day when Caleb was inspecting his winter wheat. Mary, Maggie, Priscila, and Enoch were working in the garden, planting, weeding, and hoeing. William was plowing a field behind two oxen to sow corn. Catherine and Sam were playing next to the garden and pretending to pick weeds, and Isaac, now just one year old, was in a basket with a cover to protect him from the Sun. He was watching his Ma and sucking his thumb. Caleb looked over the whole scene from his field and wanted everything to stay the same forever.

The Squatter Sovereign

John Stringfellow, Charley Dunn, and a few hired hands helped Robert Kelley move his Liberty, Missouri newspaper to the new town of Atchison in the early days of February 1855. John Stringfellow and Robert Kelly were partners and owned the newspaper. David Atchison had loaned them the money to get the newspaper started. Kelly's combination house and print shop building was already built, all he needed to do now was move his family, furniture, and printing press into it.

Kelly's wife and children were still in Liberty but would move to Atchison in about a month. Stringfellow and Kelley meant for Atchison to be a stalwart pro-slavery community and they wanted to be its voice. Kelley renamed his newspaper the *Squatter Sovereign*. "Squatter sovereign" at the time meant that once a man claimed his 160 acres and built a farm, he was a sovereign of the land, independent, self-supporting, and free. Private property was the key to freedom in their view. The first issue of the new paper was published on 20 February 1855, and it proclaimed:

"Negro Slavery is not only no Evil, but a Blessing to the White man and to the Black man."

The newspaper quickly became the principle proslavery newspaper in the Kansas Territory, although the *Leavenworth Weekly Herald* was also popular. The latter paper wrote the following on 15 September 1854:

"The question whether slavery shall exist or be prohibited is to be decided at the ballot-box, by freemen of Kansas and it would be a departure from the spirit and meaning of the [Kansas-Nebraska] bill establishing the territory for a Newspaper to attempt to dictate to any faction. ... We shall set forth the issue ... and treat both sides with fairness without hesitation."

While the *Leavenworth Herald* tried to remain neutral, they were proslavery and so was the town. Proslavery feelings dominated in the summer of 1854 and Missourians were in control, but settlers from the northern states were pouring into the territory and they resented the influence of the nonresident Missouri squatters. The distinction between full-time resident settlers and part-time residents caused a lot of conflict.

Meeting Pardee Butler

In March 1855 Pardee Butler arrived in Ocena, he immediately looked around the small town and quickly found out that the land east of the May farm was unclaimed. After a quick look at the land from the road, he rode to the May cabin and found Maggie working in the garden, "Hello, my name is Pardee Butler, I'm new here and looking for a claim. I used to be a minister in the Disciples of Christ Church, but now I'm just a farmer. I have a family, but they are back in Iowa and not with me right now. I understand the land to the east of your claim is available, can you tell me anything about it? Is it OK if I look it over?"

Maggie was in her gardening dress and old lace up ladies' boots and wearing a straw hat tied with a strip of cloth that matched her dress. She also had her gardening gloves on. She pulled them off and wiped a wisp of her hair from her face, and replied, "By all means, please do. We would love to have you, and your family join us here. Let us know if you need anything. Your name is unusual, do you mind my asking where it is from?"

"I was named for my mother's family, the Pardees, who were originally from Norfolk, Connecticut. My father was Phineas Butler, from Saybrook, Connecticut."

Caleb had been in the barn and saw them talking, so he joined them and introduced himself to Pardee, then said, "So you will move here?"

"Yes sir, I want to check out that land next to your claim, it looks like a very nice place."

"It certainly is Mr. Butler, the land is rich, there is plenty of water, and the hunting is excellent. We always have meat in our smokehouse."

"My father was a great hunter, but I never took up hunting and I don't own a gun."

Maggie said, "My Caleb here is fond of both guns and hunting. He keeps us well supplied with meat, and we always have meat left over, you will not need to hunt to have meat here."

Pardee laughed, and said, "That sounds pretty good to me."

Despite their differences on hunting, Pardee and Caleb were to quickly form a life-long close friendship. Their mutual respect was due to a shared religion, but also due to their shared deep devotion to honesty, honor, and integrity. It didn't hurt that they were both vehemently against slavery and both advocated temperance.

Caleb then offered to show Pardee the land to the east of his claim. They walked a quarter mile to the edge of Caleb's claim and Caleb stood next to the stake that marked the northeast corner of his land. This was on the edge of a small tributary of Stranger Creek that flowed northeast.

Then Caleb said, "You don't have to make this stake a corner of your land, and I don't recommend it. The trees are mostly north of here along this creek, you could put your northwest stake about a quarter mile north of this point, and next to the town, then pace off your claim from there. That way you are next to the town and don't need to buy a lot."

Pardee followed Caleb's advice, and they paced off and staked Pardee's claim that same day. It adjoined Caleb's on the east but was offset to the north. There was a nice small hill next to the creek where Pardee decided to build his cabin. It was just across the creek from the town.

Caleb said, "I heard you say you are from Iowa; I've heard they are an anti-slavery state."

"Yes sir. In Iowa slavery is not only illegal, but escaped slaves are protected and cannot be returned to their owners. This is in defiance of federal law."

"It happened because in 1839 the Iowa Supreme Court ruled that a slave named Ralph had to be released because his master had given him permission to travel to Iowa. The court said that permission was also permission for the slave to go free, since Iowa is a free state. The court ruling conflicts with the Federal Fugitive Slave Acts of 1793 and 1850 but it is used to defend and free runaway slaves anyway."

Caleb replied, "Makes sense to me, if the slave is told to go to a free state, what does his master mean? He means to free the man."

Butler replied, "Yes sir, sounds like that to me as well."

Butler continued, "I was born in New York and used to be a minister affiliated with the Disciples of Christ Church. But they were running out of money and had to let me go. That was when we decided to move here and start over."

"We are Disciples of Christ; we would encourage you to open a church here."

"Not right now, I need to get a farm going and get my family here first. Maybe sometime in the future."

Pardee was nearly as tall as Caleb and the same age, since both were born in 1816. But, while Caleb was lean and muscular, Pardee was a bit overweight, with a paunch, was considerably grayer, and had a receding hairline. Unlike Caleb, Pardee shaved his mustache. Pardee had intelligent light brown eyes and a clear voice with a New England accent.

Caleb said, "Well, I am happy you have chosen to make your claim here, we will help you build a cabin, and you must stay with us. It will be an honor to help you Brother Butler. I was born in Kentucky where our church was founded."

They made Pardee feel very welcome. He wrote down his impression of Caleb in his journal not long after first meeting him. On the first day, Caleb told Pardee, "I'm descended from Pocahontas, and have Indian blood." Pardee noted Caleb's evident pride in this fact and then continued to write:

"Born and reared on the frontier, tall, muscular, and raw-boned, an utter stranger to fear, a dead shot with pistol or rifle, cool and self-possessed in danger, he had become known far and near as a desperate[10] and dangerous man when meddled with. But he had been converted, and had become a member of the Christian Church, and according to the light that was in him he did his best to conform his life to the maxims of the New Testament, and conscientiously sought to confine all exhibition of 'physical force' to such occasions as those in which he might be compelled to defend

---

10 In the 19th century, "desperate" could mean violent, angry, or excessively aggressive (Oxford Dictionary, when referring to a man or a fight). It might draw this meaning from a famous 1843 painting by Gustave Courbet, *Le Désespéré*.

himself, his family, or his friends. Then it was not likely to be a healthy business for his antagonist."[11]

While Caleb and Maggie May were mostly illiterate, they could and did read when they had something to read, although neither could write well. The Reverend Pardee Butler was an accomplished writer, and often contributed to both popular and religious newspapers. He had published many articles in the famous *New York Tribune*, the leading U.S. newspaper of the time.

Prior to moving to the Kansas Territory in 1855, Pardee and his family lived in Iowa for a time. While there, in July of 1854, Pardee's youngest daughter passed away. It was a devastating loss for Pardee and his wife Sybil. The following fall, Pardee lost his job with the Disciples of Christ ministry. It was then that Pardee and Sybil sold their Iowa farm. That winter Pardee finished memorizing the entire New Testament of the Bible and wrote several popular articles on the New Testament as it related to grief.

Pardee, Elijah Smith the store owner, and another farmer named Andy Elliot were among the first families to settle in Center Township, Kansas Territory early in the spring of 1855.

While Caleb and Pardee were surveying Pardee's new claim, Caleb told him "I have been stockpiling logs, lumber, and nails. I also have a large store of crushed limestone for making cement and shaped limestone building stones. I can sell you these items and if you buy my crushed limestone, I will make it into a good cement for you to use in building your foundation, chimney, fireplace, and stove."

Pardee replied, "That is wonderful, I had no idea all of this was available here."

As time went on, Pardee and the other neighbors were amazed at Caleb's knowledge and skill in making cement and how he could customize the recipe correctly for different uses. Normally, settlers had to use mud and clay to seal their houses, Caleb's cement, concrete, and mortar were a huge improvement.

Caleb told Pardee, "One of the main reasons I chose to stake my claim here was it has everything I need to make cement, no need to buy

---

11 (Butler, 1889, pp. 48-49)

anything, this claim has the right clay, sand, and nearly pure limestone everywhere."

Caleb and William helped Pardee build his house. Caleb would take no pay, but Pardee insisted on paying William fifty cents a day, which was about half the going wage in Missouri and Caleb approved of that. While building his house, Pardee stayed with Caleb and his family and shared in their meals. Caleb thought it was wrong to take payment for food, but Pardee said, "I must pay Maggie and Mary for their work, they deserve that."

Caleb eventually agreed, "Maggie will use the money to buy nice things for the house, herself, and the girls."

Maggie was a bit indignant at that and said, "Nonsense Cale, the money will go straight into the box with all our other money. It will be spent on necessities we all agree we need, just like always."

William asked, "Will my money and Mary's go into the box also?"

Maggie replied, "Of course it will son, but we will remember where it came from, and you and Mary will have a big say on how it is spent. We don't have much money, William; we must be careful with it. It is only spent on things we need, the rest we save for bad times. Bad times always happen eventually, we must prepare for them."

Caleb added, "Listen to your Ma, William, the money we make always goes to her. She has the final say."

William thought, "It's my money!" But he kept silent and took heed of his Ma and Pa. The family always comes first, he might be 15, with all that means, but he knew that.

With the finances settled, they worked on a new cabin for Pardee's family. William helped every day and Caleb helped occasionally, as he could. At night they discussed their day and current events.

Crossing Missouri

Pardee led them in prayer before each of their meals. The Mays were honored and grateful to have a reverend staying with them. Pardee knew the May family were anti-slavery, as he was, and that they opposed liquor. They were kind people and Pardee felt fortunate to have found this place.

After dinner, a few nights after he arrived, Pardee told the Mays about his journey to Kansas. Pardee said, "My first stop was in Linnville, Missouri, I had heard that a congregation of Disciples resided there. I stopped to visit one of the members and he told me he had heard of me and had read my articles in the *Christian Evangelist*. But, when he discovered I was traveling to Kansas, he turned decidedly cool. I noticed the change and left."[12]

Caleb asked, "He was upset you were going to Kansas Territory? Why?"

Pardee replied, "I think that was the problem, he knew I was coming from Iowa and traveling to Kansas. I was from a free state and traveling to a new territory. He thought I was coming here to vote Kansas a free state."

Caleb said, "Maybe so."

Pardee continued, "Later, after nightfall, I found an old man who kindly took me in, fed me, and allowed me to sleep in his cabin. The next morning, I discovered the man's cabin was surrounded by negro cabins, and we fell into a conversation about slavery, the topic of the day. I admitted that I didn't approve of slavery and the old man became angry and told me that if I talked that way in Kansas, they would hang me."

William asked, "Really? He said they would hang you?"

Pardee answered, "Yes sir, he said that. I laughed at the thought and told him you cannot teach an old dog new tricks. I have spoken my mind for so long, I shall continue to do so until they do hang me."

Maggie spoke up, "Pardee, you must be careful. This is a dangerous land, especially for people who disapprove of slavery."

Pardee said, "Yes, Ma'am." then continued, "The next day, night came before I reached St. Joseph, and I found accommodations at a private house owned by a nice old man. I saw no books or newspapers in the house, but the owner was well informed, and we discussed the Kansas-Nebraska bill, which had opened the Kansas Territory to settlement. Then he asked me about the 'Black Republicans,' a name given to Republicans opposed to slavery.

I told him what I believed, and he listened intently."

---

12 (Butler, 1889, p. 37)

Then he said, "I am originally from Pennsylvania and agree with you. But I must advise you to be careful how you talk to other men as you have talked to me. There are many men around here who would shoot you for saying such things."[13]

Caleb asked Pardee, "Do you need a gun for protection?"

Pardee replied, "I do not. As I mentioned to you a few days ago, my father was a hunter, and taught me how to use guns, but I am uncomfortable with them."

Caleb told Pardee, "I need to tell you of a man called Charley Dunn. He and two of his friends forced William to drink whiskey when William was only 15! I had to beat them severely to make sure they did nothing like that again.

Not long after that reprehensible act, Dunn stabbed a man called Isaac Cody at Rively's Trading Post in Kickapoo. Cody's only action was speaking against slavery, and he was stabbed for it. Dunn was not charged for the stabbing or attempted murder, and he certainly should have been. There were dozens of men who witnessed the assault. That poor man, Isaac Cody, is now living in Grasshopper Falls. He has not fully recovered from the stabbing to this day.

We are against slavery and against bringing any slaves or black men into Kansas Territory and support your home state of Iowa and their laws, this is what we want for Kansas. But this is a dangerous place to talk of such ideas. I keep my own council, which we must do, to live here in peace. We own some guns, should you need one to protect yourself, we will loan you one. I can shoot well, so can William, we can help you. Our guns are older flintlocks, but given the times, we have discussed going to the new town of Lawrence, where the New England Emigrant Aid Society sells the new Sharps rifles and the best Colt revolvers. I very well might buy one of each."

Pardee replied, "Those are shocking stories. But I'm OK for now. Thank you for your offer."

Maggie said, "Cale won't say it, but even the roughest men in Missouri are afraid of him. I doubt they will bother us, regardless of what we think about slavery. But you cannot always be here, and anything you

---

13 (Butler, 1889, p. 41)

Crossing Missouri

say will travel. I encourage you to buy a gun, or borrow one of ours, and keep it with you. There are dangerous men about."

William nodded in agreement, and added, "You must be careful sir."

That night, Pardee wrote to his wife Sybil.

"Dearest Sybil,
My new neighbors are kind and welcoming people. I greatly admire them and enjoy their company. The father, Caleb May is widely feared and respected both in Kansas Territory and in Buchanan County Missouri. He is a Godly man and against slavery. Although he is feared, especially by the proslavery men, I find him to be kind, neighborly, quiet, and hardworking. Caleb is always ready to defend his family, friends, or the poor and downtrodden. It is a blessing to know him, I know you will like him and his lovely wife Maggie when you can join me here."

March 1855

March 30, 1855, was election day. Each district was to vote for their delegates to the new territorial legislature. Everyone loved the idea of being a squatter sovereign and to be free and independent. Now, through the election, they were to decide their institutions by themselves. Yet when the election day came every election district in the Territory was overrun by Missouri ruffians. The election was not decided by the new settlers, but by invaders.

The proslavery forces in Missouri, under the leadership of David Atchison and his lieutenant Charley Dunn, had carefully prepared for this election. They wanted the Kansas Territorial Legislature to be populated with a majority of proslavery legislators. Prior to the election, Atchison gave a speech in Weston in front of a crowd gathered by Charley Dunn, Ben Stringfellow, and the Platte County Self-Defensive Association. In the speech he said,

"The law of the Territory is created by the people who reside in it, they have the power, through their legislators, to form all municipal regulations. In these regulations, they can either admit or exclude slavery, and this is the only question that materially affects our interests.

If the New England Emigrant Aid Society, from a thousand miles away, can spend many thousands of dollars sending hundreds of abolitionists to the Territory, and exclude the slaveholders here when they have not the least personal interest in the matter, what is your duty?

You live one day's journey from the territory, and your peace, your quiet, and your property depend upon your actions. You can, without exertion, send five hundred of your young men to vote for your institutions. If we do this, we can decide this issue quietly and peaceably at the ballot box.

The abolitionists have nothing to gain or lose. This is an abstraction to them. We have much to gain and much to lose. I say, if you burn my barn, I sustain a great loss, but you gain nothing. So, it is with the Emigrant Aid Society and the dupes they send to abolitionize Kansas."

Then Atchison became prophetic and continued:

"If abolitionism, under its present auspices, is established in Kansas, there will be constant strife and bloodshed between Kansas and Missouri. Negro-stealing will be a principle and a vocation. In a hybrid state we cannot live; we cannot be in a constant quarrel—in a constant state of suspicion of our own neighbors. We must be willing to punish negro thieves, they must be hanged. To avoid a civil war, we must try to settle this issue according to the principles of the law. That way, such actions are not needed."[14]

The election was held a few weeks after Atchison's speech. At first the election proceeded normally and quietly, then companies of more than ten men came riding in from Missouri and took over nearly all the polling places. They voted, and would let no one else vote, unless they swore to vote for the proslavery candidate. In the Center Township polling location, whiskey flowed like water, the men got drunk and made such chaos that every settler went home.

Pardee Butler wrote in his journal, "My neighbors told me with pain, shame, and resentment, that they had gone to vote and were interrupted by a mob of noisy, drunken ruffians who took over the polls and did all the voting."

---

[14] Substantially paraphrased version of a speech given by Atchison on November 6, 1854, as reported in the Platte Argus. (Connelley, 1918, pp. 384-385)

Caleb did not arrive at the polls until late in the day and when he heard the stories from his friends he threw his hat on the ground and in a "towering rage" said he would no longer vote for the Democratic Party, a party that would treat people that way. Caleb had been a lifelong Democrat, but no longer. He joined the new Free-Soil Party, and a few months later, he joined the newly formed Free-State Party, as did his friend Pardee Butler.

Pardee and Caleb did nothing to fight back that day, and neither did any of their neighbors. Caleb didn't even go to the polling place, if he had he would have seen his nemesis, Charley Dunn. Charley had installed his own district judges by then and the new judges did not ask if potential voters were residents, as required by law. They also excluded voters they thought were anti-slavery. The new judges, installed by Dunn, took possession of the ballot box, and delivered it to Fort Leavenworth where the votes were counted. A later Congressional analysis[15] of the election showed that over 73% of the votes cast in the election were illegal. In Caleb and Pardee's district, there were 12 legal votes and 230 illegal votes.

June 1855

Charley Dunn was summoned to Atchison's office in Platte City, when he showed up, there were some other men there already. Atchison said, "Charley, these men are here to appoint you to be the new postmaster for Weston, Missouri, if you want the job."

Dunn replied, "Oh! Yes sir, that would be wonderful."

Atchison then told him, "You've done an excellent job for me recently, and this job is well earned, congratulations!"

One of the other men stepped up and smiled at Charley and issued him his oath of office. In addition to Charley's other duties, he was also a construction sub-contractor and Atchison made sure good projects made their way to Dunn's company. In short, Atchison made sure that Charley was well rewarded for his work to drive anti-slavery people out of Kansas and stuff ballot boxes.

---

15 (Howard & Oliver, 1856, pp. 9-35)

While Dunn was receiving his reward, the settlers felt betrayed. Caleb told Pardee, "I am sick at heart. I feel a deep, bitter, and shame-faced feeling, because my old neighbors in Buchanan and Platte Counties in Missouri did this."

The legislature elected on March 30th was forever after known as the "bogus legislature." Yet, it created the initial laws of the Kansas Territory.

The prevailing sentiment among the squatters from Missouri, including Caleb, was that Kansas should become a free white state. As Caleb explained to Pardee, "I will work to make Kansas a free white State; we will admit no Negroes into it. I was born poor and to a life of toil, and the Negro has made labor a disgrace. I have only six months of school, because my father died when I was 14-years old, and I had to help run the farm. My children will have more education than I received, but less than they should have, and the Negro is the cause of it. An aristocracy in the South has assumed control of public affairs, and the Negro is the cause of that. Kansas must be a free white state, like Iowa, and shut out the Negro, who has been the cause of all our calamities."

Pardee replied, "Negros are children of God, just as we are. They did not come to this land; they were sold to slave traders in Africa and brought here against their will. Slavery, itself, is your enemy Caleb, not the Negro. While it is true that poor white men in slave states have no future, black men did not cause that."

Caleb said nothing, but quietly considered what his friend said. It made some sense. Many in Kansas, who were against slavery, thought as Caleb did in 1855. The coming blood and turmoil would cause many of them to abandon that view and adopt Pardee's. White American's views on slavery and black men were in the process of changing.

Pardee Butler's farm came together a little quicker than the May farm. He had William's experienced help and the benefit of Caleb's stockpile of limestone, cement, nails, tools, and logs. Further, he had some money from the sale of his farm in Iowa, and stores to buy goods from. There was Elijah's small store in Ocena, and stores in Atchison and Rively's Trading Post near Kickapoo, nearly anything he needed could be found in one of those stores.

By June 1855 he was reasonably settled and had built a small log cabin on his land. Unlike Caleb, Pardee owned a nice twelve-pane glass window, and he installed it in one wall of his cabin. It was the only one in the township. With William and Caleb's help he also built a chicken coop, a hog pen, and a small barn. Unlike Caleb, Pardee had brought no stock to Kansas, only three horses and a buggy. But he bought some animals from his neighbors, as well as hay for them.

Many other Disciples lived in the area, and they all called on Pardee. He knew there were enough people for a church, but he was trying to prepare his farm for his family, who were still with his sister-in-law in Illinois and the times were stormy.

Originally, he had no plans to start a church, but Caleb and his other neighbors convinced him to start one. He delayed his first sermon until June. That year June was gorgeous. While the southern part of the state was still in a drought, the area around Stranger Creek had refreshing showers, singing birds, and abundant blooming wildflowers. His farm was nearly ready for his family, and it was time.

Pardee's Sermon

So, on the forested eastern shore of the Stranger Creek tributary that lay between Caleb's house and his, Pardee planned his first church service. It was to be in the open air. People came from all over the township and beyond, they were excited, many had not been able to attend a religious service for many months, even years in some cases. They wore all manner of clothes, some in Kentucky-jeans, some in broadcloth, some men had shaved, and some had full beards, all were dressed in the best they owned, whatever that was.

The women and girls wore their best dresses and all the jewelry they owned, their shoes were not fancy, but clean, polished, and practical. The women drew back their hair in a bun or braid and wore their nicest bonnet or hat. The hats were secured against the Kansas wind with their best ivory, silver or gold hat pin. The young girls wore their hair down, but it was secured into one or two ponytails or braid with colorful cloth ribbons. All the girls wore nice, clean bonnets that were tied below their chins.

Maggie had her fine silver hat pin well placed through her bonnet and into her hair. Both Caleb and William told her how beautiful she looked. After she was ready, it was time for her girls. Maggie spent a lot of time dressing them and fixing their hair. The girls were not patient, and Maggie had to use her "Ma" voice to keep them quiet as she worked on their hair and clothes. Finally, everyone was ready, and they walked the short distance down to the open-air meeting next to the small tributary.

After it seemed everyone had arrived, the Reverend Butler came before his neighbors and led them in song. He wrote in his journal later that the singing was awful, but sincere and enthusiastic. Then Pardee began his sermon:

"My friends and fellow citizens, I have never seen trees clothed with leaves so rich a green as those above our heads. I have never seen prairies robed in richer verdure than the prairies around us. ..."[16]

He went on to discuss the birth of Protestantism and its importance in the formation of the United States and Kansas. Of Kansas he emphasized that he expected it to become a great state. Most of his audience were entranced by his sermon and appreciated Pardee's skill and knowledge of the Bible. However, two young gentlemen from New England, who were on their way to the new town of Lawrence being built by the New England Emigrant Aid Society, snickered at the open sky meeting and the congregation. They kept up a distracting running commentary between themselves on the sermon and how the other people attending looked. Pardee became annoyed, so he turned to them and said, "Young gentlemen, you profess to be men of good breeding, and it is understood that well-bred people will behave themselves in meeting."

The two men were embarrassed and angry at the rebuke. They left early to continue their journey. They were well dressed in nice suits made of fine cloth and riding in a fine buggy, pulled by two horses, that they had purchased new in Leavenworth.

On the way, several Missouri border ruffians attacked them and stole all their possessions. The ruffians were dressed in rough clothing. Some of their shirts were in a variety of loud colors. They were all armed with pistols and knives. This sort of highway robbery was always a risk at the time. Everyone knew that Lawrence was a Free-Soil community of

---

[16] The full sermon can be read in Butler's book. (Butler, 1889, p. 55).

anti-slavery immigrants from New England. Well-dressed newcomers with Yankee accents heading toward Lawrence were considered fair game in those days.

The leader of the proslavery border ruffians told them, "We are pressing your possessions into service. We will use them to protect the sacred institution of slavery."

One of the young New Englanders said, "But stealing is wrong, it is always wrong! You are taking everything we own."

The leader said, "You have traveled here to invade our land to vote Kansas a free state! That is also wrong. What we do is justifiable theft. You should go back to where you came from and forget this place, it is not for you."

The two young men continued to Lawrence on foot, but as soon as their families sent them tickets, they returned home. Kansas was just too wild and dangerous for them.

This sort of problem, encouraged by Atchison, and carried out by Charley Dunn and his men, plus the awful election of the bogus legislature led to deep divisions and discontent in the settler population. Some new settlers stayed and fought, but many simply turned around and went home.

Governor Andrew Reeder

President Pierce appointed Andrew Reeder to be governor of the new Territory. Reeder arrived at Fort Leavenworth in the fall of 1854 and was a Democrat, like Pierce. Because Reeder was from Pennsylvania, which allowed no slaves, he was something of an unknown. However, the powerful southern wealthy Democrat elite, that had helped Pierce become elected, expected Kansas to enter the Union as a slave state. Likewise, they expected Nebraska, bordered by Iowa, a free state, to enter the Union as a free state. This was the deal they made to support the Kansas-Nebraska Act, a bill proposed by both Senator Stephen Douglas and Senator David Atchison.

So, when Reeder was briefed on his new position early in October of 1854, by President Pierce, he was told to expect trouble from the "lawless actions" of the New England settlers brought in by Eli Thayer's Emigrant Aid Society. The President told Reeder, "These emigrants have moved to Kansas in large numbers to vote down slavery in the Territory."

The newly appointed Governor Reeder then asked, "I should fully expect that the New England Free-Soil settlers will be the most important problem I will have?"

The President replied, "Yes, keep a close eye on them. Remember, our fealty to the U.S. Constitution precludes us from considering whether slavery is morally right or wrong. Our duty is only to the Constitution and the law."

Reeder responded, "Yes Mr. President."

The election aftermath

Pardee, Caleb, and their friends in Center Township followed the news of the terrible election and the aftermath closely. Sharing the news as they heard it. Pardee received hopeful news in April, a few weeks after the election.

Pardee told Caleb, "Governor Reeder has been besieged with complaints about the election. He knows the threats of violence from the ruffians kept honest settlers from voting. The Governor is upset at the lawless acts by the Missourian invaders, since he explicitly ordered that only bona fide settlers should be allowed to vote. Once he found that Missourians came to Kansas to vote and then returned to Missouri the same day, he investigated the problem and set aside the results from four districts!"

Caleb simply replied, "Thank God."

Pardee went on, "He has set a special election in the four districts for May 22."

Caleb replied, "It is getting dangerous Pardee, have you noticed nearly everyone is armed all the time now."

"Yes, Caleb, I have noticed."

Caleb said, "Everyone is jumpy now, a fight erupted in Leavenworth, and someone was shot and killed. A lawyer named Phillips was taken into Missouri and tarred and feathered. It is getting ugly. I will speak with Maggie and see if it is time to buy more modern guns for William and me. I understand that Sharps rifles and modern Colt six-shot revolvers can be purchased in Lawrence for $2 each. Do you want me to buy you a revolver?"

Pardee said, "No, I don't need a revolver."

Caleb answered, "I will buy an extra revolver, just in case you need one in the future. Remember that I have it. I think there will come a time when you need it."

Pardee said nothing but looked away from Caleb and seemed thoughtful.

Caleb excused himself and went to find Maggie to see what she thought. Once he found her, he explained, "Maggie I only have old single shot muzzle loaded pistols and flintlocks. I'm afraid of being outgunned in a fight. It is getting dangerous, and I am afraid fighting is inevitable after this travesty of an election."

Maggie thought for a while and said, "I agree Cale. It is getting very dangerous, and we must always be prepared for a fight. The timing is good, we've made a lot of money selling cement, logs, limestone blocks, and shingles. I'll give you $20 for the guns and ammunition. You'll get William a revolver and teach him to use it, right?"

Caleb answered, "Yes Maggie, I will. Pardee doesn't want one now, but I will buy another to keep for him. That way it is ready when the time is right. You and I both know he will eventually need it. I'll ride to Lawrence tomorrow."

Maggie said, "OK, please be careful, I love you."

Caleb said, "Love you too. We'll get through this, but not without a fight."

Next, they discussed the decision with Mary and William. They both agreed, and William said, "The reputation of the rifle frightens even the boldest of the Missouri ruffians. It is a deterrent even before you fire it."

Mary said, "We need what we need to protect ourselves."

Caleb said, "I know little about Lawrence, but I've heard that if I'm anti-slavery I can buy modern guns there at a good price. The man in charge is Charles Robinson. He has a rough reputation, supposedly he had some problems in California some years ago. Tomorrow I will go find him and see what kind of deal I can get."

Charles Robinson

With everyone agreed, Caleb set out for Lawrence and made the 40-mile trip in one long day. It had rained some in the past few days, so the roads and paths were a bit muddy, but the sun was out, the air was clean, and everything was green. After reaching Lawrence, he was sore, but even so he enjoyed the nearly 12-hour ride, including time for two rest stops.

The Robinson house was located on top of a large hill called Mt. Oread. It had a beautiful view of the Kansas River valley and was surrounded by large oak trees.

He arrived at the house just before sunset, and immediately walked up to the front door of the large house. Shortly after he knocked, the New England Emigrant Aid Society agent, Charles Robinson and his wife Sara, opened the door. They greeted him warmly.

Caleb said, "Hello Mr. and Mrs. Robinson, I'm Caleb May from Ocena in Center Township near Atchison. We are a small Free-Soil community and threatened by Missouri ruffians and the proslavery men in Atchison. I'm here to try and purchase a Sharps rifle and some Colt revolvers for our protection. I'm told you have some for sale."

Charles Robinson said, "Caleb May, I've heard of you!"

Caleb was surprised, and asked "How did you hear my name?"

Robinson replied, "Charley Dunn has been in town and mentioned you. He doesn't like you much, I guess you had a fight with him and broke his nose? His nose is still crooked, and he claims he is going to 'get you' for that."

Caleb laughed and said, "He can try."

Caleb added, "Dunn and his friends held down my boy and forced whiskey down his throat when he was only 15 years old. They needed a serious lesson in manners, and I gave it to them. The sheriff investigated and decided I was in the right."

Charles laughed and said, "I like you! I sure could have used you in the troubles I had in California."

Caleb said, "I heard stories about you in California. What happened there?"

Charles said, "In California I joined a movement to secure the legal rights of the citizens against unscrupulous speculators and sharpers and was thrown into prison by one group of scoundrels and then elected to the California Legislature by another. It is a long story that I will have to tell you some day."[17]

Caleb said, "I can see you are no stranger to troubles with bad men. We have that in common."

Charles smiled and said, "Indeed, I suspect we do. Have you joined our new Free-State Party?"

Caleb said, "Not formally, but I wish to. So does my neighbor Pardee Butler."

Charles replied, "Pardee Butler? The famous writer?"

"Yes, one and the same, although he has been busy improving his claim and has not had much time for writing lately."

"Excellent, my good man! It is outstanding that Mr. Butler is in the territory, I'm pleased. We are having a convention in Big Springs on September 5, please come if you can and bring Mr. Butler. We will formalize your membership in the party there. At the convention we will try and form a Free-State government to counter the bogus legislature. Your claim is in Center Township?"

Caleb replied, "Yes sir, west of Atchison."

Charles says, "Atchison? That is where that damned *Squatter Sovereign* newspaper is published, correct?"

Caleb replied, "Indeed, it is an awful paper, published by awful people. It is run by Dr. John Stringfellow and Robert Kelly; both are proslavery and incessantly threaten to hang all Free-Soilers with a hemp rope. Their mantra is 'All right on the hemp.' I stay away from Atchison as much as I can."

Charles said, "We will try to help you with that. I don't think we have any Free-State members up there, you will be very welcome."

Caleb says, "It is getting dangerous in our area, that last election has everyone up in arms. Literally everyone I see has a gun, or more than one. A man in Leavenworth was shot to death a few days ago in a fight in a saloon, another was dragged into Missouri and tarred and feathered. Robberies on the roads are common. Currently, I only have an old flintlock rifle and single-shot pistol, as well as a shotgun. Nothing

---

17 See here for a short description of Dr. Robinson's California adventures:
https://sactoconfluence.com/2015/05/22/from-sacramento-to-bleeding-kansas-the-struggles-of-doctor-robinson/

strikes fear into a border ruffian's heart like a Sharps or a Colt revolver, I need them."

Charles replies, "I do have them, I will sell you a Sharps for $2, which is my cost along with cartridge papers, lead, a matching bullet mold, and some fine gunpowder that is perfect for a Sharps."

Caleb said, "Wonderful, and what types of revolvers do you have?"

Charles replied, "I have some 1851 Colts, both the smaller pocket Colt and the heavier Ranger size Navy model. You get the Free-Soil discount; I will sell you either of them for $2 each. All are new and we can fire them until you are comfortable with them."

Charles then went into another room and brought the rifle and pistols out. Caleb was pleased; they were unmarked, new, and beautiful weapons. Caleb, said, "I don't know what to say, they look great."

Charles said, "We're on the same side Caleb, and you are in a dangerous place, we want to help you. It is late, and you've had a long ride. Let's bed your horse and turn in ourselves. In the morning, we will shoot the rifle and pistols, and I will show you how to load and fire them properly, then we will pack up your supplies and get you ready for your ride home."

Then they sat down for some dinner with Sara. Sara was a nice looking, slender woman, but with a serious expression. She was dressed well in nice clothing which was all in various shades of gray. This gave her a serious, no-nonsense look. Her hair was in a pigtail that she had wrapped over her head, adding to the look of seriousness.

Sara talked about the book on Kansas that she was writing and asked Caleb about the area where he lived. Caleb described his family, their claim, the town of Ocena, and his neighbors. Sara listened intently and took some notes in a notebook. It was a pleasant meal and good conversation, but it was not jovial.

The next day, after some coffee and bread, Charles showed Caleb all he needed to know about shooting and caring for the Sharps rifle and the revolvers. The new .52 caliber Sharps had a rifled barrel and was accurate at 300 yards, even 500 yards by an expert marksman with good eyesight. The large .52 caliber bullet had a muzzle velocity of 1200 feet per second and struck the target with devastating force. In contrast nearly everyone in the area, including the Missouri ruffians, were armed only with old smoothbore muskets and pistols shooting balls

Charles Robinson

that were notoriously inaccurate, even at 50 yards. And, even if they hit someone with one of their balls, it was unlikely to stop them.

Robinson's company, the New England Emigrant Aid Society, bought most of the first lot of Sharps slant-breech 1852 model .52 caliber rifles. The deal was made for two reasons, the manufacturer, Robbins and Lawrence, was in financial trouble and needed startup money to equip their factory to build the new model. At the same time, the Emigrant Aid Society wanted a lot of weapons to send to Kansas. They struck a deal where the Aid Society paid for all the guns they wanted months in advance of their manufacture and received nearly all the first lot of rifles for one dollar each. This was just over the cost of manufacture. In essence, Robbins and Lawrence were given an interest free loan to build their manufacturing facility.

The rifled 1852 Sharps barrel fired a perfectly matched bullet in a straight and flat trajectory. Each rifle came with its own custom precision bullet mold perfectly matched to the rifle barrel. Due to the technology of the time each rifle barrel could have a slightly different diameter, thus the custom bullet molds were a key factor in the rifles' accuracy. The large bullet and high velocity will kill any man it hits in or near a vital area. The gun justly terrified the Missouri ruffians, it was a full generation ahead of anything they had available.

The 1852 Sharps was a single shot rifle, it used a paper or cloth cartridge with a precise 50 grain gunpower load. A measuring cup for gunpowder was included. This model had the newly patented pellet primer system with a unique feeding mechanism for a ribbon of pelleted primers. All Caleb had to do was insert the paper cartridge into the breech, with a bullet glued into the end, aim and fire. The rifle could use standard percussion caps that were individually fitted to the cartridges, but the pellet feeder was much faster and easier to load.

Charles advised Caleb to cover each cartridge with a thin coating of beef tallow. When the handle was lowered, the breech opened and a cartridge was inserted in the top of the breech, this allowed the gun to be fired more rapidly than muzzle loaders.

Charles carefully went over all the details with Caleb. He made sure that Caleb knew the breech of the gun was not always a perfect seal and would sometimes spray smoke near his face when it was fired. The block needed to be kept clean and oiled, or an accident could blind him temporarily, or even permanently. Robinson told Caleb to always carry a cloth to wipe the gunpowder residue out of the breech. Charles was impressed with Caleb's shooting skills, and said, "You are one of the best shots I've ever seen."

Caleb simply said, "My son William is better than I am."

Charles said, "I do want to meet him, then!"

Caleb smiled and said, "I hope you will, I would like him to meet you as well."

They also went over both pistols, the larger .36 caliber "Navy Colt" and the smaller .31 caliber pocket Colt. They were nearly identical, but the pocket version was smaller with a shorter barrel and a smaller caliber ball. Both were "cap and ball" smooth bore revolvers. Both revolvers had built in loading levers that made reloading easier. He cautioned Caleb that the Colts usually shoot a little high, they would need practice with them to be effective. Caleb test fired the smaller gun and saw that Charles was correct, a couple of inches high at 20 yards.

After the demonstration and lesson were over, they discussed what Caleb needed. Caleb said, "I will definitely buy the Sharps, but the pocket revolver feels too small, it is hard to hold. I think it will be for William as well. So, I'll buy two of the larger Navy model revolvers. They are more accurate and fit well in my hand."

He added, "But I need another revolver that my wife and daughter can shoot, I think they will be more comfortable with the pocket model. It is lighter and has less kick." Caleb thought to himself that if they ever needed to loan Pardee a revolver, he might like the smaller one as well.

The Colt pocket revolver was not powerful, had a low muzzle velocity, and a small round ball, but it did fit in a pocket, was reliable, and reasonably safe if handled and loaded properly. It was accurate and effective for up to 20 yards with practice. This Colt was the most popular revolver of the time. The larger Navy model, had a longer barrel, was more accurate, and had a larger ball, but it required a holster, was heavier, and had a ferocious kick.

Charles gathered the three pistols and the rifle, the bullet molds, three bars of lead, a bag of gunpowder, and cartridge paper. Caleb bought several containers of primer pellets (caps), as well as more of the paper housings for the Sharps' cartridges. Charles told him if he ran out, he could use cloth.

Caleb paid him with the $20 gold piece that Maggie had given him and marveled at the deal he had received; anywhere else he would pay $20 just for the Sharps rifle.

Charles bragged, "We got a better deal on the new 1852 Sharps rifles than the Army did, by paying for them months in advance and buying them directly from the manufacturer.

We also negotiated a low shipping rate with the railroads and shipping companies. We had to do this to keep David Atchison's Missouri ruffians at bay. We also negotiated a special price for the Colt revolvers directly with Samuel Colt himself."

Caleb paid Charles and thanked him. He then said, "I will see you on September 5 if possible. I'll bring Pardee Butler with me if he will come."

Charles added, "We are forming a Free-State militia for self-defense, it is called the Kansas Legion. We need men to recruit militiamen in their areas. Maybe you can talk to your friends and see if you can form a militia? If you can we will help you equip and train them. We can discuss this more in Big Springs, but please consider this request, to survive here we need to organize. Tell as few people as possible about the Legion, we want to keep it a secret society."

Charles then helped Caleb pack his new possessions onto his horse and they said their goodbyes. Sara joined them and bid Caleb farewell. After Caleb left, Charles said, "I like that man."

Sara replied, "I do too, he's not educated, but he is a good man. He has a dangerous look about him, but you can feel that he is good to the core. I think he likes you as well."

On the way home Caleb considered Robinson's request to form a Kansas Legion militia in Ocena. He would try and recruit members. He said, out loud to himself, "I will see what I can do."

A Special Election

The special election occurred with only minor problems in three of the districts and they all elected free-state legislators. However, the 14th district in Leavenworth was overrun by hundreds of Missouri men that crossed the river on the steamboat, Kate Kassel. A majority of the Leavenworth judges that day decided that for a man to vote, he only had to have some interest in the territory, effectively removing the residency requirement.

David Atchison was not happy that six free-state legislators were elected in the special election to be added to the two already elected. But they had eighteen proslavery legislators, and his loyal John Stringfellow was one of them. He thought he had control of the Territorial Legislature. He met with Charley Dunn and John Stringfellow to discuss what to do next. He said, "OK, we have a majority in the Territorial Legislature, what can we do to shut down the Free-State faction?"

He continued, "I've written to President Pierce and my old friend Secretary of War, Jefferson Davis, to lay out why Missouri sent so many to participate in the recent Territorial elections. First, the New England Emigrant Aid Society sent hundreds of men to vote in the election. They had no women or children; they just came to vote and then return to New England. Second, anti-slavery organizations in many other states, especially Illinois and Iowa, sent men here only to vote. Third, Governor Reeder purposely postponed the election to allow these men time to get to Kansas."

Stringfellow answered, "All true and we have evidence. The Governor says that the charges are false. He says some of the immigrants became disenchanted with Kansas and went home for that reason, but they did not come to Kansas just to vote, nor did they leave only because they had voted. As for the last item, he says the vote had to take place after the census was taken and that was the only reason it was delayed. We are not so sure about that, something more is involved.

As for what to do next, I have some ideas. The first meeting of the new legislature is to be in Pawnee City in July. That is over a hundred miles from here! So, our first order of business will be to move the meetings to Shawnee Mission, which will be much more comfortable.

I recommend we base our laws on the laws of Missouri, but with one major change. The right of free speech will be curtailed on the subject of slavery. Discussing slavery or ending slavery will be called "circulating incendiary sentiments," and punishable by a term in jail or expulsion from the Territory. This will apply to newspapers as well.

We will appoint a panel of 30 men to observe and report on all such persons that violate this law. I've already discussed this with Justice Lecompte and he approves of it."

Atchison thought a moment, and said, "This is going to really upset a lot of people. I'm not sure the President will allow it. But I understand the necessity. Ending free speech on the topic of the day? Not sure, it might backfire. Let me write to the President, maybe I need to go to Washington to discuss it with him. But don't let my doubts stop you. If you can get a vote to approve such a law through the legislature, do it. That bastard Reeder will probably veto it anyway."

President Pierce

Governor Reeder was seen as a traitor by the proslavery legislators, and he received many death threats. As a result, he returned to Washington and met with the President. Once in the oval office, he told the President, "Kansas is a powder keg, I need your support and an affirmation of my authority. The Missouri Democrats are threatening to kill me, and the Free-Soil settlers are insisting the new legislature is bogus. Both are ready to revolt."

The President replied, "Is it really that bad? Surely not."

Reeder replies, "The whole country knows that the election was unfair, that the polling places were overwhelmed by armed ruffians, that ballot boxes were stuffed, and legitimate voters turned away. I must have the authority to hold a new election and sufficient federal troops to protect the polling places. If I cannot have a fair and accurate election of a legislature, I must, regrettably, resign."

The President replied, "Governor, many Democrats here in Washington support you, you are quire correct to resist illegal voting, but the southern Democrats feel betrayed. To them the New England settlers are invading and taking a state they feel is theirs by right."

Reeder replied, "The law is clear, the settlers will decide free or slave. No nonresident, even from a one-day ride away has any say and should not vote. They certainly cannot prevent a bona fide settler from voting. George Smith, a legislator in Missouri has publicly said, that as important as slavery is to him personally, he would never violate the law to make Kansas a slave state, or words to that effect."

The President replied, "Yet, Jefferson Davis, my Secretary of War, and a critical ally, wants me to fire you. He says that the New England Emigrant Aid Society is sending in nonresidents to vote."

In the end, the President asked Reeder to return to Kansas, but only after a lengthy discussion about how to handle Reeder's resignation. The President didn't seem to know what to do, but somehow decided sending Reeder back to Kansas was better than letting him resign in Washington. Reeder had no idea why his return was needed, or why the President wanted it. He later thought he would have been better off resigning on the spot, in spite of Pierce's request, but he didn't have that in him. He was a patriot and felt duty-bound to follow the President's orders even if he was going to quit no matter what or when. On the other hand, Reeder could easily see that President Pierce was between a rolling rock and a brick wall. Pierce clearly didn't know which way to turn.

Reeder then began his journey back to the Territory. His residence and, the capital, was the Mission in the Shawnee tract, usually called Shawnee Mission. This is in the present-day town of Fairway, Kansas and only one mile from the Missouri border. While some of the Indians in Kansas retained their traditional dress and customs, the Shawnee were very westernized. They lived in modern houses, farmed their land with modern tools, owned stores, and sawmills, and wore western clothes.

Reeder returned to Shawnee Mission, but without the presidential support he wanted. When Reeder reached the Missouri River, north of St. Louis and boarded the Polar Star for the final leg of his trip to Kansas City, he was instantly recognized. He was accosted and harassed nearly continuously on the trip by proslavery Missourians. They had seen articles in the southern press that portrayed him as an abolitionist and a Free-Soiler, even though he was a Democrat.

One man can do little

Pardee excitedly explained to Caleb in June of 1855, "The original bogus legislature has decided not to certify the legislators elected in the special election and will seat only those legislators elected in the original March election."

Caleb responded, "Then the legislature has no validity, it does not represent the settlers. Even the special May election had over 500 illegal votes."

Pardee then said, "This is true. Legislator Martin Conway told the Governor that no settler would obey the authority of a foreign government. He refused to lend any legitimacy to the current legislature."

Caleb said, "Properly said. We must and will resist any, every, and all laws that this bogus legislature passes."

To which Pardee replied, "Agreed."

Caleb said, "You know I am trying to form a militia under the leadership of the Kansas Legion. Andy Elliot and Elijah have already joined. It is just for this sort of thing that we need to organize, will you change your mind and join?"

Pardee replied, "I'm still considering it, give me some time."

Caleb responded with a smile, "Well that is a more positive answer than last time, we will keep working on you."

Pardee laughed and said, "Maybe, we'll see. Dark times are here, and we do need to organize. One man, by himself, can do little. When men organize, they can do anything."

None of the Free-Soil settlers considered the legislature valid and vowed not obey any laws they passed. What else could they do? After expelling the free-state legislators from the special election on May 22nd, only two were left, and both promptly resigned in protest. In Samuel Dexter Houston's resignation speech, he announced, "This legislature is an illegal body, and by moving from Pawnee City, it has nullified itself."

Once all the drama was over and the free-state legislators were gone, the legislature was constituted. Governor Reeder had wanted the meeting to be well west of Missouri, in Pawnee City, Kansas, and chose a spot where he owned land. This led to the proslavery settlers crying fraud, as well as Reeder's enemies in Washington, like the Secretary of War Jefferson Davis.

The legislature quickly voted to move their meeting place to Shawnee Mission, right across the street from Governor Reeder. Reeder warned them that the laws they made in Shawnee Mission might not be legal, since he had told them to meet in Pawnee City, but the legislature ignored him.

They enacted the laws that John Stringfellow had planned for them. Nearly all the laws were the same as those in Missouri. The intent of the laws was to protect slave owners and establish slavery in the Kansas Territory. The special John Stringfellow law limiting free speech with regard to slavery was passed exactly as he described it to David Atchison. As Pardee explained to Caleb, after dinner on a pleasant July evening, "The legislature passed a law that made writing or circulating anti-slavery material illegal and punishable with two-years at hard labor."

Caleb asked, "What about our Constitutional right to free speech?"

Pardee answered, "Indeed. Such a law would seem to me to be unconstitutional."

Pardee continued, "Stealing or aiding in the theft of slaves can result in imprisonment or death. Instigating a slave rebellion is punishable by death. Finally, they have made a law that no one who is opposed to slavery can sit on a jury in any trial."

Caleb, replied, "They have insured that they can imprison or kill anyone that does not agree that slavery is a good thing."

Pardee said, "Very true. I'm told that all copies of George Brown's Lawrence newspaper, *Herald of Freedom*, sent to Atchison, including my copy, were sent back by the postmaster. This was without our consent. The postmaster sent a letter with the returned newspapers that said Brown must keep his rotten and corrupt effusions from tainting our pure air."

Caleb replied, "So, freedom of the press goes away, along with freedom of speech. And the sanctity of the post is defiled. I was always told that postal workers must respect all mail."

Pardee said, "Apparently that is not the case anymore. The *Daily Pennsylvanian* had an article that supported Governor Reeder's resistance to the Missourians. The paper said they stand by the rights of the South, but will not abide their wrongs, and that slavery is not God-descended."

Caleb said, "Amen to that. I foresee there will be trouble. I've bought a Sharps rifle and three pistols, one for me, one for William, and one for Maggie. I can buy one for you or loan you one of ours. You might need it on your trip to pick up your family."

Pardee said, "No thank you. I've never needed a gun before, although I see why you want one. I support your decision, but I am not comfortable carrying a gun."

Caleb said, "We have not seen times like these before Pardee, this is a different time, and it cries out for different methods and actions. My old Democratic Party is being torn apart, and the rip of that tear runs right through Kansas Territory. Our founding fathers wisely gave us the right to have guns for self-protection. This right is not just to protect us from thieves and killers, but also an illegal and corrupt government when necessary."

Pardee simply said, "You may be right, but no gun."

Caleb said, "Maggie said that the Governor vetoed all the laws the legislature passed."

Pardee said, "He did, but it made no difference. They overrode his veto."

Besides overriding Governor Reeder's vetoes, the legislature also voted to send a petition to President Pierce to fire Reeder. Pierce accepted the petition and fired Reeder only a week later on July 21, 1855. This was well after Reeder had already requested to resign.

Reeder's last day was August 16, 1855. He was replaced by the state secretary Daniel Woodson, a proslavery Virginian. Woodson was a proslavery journalist who had attracted the attention of President Pierce. Pierce was impressed by Woodson's editorials supporting slavery and as a result, he appointed him to be the secretary of the Kansas Territory on June 29th, 1854. Woodson remained acting governor until the arrival of Wilson Shannon in December 1855.

Governor Reeder, freed from his office, became a loud and influential voice in the newly formed Free-State Party. He was always given a good welcome in the anti-slavery northeast. Reeder became an effective fund-raiser for the new Kansas Territorial Free-State Party and movement.

Sam and Caroline Moore

This was the summer of 1855 and Ocena was a growing town. New settlers arrived almost every week. Almost all of them were Disciples of Christ that were excited about Pardee Butler's new church. The permanent church building had not been completed yet, but they had a temporary, partially enclosed church that worked after a fashion, as long as it was not raining. The town wanted something grander when they could find the time and money to build it. All the settlers were anti-slavery and knew that Pardee was the only town in this very fertile area that would accept them wholeheartedly.

Elijah Smith had been in Ocena for several months and was delighted that so many were settling in the new town. His store did a thriving business. Sam Moore and his family arrived during the summer, a few months after Elijah and his family. Sam was most charitably described as not handsome. The best descriptor for him was rugged, he was a muscular man, and a little dangerous looking due to his nearly perpetual frown or scowl, depending upon the day. He was about 40 years old and had seen his share of troubles.

He was married to Mary, who was 32 years old. Mary had indifferent looks, but she was such a pleasant and outgoing person she charmed everyone she met. Their marriage was the poster child for the saying that "opposites attract." Their daughter Caroline defied the mold. She was 17 and an outstanding beauty. She had long brown hair, a perfect figure and complexion, and a face that immediately caught everyone's attention. Thankfully, she took after her mother in the personality department, she was nearly always smiling and brightened any room she walked into.

Their other child was Michael, who was five years old. Michael was a good-looking child, although not as handsome as his sister was beautiful. He was nearly as cheerful, outgoing, and pleasant as his mother and sister.

Sam's whole life revolved around his family, and he was very protective of them. He constantly worried that he would fail them somehow or not provide adequate food or shelter. His greatest fear was that he would somehow let them down. Like Caleb he was a teetotaler and never touched alcohol. He was a skilled blacksmith and gunsmith, and next to his family his greatest joy was successfully repairing things, whether it was a wagon wheel, plow, or gun. A job well done was his reward.

He arrived in time to stake a claim north of Pardee and buy one of the remaining original town lots, but his focus was not farming, he was anxious to set up a blacksmith shop and a gun store. He would farm enough to keep the land but look for a hired hand or sharecropper to farm it.

The Moore family lived in a tent while Sam built the cabin with help from Caleb, Pardee, William and the other settlers in the town. The stern Caleb and the dour Sam formed an early bond and a firm friendship, some in town called them the "dour twins," although not to their faces.

Caleb and Sam were working the ends of a large two-man saw and cutting logs for the cabin when they struck up a conversation. Caleb told Sam, "You have a fine-looking family Sam."

Sam said, "Yes, sir. I do. I hope everything goes well for them here. It hasn't always been easy for us. We needed more land and more income. I want to provide them with more than I had."

Caleb replied, "I wanted more for my family also. We have it now; we are doing well. Will you be in church on Sunday?"

"We will, we are so looking forward to Pardee Butler's sermons. He is famous you know?"

"How so?"

"He has written some fine essays in the *Christian Evangelist* and in the *New York Tribune*. In truth, one of the reasons we came here was because Pardee Butler preaches the gospel here."

Caleb beamed, "I'm so glad to hear you say that! Brother Butler is a wonderful person and a great speaker of truth."

William was chopping down trees from the nearby woods when he first noticed Caroline Moore. He was thunderstruck, he had never seen a more beautiful girl in his life. She turned to look at him, and he turned beet red from embarrassment, but could not take his eyes off her.

Caroline, being Caroline, could not let the moment just pass. She walked straight over to him and said, through a dazzling smile, "Hello, I'm Caroline Moore. I'm Sam Moore's daughter, this cabin will be ours."

William replied, "I'm, I'm ... I'm William, Caleb May's son." He was flustered and didn't know how to continue.

Caroline ended his embarrassment by responding, "Nice to meet you! It seems my Pa and your Pa like each other. They are talking more than sawing." Then she and William both looked at their fathers and laughed. The ice was broken.

Caroline then told William, "We came from Illinois, Ma and Pa wanted more land and a better life for us."

William relaxed a little, and said, "I think you will find that here. This is a nice place and I'm so happy you came."

Afterward, William and Caroline talked a while longer. William was completely smitten. When he regained his composure, he noticed she had long auburn hair partially covered with a yellow bonnet that was tied under her chin. The hair was pulled back into a ponytail, held in place with a matching yellow ribbon. Her yellow bonnet matched her dress, which was gathered around her small waist, but billowed out from her waist down. It had subtle vertical stripes of light yellow in between stripes of darker yellow. William noticed it was very flattering on her. She wore lace-up brown boots, that were mostly covered by the dress.

They discovered they were about the same age, Caroline was more than a year older than William, but William was much taller and getting more muscular by the day with all the hard work he did. Caroline was attracted to him, but cautious. They agreed to try and sit together at church on Sunday.

The ever-watchful Sam Moore saw his daughter talking to William and said, "Caleb, looks like your boy and my Caroline are having a conversation of their own."

Caleb looked up and saw them, he instantly saw that William looked star struck. He chuckled and said, "I think my William is smitten by your daughter. Not that I'm surprised, your Caroline is a real beauty Sam."

Sam said, "She is. I must watch out for her all the time. Your William seems like a nice young man, what is he like?"

Caleb answered, "He is a good young man Sam. Very devoted to his mother and brothers and sisters. He's never been any serious trouble for us, like some young men his age can be. He's smart and hard working. He reads well, can write, and do his numbers. He came to this claim with me while the rest of the family stayed with my brother in De Kalb and worked as hard as I did to build our cabin and dig the well. Did a good job. He is an excellent shot with either a Colt or a rifle. He and I do a lot of hunting together."

Sam said, "He sure is working hard here. I'll talk to Caroline and Mary and see if they want him to come to Sunday dinner, if that is OK with you."

Caleb said, "Oh good Lord! You think William is old enough to be calling on a girl?"

Sam said, "How old is he."

Caleb said, "He's 16."

Sam said, "Caroline is 17, but that is close enough. I don't see a problem. Besides, we just got here, Caroline needs some friends to get settled. I can see from here that they like each other. I'd rather her first friends were from solid stock, like you and Maggie."

Caleb said, "Why, thank you, that is a nice thing to say. I'll have to discuss this with Maggie and let you know. I just don't know if he is old enough or established enough to be calling on a girl."

"OK."

"One more thing Sam, I'm forming a militia to defend the town. These Missouri border ruffians are becoming a problem, especially around elections and I think we need to organize for defense. There is a new group being formed in Lawrence by Charles Robinson called the Kansas Legion. They will help us get arms, like Sharps rifles and Colt revolvers at a steep discount, they will also help with training. Would you be interested? Andy Elliot and Elijah have joined."

Sam became thoughtful, then said, "Sure. Let's discuss it. I would certainly like to buy a Sharps and some Colts. Let me know the price and where and when we meet."

"OK, good. You can tell your wife about the Kansas Legion, but otherwise don't discuss it, we are trying to keep its existence secret."

"Sure, no problem."

Maggie and Mary Moore also conferred and discussed the proposed arrangement between Caroline and William. They eventually agreed, and when Sam and Mary asked Caroline if they should invite William to Sunday dinner, she enthusiastically said "Yes!" Then she asked them about the age difference, "He is more than a year younger than me, is that a problem?"

Mary said, "No, you are about the same age, that can work fine. But for now, just think of William as a friend. Other things are far in the future, don't get in a rush."

With everyone in town helping, the cabin was built in a few days. Just like every other settler, Caleb sold Sam cement and limestone blocks for the foundation, and he helped lay it and build the chimney and stove. Caleb's idea for a business had worked out and he made quite a bit of profit on his sales of crushed and block limestone and cement. No one charged Sam for their labor, only for the materials. It was the same with all the cabins in the town.

Once Sam and his family moved into the cabin, which was a half mile north of the town, Sam started working on his blacksmith and gunsmithing shop. He built it on a lot he had purchased from Caleb in the town. In the evenings he first worked on fencing his animals and on a chicken coop, then he worked on a garden for their vegetables. He and Caleb were the hardest working men in the whole town.

On Sunday, the May's and the Moore's met each other outside the small, crude and not quite completed church that the town had erected for their minister, Pardee Butler. Pardee stood at the door to greet each person that entered the church. As he looked over the crowd excitedly greeting one another and waiting to enter the church, he smiled. He thought, "These men and women are not refined and educated, yet they all have the qualities that our Lord found in the fishermen of Galilee."[18]

Caroline and William sat together during the sermon, surrounded by their families. Pardee Butler's sermon that day was extemporaneous, and he did not write it down. But it was inspiring and both families were uplifted by it.

Mary Moore had completed the eighth grade as a child, an unusual accomplishment for the time. So, she opened a school and taught students for one dollar per student per year.

Her school was held outside Sam and Mary's cabin in a detached open porch that Sam built specifically for a school. At a later date, and before winter started, he planned on enclosing it. Caleb and Maggie gladly paid the tuition for William, Mary, Priscila, and Enoch. School was every morning, except Sundays, from 8AM to 11AM and the May children walked over half a mile north to attend. Both William and Mary had gone to school in De Kalb but had not been able to attend since they left. Maggie and Caleb knew the frustrations of illiteracy and wanted to make sure that their children knew how to read and write well and how to "do their numbers."

---

18 (Butler, 1889, p. 49)

Mary Moore had three textbooks and William and Mary May each had one, they didn't match, but at least they had five grammar school textbooks for the school. They were better off than most schools in the area at the time. Mary Moore spent some of her tuition money to order more textbooks through Elijah Smith.

Chapter 5
Pardee's trip

A few weeks later, in the middle of August in 1855, with Pardee's cabin completed and his new farm and garden in reasonable shape, he was ready to go get his family. He traveled to Atchison to catch a Missouri River steamboat to St. Louis for the first part of his journey to Illinois.

Due to the new laws passed by the "bogus" territorial legislature, most free-state newspapers had been shut down due to their anti-slavery content. Proslavery papers, like the *Squatter Sovereign*, continued unmolested and became even more outrageous than they had been in previous months. The *Squatter Sovereign* wrote the following about Caleb May after he supposedly complained about the language in the paper:

"We learn that one Caleb May, an ignorant and fool-hardy abolitionist, living about ten miles from Atchison, has been boasting of coming into this place and using insulting language to the editor of this paper [Robert S. Kelley] – also proclaiming himself as abolitionist in our presence. As the report is credited this neighborhood, we feel it due to ourself to brand the assertion as a base and malicious lie. We do not allow ourself to be insulted by anyone, much less an abolitionist ... No, this same cowardly skunk – we mean Caleb May – has we are told, been in this city, but not very recently. During his stay here, he was very quiet and civil, which was all very proper. No person who visits this place and attends strictly to his own business will be molested. Those of our friends who have expressed surprise that we would let such an outcast as May insult us, are informed that he has had no interview whatever with us ..."[19]

---

19 Moved up in time for this story, the actual *Squatter Sovereign* article was 1 July 1856.

Pardee was simultaneously amused and horrified by the newspaper. He simply had to buy some recent copies to take home to his family. If he didn't, they would never believe his descriptions of the stories. So, he stopped at the *Squatter Sovereign* printing office to purchase some back copies of the newspaper to take to his family in Illinois. He was waited on by Robert S. Kelley, the editor. Pardee describes Robert Kelley, or Bob Kelley as he was often called, as a handsome, well-built man, with a fair complexion, and blue eyes. Kelley radiated a personal magnetism that drew people to him. He was also an eloquent and passionate speaker. After paying for the newspapers, Pardee told Kelley, "I should have become a subscriber to your paper some time ago, only there is one thing I do not like about it."

Kelley asked, "What is that?"

Butler replied, "I do not like the spirit of violence in the articles."

Kelley replied, "I consider all Free-Soilers rogues, and they are to be treated as such."

To this, Butler said, "Well sir, I am a Free-Soiler; and I intend to vote for Kansas to be a free state."

Kelley fiercely replied, "You will not be allowed to vote."

Butler's friend and fellow Disciple, Brother Elliot, had accompanied him to the printing shop and after they left, he told Butler, "Brother Butler! You must not say such things; they will kill you!"

Butler replied simply, "If they do, I cannot help it."

"Brother Butler, you only demonstrate that you have more courage than common sense."

"Perhaps so, I've been told that before."

Pardee's boat was delayed, and he had to spend the night in Atchison in a boarding house. The remainder of the day Pardee, being Pardee, conversed freely with several people about his conversation with Robert Kelly. He told them that Kelly's attempt to silence him would not work, and it was his right to speak freely about his beliefs. Needless to say, his views and beliefs did not sit well with some, and they spread about the town like wildfire. Besides, technically within the Territory, his vocal support for the Free-Soil Party and against slavery was illegal.

That night a public meeting was hosted by Robert Kelly to decide what to do with Butler. The meeting went well into the night and Butler was not present or told about it.

Later, the same evening, Pardee was informed that his boat was not expected to arrive until noon the next day. So, the next morning, he had some unexpected free time, which he spent in the boarding house writing letters in an upstairs writing nook. While there he heard someone call his name. He rose and went downstairs where he was met by six men with revolvers and bowie knives. They were led by Robert Kelley and they escorted Pardee back up the stairs to his room. There they presented him with a list of resolutions that denounced Free-State men, abolitionists, and northern emigrant aid societies. They demanded he sign it.

The resolutions were cut out of the *Squatter Sovereign* newspaper. The Jim Kelly referred to in these resolutions is not related to Bob Kelly, the editor and publisher of the *Squatter Sovereign*, the resolutions were as follows:

"Whereas, by recent occurrences it is now known that there are among us agents of the underground railroad, for the express purpose of abducting our slaves; and, whereas, one Jim Kelly, hailing from some infernal abolition den, has, both by words and acts, proved himself a worthy representative of such an association; and whereas others in the vicinity, whose idle habits and apparently plenty of money, induce us to believe that they are hirelings of some such infamous society; believing it due not only to ourselves, but to the adjoining portion of Missouri, to rid ourselves of so great an evil, and for the furtherance of this end:

Resolved, 1st. That one Jim Kelly, hailing from Cincinnati, having upon sundry occasions, denounced our institutions and declared all proslavery men ruffians, we deem it an act of kindness to rid him of such company, and hereby command him to leave the town of Atchison in one hour after being informed of the passage of this resolution, never more to show himself in this vicinity.

Resolved, 2nd. That in case he fails to obey this reasonable command, we inflict upon him such punishment as the nature of the case and circumstances may require.

Resolved, 3rd. That other emissaries of the Aid Society who are now in our midst tampering with our slaves are warned to leave, else they too will meet the reward which their nefarious designs justly merit—hemp.

Resolved, 4th. That we approve and applaud our fellow-townsman, Grafton Thomasson, for the castigation administered to the said Jim Kelly, whose presence among us is a libel on our good standing and a disgrace to the community.

Resolved, 5th. That we have commenced the good work of purging our town of all resident abolitionists, and after cleansing our town of such nuisances, shall do the same with settlers on Walnut and Independence Creeks, whose propensities for cattle stealing are well known to many.

Resolved 6th. That chairman appoint a committee of three to wait upon the said Kelly and acquaint him with the action of this meeting.

Resolved, 7th. That the proceedings of this meeting be published, so that the world may know our determination.

On the motion of Henry Allen, copies of these resolution were ordered to be made out, and a committee of three be requested to circulate them, with a view of obtaining signatures, thereby showing who are abolitionists"[20]

The resolutions are the result of an argument between Jim Kelly and Robert Kelly and the local border ruffians. Apparently, Jim Kelly criticized Grafton Thomason, a slaveowner, by claiming he improperly buried a slave he owned that had passed away. Thomason then severely beat the smaller Kelly with his fists and a rock until his face was so swollen, he couldn't see. That night he was cared for by a kind local family. The next day he was ordered to leave town, he obeyed the order and never returned.

Pardee was told about all this in graphic terms by Robert Kelly and was terrified and afraid to speak. If he did, he was sure his voice would shake. He sat down in a chair by the window and noticed a crowd was gathering in the street. He then pretended to read the resolutions, although he already knew what they said, as he had read the original article in the *Squatter Sovereign*. Then he started to read them aloud to the

---

[20] The resolutions can be found here (Howard & Oliver, 1856, pp. 961-962). The whole story is paraphrased from Butler's testimony to the Congressional committee. And from (Butler, 1889).

men, but they were impatient, and Kelley said, "We just want to know, will you sign these resolutions?"

Pardee glanced at the growing crowd in the street and wanted to be among them. He felt whatever was about to happen should happen in public. He quickly got up, moved into the hallway and down the stairs. The men caught up to him there and grabbed his wrists and demanded "Will you sign?"

Pardee then answered, "No!"

Then they dragged him to the Missouri River shore, cursing him and telling him they were going to drown him. When they reached the river, some little boys, anxious to see what was going on, asked Pardee to stand on a nearby stump and defend himself. Pardee replied, "But, I don't know what I am accused of yet."

This broke the silence and Kelley asked him, "Did the Emigrant Aid Society send you here?"

Butler replied, "No; I have no connection with the Emigrant Aid Society."

Kelley, then asks, "Well, what did you come for?"

Butler says, "I came because I had a mind to come. What did you come for?"

Kelley, "Did you come to make Kansas a free state?'

Butler, "No, but I will vote to make Kansas a free state."

Kelley, "Are you a correspondent of the abolitionist *New York Tribune*?"

Butler, "No; I have not written a line to the *Tribune* since I came to Kansas."

By this time a large crowd had gathered at the river and many of the men took turns questioning Butler.

A man in the crowd said, "Slaves are property, and we have a right to take our property to any state in the union and have it protected."

Butler responded, "Free-State men have a legal right to move to Kansas and make it a free state with their votes."

Ira Norris, an old man, then approached Butler and whispered to him, as a friend, "You are to be set free, for your own good, when you get away, stay away."

Norris had a northern accent and was a government official in Platte County Missouri. He stepped away, but looked at Butler carefully, as if to say, "Mind what I say!"

Many of the others wanted Butler to leave Kansas and stay away, but he refused saying, "Gentlemen, there is no use in keeping up this debate any longer; if I live anywhere, I shall live in Kansas. Now do your duty as you understand it, and I will do mine as I understand it. I ask no favors of you."

The men then walked away and met to discuss what to do with him. Dr. John Stringfellow, Robert Kelley's partner in the *Squatter Sovereign*, was out of town, attending the "bogus" Territorial Legislature, when these events occurred. But Kelley told his friend and partner what happened during the meeting. Stringfellow later described what Kelly told him:

> "A vote was taken upon the mode of punishment which ought to be accorded to him, and to this day it is probably known to very few persons that a decided verdict of death by hanging with a hemp rope was rendered; and furthermore, that Bob Kelley, calmed the excited mob, and saved Mr. Butler's life. Then the crowd decided to send Pardee Butler down the Missouri River on a raft."[21]

Robert Kelley may have saved Pardee Butler's life, but he was also famous for having written, "No northern man was fit to govern Kansas." And "I will never die happy until I have killed an abolitionist. If I can't kill a man, I'll kill a woman, if I can't kill a woman, I'll kill a child." This was the state of journalism in Kansas at the time, anything to make a fuss and sell newspapers.

The local dentist, Mr. Peebles, supported Kelley in saving Pardee's life. He said:

> "My friends, we must not hang this man; he is not an Abolitionist, he is what they call a Free-Soiler. The abolitionists steal our slaves, but the Free-Soilers do not do this. They intend to make Kansas a free state by legal methods. But in the outcome of the business, there is not the value of a picayune of difference between a Free-Soiler and an abolitionist; for if the Free-Soilers succeed in making Kan-

---

21 (Butler, 1889, p. 70)

sas a free state, and thus surround Missouri with a cordon of free states, our slaves in Missouri will not be worth a dime apiece. Still, we must not hang this man; and I propose that we make a raft and send him down the river as an example."[22]

The group decided it should be a two-log raft, then built one and placed Pardee on it. Before sending him down the river they painted an "R" (for rogue) on his forehead with black paint. Flags were affixed to his raft that said, Horace Greely to the rescue, I have a slave; Eastern Aid Express; and Rev. Mr. Butler, agent for the Underground Railroad.[23] The *Squatter Sovereign* later notified their readers that "the same punishment will be awarded to all Free-Soilers, abolitionists, and their emissaries."

Butler had a purse of gold in his pocket and was worried that if he drowned it would be lost forever. He took it out and asked a local storekeeper he had dealt with before, "Please take this gold and send it to my wife. I don't want to lose it."

The storekeeper said, "I'm sorry Pardee, I can't do that. You will need to keep it as safe as you can."

Later the storekeeper told Pardee he was afraid of the other men and that was why he refused. They used a boat to pull the raft out into the middle of the Missouri River (the river is normally over 1,000 feet wide at Atchison). Once there, Pardee told them, "Gentlemen, if I am drowned, I forgive you; but I have this to say. If you are not ashamed of your part in this transaction, I am not ashamed of mine. Good-bye."

They left Pardee on the raft and rowed back to shore. Pardee then looked around him and saw the flag on the end of the long log of his two-log raft. The men had left him with his pocketknife, so he crawled down the long log and used it to cut down the flag, then he shaped the flagpole (a forked sapling the men had cut down and tied to the longer of the logs) into a crude paddle by using part of the flag to bridge the fork in the sapling. He used the crude paddle to row ashore several miles downstream of Atchison. Once back on land, he made his way south to Port Williams where he had a friend and brother Disciple that

---

22 (Butler, 1889, pp. 70-71)

23 We have softened the original language for this book, both here and in other quotes.

ran a sawmill and asked him for help. He explained what had happened and told his friend, "Now if you do not want to lodge me, please say so, and I will go somewhere else."

His friend replied: "You shall lodge with me if it costs me every penny I am worth." Then he added that he had leased the sawmill from men who were very bitter, and extreme in their views, and they might be so angry with him they would turn him out of the mill. So, he said: "There is Brother Oliphant living in the bluffs; he is under no such embarrassment."

Brother Oliphant and his friends treated Pardee well and listened to the whole story with sympathy and understanding. Pardee stayed two days in Port Williams, as his story spread throughout the community.

Pardee shared his story with Oliver Steele, the local Disciples of Christ minister, who made the story the central part of his sermon the following Sunday. This caused the story to spread to a much larger area, and all heard what had happened to Pardee Butler. They came to pay their respects and told Pardee how upset they were that he had to endure such an injustice. Once his stay and recovery were complete, he traveled to Weston, boarded the *Polar Star* and continued his trip to Illinois to meet his family.

His story was told and re-told across the country and was in every newspaper. It inflamed passions on both sides.

This is a memorable day

It was well that Caleb was preparing for trouble. When Caleb's neighbors and family told him what had happened to Pardee in Atchison he immediately went to Atchison, stood in the middle of the street, in front of Robert Kelley's *Squatter Sovereign* print shop and yelled, "I am a Free-State man: now raft me!"[24] No one had the courage to take him up on his offer. Everyone fled the streets and left Caleb, his face red with rage, and his eyes blazing, on the street alone. Robert Kelly was a big man, younger than Caleb, and no stranger to violence, but even he dared not accept Caleb's challenge.

---

24 (Butler, 1889, p. 75)

Probably the two Navy Colt revolvers in holsters hanging from his belt and the Sharps .52 caliber rifle he was waving around as if it were a feather had a little to do with Bob Kelley and his friends staying inside.

So, unopposed and a little disappointed, Caleb simply made this proclamation, "If there is any more of this business done here, to any Free-State man, I will go to Missouri and raise a company of men to clean out this town!"[25]

They knew Caleb as a man of his word and took his warning to heart. Due in part to his encounter with Charley Dunn, Caleb was well known and feared in both Kansas and Missouri. Border ruffians, who regularly stole from Free-State settlers, would not touch anything on his property, and they avoided meeting him face-to-face. Caleb's neighbors, including Pardee, put their horses and cattle on his property during the troubles because they knew they were safe there and would not be stolen. Pardee's oldest daughter, Mrs. Rosetta B. Hastings, tells the following story in her book on Pardee and Caleb:[26]

"One day Caleb May saw quite a company of men riding toward his place. He and his son, William, and his hired man stationed themselves under the bank of a nearby Stranger Creek tributary, where both the house and the ford would be in range of their guns. Mrs. May was to talk to the horsemen as they rode past the house, and, if they were Border Ruffians, she was to shut the door, as a signal to the husband to be ready for an attack. When they rode up, however, they proved to be Mr. Speck, and about twenty other neighbors from the lower neighborhood, who had brought their horses up to Mr. May's to keep them from the Ruffians, who stood in great fear of Mr. May."

Caleb eventually calmed down and left. He was spoiling for a fight and was disappointed no one would face him.

While no one stole Caleb's horses or cattle, the *Squatter Sovereign* regularly insulted him in front page editorials. But Robert Kelly had to be careful, besides Caleb's fearsome reputation, he had a large and loyal family in the Rushville and DeKalb area across the river.

---

25 (Butler, 1889, p. 75)
26 (Butler, 1889, p. 271)

Governor Reeder's last day, August 16th, was the day Pardee Butler was rafted. Reeder remembered the prophetic words of John Wakefield to the territorial "bogus" legislature after the ouster of the Free-State legislators in Pawnee, Kansas, and thought of them often:

"Gentlemen, this is a memorable day and may become more so. Your acts [kicking out the Free-State members] will be the means of lighting watch-fires of war in our land."[27]

Reeder believed Wakefield and dreaded the coming war. He had invested in the Kansas Territory and was worried about both the Territory and his land.

Big Springs

Caleb was delighted to see his new friend Dr. Charles Robinson when he arrived in Big Springs for the Convention on September 4th. They greeted each other with broad smiles and a hearty handshake. Charles said, "I recognize those pistols!"

Where Robinson was well educated, eloquent, confident, and tough; Caleb had had little schooling and, although he read well, his writing and speaking skills were poor. But both were confident in themselves, tall, muscular, and familiar with fighting and trouble. Both were fearless, and it was this mutual trait that bonded them. It was appropriate that their first discussion was about the revolvers that Charles had sold Caleb.

Caleb raised his arms, so Charles had a clear view of his revolvers and replied, "They are indeed those you sold to me. Both my son and I have tried them. As you said, they do shoot a little high, but we learned how to compensate for that. I was worried about the trip and thought I should bring them. It is dangerous to travel these days."

Robinson asked, "Mr. Butler was unable to come?"

"No sir, Pardee had to return to Illinois to collect his family and bring them to Kansas. You may have heard about his troubles on his way back. He was sent down the Missouri on a raft by those proslavery ruffians in Atchison."

---

27 (Kansas Historical Society, 2019)

"I did hear about that, is he OK?"

"As far as I know he is, but he has business to settle in Illinois and Iowa, so he will not be returning for few weeks. I am forming a militia for your Kansas Legion in our town and have some solid men, including Pardee's brother-in-law who has just arrived, already signed up. I do need to pick up some weapons from you for them. I have the money with me. I need six Sharps and eight Navy Colts."

"Sure Caleb, no problem I have them at my house back in Lawrence. After the conference we can go get them. By the way, we have elected James Abbott to be General of the entire Kansas Legion, he will be helping you train your men. He will be here tomorrow, and you can meet him."

"Looking forward to it sir."

Because it was the afternoon of the 4th, they had time to talk. The Convention did not start until the next day. Charles explained what was going on. He said, "In July we realized that Governor Reeder was about to be fired, and that he will be replaced with a proslavery Governor, who will be Wilson Shannon, a totally useless individual. Many of us met in Lawrence in August, just before you visited, or I would have invited you to attend. We had the idea to formalize the Free-State Party, which we will do during this convention."

Caleb said, "I will join your new party. The Democratic Party is now only a proslavery party, and I cannot abide that."

Charles replied, "Thank you. Our meetings in both July and August were filled with talk of revolution. Many wanted to launch an armed revolt against the bogus legislature. The most prominent was Jim Lane, who you will meet here. In the August meeting, it was clear that only a Convention to set up a Free-State Party and the election of a separate Free-State government would dissuade the radicals in our party from all-out war."

After a brief pause, Charles continued, "Jim Lane has been a life-long Democrat and tried to start a Kansas Democratic Party, but we convinced him it would never work and that the Democrats would never give up slavery. The rest of the public are willing to help form and support a new Free-State Party. But they want it to be separate from the Free-Soil or Republican Parties."

Caleb asked, "Why is that? Why a new party?"

Charles said, "Basically a large faction of our group are against allowing Negros to settle in Kansas and they are against the abolitionists, who want to eliminate slavery in the whole country. These views of the Free-Soil and Republican parties they cannot abide. The Free-State Party wants no slavery in Kansas, but they do not wish to tell Missouri to free their slaves."

Caleb responded, "I can see that, those are my views as well. I want no slaves in Kansas, I certainly do not wish to tell Missouri they have to free their slaves. I'm also pretty sure I want no Negros in the state, but I listen to my neighbor Pardee Butler, who believes that all Negros should be free and should be allowed to go wherever they please. So, I'm persuadable on the settlement issue, but for now I think it is best not to allow Negros into Kansas. If they can escape Missouri and come to Kansas, I will help them get to Iowa, but I do not want them to stay. Mostly because it will just cause trouble."

Charles responds, "I agree with your neighbor Mr. Butler, but to form the party, we must focus on what we agree upon and remain united. The issue of Negro freedom is important, but it can't keep us from being united in this fight."

After a pause, Charles continued, "In July, we came to realize that the Territorial Government formed this year is an utter failure. It only supports the proslavery views and makes any debate on the vital issue of slavery in Kansas illegal. No law that makes honest debate or publishing views contrary to the majority view illegal can be allowed. It is a violation of the first amendment of the Constitution and against the spirit and intent of the Kansas-Nebraska Act. That the President and new Governor support the censorship law is a miscarriage of justice."

Charles was sad and frowning as he talked, then his expression brightened suddenly and he said, "I quite like your holsters. Where did you buy them?"

Caleb replied, "I went to Kickapoo, where some of the Kickapoo women are very good at making leather goods and bought these holsters and a saddle holster for my Sharps. I also bought holsters for my wife and my son. My son has the Sharps rifle, and my wife has the Pocket Colt at home for protection."

"They did a nice job didn't they? They also added a horizontal sheath for my knife on the back of the holster belt. Everything is secured with thongs and straps and can be worn comfortably while riding a horse, without anything falling out."

"They make lots of these holsters and have a thriving business. You should go to Kickapoo when you can. Nobody's better than a Kickapoo with leather."

Caleb turned slightly so Charles could see the full gun belt, his knife, and the built-in compartment for cartridges. Caleb didn't have any of the new brass cartridges, but he did make paper and cloth cartridges for his colts.

Charles replied, "I'd love to have holsters like that, if you have time could you have a set made for me?"

Caleb said, "Absolutely, I go to Kickapoo often, next time I'm there I'll have them make you a rig just like this."

Next, Robinson introduced Caleb to General Jim Lane. Lane's most notable characteristic is he cannot stop talking. One didn't have a conversation with Lane, one could only listen to Lane.

Lane first asked Robinson for his support in securing a government office, ideally a Senate seat, when Kansas became a state. Charles looked a little pained Caleb thought, but he agreed. Then, Caleb got the distinct impression that his friend Robinson steered them away from Lane a bit too quickly. That said, he was grateful, Lane could be a bit hard to take.

He also met the ex-governor Andrew Reeder. Reeder was the dead opposite Lane. He was quiet and unassuming, but friendly and attentive.

Reeder said to Charles and Caleb, "At this convention we must repudiate the bogus legislature, nominate our own delegate to Congress, which I wish to be me, and initiate the process of writing a state constitution so we can apply for statehood."

Charles and Caleb nodded after Reeder had spoken, and Caleb ask him, "If you are a delegate to Congress, what will you do?"

Reeder answered, "My first task will be to initiate a Congressional investigation of the March election. We have sufficient evidence that it was an illegal election, and we need a Congressional investigation to prove it."

Charles said, "Do you really think they will launch a formal inquiry."

Reeder said, "Yes, I am assured there are sufficient votes to start an inquiry, we just need to give them a little push. I'm already gathering

Big Springs 101

statements and affidavits that I will take to Congress to give our allies the ammunition they need to set up a committee."[28]

Like Caleb and Robinson, nearly all the delegates arrived at the convention heavily armed since they were not sure what might happen on their journey or after they reached Big Springs. One landlady refused to retrieve a man's coat, saying, "Go in and get it yourself, I would not touch that armory for all the property in the room."[29]

According to the *Herald of Freedom*, the convention recommended forming militia companies for defense.[30] This was a good idea as the Free-State men were accused of treason for ignoring the territorial laws against speaking out against slavery.

Andrew Reeder pushed to ignore the Territorial Legislature and create a new Free-State legislature, governor, and delegate to Congress. Reeder was voted to be the delegate to Congress by acclamation.

The Big Springs Convention knew they were committing a "State Prison offense" just by meeting and discussing the elimination of slavery and opposing the Territorial Legislature and its laws. This was amplified when the Missouri press labeled the Free-State people "revolutionists."[31]

Caleb May was nominated to be a delegate to the Topeka Constitutional Convention for his voting district in the Center Township of Atchison County. He won this position later in the district Free-State election, held on October 9. The Free-State constitutional convention was to be held in Topeka on October 23.

After the convention Caleb drove his buggy to Lawrence from Big Springs, about 15 miles, and bought the Sharps rifles and Navy Colts he needed for his men. Just in case, he bought two more rifles and two more Navy Colts than he had committed to buy, since newcomers were still arriving in Pardee, and times were tough. "Be prepared," as Maggie always told him. The extra weapons, gunpowder, lead, caps, and papers he bought would be kept in a shed that he built that he called the "armory."

---

28 The Congressional investigation was initiated by an act of Congress that was passed on March 19, 1856; their report was published in July of 1856. (Howard & Oliver, 1856).

29 (Etcheson, 2004, p. 71)

30 A Lawrence, Kansas Free-State newspaper on September 8, 1855.

31 (Etcheson, 2004, p. 73)

The Topeka Convention

It was bitterly cold on October 21, 1855 when Caleb mounted his horse and headed for the Topeka Constitutional Convention from his farm. The family gathered in front of their cabin to see him off, they looked sad, and Caleb felt guilty, but knew it was important to go. He decided to take his double-barreled shotgun and Colt pistols and leave the Sharps and the musket for the boys to use for hunting and to protect the family. William was better with the Sharps than he was anyway, and Caleb knew he would take good care of it. Maggie looked worried, and asked, "Be careful Cale."

Caleb replied, "I will dear Maggie, I will."

The trip to Topeka was a long day's ride, a good 40 miles, but he was looking forward to it. He hoped to be able to talk to Old John Brown and his sons while there. He had met the Brown sons in Big Springs but had not yet met Old John Brown who had just arrived in Kansas on October 9th. The stories he had heard in Big Springs suggested that he was a strong abolitionist. He and his son, John Jr., were in favor of freeing all slaves and inviting free Negros to settle and vote in Kansas, an issue that Caleb wanted to learn more about.

The Topeka Constitutional Convention attracted nationwide attention, as did nearly everything that happened in Kansas Territory. The whole country was debating slavery, was it right? Or was it wrong? Were slaves property, or people? Everyone had an opinion and there was no consensus on the issue.

National politics itself had devolved into nothing but the debate about slavery. The *New York Daily Tribune* was the largest newspaper in the United States in 1855, and they sent William A. (Bill) Phillips to report on the daily events at the convention. Phillips attended the full convention, and he described Caleb May as follows in one of his dispatches:

"Caleb May is a character; a Missourian [but originally from Kentucky], tall, dark-visaged and stern. He is one of those men you would not like for an enemy. He was a free-state man, of the black-law school, but had a remembrance that he had once been a Democrat. He was a good and true man, however, but rigid and stern."[32]

---

32 (Phillips, 1856, p. 134)

Phillips phrase "black-law school" simply meant that Caleb wanted to exclude black people from Kansas. The convention was to meet October 23 at noon for the first time in the new Constitution Hall building, built for the convention by the town.

Topeka, in late 1855, was a sparsely settled prairie town where almost all the residents lived in log cabins. The convention attendees mostly arrived late on the 22nd of October, with a few arriving the morning of the 23rd. There were only three small boarding houses in Topeka, and it was very cold, the attendees had to sleep in hammocks strung up between the interior walls of the boarding houses, with as many as 12 in a small room. Every room did not have proper glass windows and often there was nothing between the cold outside air and the room but a cloth cover.

The convention had 40 Free-State Party members and no proslavery members. Jim Lane was elected president of the gathering. Among the attendees, were twelve lawyers, thirteen farmers, two merchants, two clergymen and one saddler. The convention decided to leave the issue of allowing blacks into the state, or not, to a vote of the people, as the convention could not come to agreement on the issue.

The dual government of the Territory was never more apparent than in October 1855. The proslavery Law-and-Order Party elected John Whitfield as a territorial delegate to Congress on October 1st. Then on October 9th the Free-State Party elected Andrew Reeder to the same position, and neither side participated in the other's election.

The Territory continued to have two governments, one proslavery and the other Free-State, for two more years. The Free-State constitution[33] was completed and signed by Caleb May and 39 other delegates on November 5, 1855.[34]

In summary, they wrote a constitution based upon other free state constitutions and included Article I, Section 6, outlawing slavery in the state. They also freed any slave that enters Kansas from another state.[35] This provision was at odds with the 1850 federal Fugitive Slave Act, but similar provisions were already law in Iowa and other states.

---

33 (Kansas Historical Society, 1855)

34 (Topeka Constitutional Convention, 1855), The completion date was moved forward to the 5th, from the 11th to help the narrative.

35 (Topeka Constitutional Convention, 1855)

State laws were stronger in the 1850s, and sometimes conflicted with federal laws. The only exception to the slavery rule was punishment for a crime, that is, a prison sentence could include unpaid hard labor.

The new Free-State Constitution was printed and circulated around the Territory and put to a vote on December 15. The second question on the ballot that day was whether free Negros would be allowed into the state and allowed to vote. Charles Robinson, John Brown Jr. and their followers encouraged a vote of "Yes" on both provisions. Jim Lane and his supporters wanted to exclude all Negros. The vote was held, and the Constitution was approved by a vote of 1731 for, and 46 against. The exclusion of free blacks was approved by 1287 to 453.[36]

Jim

A few days after Caleb returned from Topeka, in the middle of November 1855, a young mulatto black man arrived at the farm. His name was Jim, and he gave no last name. He was looking for work and seemed a pleasant sort of fellow. Caleb warned him, "It will be dangerous for you in this area. Black men are often kidnapped, taken to Missouri, and sold into slavery."

He added, "I've helped some black people get to Holton, Kansas where they will be safely taken to Nebraska City and on to Iowa. I can do the same for you. But, if you want to stay and work, it is OK. I'll pay you fifty cents a day and give you a bed and three meals a day."

Jim replied, "I hear this is a good Christian town and I should be safe here. I know carpentry and farming, I can help you a lot, and fifty cents a day sounds mighty good to me. Thank you, sir."

"Carpentry, you know carpentry! Well, your first job is to build yourself a room next to the barn over there."

Caleb pointed to the end of his crude barn, and said, "I just got back from a territorial constitutional convention, and there may be a vote soon to exclude black people from the state. So, it may not be easy for you to stay here. They call the idea to exclude blacks from Kansas the 'black law.' I'm unclear how I feel about that law, but my neighbor

---

36 Both vote counts are from (Etcheson, 2004, p. 75).

Pardee Butler, our minister, wants black people to settled wherever they want to, just like white folks. You will find that Brother Butler is highly respected here, and he will help you. He is also my best friend, and I will help you too. But you need to know the situation here. Knowing all that do you still want to stay?"

Jim answered, "I have nowhere else to go. You seem like an honest and straightforward man, and fifty cents a day, three meals, and a room sounds like a fortune to me. Yes sir, I want to stay."

"OK Jim. We'll make this work. By God, I'm glad you know carpentry! I have many projects for you."

Jim was not quite 25 years old, and a strong, gentle, and pleasant man. Caleb could see all that. Black or not, Jim needed help. Caleb expected problems with some of his neighbors in the growing town, but everyone needed a trained carpenter, and he knew Pardee would help ease Jim into the town. Besides, he and William simply couldn't do all the work that was needed on his farm and neither of them knew enough about carpentry.

Caleb continued with his warning to Jim, "Most of my neighbors, except for Pardee Butler, are against black men settling in the area or in the town. But you aren't staking a claim. You are just a hired hand. You seem pleasant enough; you are a strong and skilled young man. I expect my neighbors will eventually accept you. If there is a problem and you must leave, I will see that you get safely to Iowa."

Jim said, "If there is a problem, it will not be because of me."

Caleb liked him and so did the rest of the family. Caleb and Maggie were doing well financially. Caleb's business of selling cement, limestone blocks, logs, and timber was going well. The farm fed the whole family, and they were growing enough to sell some of their crops. The new settlers in Pardee needed everything Caleb and William could make or grow. So, paying and feeding Jim was not a problem.

Caleb invited Jim to church with the family every Sunday, and Jim was delighted to go, he had not been to church in many years. He was afraid of being shunned because he was a black man, but the Reverend Pardee Butler took care of that by enthusiastically welcoming Jim at the church and making a point of starting a conversation with him before every Sunday meeting.

After a few Sundays, Jim was accepted by nearly everyone and a respected member of the little town. A few members of the church quietly complained about a black man attending the meetings, they even made sure that Pardee, Caleb, and Jim knew they were displeased. No one in the church supported slavery, all thought it was wrong, the disagreement was over the acceptance of black men in the community.

Neither Caleb nor Pardee would put up with any shunning or exclusion of Jim in any church activities. Pardee told Caleb, "I'm pleased to see that you, my best friend, and your family see Jim as a man, and not a black man. He is a person in God's eyes, just like we are. I am determined to make sure the rest of my flock see him the same way."

Caleb answered, "And you are hardheaded enough to do the job!"

Pardee laughed out loud at that and replied, "Yes sir!"

Jim was delighted with how things were working out for him, and later when they were alone, he startled Caleb when he said, "Mr. Caleb this is the best time of my whole life."

Caleb was surprised to hear Jim say that but wondered about what had happened to Jim in the past. Not that he would ever ask Jim about his past, this was just not done. But he did wonder.

Not asking anyone about their past was customary at the time in Kansas. Many people in Kansas had problems in their past that they were running from, and while they could volunteer information, no one would ever be so impolite as to ask.

***

While Jim had been born a free man in Pennsylvania, his entire family was kidnapped when he was only seven and sold into slavery in Virginia. Jim was taken from his family two years later and sold to a farmer in Missouri. In Missouri his master was better than most and taught the young Jim how to farm and carpentry. But Jim was born a free man, and he wanted his freedom again.

Thirteen years later, Jim told his master that he wanted to buy his freedom, and he was told no, he was a slave and would remain a slave. The man whipped Jim just for asking. It was the first time the man had whipped Jim, and while he did it, he told him not to even think about running. The whipping was hard enough to bruise and bloody Jim's back, but not hard enough to disable him, it definitely could have been worse, and Jim knew it. He thought his master wanted to make his point but was not enthusiastic about whipping him. It didn't matter to Jim, he was humiliated by the whipping, and more determined than ever to get away.

Not long before the whipping, while shopping for lumber and nails for his master, Jim was surreptitiously given very specific directions from a Free-Soiler in Odessa, Missouri on how to escape. He didn't tell the Free-Soiler that he was planning to escape, and the Free-Soiler didn't ask, he just volunteered the directions and told him about a specific barbershop in Lawrence, Kansas where he could get help. Jim didn't know the man, or his name, but the story felt like the truth. It eventually turned out that the directions, which Jim had memorized, were accurate.

From the Free-Soiler, Jim knew Kansas was only 40 miles west and he knew that Lawrence and Topeka, both free cites, were only 30 miles or so west of the border. He was young and in good shape, he knew he could run to Kansas in one night if he had to. Then another day to Lawrence.

He waited until his master was out with his friends one evening, and then waited for the mother to put the children to bed and take a drink of whiskey and go to bed herself. He had packed some food and water and one change of clothes. It was cold, so he bundled up, thankful that he had a good coat, hat, and scarf. Then he strapped his food, water and extra clothes to his back and took off. Except for several short breaks to catch his breath, rest a bit, and sip some water, he didn't stop running until he reached what he knew from his benefactor was the Shawnee Mission.

He gave the Mission a wide berth, he knew that the owner of the land there, Thomas Johnson, was a slave holder and would capture and return him if he could. He was now in Kansas Territory, but not safe yet, he needed to get to Lawrence.

He headed south toward Olathe, sticking to the woods and avoiding the roads. He knew Olathe was a mixed town, with both anti- and pro-slavery settlers, but he didn't know anyone there and had no place to go. So, he skirted the northern edge of the town.

It took all day for him to get to Lawrence, but once there he went straight to the barbershop, that the Free-Soiler in Odessa had described. The Free-Soiler had told him he would be safe in Lawrence, and sure enough, no one paid much attention to him as he looked for the barbershop. It was closed by the time he got to it, but he knocked, and a black man came to the door.

The man greeted him, and said, "No names, no details. You here from Missouri?"

Jim replied, "Yes sir. Looking for safety and work."

The man said, "I got no work for you here, but I got a blanket and a safe place to sleep. It's cold out, please come in." I can give you water and dinner. Tomorrow we'll see what happens next."

Jim said, "Thank you sir."

The barber and his wife fed him some bread and venison stew and asked no questions but told him a lot. The man said, "You can stay here in Lawrence or in Topeka and find work for 25 cents a day and room and board, but there have been a lot of kidnappings of blacks lately, it isn't safe."

The barber's wife chipped in, "Just a kidnapping yesterday, story is they got a black man helping them. The black man leads the victim to the kidnappers who take him to Missouri for the reward or to sell him."

The barber said, "Yes sir, that's the story, this is what we've come to. Now our own are helping in the kidnapping. They are taking money to betray their own. Anyway, due north of here, about 35 miles, there is a Disciples of Christ minister named Pardee Butler who is very anti-slavery and has helped many of our folk get to Iowa. His neighbor and best friend, Caleb May, helps him and is a real bad ass. All the proslavery ruffians are afraid of him. If you think you can make it, I recommend you go there. But be careful, the towns of Atchison and Leavenworth are close by and dangerous for black men."

"Pardee Butler was recently sent down the Missouri River on a raft just because he is against slavery. He is now famous and admired among all Free-Soilers and black folk. The people of his town changed the name of their town to Pardee in his honor."

Jim asks, "So you say it is due north? If I left tomorrow night and followed the North Star, I would get there?"

"Yes sir. Just be careful, these are troubled times."

Jim finished his stew, chatted a bit more, then went to bed. The next morning, he slept in, he was exhausted. The barber and his wife were up early, but the barber said to her, "We should be as quiet as possible, the boy needs to get some sleep today, the more he gets the better."

Jim awoke in the early afternoon and made his decision. He told the barber and his wife, "I want to try and get to Pardee, I like what you told me about Mr. Butler and Mr. May. I'd like to leave at sunset."

Jim continued, "Bless you, I never could have gotten away unless I had heard that you are here."

The barber drew a crude map of the route and gave it to Jim.

Then as Jim was leaving that evening, the barber told him, "Most of the towns you will pass are fairly safe, Oskaloosa is first and it is nearly all anti-slavery, next is Nortonville, which also nearly all anti-slavery. Once you pass Nortonville you will be only five miles from Pardee, Pardee is just a little east of due north from there."

***

After working with Jim for a few days, Caleb found he was a good hired-hand and very skilled. The day after Caleb hired him, he took Jim to Elijah Smith's store in his wagon and bought some milled lumber and tools.

While at the store, Jim described some tools he would need that Caleb didn't already own. He said, "Mr. Caleb and Mr. Elijah, to do a good job I will need a draw knife, a caliper, a square, chisel, and a brace."

Elijah replied, "I have a draw knife, but I need to order the other items. Can you describe them?"

Jim answered, "OK, the square is two flat pieces of metal joined in a perfect 90-degree angle, it is used to make square joints. A caliper is two thin knives joined with a piece of wood and the knives can be moved back and forth, then fixed in place with a thumbscrew, so they are different distances from one another, it is used to make circles or curved arcs. A chisel is used to shape a piece of wood, I'd like a wide one and a narrow one. A brace is used to drill holes, I need one with two or three steel bits of different sizes."

Elijah said, "OK, I should be able to get those tools in Leavenworth, I'm going there tomorrow. Caleb, should I buy them for you?"

Caleb said, "If they aren't too expensive, please do."

Jim started working on his quarters that same day and received his new tools from Elijah with great delight two days later. He used the tools and the lumber to complete his quarters and then built a new bedroom, with a new bed off the main cabin for Maggie and Caleb. He also expanded and improved the lofts where William, Enoch, and Priscila often slept. Sam and little Catharine slept in the bed in the main room, and baby Isaac would sleep in the new bedroom with Caleb and Maggie. He also made some new furniture for the expanding house. The house was taking shape, thanks to Jim's skill and hard work.

Most of the kids only slept in the stuffy, poorly ventilated house when the weather was bad, they liked sleeping outside on the airy sleeping porch that Caleb had built the previous winter. Caleb had also built a second fireplace for the porch, so it was comfortable except on the coldest winter nights. Caleb and Maggie often joined them. But this was November, so they were inside almost every night, and Jim's additions were very welcome.

Caleb and Maggie finally bought some glass windows for the cabin and Jim installed them. The glass windows already had sashes and casements, but would not stay up when opened, so Jim made two hinged dowels for each window to use to prop them open so a breeze could air out the cabin. Jim proudly demonstrated them to a pleased Maggie and Caleb.

Maggie smiled her big smile and said, "I'm astonished Jim! Such a wonderful creation, I never dreamed I would have such a luxury. Look at how much light and air they let in! It brightens the whole house."

Jim worked quickly, was a hard worker, and did a wonderful job. He had an engineer's eye for what would work and what wouldn't. Once the additions and improvements to the house were completed, Maggie squealed with delight and with uncharacteristic exuberance said, "Jim, you are God sent, bless you, this is wonderful!"

Jim simply said, "Thank you Ma'am. Anytime Ma'am."

Maggie then said, "What is your favorite dinner? Do you have a pie or cake you are partial to; I must reward you! This is your night."

"No need for a reward, ma'am. But I am partial to strawberry pie."

"Then you will have it! I have canned strawberries in the pantry, and Priscila and I will make a pie, two pies! I love our new house, bless you brother Jim."

Jim's eyes teared up a bit, and he turned his head in embarrassment, in a low voice, he said: "Thank you ma'am."

Maggie noticed the tears and thought, "This man has seen some hard times." But she was too polite to say anything.

Maggie and Priscila found the jars of strawberries in their cupboard and set about making the strawberry pies for Jim and the family. They had some sugar and cinnamon that they had bought from Elijah's store, and they had plenty of their fine homemade cornstarch. They added one cup of their homemade apple-cider vinegar, a cup of water, and a little home churned butter.

They combined the vinegar, water, sugar, cornstarch, cinnamon, and butter in a skillet and brought it to a boil. Then they used their stored lard, water, a pinch of salt, and fire dried and sifted flour to make the dough for the pies. After partially baking the dough carefully in two round pans on the wire grate over the fire they added the canned strawberries to the skillet for a few seconds and let the filling cool before adding it to the pans, covering them with more dough, and baking the pies over the fire.

It was not an easy job over an open fire, but the pies came out perfectly. As Maggie told Priscila, "Strawberries are very healthy and can stave off scurvy. But we always add vinegar to all pies, especially in winter, to make sure no one in the family gets scurvy. Scurvy is all too common in the deep of winter when we have little fruit to eat. These pies, besides pleasing Jim tonight, will keep us all healthy."

Later, after dinner, when Maggie was alone with Caleb, she mentioned Jim and his tears earlier in the day, "Cale, Jim is a good man, but some bad things must have happened to him."

Caleb replied, "He never speaks of his family or his past, I think he is all alone and we need to be mindful of that. He knows he looks different from us, but I think we are all he has in this world today. He doesn't feel like he can get too close to us, but everyone needs someone.

He is a stranger in a strange land, like the descendants of Abram. He may not find peace for himself, but maybe in the future, for his descendants.

The good book says, 'Do not neglect to extend hospitality to strangers, for by this some have entertained angels.' It is our Christian duty to help him and comfort him. He is a black man, and in a strange world, but brother Pardee says we are all the same to the Lord."

Maggie said, "I agree Cale, we will love the stranger."

The next day as they began their work after breakfast, Caleb went to Jim and said, "Jim do you know how to shoot?"

"No sir, I've never held a gun."

"Well time to learn, my good man. If you are going to stay in these parts, you need to know how to use a gun."

Caleb grabbed his Sharps and his Navy revolvers and showed Jim how they worked, then he had Jim fire and reload both and fire them again. Jim wasn't the best shot, not like Caleb or William, but good enough to help in a fight.

Jim was a big man, nearly as tall as Caleb. He was also well built but had no experience fighting. So next, Caleb gave Jim a quick lesson in how to handle a bowie knife, how to wrestle, and box. He told Jim, like he told William, "Jim, avoid fighting when you can, but don't back down. Once the fight starts, it is all about winning, put the man down as fast as possible and make sure he stays down. Never turn your back on him, once he is down and you think he will stay down, back away from him carefully and watch him closely."

"Yes, sir."

After a little work, Caleb pronounced Jim ready to go. He said, "Work on those moves, ask William to help you practice. We all need to know how to defend ourselves here on the frontier, maybe you even more than us."

Jim only said, "Yes sir. Thank you, sir."

Caleb looked straight at him, thinking, "Maybe Pardee and Charles are right, maybe excluding black people from Kansas is wrong."

Jim saw the look, and said, "Is everything OK sir, did I do something wrong?"

Caleb cracked a rare smile, and replied, "Oh, just thinking Jim, everything is fine, you are doing well. We are happy to have you here."

Pardee's family

Pardee Butler collected his family in Canton, Illinois and brought them and his sister Beth, Milo Carlton's wife, to the newly renamed town of Pardee early in November of 1855. Pardee and his family arrived while Caleb was returning from the Topeka Constitutional Convention and just a few days before Jim arrived. While Pardee was away Caleb and his new town council had renamed the town of "Ocena" to Pardee in his honor, with the full and unanimous support of the rapidly growing community. Pardee Butler was a celebrity in the Disciples of Christ community, and stories about his being rafted down the Missouri River because of his support for the Free-Soil Party were now in every newspaper in the country. Caleb thought it was a perfect name, it honored his friend, declared that the community was a Disciples of Christ town, and had good advertising value.

Word of the newly renamed town spread quickly, and new Free-Soil settlers flocked to the area. There were still unclaimed 160 acre lots available close to the town, and the town now had a new church under construction, funded partially by the Disciples of Christ, partially by the town, and partially by Maggie and Caleb. When Jim arrived, he immediately became involved in the construction and design of the new church. It later became a beautiful new building, and the showpiece of the town.

Elijah's store had expanded from one room to three, and Sam Moore's blacksmith shop was now equipped for gunsmithing as well as blacksmithing. Sam had expanded his shop to two rooms.

Pardee made a fuss and didn't want the town named for him, but his neighbors and his kids changed his mind. Eventually he got over his embarrassment and rather liked having the town named for him. Plus, it promised to increase the attendance at his sermons, always a good thing.

After visiting his neighbors, Pardee showed his family their new home and started to get them settled into the cabin.

Pardee loved the new church once it was completed early in December; and publicly thanked Jim and the town for building it. He said, "This beautiful new church is a joy to behold, and a testament to your devotion to God and his son. It shows that the town can come together and achieve great things. It is clear evidence of the extraordinary talents that Jim and all of you possess. Thank you, Jim, and a big thank you to everyone involved."

Pardee's brother-in-law, Milo Carlton, had come ahead of his family to build a cabin with community support as well as a lot of help from William. As Pardee had done, Milo paid William for his work. The cabin was completed, but there was still a lot of work needed. But at least Milo and his wife, Beth, had a place to stay. Milo also joined Caleb's militia and purchased a Sharps rifle and a Colt revolver. Most of the adult male newcomers joined the militia and ordered Sharps and Colts from Caleb. They were a Free-State town in the middle of a proslavery county and needed to organize their defense, as Caleb constantly told them.

Due to the rafting incident and threats from Robert Kelly and the others in Atchison, Pardee brought his family and sister back via the ferry terminal at Iatan, Missouri, rather than the new port in Atchison. But this created a new problem, because his buggy and two of his horses were still in Atchison.

Judge Tutt presiding

After a few days at home, he decided he needed to go to Atchison to get them. He suspected he would be OK, as long as he went in the daylight and entered and left quickly. He foolishly did not tell Caleb what he was doing, Caleb would have been happy to go with him.

He quietly passed through Atchison, and went straight to the stables, paid the stable master, and retrieved his buggy and horses. As he prepared to make the journey home, he was accosted by Robert Kelley. Kelley then led him to a saloon and put him on trial before a group of South Carolinians. Some of the men called for Butler to be killed. They intended to hang him for being an abolitionist. They had a rope and were ready to proceed when they were interrupted by a Missourian named Judge Henry Tutt, a judge and lawyer from St. Joseph. He said:

"My friends, hear me. I am an old man, and it is right you should hear me. I was born in Virginia and have lived many years in Missouri. I am a slave owner and desire Kansas to be made a slave state, if it can be done by honorable means. But you will destroy the cause you are seeking to build up. You have taken this man, who is peaceably passing through your streets and along the public highway and doing no harm. We profess to be 'Law-and-Order' men and ought to be the last to commit violence. If this man has broken the law, let him be judged according to law; but for the sake of Missouri, for the sake of Kansas, for the sake of the proslavery cause, do not act this way."[37]

At that, they took Pardee to another building and appointed a moderator to conduct the proceedings. Robert Kelley told his story and then

---

37 (Butler, 1889, p. 107)

Pardee rose to tell his, but he was jerked back into his seat before he could get a word out. Judge Tutt then spoke and pleaded for Pardee's freedom.

Kelley asked Tutt, "Do you belong in Kansas?"

Tutt replied "No, but I expect to move here next fall and in this matter the interests of Missouri and Kansas are identical."

Two other Atchison residents, Chester Lamb and Samuel Dickson, both proslavery, then spoke up in defense of Tutt and ask for Pardee to be set free.

Robert Kelley then said, "We will not hang Pardee Butler, but only tar and feather him."

The moderator replied, "It is moved that Butler be tarred and feathered and receive thirty-nine lashes."

A majority shouted, "Aye" although there were some scattered "No's."

The moderator then said, "The affirmative has it; Butler is to be tarred and feathered and whipped."[38]

There was a good deal of whispering and quiet discussion around the room, then the moderator again came forward and said, "It is moved that the last part of the sentence be rescinded."

The South Carolinians were upset and said they should have just shot Butler right off and not messed with all this. The leader said, "I did not come all the way from South Carolina, spending so much money to do things up in such a milk-and-water style as this."

Then they stripped Butler naked to the waist and covered him with tar. They had no feathers, so they covered him with cotton. Then they threw his clothes onto his buggy, put him in it, tied his extra horse to the back, and sent him on his way. It was cold that day, so Pardee stopped outside town and tried to clean himself up. Then he put his clothes back on. Butler was asked many times, "Why did this happen?"

His reply is always the same, "It was done because I declared myself a Free-Soiler in the office of the *Squatter Sovereign*."

Caleb, Maggie, and Sybil were furious with him, as they discussed the whole affair over Pardee and Sybil's dinner table. Caleb said, with some irritation in his voice, "Why did you not ask me to go with you? You know I would go. All this could have been avoided."

---

38 (Butler, 1889, p. 108)

Pardee answered, also with irritation in his voice, "I am a man, and I can take care of myself, I don't need a caretaker."

Caleb shrugged, then said to his friend, "Oh well, I've been guilty of foolish pride as well. Just know, you can always ask for my help, Brother Pardee. Believe me, no one in Atchison will bother you if you are with me."

Pardee calmed down a bit, looked at his friend and said, "I know I can Caleb, and I will next time, I cannot afford to lose any more clothes!"

That got a laugh from everyone and cleared the air. Sybil looked at Caleb with great gratitude, grasped his hand from across the table, and said, "We are grateful for everything you've done for us Caleb. If my man does anything this foolish again you can thrash him, I'll hand you the whip myself!" That led to more laughter.

A few evenings later, a group of South Carolinians camped near Caleb May's house and Pardee Butler was warned about it by one of his flock. He immediately left to tell Caleb. While Pardee was gone, Milo, his brother-in-law, nailed some shakes over the Butler's prized 12-pane window, cleaned his new Sharps, and loaded it. Pardee's sister, Beth, molded more bullets over the fire and Sybil grabbed a butcher knife and shielded the lantern. Then they all took turns standing out in the darkness, near the corner of the cabin to keep watch.

Pardee came home around 11PM and told them that the South Carolinians had asked Caleb if they could sleep in an empty shed on his place and Caleb told them it was OK. Pardee and Caleb went to the shed, which was close to a creek, and on stilts. They crawled underneath the floor and listened; the men seemed to be sleeping soundly. Things seemed safe, so the Butler family went to bed, but Pardee's daughter, 9-year-old Rosetta, noticed her father put a loaded pistol under his pillow before going to sleep.

The next morning, she sought out her friend Priscila, also nine years old, and asked her about the gun. Priscila and Rosetta were both thin and pretty. Priscila had her mother's straight brown hair and Rosetta had curly red hair. They both wore floor length dresses with matching bonnets that their mothers had made and lace-up boots.

Rosetta said, "Prissy, I've never seen my Pa with a gun before. What is going on?"

Priscila answered, "After they went to the shed, they came back to the house and my Pa gave your Pa Ma's Colt. Your Pa hesitated, then took it."[39]

The proud Pardee Butler was much more inclined to listen to his friend Caleb May after being rafted and tarred and feathered. The next day, Pardee wrote an account of all this for the Lawrence *Herald of Freedom* newspaper.[40] He then bought his own revolver from Caleb and returned Maggie's. He also finally joined Caleb's Kansas Legion militia which had ballooned to 30 men, with more joining every week.

The Quilting Bee

After church the next Sunday, William walked to the Moore cabin with Caroline, as he now did every Sunday. William, Caroline, and her family enjoyed a wonderful meal of venison stew, and a dandelion salad sprinkled with apple cider vinegar. Desert was a wonderful venison mincemeat pie made with apples, vinegar, and raisins made from wild grapes. The pie was flavored with sage and ginger. Caroline had made the pie, and her mother made the stew.

The conversation revolved around Butler's sermon and his experiences in Atchison. They still thought Kansas' future was bright, even considering the Reverend Pardee's recent problems.

After the meal William walked Caroline and her mother to a newly organized sewing bee in Sybil Butler's cabin. The bee was informal and the women who came brought their mending or helped with a quilt that Sybil had designed and wanted to make.

Caroline, her mother Mary, and William talked as they walked about three-quarters of a mile south to the Butler cabin. They had become more comfortable with one another over the past few months, although William was still somewhat star-struck by Caroline's beauty. Caroline had grown to like William, but perhaps not romantically, at least not yet.

---

39 (Butler, 1889, p. 266).
40 (Howard & Oliver, 1856, p. 104) and (Butler, 1889, pp. 106-109).

After leaving Caroline and her mother at the Butler cabin, William went home. As he walked into the cabin the twins, Enoch and Priscila, danced around singing "William has a girlfriend, William has a girlfriend!" After a bit of this Caleb told them, "Enough is enough children, leave your brother alone!"

At first William was embarrassed, but he recovered quickly and just laughed. He said, "I like Caroline, and we are friends, but she is not my girlfriend."

Maggie had prepared a nice Sunday meal for her family, but it was without William. After the meal she left the dishes and clean-up to Mary and Priscila and headed to the Butler cabin for the sewing and quilting bee. This was a major new event in the town. It occurred every Sunday after family dinner and all the women of the town were eager participants. Every woman in town looked forward to the "bee." It was a chance to talk, share the stories of the week, have some fun, and laugh. In addition to the fun, they could work on their joint quilting project or catch up on the endless mending of their family's clothing.

This was the women's time, so Pardee left the house after their dinner and joined Caleb outside his cabin for some lemonade. Caleb's lemon trees were not producing fruit yet, but he had some lemons left over from a recent visit to his brother Isaac in De Kalb. Isaac had given Caleb two bushels of lemons for the family, and he still had some left, so he used them to make some Sunday lemonade.

Pardee told Caleb, "I'm not allowed in the house now, they are having their 'stitch and bitch.'"

Caleb smiled and replied, "That they are, I'm not sure we want to hear what they are saying about us anyway."

"True, best I stay here and out of the line of fire."

In the meantime, Sybil was explaining the quilt she wanted to make with the women who came to the bee, "Ladies, I want us to try and make a double wedding ring quilt. It is one of the most difficult quilts to make, but also one of the most beautiful. I have made paper templates for the fabric pieces we will need for the quilt top."

Sybil then passed out the pieces of paper to use as templates and told the women, "Please find your scraps of fabric that are large enough and cut out these shapes, exactly to size. Once we have enough, we will piece together the quilt and begin sewing the top of the 'quilt sandwich.' We will also need your old, unusable blankets and fabric pieces for the batting that goes in the inside of the quilt. I'll worry about the backing fabric later, I may buy that, it should be a nice fabric since it is next to the skin. Those of you with mending or embroidery to do just carry on."

Maggie spoke up enthusiastically, "Oh Sybil, this is so nice! What a wonderful way to spend time with friends. Just the chance to get away from the house for a few hours with neighbors and friends makes me so happy."

The entire group agreed, and Sybil responded, "We did this in Illinois, and everyone left every Sunday evening happier than when they arrived. My Pardee sometimes even enjoys his exile."

Everyone laughed, and Maggie said, "My Caleb doesn't like not having me to order around for such a long time. He might be tough enough to handle being away from me, but I'm not sure."

That caused everyone to roar with laughter, and Mary Moore said, "My Sam gets dourer when I go every Sunday, but no one can tell but me."

Even louder laughter at that. The laughter and joking continued the whole time they worked on cutting the pieces from old worn-out clothes that could not be mended or mending those that could be saved.

Mary May, only 11, joined the group after she finished the dishes at the May cabin. She wanted to embroider a design on her nicest church blouse, and Sybil and Rosetta Butler were showing her how. Maggie was pleased that Mary had this opportunity to learn from such skilled seamstresses.

The women got a lot of work done and had a good time doing it. The Sunday bees were a welcome relief from their often hard, tense, and tedious lives. They left the bee feeling refreshed and renewed. Nothing like laughter and companionship to boost the spirit.

A Cold Winter

On the 21st of December, rumors circulated around proslavery Atchison that Caleb May was the leader of a conspiracy to burn down the town. Caleb's farm is only about 10 miles west of the town, and when he heard the rumors, he was infuriated. He wrote a letter to the Atchison *Squatter Sovereign*,[41] denying it was true and offering to duel with the man who started the rumor. The paper made an issue of the fact that Caleb was a "traitor" who had signed the "abolition production" of the Topeka convention. The newspaper recommended a "*Hemp necklace*" for his abolitionism.

Despite the tensions of the time, the mistreatment of Pardee Butler, and the fact that Atchison County was nearly all proslavery, no one ever confronted Caleb directly. As already discussed, he was known as a man who could and would defend himself and his family, and he could be a vicious enemy when he or his were threatened.

The weather at the time was terrible, temperatures dropped to 17 degrees below zero Fahrenheit on Christmas Eve, it had been snowing since the 22nd and the snow was drifting and very deep. In Atchison County on Caleb's farm they could not stay warm and had to tend the fire in their concrete-sealed log cabin in shifts all night, so it did not go out. But, even with the fire and their blankets they were cold. It was the same in the Butler cabin.

Jim's little shed had no fireplace, so he moved in with the family on the 21st. But Jim also became concerned about the animals. He told Caleb, "It is so cold they will die; we must do something to keep them warm."

To try and save all the stock, Jim, William, and Caleb worked hard to enlarge and better seal the walls of the barn. They also joined it to the hog pen and chicken coop.

It wasn't enough, it was just too cold. The animals were in danger of freezing to death, even in their enclosures. Using limestone slabs they had pulled from their fields and stored for future sale or construction, and cement they made in their improved kiln, they built a crude chimney and fireplace in the barn.

Thanks to Caleb and Maggie's "always be prepared" natures, they had everything they needed stored and ready to go. So, the three of them were able to build what was needed to save the stock.

They started a fire in the new fireplace and hustled all the animals into the barn to keep them warm, Jim tended the fire constantly and stayed in the barn with the animals to protect them and make sure they

---

41 *Squatter Sovereign*, January 1, 1856, "A Literary Production."

had water and food. He brought in snow and ice and put it in a large pot that he placed near the fire on the crude hearth that he and Caleb had made. At night water would freeze solid in a few minutes unless the pot was right next to the fire on the hearth.

The fire heated the limestone blocks and mortar of the chimney, and the animals huddled around it to stay warm. Jim had to keep the animals moving so they all had a turn close to hearth and the water.

With all the animals in the barn, it began to stink badly. Jim, William, Sam, and Enoch had to share the duty of cleaning out the animal poop and pee from the barn. Then they had to re-cover the floor with hay to collect the next round of poop and pee.

The Butlers and the other neighbors around Pardee all lost some livestock that winter, but Jim, Caleb, Enoch, Sam, and William managed to save all the May stock. Caleb thanked God for his stockpile of limestone blocks, crushed limestone, timber, and mortar. He was a man who stockpiled what he could, when he could, and never threw anything away.

It was lucky they built the fireplace in the barn because temperatures dropped further on Christmas night to 30 degrees Fahrenheit below zero. Outside it was painful to breathe. The bitter cold remained until New Year's Day, when the air was still cold and below zero at night, but not the painful, bitter cold of Christmas Day and the following week. There were no clouds on New Year's Day and when the sun was out during the day it was pleasant after what they had endured. Caleb and Pardee later learned that the ice on the Mississippi River was over two feet thick for two weeks around Christmas in St. Louis. The balmy zero degrees Fahrenheit of New Years Day 1856 was welcomed by the whole family.

The Topeka Constitution

David Atchison held a meeting in his office in early December with John Stringfellow and Charley Dunn. He asked them about the "damnable new Free-State Constitution" and pointed out that the Free-State vote to ratify it would be December 15.

Stringfellow answered first, "The official territorial government is in place in Shawnee Mission. Work on the official Territorial Constitution will begin soon. This idiotic Free-State Constitution has no validity, an election to approve it is not legal under our laws. I think we should ignore it, to oppose it would only make it seem more legitimate, and more than it is. It is nothing and we should treat it as nothing."

Dunn then said, "The vote is illegal, assemblies to discuss or promote any anti-slavery movement are against our laws. I think we should seize the ballot boxes. Law and order must be upheld."

Atchison thought for a moment, "Charley, you are now the appointed Sheriff of the Territory for the Leavenworth and Atchison area. You do what you determine your duty requires. John, I agree to the extent that we should not organize a Territory-wide disruption of the vote. This damnable Constitution just isn't worth the trouble. But Charley should make a public statement, so the public knows that the Free-State vote is clearly illegal."

Stringfellow then said, "We do need to hold a convention of our own, however. Ours will publicly announce our new Law-and-Order Party and introduce the new Governor, the solidly proslavery Wilson Shannon. That should take some of the wind out of the sails of the Free-State Party. I'll start working on that, the meeting will be on the day Shannon arrives and soon after the Free-State Convention."

Due to Atchison's decision, proslavery interference in the December 15 Free-State election was minor, except in Leavenworth. In the Leavenworth polling place, voters voted outside a grocery and passed their votes through a window to the district voting judges. Charley Dunn, now a captain in the local Leavenworth militia, and a group of his men showed up at the window and demanded that the voting stop. The district judges said they would not. Dunn then shouted, "Under the authority of the territorial laws I order you to stop this election!"

The judges refused, and Dunn then shouted, "Turn the ballot box over to me immediately!"

They refused, and Dunn grabbed the sash of the window and ripped it and the enclosed glass window off the building. Then Dunn and his men climbed through the opening into the room with the judges. They were armed with revolvers and bowie knives.[42]

---

42 (Howard & Oliver, 1856, pp. 978-981)

The judges all fled, but one of the voting clerks, George Wetherill, who owned the grocery store, grabbed the ballot box and ran into an adjoining room and threw it under a counter. He then headed out the backdoor of the building. Dunn chased him but didn't see him dump the ballot box.

Dunn grabbed him by his throat, and immediately saw that he no longer had the ballot box, so he pushed Wetherill up against the outside of the building and said, "Where is the damn ballot box, turn it over now!"

Wetherill replied, "I do not have it."

In response Dunn smashed his fist into Wetherill's face. Another of Dunn's men then struck him in the head. Then they threw Wetherill to the ground and began viciously kicking him. Some free-state men arrived and fought off Dunn and his men and carried the beaten Wetherill to a doctor. Wetherill mostly recovered in a few days, but the beating was so severe he was never completely well afterward.

Shortly afterward Dunn's men went back into the grocery and found the ballot box and carried it off. As they left, Dunn stopped and turned to face the crowd and announced, "This vote is an unlawful assembly under the new Territorial laws and the votes are all illegal."[43]

Dunn and his men then carried the ballot box away. It was never seen again.

The Leavenworth vote and the brutal attack by Charley Dunn and his friends in Leavenworth were widely reported in the rest of country. It was now clear that Dunn's proslavery Law-and-Order Party and the anti-slavery Free-State Party were at war.

On December 27, 1855, in the middle of the coldest period of the coldest winter in memory, the Free-State leaders proclaimed the Free-State constitution, now ratified by the voters, was in force and called for an election of territorial officers on January 15th.

The Topeka Constitution attempted to give legitimacy to the Free-State movement. The proslavery settlers thought it was a joke and didn't take the Constitution or the vote seriously. They believed that Kansas Territory was theirs. They had more people in the area, the Ter-

---

43 (Howard & Oliver, 1856, pp. 979-980)

ritorial Legislature, Governor Shannon, and the full support of President Pierce. No piece of paper could stand up to that.

The proslavery settlers held a convention on December 11, 1855, in Leavenworth.[44] They invited all settlers, but the attendees were mostly proslavery. Governor Wilson Shannon arrived in Leavenworth the same day, and was escorted to the meeting by Charley Dunn, John Stringfellow, and some of their friends. He was quickly elected the party leader and presided over the convention.

In his address to the convention, the new Governor said, "All of President Pierce's Territorial appointees are in attendance. We insist that all the laws passed by the Shawnee Mission Territorial Legislature will be fully enforced! Many have called this legislature a bogus legislature, but I am here to tell you it is real, it is legal, and its laws are the laws of the land!"

The Governor continued, "The so-called Free-State Party is a radical faction and is an illegal organization. The Free-State leaders claim that 75% of the current legal residents voted for delegates to the Free-State Convention held in Topeka. But this is a lie!"

While the Free-State Party probably did represent the bona fide settlers counted in the 1855 census, the Law-and-Order Party claimed more people in the area were with them. In other words, they counted those that still resided in Missouri but traveled to the Kansas Territory frequently for business or work. Both statements might have been correct, and federal law was unclear on who could vote and who could not.

General John C. Calhoun of South Carolina, who was the seventh Vice-President of the United States under both John Quincy Adams and Andrew Jackson, addressed the Law-and-Order Party Convention and his address included the following:

"Shall abolitionists rule you? No, never! Give them all they demand, and abolitionism becomes the law of the land. You yield, and you have the most infernal government that ever cursed a land. I would rather be a painted slave over in Missouri, or a serf to the Czar of Russia, than have the abolitionists in power. (Tremendous cheers.) Look at the outrages mentioned in their journals, of babies shot

---

44 (Alexander, 2022)

through the sides of houses, etc. There is nothing so low or mean but abolition papers are found to tell it. We, the Union-loving and State-rights party, of Kansas, have kept too still, and allowed the nullifiers to proclaim millions of lies. This is a great question for abolitionists to make capital out of. We must not allow it to go on here. We must stop its growth. It tramples upon the laws of the land. Say to your governor, 'Enforce the laws; we will stand by you, and, if necessary, we will spill our life's blood to enforce them!' The governor will be with you. The governor calls for all to help him, except abolitionists. He calls to men of all states; but he don't want abolitionists."[45]

The Kansas Legion was originally formed in February 1855 to counter David Atchison, the Stringfellow brothers, Dunn, the Platte County Self-Defensives, and other similar proslavery organizations. It was charged with protecting Free-State ballot boxes and voters from invaders. So far, it had a mixed record in this regard, but now that James Abbott was the General and the membership had grown, the members of the Legion hoped they would have a larger impact.

It was a secret society, the members wore black ribbons on their shirts, had passwords, and special handshakes. They also had secret signals, like rubbing the corner of the eye with the left little finger.[46] Wealthy eastern men, like Amos Lawrence (for whom Lawrence Kansas was named) and Eli Thayer, collected money, bought, and shipped the latest Sharps rifles, Colt revolvers, and other arms to the Kansas Legion and their company agents (like Charles Robinson) in the Kansas Territory. These shipments were often in crates labeled as books or farm tools.[47] The shipments increased, as anti-slavery funding in the Northeast increased. The enthusiasm to keep Kansas free was high in New England, and contributions to the emigrant aid society grew rapidly. Tensions were high.

---

45 (Robinson S. T., 1856, pp. 114-115)
46 (Etcheson, 2004, p. 76)
47 (Etcheson, 2004, pp. 76-77)

Easton

Caleb formally joined the Kansas Legion in the fall of 1855 at the Big Springs Convention. After the convention, he recruited most of the men in Pardee and formed a company of militiamen from his neighbors and the new arrivals. He was given the title of Captain by a vote of his men. The brutal attack by Charley Dunn in Leavenworth convinced the free-state men that if they were going to have elections, they must protect their chosen poll locations. Caleb and the other officers divided up the polling locations among themselves and Caleb was assigned to the Easton, Kansas location for its January 17th, 1856, election of Free-State Territorial officers.

The election was supposed to have been held in all the districts on January 15th, and in many districts, this was the case. But a rumor circulated that the Kickapoo Rangers, a proslavery militia, was mustering to come to Easton to disrupt the voting.[48] Caleb sent word that he needed a couple of days to gather more men and asked the district judges to delay the vote until the 17th.

Caleb raised sixty well-armed men. He wanted to have such an overwhelming force that the Kickpoo Rangers would back down without a fight. Nothing like what Dunn had done in Leavenworth the previous month was going to happen in Easton while he was in charge.

Before dawn, on the 17th, Caleb mustered his men and said goodbye to his family and Jim. He took his revolvers and Sharps, but left Maggie's pocket revolver, the shotgun, flintlock rifle, and two spare revolvers for Jim and William to use to protect the house. After kissing Maggie and saying goodbye, he and his men headed to Easton.

They arrived in Easton before 9AM, and the polls were to open at 10. The men set up a camp next to the Free-State voting location at Edward Minard's house in Easton. They brewed some coffee and ate a nice breakfast of biscuits and eggs that Mrs. Minard helped them fix.

Minard's house was less than one-half mile, a short walking distance, from where the proslavery Kickapoo Rangers and some local proslavery men were gathered at Dawson's General Store and saloon. The vot-

---

[48] This account is fictional but based on a real conflict in Easton on January 17th, 1856 as described here: (Howard & Oliver, 1856, pp. 981-1020).

ing went on all day and the votes and voting ledger were kept in an old hat of Minard's, because the official ballot box was not delivered as planned.

Caleb and his men guarded Minard's house in shifts, they were all armed with Sharp's rifles, Bowie knives, and Colt revolvers. Around 6PM, a large group of men on horseback approached the house. Before the proslavery men were in earshot, Caleb said, "Men, silence and vigilance are the most intimidating action. They provoke no one and frighten all."

Then the leader of the horsemen, said, "Give us the ballot box, we will have it if we have to shoot every man here."

No one answered them.

Then all the men came out of the house with their arms at the ready. Captain Caleb May was in front. He said nothing, he just stared at the men on horseback. The men paused, then retreated, leaving three of their number about halfway between Minard's house and Dawson's store.

After they left, Caleb said, "We need to find out how many men they have."

He counted out fifteen of his men and said, "We will walk easy men but ready to fight. All we are going to do is go to Dawson's store and count the men."

As they approached the store, some men came out of it and stood in a line blocking the entrance. Caleb counted 20 of them, so did the men on either side of him.

Caleb and ten others stayed outside, opposite the Kickapoo Rangers, while five pushed themselves through the line to go inside the store saying, "If you do not mind, we want to go inside and get a drink of whiskey."

When they returned a few minutes later, one quietly reported to Caleb that there were at least 30 more men inside. Caleb was satisfied. His men who went in reported that most of the Rangers were drunk and few had Sharps or revolvers, most had muzzle loaders of one type or another.

Caleb moved to the front of his men, just a few feet from the Rangers. He was carrying his Sharps rifle, and his coat was open, so his new Navy Colts were clearly visible. He quietly said, "We have come here to have an election and to vote and will not be molested. We are armed for resistance, should that be necessary."

None of the Rangers responded to the threat. Dr. Edward S. Motter, a physician born in Maryland, who had his office in a room next to the store, immediately came out and addressed Caleb, "You should leave here, you are in serious danger and you are putting all of us in serious danger."

Caleb tipped his hat to Motter and replied, "Dr. Motter, I believe, I am Captain Caleb May. We intend no harm to anyone here, we just want to have our election in peace, and then go home."

Motter did not reply. Caleb then left with his men and returned to Minard's house. After he left, the Kickapoo Rangers continued drinking, and loudly denounced the "illegal" Free-State election.

Mrs. Minard had so many guests, she found she had to go to the store to buy some essentials. Since she was a woman, she did not expect any trouble from the men at the store, even though her husband was hosting the election. Even so, she approached the store with some caution. But the men did not bother her and even tipped their hats to her politely.

The clerk, Sam Kookogey, a proslavery immigrant from Georgia and Dawson's Store clerk, waited on her and helped her collect what she needed, then he escorted her to her home for her safety and to help her carry her purchases. There were Free-State sentries posted around the home and Kookogey only recognized a few of the men as being from the area, the others were strangers. He counted about sixty or seventy men around the house.[49]

Later that evening, Kookogey found out that Dawson had been appointed postmaster of Easton from John W. Whitfield (the proslavery House of Representatives member) who had stopped in Easton to see how the voting was going. So, Kookogey walked back to Minard's house to tell them the news. He was accompanied by a young friend, a surveyor named Joseph McAleer. As Kookogey was speaking with Minard, McAleer said, a bit too loudly, "You men had better turn over the ballot box. It will go badly for you if you do not."

---

49 (Howard & Oliver, 1856, pp. 1016-1017).

Stephen Sparks, an immigrant, from Union County, Indiana and a Kansas Territory Free-State legislator, heard this and said, "We should hang McAleer! He cannot threaten us like that."

Tensions rose rapidly, and insults flew back and forth. The rest of the evening threatening notes and insults flew back and forth between Dawson's Store and the Minard house.

In the meantime, Sparks rode out and gathered up more Free-State neighbors and asked them to grab their guns, then he marched them to Easton. Sparks also sent one of his sons to Lawrence to ask for help from the free-state leaders there.

At around 9PM, Caleb and some of his men returned to Dawson's Store, but did not go inside. Both Kookogey and Dr. Motter came out and asked them to leave to avoid violence. Caleb replied that "I've already seen one ballot-box taken, and I'll be damned if I'll see another taken unless they carry it out over my dead body."[50]

Later, near midnight, Stephen Sparks, his fifteen-year-old son Greene and Stephen's nephew left the Minard's cabin to go home. Rather than walk over the snow on the broken ground directly southeast to his home, Sparks deliberately walked due east past Dawson's Store so as to stay on the Fort Riley Road where the walking was easier. He carried his double-barreled shotgun on his shoulder. A mob gathered and surrounded Sparks, who was cursing and daring the men to shoot him. Dr. Motter and Kookogey were in the Doctor's office next door and came out when they heard the commotion. Dr. Motter didn't like the tension and animosity that he observed and yelled to the mob, "As Mr. Sparks is on his way home and got thus far, let him go."[51]

Stephens young nephew ran back to Minard's house and told them what was happening. Caleb told his men, I want 30 of you to come with me, we must ensure Sparks gets home. The men divided themselves and thirty went with Caleb.

The men stood at the ready, while Caleb, armed with his pistols and Sharps rifle walked up to the drunken mob standing just off the road in a lane that went north. The lane was bordered by two wooden fences one on each side of it. Caleb shouted from the head of the lane, while

---

50 (Howard & Oliver, 1856, p. 1017)
51 (Cova, 2012, p. 154).

standing in the Fort Riley Road, "Sparks and his son will come to me now."

The mob could see Caleb and all his men blocking the head of the lane and the road, May clearly had the advantage. They parted and allowed Sparks and his son to walk to Caleb while loudly complaining about the release. Some in the mob said it was no matter, as soon as they caught old Sparks alone, they would shoot him. Caleb did not respond and led the pair back to his men.

All the Free-State men were armed and at the ready. They began to walk slowly backwards and by side-stepping over the snow away from the mob. They moved south of the road and west-southwest toward Minard's house and a neighboring log cabin. The proslavery mob moved west, keeping north of the road until the road forked. Then the mob moved toward Dawson's store on the north fork and Caleb's men took the south fork towards Minard's house. The two groups kept a close eye on one another, and Caleb warned the Kickapoo Rangers not to fire, "If you fire, we will return the fire."

When the western end of the line of Kickapoo Rangers reached Dawson's store and were about 80 to 90 yards from Caleb and his men, one of the Rangers fired. No one knew who had fired, but Sparks saw a flame from a gun fired from near the store to the northwest of him.

Caleb yelled, "Boys, they have fired on us, take cover!" Caleb dove for the snow-covered ground and raised his rifle to take aim.

A gunfight started, as everyone took cover and returned fire. Most of the Free-State men took cover behind a nearby house and in a creek bed. Everyone had fired, so they now reloaded. The Free-State men already had pre-made cartridges in their pockets, so they simply opened the breeches on their Sharps, brushed out the breech and loaded the next cartridge. The distance was too far for revolvers and pistols.

The proslavery men took cover behind Dawson's Store or dropped to the ground. The battle lasted ten to twenty minutes, Greene Sparks was grazed on his head and arm by a musket ball, but the wounds were minor. One of the Rangers, named John Richardson, was shot in the leg. Another Ranger, named John Cook was in front of Dawson's Store and had just fired his musket at the free-state men. He paused to reload and was shot in the abdomen just as he finished reloading and was raising his musket to fire. Dr. Motter got to him quickly and found that the bullet had lacerated his colon, kidney, and spine. Kookogey and Dr. Motter dragged Cook into the store, and eventually to Motter's office. Unfortunately, there was nothing he could do for the poor man. He died two days later.

Caleb and his men retreated to Minard's house. None of them were seriously injured.

Dr. Motter and Kookogey sent messages to Kickapoo and Leavenworth asking for help. U.S. Army Captain John William Martin received Dr. Motter's letter at sunrise on the 18th. It said Cook had been seriously shot in a gunfight, and that he had not yet died but Dr. Motter expected him to soon. A posse of more Kickapoo Rangers were mustered under the command of Captain Martin, no regular U.S. Army soldiers, other than Martin, accompanied them.

Caleb and his men went to Minard's home with the Sparks and spent the night. Stephen Sparks left early the next morning and went to Lawrence, where he immediately wrote to his brother and said, "To Caleb May's gallantry I owe my life."

Most of Caleb's men left immediately after Spark's departure and went their separate ways, but Caleb and seven of his men accepted Minard's invitation to have breakfast and then headed out on the north road toward Atchison. They were either in Caleb's wagon or riding alongside on horseback.

Most of the men in the battle, on both sides, believed it was Caleb who fired the fatal bullet into John Cook and word spread quickly. Caleb was the best shot in the area, and it was over 80 yards, in the dark, who else could have made that shot? The moon was up and lanterns were lit at Dawson's store and cabin, but the light was still poor.

The Free-State settlers were pleased. They realized that Cook had been one of the mob that was intent on hanging Stephen Sparks and deserved what he got. Further, some of them could clearly see Cook had fired and was reloading his musket when he was hit. But the pro-slavery settlers felt that Cook was murdered and, worse, with a Sharps rifle. To them the Sharps rifles were an unfair advantage over their primitive flintlock muskets. Sharps were many times more accurate, far more deadly, and could be reloaded faster.

Captain Martin's company of 50 Kickapoo Rangers, in four wagons and on horseback, were on their way from Kickapoo to Easton. The last part of the journey was south on the north road out of Easton. The first wagon of men passed Caleb and his seven men who were moving northward. They asked who Caleb and his men were and where they were going. Caleb did not respond and simply passed them on the double track road. Then another wagon and more men on horseback appeared to the north, and all the men were yelling. The men south of Caleb's wagon turned around and the men north of his wagon advanced until Caleb's wagon was surrounded. Caleb and his men got out of the wagon guns at the ready. Caleb asked, "Who is in charge here?"

Captain Martin approached riding on his horse and said, "I am."

The Rangers advanced to Caleb's wagon, and Caleb told Captain Martin, "Keep your distance, we are well armed and will defend ourselves."

Captain Martin said, "We are here because of the attempted killing of John Cook last night and we must take you to Leavenworth to stand trial."

Caleb replied, "If Cook is dead, it was in self-defense. He had already fired at us and was reloading his musket to fire at us again when he was shot himself. We all have Sharps and were firing, it was dark, and we have no idea who shot him."

Martin then said, "None-the-less an investigation is necessary. You will all be well treated as prisoners."

Caleb considered their situation, they were only eight total and facing at least 50 well-armed men, so he said, "We will give up, if you treat us as prisoners should be treated."

Almost immediately after the surrender, there was a loud howl, and a man named Robert Gibson charged at Elijah Smith, the Pardee store owner. Gibson knocked Smith to the ground and swung his hatchet at his head. Smith saw the hatchet and moved just enough so it missed his head and only knocked off his hat. Gibson tried to strike at Smith again with a second blow, but was restrained by Sam Moore, the Pardee blacksmith, and some of the Rangers. Moore quickly pulled Captain Martin aside and said, "Captain Martin, Gibson is intent on killing someone, you must restrain him."

Captain Martin ignored t his, and in the meantime, Gibson took Smith's Sharps rifle from him.

They took the men back to Easton, to conduct the investigation. Several of the men (both from Martin's Kickapoo Rangers and some proslavery men who lived in Easton) were tying nooses to hang Caleb and all his men. Others objected to this and any violence, including Captain Martin.

All the men were detained in Dawson's Store with a small body of guards, except Caleb, who was taken into Dr. Motter's adjoining office and drug store for interrogation. Once there, Caleb was seated in Motter's chair and asked why he came to Easton. He replied, "We came to Easton to vote and to defend the polls, if necessary. We understood that the Kickapoo Rangers, or other proslavery men, were intent on stealing the ballot-box and we were here to prevent that."

Dr. Motter asked Caleb, "Are you the head of the free-state men who were here last night?"

Caleb, simply said, "Yes."

Dr. Motter asked him, "Who fired the first shot last night?"

Caleb said, "I do not know who it was, but the first shot came from the other side. We did not fire first. It came from the general direction of the store."

Captain Martin announced, "These men are to be taken to Leavenworth to be put on trial for the murder of Cook, under the law." Martin's men had already hit the liquor in the store pretty hard and many of them were already drunk, although it was still early in the morning. There was not enough room in the store for all of Martin's men and some were outside yelling about hanging Caleb and all his men. The tension among Martin's men was very high, and just as Martin made his announcement the door from the store burst open and Gibson and many other men rushed into Motter's office.

Gibson ran straight for Caleb with his hatchet in a rage. Caleb saw murder in his eyes and stood up from his chair and tried to grab the hatchet, but only deflected it to his left, so it hit the left side of his head a glancing blow. The hatchet's sharp blade missed its mark, but it did make a mess of his scalp and hair. Because it was a head wound, it bled profusely and looked much worse than it was. The hatchet blade missed Caleb's shoulder, but the handle did not, leaving a bruise. The blow was hard, but not hard enough to cause unconsciousness.

Gibson was swinging as hard as he could and expected to strike Caleb's head. When he didn't and only hit with a glancing blow, it threw him off balance, and he wound up leaning heavily on his right foot. Caleb was frightened and in pain from the blows to his head and shoulder, but he was not one to miss an opportunity like this in a fight. He kicked straight at Gibson's groin with his right foot as hard as he could and connected perfectly. Gibson was in so much pain he couldn't even groan, but his ashen face betrayed his agony. He collapsed to the floor and dropped the hatchet.

Caleb immediately grabbed it and swept it in a large arc to keep the other men away. He yelled, "This is the way you treat prisoners?" He then looked directly at Martin with blazing eyes through his own blood. With those eyes and his head covered in blood, he looked like the devil himself.

Caleb then yelled, "You will all back away now and leave us in peace, we are going home. You will not molest us. If you set a date for trial and deliver a warrant for our arrest, we will appear when notified. But you have broken your promise to treat us fairly, and you have no warrant for our arrest, so this ends now!"

Captain Martin was disgusted by what had just happened. He drew his revolver and stood next to Caleb, he said, "This man is correct, we have no warrant, we have mistreated him and his men, and have disgraced ourselves."

"You men will all leave this building now. You are all drunk and disgusting."

Gibson still couldn't move so they carried him, moaning loudly, from the building. Martin then told Caleb and his men to quickly retrieve their weapons and join him in Dr. Motter's office.

Once in the office, Martin said, "Dr. Motter please tend to Captain May's wounds."

Caleb objected, but Martin insisted, "Sir, my man did this, and medical treatment is part of fair treatment."

Dr. Motter added, "That wound will not heal correctly and could become dangerous if it is not treated immediately. Please sit down, sir. We do not want this to become worse than it already is on so many levels. What a mess."

Caleb scowled, and said, "Oh very well, but be quick about it."

Dr. Motter carefully examined the wound, and said, "This is going to hurt, but I must clean the wound, move the skin back into place and stitch it up. Please be still."

With that, he washed the wound first with water and then with whiskey, Caleb winced, but did not cry out or move. Then the doctor carefully moved the skin into place and stitched the two flaps together, making a lot of small stitches. Part way through he asked Caleb, "Do you want some whiskey for the pain?"

Caleb replied, "No Doctor, I don't drink."

Dr. Motter replied, "Well no one will blame you if you start today. You are doing well; but I know this hurts a lot."

Except for Caleb, who frowned, everyone laughed at that.

Caleb said, "I will admit, getting hit with the hatchet didn't hurt this much!"

"Captain, stop acting like a baby."

Much more laughter, even Caleb smiled at that.

Once the stitches were in place, the doctor poured more whiskey on the wound and then wrapped a bandage around the whole head. He told Caleb to leave the bandage in place for at least two days and try to keep it dry if possible. Then remove it, clean the wound with as little water as possible to protect the stitches and rebandage it. Continue in that way for at least a week, probably two to be safe, then remove the stitches with some scissors and tweezers.

Caleb's men wasted no time retrieving their weapons. Some of Martin's men helped them. They were embarrassed by what had happened and Captain Martin's harsh words had stung. They returned all the weapons and let the men return to Dr. Motter's office. They also retrieved Caleb's pistols and Sharps rifle and took them to Caleb while he was in the office being treated.

Once they had collected their things, they regathered in the office where Captain Martin asked the men to give him their names and attest to the fact that they had all their property back. He wrote all this down and put the list in his pocket. He said their horses and the wagon would be returned and they were free to go. He would contact them regarding the shooting of John Cook in due time.

In the meantime, Gibson had mostly recovered and started ranting about revenge. Most of Martin's men had had enough so they mounted their horses and left, but a few stayed and drank even more whiskey, making them reckless.

Dr. Motter told Caleb he would have headaches, but he thought the wound would heal well, fortunately the hatchet had not penetrated the skull and the bruise on Caleb's shoulder did not look bad. He thought the skull might be cracked a little and he was fairly sure Caleb had a concussion, but it should heal with time. Caleb was reminded to keep his head wrapped in clean dry cloth for two weeks.

Just as Dr. Motter was ready to release Caleb, Captain Martin heard a commotion outside and went out to see what was going on. By now Gibson and the others were drunk and ranting about hanging all the damned abolitionists. Martin told them, "Go home, there will be no more business today. I need to go to Fort Leavenworth and discuss the next steps with the Territorial authorities there."

Gibson then yelled, "Captain Martin, you are a traitor and no better than an abolitionist. I will kill you like I would any traitor!"

Gibson reached for his pistol, but Captain Martin drew his revolver much faster and shot Gibson in the chest, just as Gibson pulled his gun out of the holster. For an instant, everyone was frozen, except Gibson, who fell to the frozen ground with blood pouring out of his chest wound. Gibson was still alive and Dr. Motter rushed to him and examined the wound. The bullet had entered the chest and penetrated to the spine, he looked up at Martin and shook his head. There was no hope for the man.

Most of Martin's men had already left the town and only about ten were left. They were drunk, and the shooting of Gibson took all the fight out of them. They were sick of the whole affair. When Captain Martin ordered them to go home for the second time, no one objected.

Dunn investigates

By now it was afternoon on the 18th of January 1856 and Captain Charles Dunn was hung over. He had been doing well at controlling his drinking, but the previous day he blew it. Atchison had ordered him to behave himself, and he had managed to restrain his drinking for several months. But after arriving in Easton very late the night before, he was exhausted and immediately hit the bottle. Like many alcoholics it didn't take many drinks for him to become extremely drunk.

He had come to monitor the election and keep an eye on Caleb May but got so drunk he wasn't even sure what had happened the night before, the events were blurred in his tortured and abused alcoholic brain. He clearly had passed out upstairs in Dawson's Store, he was there now. He didn't recall hearing or seeing anything going on the night before or earlier that morning. He remembered nothing, maybe his memory of the previous night's events would come back, maybe not.

He came downstairs and Dawson gave him some coffee and told him what had occurred in Easton the previous night and that morning. By then, everyone was gone, except for Gibson who had just passed away a few hours earlier and Cook, who was barely hanging on. Dunn was the Sheriff and had to investigate both shootings.

The coffee revived Dunn a bit and he asked Dr. Motter for the details and carefully listened. Once Dr. Motter finished, Dunn asked him, "So they let both Caleb May and John Martin go?"

Motter replied, "Yes, sir. They all headed north from here a few hours ago. Given the rough treatment of Caleb May by Bob Gibson, Captain Martin felt he had no choice. He had promised May and his men fair treatment as prisoners, then Gibson nearly killed him. Further, Captain Martin had no warrant to arrest them in any case. He thought it best to let them go, although he wrote down all their names."

Dunn asked, "I see his point, I just wish Gibson had finished the job. That May is a tough hombre though, Gibson didn't have a chance against him. Martin is a U.S. Army Captain, and I probably have no jurisdiction over him, but was his shooting of Gibson clearly self-defense?"

"Yes sir, Sheriff, everyone saw Gibson go for his gun first. But the Captain was faster."

"OK then, nothing to do on that one, I'll just report it to the Governor and the Fort commander. What about this Sparks, the one May rescued?"

Motter said, "Stephen Sparks left Minard's very early today and went south, that is all I know. His claim is a few miles south of here. He took his boy, who was wounded, and his nephew."

"You said that besides May, Sparks was the biggest troublemaker, is that correct?"

"Yes sir, Sheriff. Sparks has a big mouth and was trying to provoke trouble in my view."

"So, give me directions to Sparks claim. I need to pay him a visit."

After receiving the directions, Dunn and some men he recruited at Dawson's Store, set off for Stephen Sparks' claim. There were ten of them and they arrived at the claim near sunset. They spoke to Mrs. Esseneth Sparks, Stephen Sparks' wife,[52] Dunn asked her, "Ma'am we are here to speak to Stephen Sparks, can you tell us where he is? We have private business with him."

She answered, "He is away on business today."

Dunn told his men, "Search the house and shoot or detain Sparks if you find him."

Mrs. Sparks said, "Wait, wait! I have an afflicted son. Any excitement and he will fly into spasms. You must not excite him. And anyway, as I said Stephen is away on business and I'm not sure when he will return."

Dunn walked into the house and drew his gun and pointed it directly at her younger son, Elias, "Boy, where is your Pa?"

Elias stood up straight and replied, "I am on the Lord's side, and if you want to kill me, kill me; I am not afraid to die."

Dunn then asked him, "Where is your Pa's Sharps rifle?"

Elias replied, "My Pa doesn't have a Sharps."

Dunn pointed to a rack of guns on the wall of the cabin and asked, "What are those guns?"

"The men take care of the guns, I'm too young."

Charley Dunn decided that he was getting nowhere and was convinced the family told the truth and Stephen Sparks was gone, so he left. He aggressively questioned Sparks neighbors as to the whereabouts of Stephen, but never determined where he was. The next day, Mrs. Sparks received a letter signed by numerous people. It was addressed to her husband, and said in part, "We believe that your further residence among us is incompatible with the peace and welfare of this community, we advise you to leave as soon as you can conveniently do so."[53]

Mrs. Sparks checked the list of people who signed the letter and found that only one of the signers was a true resident in her area, the others were all Kickapoo Rangers and Missourians.

---

52 (Howard & Oliver, 1856, p. 1019)
53 (Howard & Oliver, 1856, p. 1020)

She talked to the men who delivered the letter. She asked, "What problem do you have with my husband?"

They replied, "Nothing personal against him, but he is too influential in the Free-State Party, and our goal is to destroy the party."

They added, "You must move your family by the 10th of March, or face the consequences." The same men returned on 8 March and searched for Stephen Sparks who was not at home. They told Mrs. Sparks that if they found him, they would cut him into small pieces.

January 1856

The New England movement to populate Kansas with Free-State settlers was proceeding and new anti-slavery immigrants were arriving, but too many quickly gave up the hard life in Kansas and returned to New England. As a result, the bulk of Free-State immigrants, who stayed in Kansas, were not from New England, but from the western states, especially Ohio, Indiana, and Illinois. But even these men and women were often armed with guns supplied by the New England aid societies, as well as some anti-slavery societies based in Chicago. This was a major concern for the proslavery men, and they started their own movement to entice southern proslavery men to immigrate to the state. Unfortunately for them, too few were willing to make the move and many who came to Kansas quickly converted and became Free-State Party members. There were also conversions from Free-State to proslavery, but far fewer in number.

Sheriff Dunn traveled to Pardee, Kansas to arrest Caleb for the murder of John Cook. It was cold, but they had camped near Pardee overnight and arrived early on the morning of the 19th. Even though Dunn had four deputies with him, he was nervous about arresting Caleb May. He repeatedly told his deputies how dangerous Caleb was. While riding to Pardee from Easton, a trip of about 15 miles, he said, "Caleb May is a big and muscular man, and he knows how to fight. Don't get into a fist fight or knife fight with him, he'll win. Shoot him if you must, but don't wrestle with him."

He added, "Once he is in custody, tie him up, don't forget this."

Neighbors saw Sheriff Dunn and his deputies coming well before they reached Pardee and sent word to Caleb. Caleb's head was still bandaged from his injury, and he had a bad headache, exactly as Dr. Motter had predicted. He was lying down and feeling guilty about not working. Once the young man arrived on his horse with the warning that Sheriff Dunn was coming, Maggie and William grabbed their new pistols and the Sharps and Maggie said to Caleb, "Cale, you must leave the house, we must tell the Sheriff you are gone, and we don't know when you will be back. William and I are armed, the Sheriff will not come into the house if we resist. Please leave quickly, take Jim with you and all these blankets, it is very cold."

Caleb protested, but he saw the logic in what Maggie was saying, after all his own rule was avoid a fight if you can. Caleb grabbed their old shotgun and his old musket, then he and Jim went to the Stranger Creek tributary about 200 yards east of the house and lay down on the snowy riverbank facing the front door of the cabin. It was cold, but they had blankets to lie on and to cover themselves.

He gave the shotgun and two additional homemade shells with caps to Jim for his protection. Caleb told him, "Jim, if they see you, they will assume you are a runaway slave and try to arrest you. If there is a fight and they try and take you, shoot them."

Jim started to tell Caleb he *was* a runaway but stopped himself. Then said, "Yes sir, shoot them."

Caleb kept the flintlock and said, "200 yards is too far for this old flintlock rifle, but I can get close enough to scare them with it."

Once Caleb and Jim were gone, Maggie quickly arranged the family in the cabin. She took her Pocket Colt and made sure it was loaded, then she buckled her holster on over her dress. William did the same with his Navy Colt and grabbed the Sharps and some spare cartridges. He gave the other Navy Colt to Mary, it was a heavy weapon for her, but she was strong, and had fired it before, even though she was only 11 years old. Nine-year-old Priscila took little Isaac over to a chair by the fire. Her twin brother Enoch, three-year-old Catherine, and 6-year-old Sam joined her there.

Maggie then explained her plan. "I will answer the door, William will stand behind me, to my left, facing the door. The door opens left to right, so he will be in clear view by the men at the door. If it looks like there will be fighting, I will move to my right to make sure William has a clear shot with the Sharps. Does this plan sound OK to everyone?"

William repeated, "I'm behind you but to your left, if a fight erupts, you move right, and I fire. OK, got it."

Maggie, "No shooting unless it is clear they are going to fire. Watch them carefully, William. Remember what your Pa always says, when a fight begins do not hesitate, but don't start the fight."

"Yes Ma. I know."

They did not have long to wait; they heard the horses arrive a few minutes later. Sheriff Dunn said, "Men dismount and be ready for trouble."

Then he walked to the door and knocked. Maggie opened the door wide and moved with it, so she was partly shielded by the open door and William was clearly visible. She said, "Sheriff Dunn, what can we do for you?"

Dunn replied, "I'm here for Caleb, send him out."

Maggie said, "Cale is gone, and we do not know when he will return."

"Well, where did he go?"

"We aren't sure, he didn't say."

"I must search the house, please, both of you, step aside."

Maggie's blue eyes became steely and fierce, she looked directly at Dunn and said, "Sheriff please present your warrant to search this house, then you can enter."

Dunn replied, "I do not have a warrant."

"Sheriff, you will not enter this house without a proper, signed judicial warrant! Less than two years ago, you forced my boy to drink whiskey, we consider that an assault, it is good reason not to allow you in the house. We do not know where Caleb is, and you and your men must leave our property now. If you don't go, we will fight you off, and not a man in this township will doubt that we have a good reason to do so."

Maggie drew her pistol and cocked it. William raised his Sharps to his shoulder and pointed it directly at Dunn's face. Their faces showed fierce determination.

By this time, Pardee with his new Colt, and his brother-in-law Milo with his Sharps were approaching the house from the east.

Dunn noticed the arriving neighbors, then took a closer look at William; this was the first time he had seen him since he forced whiskey down his throat nearly two years prior. Good God, he thought, that boy has grown. That heavy rifle was steady as a rock, William's face betrayed no emotion, just determination. He's as dangerous as his Pa, Dunn thought. Maggie looked even more dangerous.

Dunn involuntarily took a step backward, then said, "Ok, we will leave, but this investigation into John Cook's murder is not over. We will be back."

Maggie simply said, "We will be here. Now leave our property and do not come back without a legal search warrant."

Dunn and his men left. Once they were gone, Maggie closed the door and she and William breathed a sigh of relief. William turned to his Ma, and said, "Ma you were perfect! How brilliant to ask for a warrant."

Maggie replied, "It made perfect sense. Even under the new bogus legislature laws a warrant is required to search a house for anything. There was no way he could have gotten a warrant in such a short time and ride all the way here."

Pardee and Milo came to the house and asked if everything was OK. Maggie said, "Dunn will be trouble, but not today. He had no warrant and with his history of forcing liquor into William he was on shaky ground. I told him to leave."

She invited Pardee and Milo in for coffee. They closed the door and joined the family at the fire, it was bitterly cold. Closing the door was supposed to be the signal to Caleb to come back, but Caleb and Jim waited a few minutes to make sure Dunn was truly gone, and then returned to the house and the warm fire themselves.

Pardee's wife, Sybil, their two sons, George and Charles, and their daughter Rosetta, came to the house to check on everyone.

Caleb did not feel well and was cold. He had a cup of coffee, then lay down on the bed. Maggie told the story to everyone, with some help from William. When she was finished, Sybil Butler asked, in a fearful voice, "What will happen next?"

Milo responded, "Sheriff Dunn will not give up, he will be back, and with more men."

Maggie agreed, "Yes, he will be back."

Milo said, "I am so glad I bought this Sharps and joined the Kansas Legion."

Pardee was just about to object, but instead said, "I'm also glad I joined the Legion and I guess it is time I bought a Sharps rifle and learned how to use it."

He looked at Sybil, and said, "We must be prepared for trouble. Sybil, do you object?"

Sybil simply said, "Thank you husband, I agree with you, we need to be ready for troubled times. This is especially true when the man we are most afraid of is the Sheriff! I think Maggie has rubbed off on you."

Most of the families in the neighborhood had arms, but they all agreed that they needed to encourage those that did not already own them to buy them. After this incident, and with Caleb feeling poorly, every man near Pardee who had not already joined the Legion, did so.

Maggie said, "We need everyone in town to be armed to safeguard all of us. Caleb will arrange, through the Kansas Legion, to get the Sharps and Colt revolvers at a huge discount. All anyone must do is ask."

The next day, Pardee and Sybil gave Caleb money for two more Colt revolvers and one Sharps rifle. Soon several other neighbors gave Caleb the money for their arms.

Caleb drove to Elijah Smith's store and sent a message to James Abbot in Lawrence detailing what he needed and told Abbott he had the money in full. Abbott didn't come himself but sent a wagon with all the requested arms to Pardee two days later. Caleb paid for them and distributed them to the men that same evening. Caleb had also requested extra gunpowder, cartridge papers, and lead, which he paid for himself and stored in the shed he had designated as the "armory." Caleb's neighbors, including Pardee Butler, were only rarely seen without their Colt revolvers.[54]

As expected, Charley Dunn returned to Pardee three days later and accosted Caleb in the street near his house. He told Caleb he was under arrest, Caleb responded, "Under whose authority?"

Dunn replied, "As Sheriff of this county."

Caleb said, "Show me your judicial warrant."

By now a crowd, all armed, had gathered and surrounded Dunn and his three men. Dunn replied, "I'll not show you my warrant, but I have one." The rest of you men have a duty, under the law, to help."

---

54 (Butler, 1889, pp. 265-266)

Caleb simply said, "If you have no warrant, I will not go with you."

One of the bystanders then carefully and silently lifted a pistol from Dunn's coat pocket and ran away with it. Dunn yelled after the man who kept running as everyone else laughed at him.

Dunn's men did not laugh, and said nothing, but one of them visibly struggled to keep from laughing. One witty bystander quipped, "You didn't specify who to help, so we helped Caleb."

This caused everyone around Dunn to laugh again, and his deputy could not contain himself anymore and burst out laughing himself, which earned him a vicious glare from Dunn. The incident was funny, and it showed Dunn that he had no authority in Pardee or in any other free-state community. He noticed all the men were armed and some of the revolvers looked new. He had not seen this when he visited earlier. He decided to back off.

Dunn and his men camped in a large tent at the edge of the small town. The Sheriff told his men, "That bastard Caleb not only helped defend the illegal Free-State ballot box in Easton but, I'm sure he is also smuggling Sharps rifles and Colt revolvers into Pardee and helping to smuggle stolen slaves into Iowa!"

He was correct on both counts, but no one in the town would ever confirm any of this. Things were not going well for Dunn. Given his circumstances, he had to give up and leave.

When back in Leavenworth, Dunn asked for a meeting with David Atchison, he needed help. He explained to Atchison what had happened in Pardee, then said, "None of the free-state communities, like Pardee, have any respect for me or the law. They blatantly ignore my orders. They are all armed to their teeth and simply stand there laughing at me. Criminals, like Caleb May, walk around with a complete lack of fear. It is getting worse with time, not better."

Atchison thought for a while and finally said, "We must increase the pressure on these abolitionists. They ignore our laws and act like we do not exist. This cannot be allowed; we have the only legitimate government in the Kansas Territory, and it must be respected. Go immediately to Kansas Supreme Court Justice Lecompte and get a warrant to arrest Caleb May for murder and another to search his farm. I will tell Governor Wilson Shannon to send some U.S. cavalrymen with you to Pardee, we will get this man."

He continued, "Weapons are flowing into Kansas like a raging river from New England, Chicago, Ohio, everywhere. We must stop this. I want to start a blockade. All riverboats headed to Kansas City or Atchison must be boarded and searched. We must have men on every road to all Free-State towns and all wagons heading to them must be searched. All weapons and supplies found will be confiscated. It is time for drastic action."

"These people will respect the law! If not, we will starve them out."

Dunn agreed, "We must do it. Nothing else will work."

As promised by Atchison, Governor Shannon sent six U. S. cavalrymen to accompany Dunn to Pardee to arrest Caleb. Shannon managed to convince the commander at the fort that this was a temporary emergency that warranted federal help. The action was later admonished by the Secretary of War. He reminded the commander that U.S. troops are not to be used for police actions.

When Dunn and the soldiers arrived, Caleb was nowhere to be found and, not surprisingly, no one seemed to know where he was. Dunn decided to stay the night in Pardee and slept in the soldier's tent on the edge of town. Dunn had an arrest warrant, but if Caleb could not be found he couldn't use it. He also had a search warrant for the May cabin, but he dreaded using it because Maggie and William would resist and regardless of how that worked out, he would have a worse problem, better to focus on Caleb.

As he told his men, "I am sure Caleb is not in or near his cabin. Trying to force our way in is not only dangerous, but ultimately fruitless."

Early in the evening, three men from Dunn's party, including Dunn, went to the town well for water. The well was the one William and Caleb dug when they staked their claim. It sits in front of the May cabin near the south edge of the town. While there, they were accosted by some locals who said some insulting things about Dunn's courage or lack thereof. Dunn overheard all this and yelled, "Here I am gentlemen!"

He was immediately fired upon by someone and the bullet went through his trouser leg without hitting him. Neither Dunn, nor the soldiers could identify the shooter in the crowd, so he and his men returned to their tent. A short time later a man who looked drunk came wandering into their tent and took a seat, but Dunn quickly ordered him to leave. Within a couple of minutes of the visit, two shots were fired into the tent and one of the shots entered Dunn's back. The soldiers later thought that the drunk was locating Dunn in the tent for the shooter. Since the interior of the tent was well lit by a lantern, his distinctive bulky frame stood out, so an approximate location was all the shooter needed. Dunn fell to the ground and moaned "I'm shot," but was unable to rise afterward.[55]

His men moved Dunn to a local Pardee boarding house and a doctor was called for. There was no doctor in Pardee, so he had to come from Camp Creek, about two miles north of Pardee. The wound was between the right shoulder and the spine and Dunn was in great pain, but the doctor successfully got the bullet out and treated the wound. Dunn soon recovered well enough to be moved. The next day he was transported to Leavenworth to recover.

A reward of $500 was offered for the arrest of the guilty party by David Atchison. Dunn mostly recovered from his wound. But he suffered from partial paralysis and back pain for the rest of his life. The shooter was never identified but rumors suggested that he was James Filer of New York.[56] Witnesses said Filer had borrowed a revolver from his roommate and when he returned it, he supposedly admitted that he shot Dunn. But he was never found, and it was rumored that he fled Kansas and returned to New York.

Regardless of the shooter's identity, the Missouri newspapers screamed that Sheriff Dunn was murdered! This had to be walked back quickly to "wounded." They blamed the attack on a secret society of abolitionist assassins. They were probably referring to the Kansas Legion but didn't know the name.

While Dunn was recovering, his principal deputy Samuel Salters was made temporary sheriff and put in charge of the search. Salters made six arrests of Pardee citizens who watched Dunn try and arrest Caleb but did not help him. Salters was quickly informed that was not a crime and he had to let them all go. Salters and his men did stay in Pardee for a few days to look for Caleb, but they never saw him and could not get anyone to help them find him.

---

55 (May, 2019, p. 99). This is based upon the shooting of Sheriff Jones in Lawrence in 1856 as reported in: (Etcheson, 2004, p. 101).

56 (Connelley, 1918, p. 538)

The population amused themselves by giving Salters false leads and then watched him chasing about the town and the surrounding countryside only to find that Caleb wasn't where they said he would be. Caleb was well hidden and had many neighbors who brought him food and told him stories of Salters' escapades. He was even able to occasionally watch Salters running wildly around town looking for him.

After a humorous two-day search, back and forth through town and up and down the surrounding ravines and hills, Salters finally gave up. His search was hugely amusing for the community and sparked much laughter and storytelling. The laughter and joking about Salters and his men was not taken well by Salters or Dunn.

Blockade!

Sheriff Dunn's convalescence from the shooting was long, but he grew better and stronger over the next couple of months as the weather grew warmer. However, he was not well enough to lead the blockade he had carefully planned with Atchison in January. That duty fell to Dr. John Stringfellow. Together with his brother Ben and Robert Kelley, they gathered as many men as they could find to participate in riverboat raids to confiscate shipments addressed to free-state communities. The men also hijacked wagons destined for the free-state communities on the highways.

That fateful spring of 1856, there were more and more raids into Kansas from Missouri. Gun battles, theft, arson, and conflicts became common. Dr. John Stringfellow was working hard to gather and pay Missouri raiders, who were often called border ruffians, to implement the blockade. The men usually took the goods they confiscated to Stringfellow, then he took a cut of the seized goods and let the thieves divide the rest. This minimized his blockade expenses. None of the stolen goods, whether weapons or not, were ever returned to the people who had paid for them.

Stringfellow was most interested in stopping the arms shipments, but since the arms were usually in crates labeled "farm tools," "Bibles," or some other innocent sounding item, he kept everything headed for

Free-State towns. He called this thievery "pressing," as in pressing the goods into "government" service.

Stringfellow even advertised in southern states asking for more immigration to Missouri to attract more men for his blockade. Some of the southern immigrants stayed and helped, some found the job too dangerous and difficult and simply went back home.

By early spring, Caleb's head wound had healed, and his headaches became more and more infrequent and eventually disappeared altogether. Fortunately, the farm did not suffer during his convalescence, between William, Jim, Enoch, Pardee Butler and his other neighbors all chores and the spring planting were taken care of. Caleb was grateful.

Besides boarding ships on the Missouri River and stopping wagons to seize cargos, the Missouri raiders also stole cattle and horses from Kansas farms in Free-State areas. This sparked retaliation, and soon gangs of Free-State men were raiding inside Missouri and in proslavery areas of Kansas to steal cattle, horses, food, and other goods. This was sometimes to steal back what had been stolen from them, and sometimes just to steal replacements for what they had lost, regardless of where it came from. The blockade was causing hunger and suffering, it was every man, woman, and child for themselves.

No one dared to steal anything from Caleb May, so nearly everyone in Pardee put their stock on his land for protection. However, necessary supplies from the Missouri riverboats nearly stopped. The town was critically low on salt, coffee, lumber, nails, tools, all manner of foodstuffs, and building materials. They were especially low on gunpowder and lead for bullets. Times were desperate. Caleb was against stealing, but he could not call on the law to get his neighbors goods back, or to help the teamsters deliver their goods, it was the law that was doing the stealing.

Then Milo and Beth Carlton's cabin was burned down along with most of his wheat crop, and all the stock he had on his farm was stolen. Of the people who attended Pardee's Church, Milo and Beth lived the furthest east. That meant they were the closest to the proslavery towns in eastern Kansas. Caleb and Pardee Butler were horrified.

Early the next morning, Caleb gathered his men, and they had a meeting. In the meeting, he heard more stories of harassment and theft that occurred around the same time as the attack on Milo and Beth. Elijah Smith, told of a teamster trying to deliver some goods to his store the previous night. The poor man was shot and killed east of town, and his wagon and team were stolen along with all the goods.

Around dusk the previous night, Elijah had ridden out on the east road to meet the wagon, and he witnessed the murder and theft. He said, "I didn't dare to intervene because I was alone, and twelve men were attacking the wagon. Once I saw what was happening, I hid in the woods and watched. I saw Sheriff Dunn with them, the bastard! Afterward I followed them, from the cover of the woods, as they drove the stolen wagon eastward. I did stop to make sure the teamster was truly dead, and he was. They had left the body in the middle of the road. I then followed the wagon to Dr. John Stringfellow's farm west of Atchison, about seven miles from here. Charley Dunn looked poorly but could ride OK."

"When I returned from the Stringfellow farm, I took the teamster's body to the cemetery, but did not bury him."

Retribution

Caleb adjourned the meeting, so they could properly bury the teamster's body. Elijah did not know the man's name, but thought he worked in Leavenworth for Russell, Majors & Waddell, a freighting company. They planned to notify them of the murder and ask that his family be notified. Caleb, Pardee, and the other men in the Kansas Legion met over the teamster's grave.

Pardee joined hands with the men around him and said this prayer, "Ashes to ashes, dust to dust, we are made from the earth, and we return to earth. We do what we can when we are alive, and if we do well, we leave the world a better place. Let us hope this poor man leaves a world he improved and will now move to his eternal reward. Amen."

The goods Dunn's men stole were desperately needed by the town. After the burial, Caleb told the men, "We must get our goods and stock back. We must send a message to Dunn and Stringfellow that they cannot steal from us, kill our teamsters, and get away with it. If we show any weakness, they will do this over and over again."

He continued, "We know who has our property and who killed this innocent man, we must take it back, and without delay. Obviously, we cannot go to the Sheriff, he helped steal it in the first place."

Pardee said, "The best information I have is that Dr. John Stringfellow is organizing the Missouri raiders and collecting at least some of the goods for himself. This is clear from what I've read in the *Squatter Sovereign*. His farm is just west of Atchison."

Caleb said, "I know his farm. Do you think he has all our stolen stock?"

Pardee said, "I don't know, but considering Elijah followed the thieves to his farm, I'm pretty sure he was involved in stealing our goods, and I'll bet he has some of it on his farm."

Caleb asked the men generally, "Are you with me? Do we steal our goods and stock back from Stringfellow?"

Milo responded, "Even if it is not all our stock, I think we are all sure Stringfellow was involved in all the raids, and what he did not do himself, David Atchison, Charley Dunn, or Dunn's men did. I think we need to take all we can carry from John Stringfellow's farm."

The men all agreed, they solemnly shook hands over the fresh grave and swore they would raid Stringfellow's farm and take all they could. They would all be on horseback and would take two wagons for goods.

Caleb said, "Take the battle to the enemy! Absolutely no killing except in self-defense. While they burned Milo's house and crops, we will not burn theirs. We take all their guns and ammunition, all their stock, and nonperishable food, but we leave the house, the women, and children alone."

The men responded, "Yes sir."

Caleb knew Milo was going with them, he asked Pardee, "Are you going?"

Pardee thought a while, then said, "I do not like John Stringfellow, but stealing is not something the Lord would want me to do. However, Stringfellow was involved in burning my sister's home, so I must go. I will go. An eye for an eye."

Caleb then addressed all the men, "Please prepare for a fight and then head to Stringfellow's farm with two wagons when ready. William and I will scout the farm and prepare a plan, we will meet you on the east road near the Stringfellow farm. Plan for an attack at sunup tomorrow morning."

After some preparation and explaining what they were about to do to Maggie, William and Caleb set off for the farm and covered the distance in just over an hour. They arrived at the farm a little after 7 PM. William had had little sleep the previous night due to the fire at Milo's house, and Caleb none at all, but both were adrenalin fueled, sharp, and showed no exhaustion. Caleb found a concealed spot in the hills around the farm where he could clearly see the front of the farmhouse and the road to it. Then he told William, "Stringfellow knows me well, but I don't think he knows you. Go up to the house and tell them you are looking for work. Then look around as best you can and see how many men there are and where they are, also look for any arms they may have. Don't tell them your name is May, if you must give a last name, say Jones, or some other common name."

William took off on his horse and rode down to the farmhouse, it was much nicer than any house in Pardee, two stories, built with milled lumber rather than logs, a large porch and nice glass windows. He also noticed a large barn and a corral.

William walked slowly up to the door and knocked. A pleasant elderly woman came to the door and said, "Hello young man, what can I do for you?"

William replied, "My name is William, and I was hoping that you might need some work done around the place, I need to earn some money."

The lady then said, "Well, the Mr. and Mrs. are gone just now, but they should return late tomorrow, can you come back then?"

William, then said, "Sure. Do you have many hired hands here, do you think there is a chance for work?"

The lady responded, "Well we have two men working here now, they are probably still in the field south of the house. You could go ask them. I think they are clearing a new field just now, perhaps a quarter mile or so south."

William replied, "Thank you Ma'am, perhaps I will do just that."

William then returned to his father and told him what he had found out. Caleb was pleased, they looked around and when they were done it was nearly nine o'clock and fully dark. Caleb thought it might be best to bed down where they were, it was concealed and close to the road the men would be on early in the morning.

The men and wagons arrived on schedule shortly after sunup. Caleb and William spotted them quickly and filled them in on the plan. It was a lucky break that John Stringfellow and his wife were gone.

They immediately set off for Stringfellow's farm. There were ten men, including Caleb, William, Sam, Milo, Elijah, and Pardee. Jim wanted to go, but Caleb thought it was too dangerous for Jim to be so close to Atchison and Missouri. He asked Jim to guard the house. They were all heavily armed, but Caleb doubted they would need their weapons. He told the men, "If we do this right, none of us should have to draw our weapons, stay cool, stay relaxed."

They reached the Stringfellow farm before eight o'clock and went directly to the front door. The same lady came to the door. Caleb told her, "We are here to steal your cattle and goods ma'am. We have seen goods and stock stolen from our farms brought here and we want repayment. We want no trouble or shooting, but we will if we must."

She went pale, then turned red with embarrassment and fear, and replied, "Take what you want but please do not hurt me."

Caleb said, "You are in no danger Ma'am, please stand aside, we will find what we need."

"Where are the two hired hands that were working here yesterday?"

The housekeeper said, "They are probably in the bunkhouse, or in the south field by now, I already gave them their breakfast."

"Are they armed?"

"Probably not, they don't usually carry guns."

Caleb had William and two men stand watch front and back and the rest followed him to the bunkhouse. They opened the door, and the two men were sitting at a table drinking coffee.

Caleb said, "Gentlemen, we are Free-State men and saw some men bring some goods stolen from us here. We are here to steal them back. We will abide no resistance."

One of the men reached for a musket propped against the wall next to him. Caleb jumped forward and pointed his Sharps at the man's head as Sam Moore pointed his at the other man, who looked startled and scared.

Caleb said, "Don't even think about it. I don't want to kill you, but I will."

The man sat back in his chair and didn't move. Then said, "It's not worth my life, Stringfellow ain't that good a man, and he certainly is a thief. Take what you want. But I need this job, please tie me up before you leave, so he knows I resisted."

Caleb replied, "OK, we will. One of us was burned out of his house two days ago. So, we will be taking some goods from the house, as well as all the goods and stock stolen from us.

We have had a lot of our stock stolen over the past few weeks and we know Dr. Stringfellow, Charley Dunn, and David Atchison are behind it. This is to pay us back for our losses. You tell him that when you see him."

"Yes sir."

Caleb led them and his men to the barn and opened the barn door. They immediately saw a partially loaded wagon.

Caleb said, "This must be from the robbery and murder early yesterday. Why else would it be loaded with crated goods?"

Pardee and Elijah took a close look at the wagon, and Pardee asked, "Elijah, is this the wagon you saw yesterday?"

Elijah replied, "Yes sir, I believe it is, it looks the same. It is much sturdier than most wagons, unusual looking."

Pointing to the side of the driver's seat, Pardee said, "Well, this plate identifies it as a Russell, Majors & Waddell freighter. It also has an identification number. Those idiots stole a Russell, Majors & Waddell wagon and killed the teamster driving it!"

Caleb whistled, "Incredible, but not surprising, the teamster was probably an employee. We will return the wagon to them as soon as we can and tell them where we found it. Maybe they can get some justice. I understand that most of their work is for the U.S. Army. Stringfellow may have bitten off more than he can chew this time. Now we have everything we need to justify our actions. Let's hope the Army goes after him."

Pardee answered, "They certainly should."

One of the hired hands became pale in the face, and replied, "That wagon is a Russell, Majors & Waddell wagon?"

Caleb said, "Yes sir."

The hired hand only said, "We only saw the wagon yesterday, we had nothing to do with bringing it here. We will tell him. But you know he will come after you hard. He will bring Sheriff Dunn."

The other hired hand walked to the front of the wagon and examined the brass name plate and said, "That is their name plate for sure, I seen wagons like this in Leavenworth before, I wanted to work for them."

Caleb said, "You two stay quiet, and you will not be harmed. Sit over there, don't cause us any trouble. We'll tie you up before we leave."

Caleb then asked, "Does Dr. Stringfellow have any slaves?"

The man replied, "No, he don't have any, but his brother Ben has two, his farm is just north of here about a mile. Look, we don't want to get involved in this slavery fight, I know you been done wrong. I know if that's a Russell, Majors & Waddell wagon, all hell will break loose here. I understand your actions, but don't drag us into a fight over slavery. I don't know about my quiet buddy here, but I may not be around this place much longer."

"I won't drag you into this, I won't even mention you to anyone." Caleb then looked at Elijah, and without mentioning his name, in a low voice, he asked, "Do you recognize these men?"

Elijah answered, also in a low voice, "No sir, I didn't see them at the robbery and murder the other day."

Then Caleb said, "I thank you men for your understanding."

Elijah and Pardee stayed with the wagon and the men, while the others went to the house. They took several revolvers and two Sharps that they found, and all the powder, caps, and lead they could find in the house. They also took all the food that would travel OK. The Stringfellows had some very nice silver tableware, and some fine items made of gold; they took all of that.

Finally, they left William with the housekeeper and went to the barn and loaded all the farm tools, some of the hay, and goods from there on the wagons and gathered up the cattle and horses from the barn and corral.

While in the corral, Elijah said, "Look at all these different brands on the cattle and horses. Some of these brands are from our neighbors." Finally, they took the pigs in the pigpen.

After the wagons were loaded and animals were assembled, the rest of the men left and started the journey to Pardee.

Caleb and Pardee tied up the two hired hands in the barn and left the barn door open for ventilation.

Caleb told them, "You should be able to work your way free of these knots in an hour or so, if you choose to."

Then Caleb and Pardee remounted and went over to the house. The housekeeper and William were watching everything carefully. Caleb asked her, "Should I tie you up?"

She replied, "Yes, sir, thank you sir."

So, Caleb tied her to a chair inside the house, then remounted his horse and the three of them followed the rest of the men, the wagons, and the stock down the road. They headed west into the now setting Sun. Caleb was happy.

He said to William and Pardee, "We will be home before it gets completely dark. We have a Russell, Majors & Waddell wagon as proof that Stringfellow was involved in the robbery and the murder. We know the slain teamster was a Russell, Majors & Waddell employee, and all that should make a big difference.

Our actions were wrong, but they were justifiable."

Once they caught up to the men and wagons, Caleb rode up to Elijah with William and said, "William and Elijah, I think it might be better to send word to Russell, Majors & Waddell that we found one of their wagons and the body of a man we think was the driver. I'd like the two of you to ride to Leavenworth tomorrow, tell them what happened, and ask them to come up here to get their wagon and the body, unless they want to leave it in our cemetery, which is fine."

"As for the goods in the wagons, those from the robbery two days ago will all go to Elijah, if they are addressed to him. The rest of the goods we will split among all of us, with a double share to Milo and Beth for their loss."

He turned to Elijah, "Elijah, you witnessed the robbery, so you give a complete report to Russell, Majors & Waddell at their office. Hopefully, you will be able to get there and back in one day, but if not, find a place to spend the night. You may have to speak to the Army at the fort also."

Elijah and William both said, "Yes sir."

Dr. Stringfellow

Dr. Stringfellow and his wife arrived back at their farm later that evening at about the time Caleb and his men reached Milo's farm, or what was left of it. When he saw what happened, Stringfellow erupted in anger and demanded from his tied-up housekeeper and men, "What happened, who committed this outrage?"

He quickly untied the housekeeper and then the two men. They knew no names for sure, but the housekeeper said, "The boy was tall and thin, blue eyes, and about 16, he called himself William. The leader was a tall, muscular man with light hair and beard, gray eyes, and there were eight others."

Stringfellow said, "Damn him! Tall, muscular well-built man with a 15 to 16-year-old-son? That's Caleb May and his boy William from Pardee. They are abolitionist scum."

The next day Stringfellow told his partner Robert Kelly at the *Squatter Sovereign* office what happened and then rode to Platte City to inform David Atchison. Robert Kelly wrote a very inflammatory article in his paper about the "vicious abolitionist robbery of Dr. John Stringfellow and the sadistic mistreatment of his housekeeper and hired hands! They even took Mrs. Stringfellows silver and gold!"

Once in Atchison's spacious office, Stringfellow said, "Senator Atchison, things are out of control. The blockade is having an effect, but the damned abolitionists are fighting back. Caleb May and his men just stole everything of value from my farm! Other Law-and-Order farms have also been robbed; it is war out there!"

Atchison replied, "Well, if they want war, it is war they will have."

Stringfellow then said, "But, what about the Fort? What about the U.S. Army?"

Atchison said, "I can take care of that, with Governor Wilson Shannon's help. This is a local police matter; the Army will not interfere or get involved."

Stringfellow added, "Just one more thing. May took a wagon my men seized on the road to Pardee yesterday from my barn. It was a Russell, Majors & Waddell wagon."

"Don't worry about it, John. Bill Russell is a good friend; he won't give you any trouble. I'll deal with him."

It was just about that time that the "damned abolitionists" were stealing six of Wilson Shannon's prized horses.

Chapter 6
Prepare for War

Elijah and William made it to Leavenworth, a 23-mile trip, by 12 o'clock the next day, and it did not take long to find the large Russell, Majors & Waddell Freight company office. Once inside they let them know they had found one of their wagons and the teamster who was driving it was dead. The men in the office were upset and wanted all the details.

They reported the wagon number from the plate on the wagon, and Elijah told them, "I witnessed the robbery and the murder of your teamster, then I followed the men who stole the wagon all the way to Dr. John Stringfellow's farm."

The freight agent then asked Elijah, "What about the teamster's body?"

"The next day we gave it a proper Christian burial in the Pardee Cemetery. Our minister, Pardee Butler, read from the bible and prayed over him."

The agent then said, "Pardee Butler? The famous minister who was rafted in Atchison?"

"Yes sir, the very same. Then after we buried him, we conducted a raid on Dr. Stringfellow's farm and recovered the wagon and all the stolen goods. They were mostly my goods; I own the store in Pardee. Can you send someone to Pardee to give us the name of the man who was killed and claim the wagon? We don't know if we have the team or not, but we do have some horses from Stringfellow's corral, if you can identify your team, you can have them back also."

"The horses on our team will have our brand on them. He pointed to a brand posted on the wall, it was simple brand, just the initials RMW, end to end. So, we will know which horses are ours. Yes, we will send a teamster back to Pardee with you to bring back the wagon. Once we determine who the teamster was, we will notify his family. It sounds like you gave the man a proper burial and we are very grateful to you for that, thank you. We will tell the family what you've done."

The freighter then asked to be excused and left the office to hold a meeting in a separate room. After a short while he came out accompanied by a distinguished looking gentleman in very fine clothes, who said, "The teamster who was murdered was Silas Monroe, he has a family here in Leavenworth and we will notify them. You say he is buried in the Pardee Cemetery?"

Elijah responded, "Yes, sir. Of course, they are welcome to come and visit the grave anytime they want to. We will add a marker to the grave with his name."

"Thank you. A temporary marker with his name is very welcome. We will have a proper stone marker made for his grave and bring it up and install it when it is finished.

This is Robert, one of our teamsters, he will go back with you to retrieve the wagon and team. I'm William Russell, you can call me Bill. I will notify the Army of this atrocity. The Army will deal with Dr. Stringfellow once we have collected our wagon. I would like to thank you and your whole town; we appreciate all you have done.

Please spend the night tonight with me in my house, we will fix you a nice dinner and breakfast tomorrow morning and then you and Robert can ride up to Pardee together tomorrow. These are dangerous times, and I think all of you riding up there in the daylight together is safer. If you leave now, it will be dark by the time you reach Pardee. I have some errands to run, but Robert can take you to my house and get you settled."

Elijah replied, "Why thank you sir. That is nice of you. We accept your generous offer."

Bill Russell was a slave-owner and a strong proslavery supporter. He was also the treasurer of the proslavery Law and Order Party. He did not go immediately to the Army. He first went to see his friend David Atchison. Atchison agreed to pay all the damages to Russell's company and to pay $5,000 compensation to the teamster's family, and Russell agreed to let the incident go. But, not without extracting a promise from Atchison that he order his men to stay away from all Russell, Majors & Waddell freighters.

In the end, the Army was never notified of the robbery and murder, so they did nothing. Charley Dunn was the official Sheriff of the area, and he was personally involved in the robbery, so he obviously did nothing. This left everything in the hands of Caleb May and his militia, there was no other recourse.

Elijah and William were very impressed by the Russell house. It was a large two-story house set on a well-manicured lawn and surrounded by a seven-foot-high stone wall. It was only a quarter mile from the freight office, workshop, and warehouse. A black housekeeper in a uniform opened the door for them. She took them to their rooms and offered them a warm bath. They both agreed. A bath sounded great after their long dusty ride. She escorted them to a large bathroom with two large marble bathtubs and two uniformed black bath attendants. The attendants warmed a large pot of water and began filling the tubs and getting them to the right temperature.

Elijah and William were in awe of the house and the opulence, neither of them had ever seen anything like this before. They were speechless and could only follow the bath attendants' instructions.

The main attendant said, "Please sirs, take off your clothes and place them in this bag. We will wash them while you bathe."

The attendants turned around, and Elijah and William did as they were instructed and got in the tubs. The housekeeper came into the bathroom and collected the bag of clothes to wash them.

Elijah and William then spent a pleasant hour washing as the attendants occasionally brought them warm water and soap. When they got out of their tubs, they were given towels and bathrobes and served lemonade.

When their clothes were ready, they got dressed and went downstairs for a delicious dinner with the Russell family. They slept well that night and had an excellent breakfast before they began their ride home to Pardee with Robert.

As they rode to Pardee, William asked Robert, "Mr. Russell must be very rich, his house was huge! He has a whole room for taking baths and so many servants. I've never seen anything like that in my life."

Robert replied, "Yes, he is rich. Our company ships millions of pounds of freight west every year. It owns three steamboats, an insurance company, wagon repair shop, meat processing plant, and several grocery and outfitting stores. Mr. Russell owns one-third of the company. All those servants that waited on you in his house were his slaves."

"They were slaves? I didn't know that. He owns them?"

"Yes sir. He buys and sells slaves in Missouri. His slaves in the Kansas Territory are protected by the U.S. Fugitive Slave Law."

After that conversation, the men became quiet. The rest of the ride with Robert was uneventful, although all of them stayed alert and watched for possible problems. Once in Pardee, they took Robert to the wagon and the corral that contained the horses taken from Stringfellow. Robert declared the wagon to be in good shape.

He then went to the corral and looked through the horses, he separated out four of them and said, "Look here, these horses have our brand and must be part of the team. Silas Monroe would have had a team of six for this wagon. Two of the original team of six are missing. But I can return an empty or lightly loaded wagon with only these four."

Next, he visited Silas Monroe's grave with Pardee Butler and said goodbye to him. He said, "Silas was a good man, he had a nice wife and two young children. I visited him and his family often, they were all good people, I will miss him."

Pardee offered to pray for Silas and his family with Robert, and said, "Please Lord, accept Silas into your graces and protect his family in their grief and in their lives. Ashes to ashes, dust to dust, Amen."

Robert was silent, but grateful to Pardee. He spent a minute looking at his friend's grave, and turned to Pardee, "Thank you for all you've done, I will tell his wife that you cared for him and treated him well. When the marker for his grave is finished, I will bring her and their children up here for a service. Will you lead the service? They will be so grateful if you do."

Pardee said, "Of course my good man, I would be honored to do so."

Robert then spent the night with the Butler family, who gave him a nice dinner and breakfast.

By the next morning, Caleb and Elijah had gone through the goods, all that were addressed to Elijah Smith and others in the Pardee area they kept. But a few were addressed to others, so they loaded them on the wagon for Robert to take back or deliver. They told Robert they were looking forward to talking to the Army about what had happened.

Robert hesitated, then said, "You are all good people and should know that Mr. Russell and Mr. Atchison are good friends, and that Mr. Russell owns many slaves. When he left the office, he was going to see Senator Atchison, not to the Fort. The Army may not be notified and may not be coming here. Don't tell anyone I said this, but I owe you the truth because you've treated poor Silas and me very well."

This startled Caleb, who could think of nothing to say. After Robert rode away, Caleb realized they were in trouble. He sent William to De Kalb to notify their family that Pardee might be in trouble, and he might need their help. Then he sent Elijah down the Leavenworth Road to notify their Free-State allies to be on the lookout for militias or large groups of men headed toward Pardee. Finally, he personally rode to Lawrence to tell Charles Robinson and James Abbott that he might need help soon. He needed men, guns, power, and lead. There was going to be a fight.

Atchison

Atchison sent messages to Kansas Governor Wilson Shannon and to Colonel Albert Boone (the grandson of Daniel Boone) of Westport, Missouri. He explained that law and order was breaking down in the Kansas Territory, abolitionist raiders were invading the farms of innocent men, like Dr. John Stringfellow, and taking everything of value. Teamsters are being killed and left in the road and their wagons stolen. Total loss of order.

When Governor Wilson Shannon received the letter from Atchison, he was thinking of the recent theft of his prize horses. He had no idea who did it but was reasonably certain they were Free-State settlers. He wrote to President Pierce and explained the problems in the Territory and told him he wanted to call out the territorial militia and the U.S. Army, as well as accept an offer of help from General and ex-Senator David Atchison's Platte County Rifle Company in Missouri. He also told the President that Sheriff Charley Dunn was gathering a company of deputies. The first target of the combined force was to be Pardee, a small Free-State town in Kansas Territory. They knew the town was holding and protecting known thieves and murderers, the primary example was Caleb May.

The territorial Governor was not technically empowered to call up the territorial militia and certainly could not invite a militia from a neighboring state to invade the territory. Only the President has that authority, and even the President needs the approval, or at least the cooperation, of the Secretary of War. The Secretary of War was Jefferson Davis at the time. Only five years later, in 1861, Jefferson Davis would be elected president of Confederate States of America.

While Pierce was sympathetic to Shannon's request, he wondered why he needed so many men to arrest a common thief. Jefferson Davis was blunter, "The territorial militia and U.S. Army are not there to arrest thieves. That is Sheriff Dunn's job."

President Pierce replied to Davis, "This is an election year, and I certainly cannot have Atchison's militia invading the Kansas Territory from Missouri! The damned Republican press would hang me in a public square."

Following the discussion with Secretary of War Davis, the President wrote to Governor Shannon and firmly denied his request. Jefferson Davis wrote to General Sumner at Fort Leavenworth and ordered the U.S. Army at the fort to deny any Missouri militias entry into the territory.

The national election was to be in November and the country was divided on slavery and Kansas. Everything that happened in Kansas Territory was under a microscope and on the front page of every newspaper in America.

Governor Shannon, David Atchison, and the now mostly recovered Sheriff Charley Dunn had other options. Firstly, Dunn could have as many deputies as he could support and entice to join him. They didn't need to be Kansas residents. He recruited far and wide, many of the new deputies were paid by David Atchison, which was perfectly legal at the time.

Secondly, the bogus Shawnee Mission state legislature had already appointed Lucian Easton General of the territorial militia and had funded him. Easton could raise men, and the law was ambiguous about how much authority he had on his own to protect the citizens. He could not disobey orders from Jefferson Davis or the President, neither could he wage war, but he had some latitude on personnel matters. For example, he could encourage his men to sign up as deputy sheriffs to protect the settlers and enforce the territorial laws.

Governor Shannon issued no orders to the militia, but he "informed" General Easton that the citizens of Pardee were causing trouble, and that Sheriff Dunn was afraid that he did not have enough men to enter Pardee and arrest Caleb May, who was now wanted for the "murder" of John Cook and theft. Easton recruited some men, all volunteers, to help in the effort. He issued the men arms from the armory at Fort Leavenworth, but the arms were old, had not been well maintained, and were of poor quality. They had little powder and lead for practice, but he tried to make sure that all the men fired their weapons at least one time. Most of the men refused the issued weapons and used their personal rifles and pistols.

Sheriff Dunn's other recruits were also untrained and had inferior weapons. However, between Dunn and Easton they raised almost 500 men. Easton also had access to cannons, but since he was not allowed to go to war, he concluded that he was not authorized to offer them to Dunn. In early April, Dunn, with the help of Easton, was ready. Due to their recruiting efforts and other public activities, Caleb was well informed of their plans. All of Easton's men were sworn in as deputies, as well as the men Dunn recruited. While Easton believed he could legally help Dunn recruit and equip volunteers, he did not think he could go with Dunn as part of his "posse." He thought if he did that, the Secretary of War would disapprove.

Pardee

The citizens of Pardee were alone, but not defenseless. Caleb, through his contacts in the Kansas Legion secured several hundred Sharps rifles and a large quantity of gunpowder and lead. They also gathered a lot of food and other supplies to be ready for a siege. They were busy preparing throughout the month of March.

It was spring planting season, but some men were able to come to Pardee to help. Caleb's brother Isaac gathered some men from the De

Kalb area and some men also came from Lawrence and Topeka. Caleb and his men organized and built defenses, with considerable help from the Lawrence based Kansas Legion. Unfortunately, General Abbott himself was in New England raising funds and arms for the Kansas Legion and could not participate in the preparations. An attack was expected at any time.

They built four blockhouses on limestone foundations, with four feet of cemented limestone block walls on top of the foundation that were a foot thick or more on all sides. The rest of each wall was built with a double thickness of logs. The roof of each blockhouse was also a double thickness of logs, with shingles on top of the logs. Each wall of the blockhouses had small gunports. They each accommodated eight men. Caleb also had his men dig well disguised fox holes on both sides of each road coming into town. These fox holes were dug every 300 feet along the first mile of each road.

Their calls for help through the Free-State community were effective; by the time Dunn and his men were on the march to Pardee, the town had almost 300 defenders under arms, and men were still arriving. The Shawnee and Delaware Indians offered help, but Caleb declined, he didn't want to give the U.S. Army any excuse to join the war.

Meanwhile in the Missouri and southern newspapers, the stories of Kansas Free-State settlers burning down proslavery settler's houses and throwing women and children out of their homes into the cold night spread and inflamed the public. Unfortunately, some of these stories were true, but the men of Pardee had not done any of these things.

In early April, word was received that 400 proslavery men were on their way to Pardee from Leavenworth and more were expected later. The invaders only made about ten miles on the first day. Caleb sent spies out along the Leavenworth Road to monitor the progress, and the first spy returned with this report:

"There are several hundred Missourians camped next to Easton in raggedy tents with poor quality food, but with no shortage of strong whiskey. A few can still stand up, but not many. It's wet and very muddy, but they don't care since they have plenty to drink. Most have smoothbore muskets and old pistols, which are rusty and ill-kept. They are no more prepared for war than my mother and her sister, who could probably whup all of 'em! And if my mother did kick them in the ass, I doubt they would even feel it."

With this the room erupted into laughter.

The reports from the other spies were similar. It seemed that Dunn had been unable to find or train quality troops. Some of the Missouri "volunteers" had good weapons because the Platte County Rifle Company volunteers had raided the Liberty, Missouri arsenal and stole (or "borrowed") some weapons for use in the conflict. However, for the most part their weapons were a poor match for the Free-State Sharps rifles and carbines. In the words of Territorial Governor Shannon to President Pierce in a letter written well after the fateful battle:

"Kansas Territorial General Easton had brought to the Sheriff a very inadequate force for his protection, when compared with the forces in Pardee. Indeed, the volunteers were wholly unorganized. The whole force in the Territory thus obtained did not amount to more than three or four hundred men, badly armed, and wholly unprepared to resist the forces in Pardee, which were nearly 300 men; all remarkably well armed with Sharps' rifles and other modern weapons."[57]

Dunn's men were able to form an effective blockade around Pardee designed to prevent some or all supplies from reaching the town. Caleb did not allow his men to interfere with the preparations, and as much as possible activity in Pardee remained normal, except commerce with the outside world was greatly reduced. All his men had over the shoulder bags packed and ready to go with food, water, and ammunition, each of them knew exactly where their assigned position was if and when the fighting started. A continuous stream of spies worked their way through the woods and fields keeping track of all enemy movements. There were 140 men prepared to go to their fox holes on the four roads to the town. They knew their personal foxhole and their duty.

---

57 (Robinson C., 1892, p. 214), the quote is heavily modified from the original.

Pardee 167

The Ladies

James Abbott spent most of his time traveling east to raise money and buy weapons, especially Sharps rifles and carbines, gunpowder, and lead to bring back to Kansas to support the Free-State effort. The money he used to purchase the weapons was mostly donated by large anti-slavery organizations, like the New England Immigrant Aid Company.

Abbott had just returned to Kansas with a large shipment of arms. He went around the blockade in Missouri by taking his wagons through Iowa to Nebraska City and then south through Holton, Kansas Territory. Abbott knew about the siege of Pardee from messages he had received along the way. He wanted to help Captain Caleb May but could not risk Dunn and Atchison's siege with his wagons. He knew Caleb and his men in Pardee had plenty of guns but was sure they could use more ammunition. Holton was 25 miles west of Pardee, which was a large distance to transport goods. Abbott took one wagon of powder and lead to Grasshopper Falls, a safe Free-State community only 13 miles from Pardee. One of the men he brought with him was Captain Sam Walker, a resourceful and reliable man he trusted. He asked him, "Sam, do you think you can sneak through that blockade around Pardee and get word to Captain Caleb May that we have some ammunition for him, if he can come and get it?"

Walker was a thin man, with a boyish face, and about medium height. He could be mistaken for a boy, except he had piercing, intelligent eyes, that always looked directly at you. The eyes were a decade older than the face. He wore two Navy Colt revolvers in a gun belt around his waist, and he knew how to use them. He thought for a moment, and replied, "I should be able to."

Walker took his best horse and loaded lead bars, cartridge papers, percussion caps, and a bag of gun powder into the saddle bags and headed northeast. After traveling about twelve miles he slowed down. It was dusk, and soon he saw a campfire. He dismounted his horse and walked carefully to work his way around it. He left the path he was following and went north, keeping the fire in sight and to his right.

Soon, a man approached him, and asked, "Halt, who are you and where are you going?"

Walker replied, "My name is Sam and I'm headed to Monrovia, which I think is just north of here, is that right?"

The man replied, "Yes sir, just a few miles north, follow this path and it will take you right there."

Walker said, "Thanks. If you don't mind my asking, why the interest? Why are you here?"

The man replied, "We are Sheriff Dunn's deputies, and we are after that murdering scum Caleb May. He killed John Cook a few weeks back, robbed Dr. John Stringfellow's farm, and probably shot the Sheriff. He is still free, but not for long. East of here is the town of Pardee, named after the vile abolitionist Pardee Butler. May is hiding out there, so we have the town surrounded. We are not allowing anyone to leave or enter the town. We plan to burn Pardee to the ground as punishment for aiding and abetting May."

Walker asked, "But I can go to Monrovia?"

The man said, "Yes sir, no problem going to Monrovia. If you see any other men, just say you talked to Joe Curlien, already and I said you can pass. Stay to the west, don't go any farther east."

Walker replied, "Yes sir."

Then Walker walked north, leading his horse. He continued walking for another half mile, and carefully listened and looked around. It was fully dark by then and a moonless night. He could hear nothing and saw no campfires. He found a path leading east, judging the direction with the North Star, which was very bright that chilly, moonless, and clear, spring night. He began following the path carefully on foot; while leading his horse, it was too dark to risk riding in the thick east Kansas woods. He traveled about two miles until he could hear some activity and saw a glow to the east indicating fires. He had just crossed a small creek and was still in a wooded area. So, he took his saddle off the horse, hobbled him, took his saddlebags, and set off quietly and carefully toward the glow and the noise.

As he approached the glow in the lower eastern sky, he encountered another small creek and quickly waded across as quietly as possible. He still saw no one, but just minute later, he heard someone say, "Who goes there?"

Walker could not see anyone, but replied, "Sam Walker sir, I mean no one any harm."

William May then stepped out from behind a tree, with his Sharps pointed directly at Walker and said, "Are you part of Sheriff Dunn's posse?"

Understanding William's tone of voice, Walker breathed a sigh of relief, and said, "No sir. I'm here to deliver a message from General James Abbott. It is for Captain Caleb May."

William visibly relaxed and said, "Very good, I will take you to him. But first give me your guns."

Walker withdrew his revolvers and gave them to William, who tucked them into his belt, then followed Walker into town with his Sharps pointed directly at him. Walker said, "You know Sheriff Dunn and his men intend to burn your town to the ground?"

William replied, "That is what they say. We'll see."

"You don't sound very concerned."

William said, "I'm not. We are well set up to fight them off, but I can tell you no more, you must ask the Captain."

"Very well."

They arrived at the May cabin and William knocked and walked in. Once in he turned to Walker and said, "Ma and Pa, this is Sam. He says he is with General Abbott, and he has a message for you Pa."

Caleb stood up and towered over Walker who was only about five and a half feet tall. He said, "Hello sir, I'm Captain Caleb May, what can I do for you?'

Walker replied, "Good to know you sir, I'm Captain Samuel Walker. General Abbott asked me to come here to bring you some lead and powder, here is what I have." He handed over the saddle bags to Caleb.

Caleb looked inside, and said, "Thank you, this will be very helpful." He turned and handed the bags to William, "William, please put these in the shed, with the other supplies and bring Captain Walker's bags back to him."

William said, "Yes, sir."

Then Caleb offered his hand to Walker, who shook it firmly, Caleb then said, "Thank you Captain Walker, you've had a dangerous journey here but made it. We are grateful."

After William left, Walker replied, "No problems on the trip, but I did talk to a man who said he was one of Sheriff Dunn's deputies, he called you a murderer and a thief and said they intended to burn this town down."

Caleb then said, "I am not a murderer, it was a gun battle and many men on both sides were firing. It is possible that the bullet that struck John Cook was from my gun, but there is no way to know that. In any case they fired first. As for their accusation that I shot Sheriff Dunn, that is impossible. I was here on this farm when he was shot and nowhere near his tent."

"I did steal goods and a wagon from Dr. Stringfellow, but the wagon itself was stolen from Russell, Majors & Waddell and most of the goods on board belonged to our local storekeeper, Elijah Smith, who has receipts for the payments he made for the goods."

"One more thing, one of our neighbors, Milo Carlton and his wife Beth, were burned out of their home and we strongly believe that Stringfellow, Dunn, and Atchison were behind it. Milo recognized one of his horses among the horses we took from Stringfellow's corral, and most of the Russell, Majors & Waddell freighter team was in Stringfellow's corral."

Walker said, "Thank you for telling me that. I will inform General Abbott."

Then he turned to Maggie and said, "Mrs. May, it is very nice to meet you, you have a fine son there. Are these, your other children?"

Maggie smiled and said, "Yes sir, Captain. These are the twins, Enoch and Priscila, our little Sam, who is 6, Catherine, and Mary is holding Isaac, who is almost 2."

"What a wonderful family, you are blessed. I have four children myself in Bloomington."

Maggie relied, "Thank you and bless you."

Walker then said, "Captain, we are returning to Lawrence with the weapons we bought in Chicago but have brought one wagon of supplies to Grasshopper Falls. We only need a way to bring the supplies in the wagon to you. Is there any way to get a wagon to Pardee?"

Caleb thought a while, and said, "I don't see how, Dunn's men are posted on every road and pathway, a wagon would surely be spotted, so would men on horseback."

The mention of men gave Maggie an idea and she spoke up, "Cale, I think Mary, Sybil, and I might be able to bring some of the lead and powder back. We could take extra clothing, after all it is very cold, and we could bring the powder and lead back in our clothing. The men

The Ladies

wouldn't dare search a woman. Even if they stop a wagon of women, which is unlikely, the ammunition would be safe. But there is no way we could bring a wagonload of lead and powder back. They would surely search the wagon."

Caleb thought a minute, then said, "Excellent idea Maggie! You could bring the shot and powder here more safely. You can take Pardee's buggy, it looks very innocent. What will you say if you are asked what you are doing?"

Maggie replied, "We'll say we are helping deliver a baby and we can carry supplies for a birthing. Usually, two or three women are needed, so it will make sense. Plus, it will suggest urgency, give us an excuse to be out at night, and the men will be less likely to delay us."

Walker said, "Perfect! That will work for sure."

Caleb agreed, "No one will harass you."

Walker said, "I will make my way back to my horse and on to Grasshopper Falls. With any luck I will be there when you arrive. One more thing, it sounds like Dunn and his men are about to attack. Are you ready, do you need anything more except for the ammunition?"

Caleb replied, "We have a good plan, and everything is set. We will wait as long as possible and strike when the moment is right. I doubt we will wait for their attack; I want to catch them unprepared. We are monitoring their movements carefully. I doubt we will need any help, but we'll be able to let you know if we do."

Walker replied, "Very well, then. I must be off."

Maggie and Mary made their way across the creek to Pardee's cabin and woke them up and explained their plan to Sybil and Pardee.

Sybil said, "Brilliant plan, it should work."

Pardee said, "It will be dangerous Sybil, you must be very careful."

Sybil replied, "Of course honey, we will be careful, but it is a good plan. Now please, hitch two horses to the buggy, we will need two coming back, we will weigh a lot more then!"

Pardee and the others shared a good laugh at that.

Nine-year old Rosetta Butler said, "Ma, can I go? I can bring back powder and lead just like Mary."

Sybil told her daughter, "Not this time honey, you are just a little too young for this trip. Besides there is only room in the buggy seat for three."

Then, Sybil, Mary, and Maggie gathered up pillowcases, extra stockings, and the largest corsets they could find. By the time Pardee had the buggy ready and in front of the cabin, they had stuffed their corsets, undergarments, and stockings full of bags, pillowcases, and other clothing and looked twice their normal size. As they walked out Pardee broke into a big grin and said, "My, my ladies, you've blossomed!"

They all laughed and loaded their "birthing" supplies into the back of the buggy and took off on the southwest road just as the Sun was about to come up over the horizon. The road was dry and in good shape, so they moved along quickly. About a mile outside the town a rider came up to them looked carefully at the back of the buggy, and said, "Hello ladies, I hope all is well, where are you headed?"

Sybil was driving, and said, "We are on our way to a birthing, we are to help."

The man replied, "Oh! Good for you. My best wishes to the mother and child."

Sybil answered, "Thank you sir, we must be off now."

He replied, "Of course, of course, be careful, I will pass the word to leave you be. You will not be delayed."

They were not interrupted again and arrived in Grasshopper Falls a couple of hours later. General Abbott and two of the ladies from Grasshopper Falls greeted them. The ladies fixed them a nice lunch, as the men brought the lead bars and powder into the house. With dinner over, all the men left, and the ladies began concealing the powder and lead under Sybil, Mary, and Maggie's clothing.

Maggie emptied a small keg of gunpowder into a pillow slip that she sewed shut and put under her outside dress. Sybil, Mary, and Maggie concealed the Sharps rifle percussion caps, cartridges, and gun barrel wipers in their sleeves, pockets and dress waists. They stood the four-inch, two-pound bars of lead up in their double and triple layers of stockings. Once they had concealed all they could carry they carefully, and a little painfully, made their way to the door, giggling about how they looked. "Mary laughed and said, "We are walking tree stumps!"

Sybil laughed and said, "I weigh more than a tree stump."

Maggie chimed in, "It will take four oxen just to get me into the buggy!"

The Ladies

Once outside, General Abbot and his men had to lift them into the buggy. Once they were situated, Maggie asked Abbot, "Has Captain Sam Walker made it back yet?"

Abbott replied, "No, I've not seen him, did he leave Pardee when you did?"

"No, he left before we did. I hope he is OK."

"We will keep an eye out; he may have been delayed somehow or maybe he had to detour around the ruffians. I'll send a search party out if he doesn't arrive soon."

"Thank you General, we liked that young man."

"We will, we like him also."

On the return to Lawrence they were stopped once, but the leader of the men who stopped them simply said, "Excuse me ladies; we thought you were men, and we have orders to let no man pass on this road to Pardee." and he then let them go. As they left, they heard one of the men say, "They must be the ladies that Isaac said were going to help with a birth."

When they got back to Pardee, Caleb, William, Enoch, Priscila, Sam, Catharine, Rosetta, and Pardee were anxiously waiting. Once they saw the buggy, they cheered their arrival. Again, the ladies found they could not safely get off the wagon and Pardee and Caleb lifted them off the buggy and set them carefully on the ground. Pardee couldn't help himself and said, "Bustles must be back in fashion, they are swelled out awful!" Sybil was not amused and slapped him, everyone else laughed, even Pardee with his red cheek.

They helped the ladies into the cabin where they were able to unload their treasures in private.[58]

Bitter cold

The previous night was cool, but not uncomfortable, but that day, early in April 1856, a strong north wind came up and blew in some very frigid air. The temperature that night dropped to well below freezing

---

[58] Based on a true story about two women, Lois Brown and Margaret Wood. (Etcheson, 2004, pp. 83-84)

and the north wind was very strong. It blew many of the invader's tents over onto the ground, and the Missouri border ruffians suffered from the cold.

Late that night, there was a knock on the door of the May cabin. Caleb was asleep, but got up, grabbed one of his revolvers and went to the door. Outside was a stranger who was very cold and did not look well. Caleb asked him what he wanted.

He said, "Mr. May, you have no reason to help me, but I am dying from the cold and wind, my fire is no help, can you please let me in to warm up some. I promise I'll leave in the morning and will not come back."

Caleb thought, "I should just shoot the poor bastard and be done with it, but he looks so pitiful, I just can't do it."

In the end, Caleb let him in but took his gun and knife first. He was thinking about the passage in the Bible that says, "Love your enemies," something easier to say than to do.

He set the man by the fire and offered him coffee, which he accepted. Caleb asked him, "You know who I am, you said my name, what is your name?"

"I'm called Tim McGee and I'm from Platte City. Thank you so much for the fire and coffee. It is bitterly cold out there and the wind is vicious. My tent blew over and the fire is no help."

Caleb asked, "You know Sheriff Dunn means to take me and hang me and burn my town."

McGee answered, "Yes sir. He does indeed, but I will not be helping him. Come morning, I'm going home."

Caleb asked, "How many men does he have?"

"We had about 400 yesterday, there will be fewer tomorrow."

Caleb, "Can you tell me where they are? Can you make a map?"

Caleb knew where all the men were from his spies, but he wanted to see what the man knew and if he would tell the truth. He was a careful man.

McGee hesitated and said nothing for a moment. Then, "I'm leaving anyway, and you are helping me, I'll draw your map. But don't you tell no one it was from me."

"I will not."

McGee spent some time making the map and gave a commentary as he went. He pointed out where Dunn was, along with most of his deputies. Then he explained where each of the roads were being blockaded. He said they had captured a young man named Walker the day before and showed where they were holding him.

Caleb asked, "This Walker, was he young in the face and kind of short and thin?"

McGee said, "Yes sir. We caught him in the woods west of here yesterday morning."

Caleb thought about this, then woke William up. Out of earshot of the man, he whispered to William what he had said. Then said to him, "Watch him carefully and do not let him leave. We need to rescue Walker."

Then they both got dressed, Caleb bundled himself up, said goodbye and left. He immediately gathered up his best men, Sam Moore, Milo Carlton, Andy Elliot, Bill Wakefield, and of course, Elijah Smith.

In Elijah's combination cabin and store Caleb addressed his men. "One of Dunn's deputies came to my cabin tonight and asked to be let in to warm up. I thought about shooting him."

The men all laughed, and Caleb continued, "But I didn't, I invited him in and set him by the fire and made him some coffee. He said he was going home in the morning; he couldn't take the cold. I don't know, but this cold may drive many of Dunn's men away."

Sam Moore said, "They are a bunch of candy asses." This caused another eruption of laughter.

Caleb, continued, "His name is Tim McGee, and he is from Platte City. He says Dunn's men captured Captain Sam Walker yesterday when he was leaving my house. He brought us powder and lead and we must help him escape. How are the preparations to drive Dunn from here going, are we ready? Can we save Walker? He is at Dunn's headquarters a couple of miles northeast of here where Stranger Creek crosses Pardee Road, not far from Camp Creek."

Sam spoke up and said, "I just looked over that camp yesterday, around noon, didn't see any unusual activity. There are or were about a hundred men, more or less. Dunn's large tent is well guarded, but we have ten or eleven two-man or three-man foxholes ready all around the camp. The foxholes are well concealed, and they all lie within 250 yards of the camp.

It is a stupid place to build a camp. It is on low ground, surrounded on three sides by thick woods, and you can walk almost right up to it along Stranger Creek completely concealed. It is easy to attack, my team has been watching them for days and they have no clue we are there."

Caleb thought for a minute, "OK, it is cold out there, Dunn's men will be moving slowly. If Sam leads us to them carefully, we can take our positions without being seen or heard. We will all have Sharps and can hit them from 250 yards, very few of them will have Sharps. We will be concealed; they will be in the open. We can hit them; they will not be able to hit us. The idea is to attack when they are in our range, and we are outside their range."

"If they have 100, we will only need 40, if we can surround them before we shoot. Sam, you lead the way. We will approach on foot, and we should be able to get there before dawn, when it is the coldest. We will surround them, and as many as possible will take cover in the prepared foxholes along Pardee Road. Do not shoot until I do, if you can avoid it. Stealth, surprise, and a superior position are key. Any questions?"

Milo asked, "How will we get there, follow Stranger Creek? The moon is not up yet, it's quite dark."

Sam answered, "Dunn's men are only along the roads, so we can cut across Pardee's claim and Milo's, then head northeast until we reach Stranger Creek. We'll follow the creek to Pardee Road and Dunn's camp is right there. We will approach the camp from the northwest. I have markers placed along the creek to guide us to the foxholes we've prepared. Once we reach the first marker we will split up, half will go east and half south. I'll lead the group heading east and Andy Elliot and Bill Wakefield will lead the group going south. It is important that we stay concealed when firing, we will be on opposite sides of the camp and we do not want to be shooting each other, don't enter the camp, shoot from a concealed position outside the boundary of the camp.

Caleb, I recommend that you keep part of the force at the northeast corner of the camp on the creek, where we will be splitting off. There is good cover there and by climbing one of the trees you have a good view of the whole camp."

Caleb said, "Good plan and good description. Men keep talking and noise to an absolute minimum, explain everything to your men before we leave. Surprise will be critical. There will be no warnings given, when I fire, everyone fires. Aim well and mind your hindsight, hit what you aim at, don't shoot over their heads. Our main goal is to rescue Sam Walker, once we have him and make it out of the camp we disengage and retreat. We will retreat in squads of six, just as we have trained. We will rejoin on Pardee's claim, east of his cabin.

When firing from the east and west positions, be mindful that I and my men will be entering the camp from the north to get Sam Walker, don't shoot us. We will keep our distance for safety, but we must go to Dunn's tent to get Sam."

Sam Moore said, "Good points. Men mind what Caleb said."

With that, each left to gather their men. They were to assemble at the muster point east of Pardee Butler's cabin. William was not with them, he had to make sure Tim McGee stayed put, no one wanted to let him go, he might be a spy. Caleb told Pardee he could go if he wanted to, or not as he chose. Pardee declined and stayed with his family but put on his holster and revolver. No matter how well or poorly the battle went, he knew there would be repercussions.

Chapter 7
Walker

There was a predawn glow behind Walker when he left the May cabin to get his horse and return to Grasshopper Falls. His horse was hobbled about a mile west in a wooded area, that was about all he knew, it had been dark, which prevented him from getting a good bearing on the horse's location. It was cold and a north wind was picking up, foretelling bad weather on the way. He remembered crossing a road when he walked toward Pardee, so he practiced what he would say when he saw Dunn's deputies. He'd say he was headed to Monrovia but got lost in the dark. Then he'd say he hobbled his horse so he could look around for the road to Monrovia. That ought to work.

He carefully worked his way west and when he saw the road, he stopped for several minutes and looked and listened. He could hear nothing and didn't see anything, so he walked into the road and crossed it. He had already crossed one creek, and he remembered he had to cross another before he was close to his horse. The area he was in was lightly wooded, but the area ahead was open ground.

It was dawn and visibility was good, he wanted to just hide for a while and wait for a better time, but it was cold, he was worried about his horse, and he wanted to get back to his men, so he set out to cross the clearing. He tried to look as innocent as possible. He was about halfway across when he heard someone yell "Halt! Go no farther."

He turned toward the voice and saw two men riding up on horses. When they got to him, with guns drawn, they asked what he was doing there. He gave them his planned response, "I'm on my way to Monrovia and got lost in the dark. I've just now figured out I'm turned around and I'm trying to get back to my horse and find the road to Monrovia."

Just then a third rider rode up and said, "Why you're Sam Walker! You are a damned Yankee abolitionist!"

Walker still had his pistols and considered drawing them and trying to fight his way out of this predicament, but they all had pistols drawn and at least one of them would shoot him, if he tried anything. So, he did nothing but say, "My name is Sam, but my last name is not Walker."

"Hell, you say, you are Sam Walker and I've just seen you in Grasshopper Falls. Men, we need to take him to Sheriff Dunn and see what he wants to do with him."

Walker said, "OK you've got me, but please let us find my horse first, he is hobbled just a mile or so west of here."

The third man said, "Can't let a horse die in this cold, ok we will get it, just give us your guns and walk ahead of us to the horse."

With that done, they walked west until they crossed the creek Walker remembered and found his horse. Walker took the hobble off the horse, resaddled it, and they made their way to Sheriff Dunn's camp, located where Pardee Road crossed Stranger Creek.

When they rode into Dunn's Camp the first thing Walker noticed was everyone was drinking and most looked drunk even though it wasn't even noon yet. The second thing he noticed was the camp was near the creek which made water convenient, but there was high ground, thickly wooded to both the west and east. There were also thick woods around Stranger Creek to the north. His immediate thought was anyone could take this camp, ten men could take it with Sharps rifles.

They took him to Dunn's tent and told Dunn who he was. Dunn said, "I know you, you live in Bloomington, what were you doing in Grasshopper Falls?"

Walker replied, "I had business there, I needed coffee, flour, and corn seed. The Grasshopper Falls store had these items and we didn't in Bloomington."

Dunn said, "Why not go to Lawrence or Oskaloosa? They are closer."

Walker said, "I knew that the goods were in Grasshopper Falls. With the blockade, I didn't know if the other towns had what I needed."

The third man said, "Why go to Monrovia? There is nothing there."

Walker said, "I wanted to visit a friend who lives there."

Dunn said, "This sounds like bullshit, you are a lying abolitionist. We whip abolitionists here. Men give him thirty lashes; we will see if that loosens his tongue."

They took Walker out in the cold, took off his shirt, and tied him to a tree. Then they made a big show of presenting their whip. The men said, "Tell us the truth about why you are here, and you'll save yourself a whipping."

Walker said, "I told you why I'm here, I have nothing else to say."

Then they brutally whipped him and told him he would be left tied to the tree until he told them the truth. There were some Kickapoo women in the camp who did most of the cooking. They took pity on Walker, covered him with a blanket, and fed him some soup and stew. He was very grateful.

The Battle

The 42-man force joined up east of Pardee Butler's cabin. It was bitterly cold, but thankfully the wind had died down a bit in the early hours of morning. It was about 3AM and they had a good thirty- to forty-five-minute walk ahead of them, the moon was just a sliver and low in the sky, it gave them little light. They made their way northeast, toward Stranger Creek, everyone was as quiet as possible.

This was the area Sam Moore and his men were responsible for, so they led the force. They moved quickly and stayed on the eastern fringe of a wood that surrounded a minor tributary of Stranger Creek. They were not expecting any of Dunn's men to be in that area, since they rarely left the roads. They were well west of Pardee Road, where Dunn's camp was. They moved north of the camp, because they wanted to approach it along the banks of Stranger Creek, which runs from northwest to southeast. The streambank and the surrounding trees were good cover.

Once they reached Stranger Creek, they worked their way southeast along the edge of the creek. The creek was frozen over, but they avoided walking out onto the creek itself in case the ice was thin. They moved single file with a couple of yards between each man.

When they got close to Pardee Road, Sam called a halt. He and Caleb talked in low tones. Sam said, "Most of the men will be drunk, but there will be guards along the road, and some may be awake. Dunn was an idiot to camp here, he is surrounded on three sides with thick woods. We'll use the fox holes for cover. There are trees that can be climbed for lookouts. You and I will go east across the road. You position your men along the north edge of the camp, and I will take mine to the eastern side of the camp and spread them out in the woods to the east."

"Bill and his men will go south and take positions west and southwest of the camp. We will have only minimal coverage south, so Dunn's men will run that way. You and your men will lead the attack into the camp from the north, come straight out of Stranger Creek moving south. Give us 30 minutes to get in position. We don't know where Walker is but will look for him."

Caleb said, "Good Plan, we will cross the road and wait thirty minutes. Everyone must be sure who they are shooting, we do not want to shoot Sam Walker or any of the women." Bill, Sam, and Caleb synchronized their watches, Sam said, "Thirty minutes."

***

It was bitterly cold and had been very windy. But the women taking care of Walker had brought him another blanket and covered him with a tarp so he wouldn't freeze to death. He was still tied to the tree, but the ropes had loosened, and his hands were now tied in front of him so he could feed himself. He was able to sit on the ground and lean against the tree, the rope tying him to the tree gave him a little freedom of movement. He thought about trying to untie himself, since in his new position it was possible, but figured it would be too dangerous with so many of the Missouri raiders around, and he didn't want to invite another beating. He did loosen the knots just in case a good opportunity to escape appeared.

He got a little sleep. The women brought him soup and coffee. Walker had no guards, and everyone in the camp was huddling in their tents to shelter from the wind and cold. Since Walker was huddled at the base of a tree and completely covered, he was almost invisible.

Caleb, Sam Moore, and their men made their way carefully across the road and saw no one. They moved through the thick woods until they could see the camp, then Caleb's men took up positions to wait for the time to attack. Caleb took out his watch, and noted he had 20 minutes left.

Sam and his men went farther east. They moved down the creek to a point well past the camp to where Sam had marked a tree many days before while spying on Dunn's camp. Once there they headed south in the thick woods, moving quietly and carefully. Then Sam spotted a man, clearly a guard, he was huddled against a tree to avoid the wind and cold and had not spotted them yet. He needed to proceed on the path he was on and one of his hidden foxholes was right next to the man.

He signaled for his men to stay down by moving his hand, palm down, up and down slowly. Then he drew his bowie knife, a particularly long and vicious looking knife. Then he signaled again with his left hand, palm down, telling his men to stay low, don't move. Then he carefully made his way to the back of the tree the man was leaning against. Just as he got within arm's reach, the man heard something and turned toward him. Sam immediately drove the knife deep into the man's upper gut, then again and again. The man fell dead, with only a minor grunt.

Sam visibly relaxed, looked around carefully, saw no one, and waved his men forward. No one made any noise or said anything. They moved the dead man farther into the woods and away from the foxhole and covered him with leaves and pine needles. Then Sam pointed to two men and the foxhole to tell them to get into it, which they did.

They made their way further south along the eastern side of the camp. Sam left two men at each of the premade foxholes, By the time they reached the end of the woods, south of the camp, they only had four men. There was no foxhole, so the three took positions behind trees and Sam climbed a tree for a better look at the camp.

At that moment Bill Wakefield and his men were about 150 yards west of them in another wood on the other side of the camp. Bill had already climbed a tree and could see the whole camp. He had a good spot in the tree, with good cover, and decided to stay put. He could not see much movement and could not see Sam Walker or Sam Moore. He didn't know Walker but had a good description of him from Caleb.

Bill checked his watch, five minutes to spare. At that same instant, Sam climbed down from his tree on the other side of the camp and checked his watch, three minutes to go, he and his men got ready.

Caleb had twenty men with him and had spread them out in a one-hundred-yard skirmish line. They were ready. Caleb had his watch out and fired into one of the tents precisely when thirty minutes were up. He and his men advanced to the tents. Everyone had instructions to keep their eyes forward and shoot any man that moved in front of them, unless it was Sam Walker.

Groggy, drunken men came out of their tents and were gunned down instantly. Caleb and his men kept advancing. Dunn's men began running south just as Sam predicted and were picked off by Wakefield and Moore's men as they ran.

Dunn emerged from his tent with a Sharps rifle that he aimed in Caleb's direction and was shot and immediately fell. Caleb ran up to him, took his gun and told him to surrender immediately before more were killed. Dunn angrily looked up at him and said, "Hell no I won't surrender to you! You are abolitionist murderers."

Dunn was bleeding from a wound in his side and upper arm and Caleb again said, "Give up fool, or we'll kill all your men!"

Caleb demanded Dunn's knife and revolver, took them, and led him south. They were well behind the skirmish line, which was moving south quickly. Caleb could see the battle was nearly over and that they had won decisively. This was a clear win, his planned retreat after freeing Walker was not needed.

All of Dunn's men were now dead, wounded, or had surrendered. Caleb's men were taking their weapons and collecting and detaining the walking wounded and those that surrendered. This outcome was far better than Caleb had hoped.

Caleb looked straight at Dunn and demanded to know where Sam Walker was. Dunn involuntarily looked east at a wooded area inside the camp, and said, "Over there if he is still alive."

Caleb saw nothing, and ordered Dunn, "Take me to him." Dunn led him to the tree where Walker was tied up and Caleb could see the blankets and tarps. He uncovered Walker and he was alive but too cold to speak. Caleb cut his ropes and freed him, but Walker couldn't stand.

Caleb asked for help and the nearby men were able to get Walker to a campfire that they stirred to life and added logs to. Then they covered him in blankets and propped up a tarp to make a lean-to to protect him from the wind.

The camp women, who were mostly Kickapoo women, had emerged from cover once the shooting had stopped. The whole battle was only 10 minutes long. Caleb politely asked the women to make some coffee and breakfast.

One of the women walked over to Walker, she was the one who had helped him the most, and said, "You too skinny, I will fatten you up."

She then found a pot and some meat and potatoes, and started to make a stew, she had dried onions, ginger, oregano, and basil that she had collected before it got too cold. Soon the fragrant stew had everyone hungry, but she shooed everyone away until Walker got a giant helping.

Caleb's men built a makeshift prison with a circle of Dunn's wagons and rope and put all the captives and walking wounded in it and posted guards. After they carefully searched the camp and collected all the weapons, they ate in shifts. The prisoners were kept under constant guard. They started feeding the captives once they had all eaten. All the Kickapoo women were cooking furiously, and the food tasted wonderful.

Caleb asked Sam Moore for a report on the battle, Sam replied, "None of our men were shot, in fact Dunn's men barely got any shots off during the whole battle. We have guards posted all around the camp and we've confined all of Dunn's men, I figure the rest of Dunn's men out there still surrounding Pardee. They will get word soon enough and come to see what was going on. I assume they will attack soon."

Caleb said, "I think you are right, expect and prepare for a counterattack. Everyone needs to stay sharp and ready."

Caleb then approached Dunn and asked, "Who is your second in command, who will be leading the counterattack?"

"I don't have a second in command, it's just me."

Caleb and Sam Moore were taken aback and looked at each other in surprise. Then Moore shook his head and said, "I'll be damned."

Caleb, just said, "I need to talk to Sam Walker; I want to make sure he is OK and ask him what he thinks."

Caleb and Moore walked over to Sam Walker, who had finally stopped shivering and could finally talk. Caleb asked him, "What happened to you and what do you think we should do now?"

The Battle

Sam said, "I was caught right after leaving the cabin and before I got to my horse. They helped me find my horse and then took me to Charley Dunn. I wouldn't tell Dunn anything, so they whipped me badly."

Caleb asked, "Can I see your back?"

Sam freed himself from the blankets, painfully and turned around. His back was striped with blood and bruises and looked awful.

Blue Tail

The short, square shaped, and dark-haired Kickapoo woman who had been helping Walker was never far from him. She saw the wounds and said to Caleb, Sam Moore, and Sam Walker, "These bad, Blue Tail fix."

Walker said, "Your name is Blue Tail? I thank you for your help, you saved my life. I'm in your debt."

Blue Tail simply said, "Yes you are, but that is OK."

Both Sam Moore and Caleb were ashen faced at the brutal beating Sam had endured and Caleb said, "Please do what you can Blue Tail, I'm concerned that these wounds will fester."

Blue Tail smiled at Caleb and then said, "Now I fix medicine. The back is bad, it absolutely will fester if I don't fix."

Caleb remembered his manners and said, "Mrs. Blue Tail, I am Caleb May, and I am very pleased to meet you."

Blue Tail said, "Nice to meet you Mr. Caleb, now I work. Give me room."

She left and in a wooden bowl she mixed some aloe vera oil, honey, dried lavender, dried dandelions, dried onion, limestone powder, some Kansas blue clay, and whiskey from Dunn's tent. Then she went to Walker and told him, "This hurt, don't move." Then she looked at Caleb and said firmly, "You hold."

Caleb, a bit startled by her order, simply said, "Yes, Ma'am." He then gripped Walker's shoulders from the front as Blue Tail moved to his back.

Blue Tail began by pouring straight whiskey onto the wounds. Caleb had his hands on Walker's shoulders, but lightly. Sam Walker grimaced but didn't yell or move. Caleb grimaced in sympathy with Walker.

Blue Tail said admiringly, "You strong and tough, like Kickapoo man."

Walker said nothing, but he had a pained expression.

Then Blue Tail took her poultice and rubbed it all over the lacerations on his back. Walker was still clearly in terrific pain but said nothing. Once his back was covered, Blue Tail took a blanket and wrapped his whole torso with it and sewed it tight with a needle and thread.

Then she told Walker, "Leave that on for three days. After three days have someone take off the blanket and look at your back. If it is going bad, or beginning to smell, rinse it with whiskey again, and rub more of this on it. The wounds are not deep, they may mostly heal in three days. There will be scars."

Then she handed him the rest of the poultice.

Walker wrapped the bowl in a cloth, tied it with string and put it in his saddle bag, grateful for Blue Tail. He asked her, "What can I do for you? How much do I pay you?"

Blue Tail said, "One dollar, if you have, if not pay me when can."

Walker gave her a silver dollar and wished her all the luck in the world. He felt better already.

With that out of the way Sam Walker, Caleb, Sam Moore, and Bill Wakefield sat down to discuss what to do next. Sam Walker said, "You will be attacked, we need to prepare. The blockade is now broken, so now is the time to bring in more men and fortify the town. I will need some men to go with me for protection, but I can go to General Abbott and ask him for help."

Caleb looked toward Sam Moore and Bill and asked them what they thought. Sam Moore said, "That works for me. General Abbott would be a huge help. We also have all Dunn's supplies of gunpowder, lead, horses, wagons, and food. I think we need to load that up as soon as possible and get it back to Pardee before Dunn's men can counterattack."

Bill looked at the prisoners, who had a lot of wounded, and said, "They will need at least one wagon for their wounded who cannot walk and a couple of horses, but except for those, we take them all, I say. We need something to compensate for the blockade."

Caleb said, "Camp Creek is only a mile or two north of here and they have a doctor, but you are right, they need one wagon for the worst of the wounded. OK, do we all agree then? We load up all the supplies we can, especially the food, weapons, powder, and lead, and carry it all back to Pardee. We ride in force, ready to repel any counterattack. Then we request help from General Abbott."

Everyone nodded in agreement. It was warming rapidly after the bitter cold of the previous night and the skies were a clear blue, spirits lifted. The men immediately got to work. Bill Wakefield sent a runner back to Pardee to tell everyone what happened and to prepare for a counterattack.

Caleb then addressed the prisoners, "Men, we are setting you free. You will take no weapons with you, nor food, nor supplies. You can keep what you have in your pockets, other than weapons. We will give you one wagon and a team for the wounded who cannot walk. We will leave you with shovels to bury your dead. To whomever you speak after this day, remember that we let you go, we let you bury your dead, we fed you, and allowed you to treat your wounded. We will allow no further blockade of Pardee. Any attack on Pardee will be met with steel and blood, beware."

The men were turned loose, issued a few shovels, and given one wagon and two horses. Dunn said, "I should at least be given back my knife."

Caleb said, "No, I'm keeping it. When I get a chance, I will give it to Mrs. Isaac Cody or send it to her."

Dunn had fury in his eyes but said nothing.

The prisoners began digging graves as Caleb's men packed the remaining wagons. Caleb then spoke to Blue Tail, "Mrs. Blue Tail, you do not have to go with them. You can go with us; we have no doctor in Pardee and can really use someone with your skills. Is it necessary for you to return to Kickapoo?"

Blue Tail thought for a moment, as Caleb, Sam Moore, Sam Walker, and Bill Wakefield anxiously waited for her response, "I go with you for now. My husband died months ago, my children grown, I came with Dunn because I had little at home and needed money. I go with you; one white man is about as good as another."

Everyone laughed with relief, they were all pleased she was coming with them. They helped her onto the first wagon.

Sam Moore organized the wagon train, with four outriders for each wagon. Each wagon left as soon as it was loaded. There were eight wagons and eight spare horses. After all the wagons were gone, Caleb, Bill, and Sam Walker rode and led the remaining horses, Milo and another four men rode ahead of the first wagon. They constantly looked for a counterattack, but none came.

General Easton did not accompany his men and the other deputies to the siege of Pardee. His orders from the President and the Secretary of War, prevented that. So, when Sheriff Dunn was taken out, there was no leader to plan and execute a counterattack. The men Dunn and Easton recruited were not professionals, but raw untrained recruits and volunteer militiamen, they had no dog in the fight. Further, as one of them said, "This was not what I signed up for. We were to ride into Pardee, arrest one man, burn the place down and leave. No one said anything about going to war! I'm going home."

That often-repeated statement expressed the sentiments of most of the temporary deputies. They simply went home. The one-sided battle at the main camp and the Sheriff being shot and humiliated drove them away.

It only took Caleb's men a little more than an hour to ride back to Pardee Butler's cabin where they all met. All their neighbors were there to greet them and cheer their success. Someone brought Milo his fiddle and he played some fun music, everyone sang, and some danced. Pardee said a blessing and led everyone in prayer, thanking the Lord that everyone returned home safely and unhurt.

Caleb then introduced Blue Tail to everyone and talked about what a wonderful medicine woman she was, and Sam Walker attested to that saying his back felt much better. Blue Tail received all the praise and hearty welcomes stoically, but Caleb thought he could detect a little happiness, and a small smile, in her expression.

Caleb's cabin was full, he asked Pardee if he would take in Blue Tail. Pardee answered, "Yes, with great pleasure."

Caleb suggested, "Men we should plan to build Blue Tail her own cabin if she agrees to stay."

Pardee agreed, "I'll help build it, we can give her one of the vacant town lots."

Sam Walker added, "I want to contribute some money toward the cabin and the lot. She is a treasure."

After Walker's offer, Caleb pulled him aside and said, "Why not stay tonight, have some dinner, get a good sleep, and I'll send four men with you tomorrow to escort you to Grasshopper Falls."

Walker replied, "Thank you so much, I agree, I am so exhausted, I don't think I could take another step. Let me take care of my poor horse, and then I'm definitely ready for bed. Blue Tail already fed me and I'm ready to collapse."

With that Walker led his horse to Caleb's barn, gave him some hay and water, rubbed him down, and went into Caleb's cabin where Maggie pointed him to a bed, and he fell into a deep dreamless sleep. He had barely slept in three days.

Caleb and the others continued the celebration for a short time, but the men, and most of the women and children had been up most of the previous night, and they were beat as well. They gradually faded away to their cabins and went to bed themselves. Blue Tail was made comfortable in Pardee's cabin by Sybil and Rosetta, who found her to be a stoic, but pleasant person.

Governor Shannon

Governor Shannon was screwed and he knew it. Sheriff Dunn had just been publicly humiliated trying to arrest Caleb May with almost 500 deputies. It was almost May, in an election year, and he seriously doubted the President would change his mind about calling up the Kansas Guard before the election. He knew Secretary of War Jefferson Davis was a "by-the-book" man and would not bend either. The steadfastness of the President and the Secretary of War tied his and General Easton's hands. They could do nothing.

However, David Atchison and Albert Boone, an ardent supporter of slavery, wanted to meet with him. He agreed to the meeting, hoping they had some good ideas.

Before the meeting, Shannon wrote to the President:

"There was great danger to Sheriff Dunn in his attack on the town of Pardee, which was strongly fortified, and had about one thousand and fifty [a gross exaggeration, May had no more than 300 men] well-armed men to defend it, with two pieces of artillery [May had no artillery], while on the other side there was probably in all nearly two thousand men [about 500 in reality], many of them indifferently armed, but having a strong park of artillery

[Dunn brought none, but could have]. Dunn's deputies had a deep and settled feeling of hostility against the Pardee townspeople, and apparently a fixed determination to attack that place and demolish it ... and take possession of their arms. It seemed to be a universal opinion in the camp that there was no safety to the Law-and-Order Party in the Kansas Territory while the other party were permitted to retain their Sharps' rifles, an instrument used only for war purposes."[59]

Sara Robinson, Charles Robinson's wife, met Governor Shannon and described him in her 1857 book, *Kansas; Interior and Exterior Life*,[60] as a tall, well-proportioned man with graying hair. He was 53 years old, had a weather-beaten, but handsome face and mild eyes. He did not have any firmness or strength in his bearing, he appeared, and later showed, that he was controlled by events and was not a controller of events.

Governor Shannon once again requested permission to use federal troops and/or the Kansas Guard from President Pierce, and he appeared to agree. Based on a vague approval from the President, Governor Shannon requested federal troops from Colonel Edwin V. "Bull" Sumner at Fort Leavenworth, Sumner refused until he received orders from the War Department. Sumner was quite new to his command and the Kansas Territory, and a cautious man. His nickname "Bull" was used by his men both affectionately and derisively. Sumner, like Jefferson Davis, was a "by the book" officer, with uncompromising discipline and had a thunderous voice. He both followed orders exactly and expected his orders to be followed exactly.

One variation on the nickname was "Bull Head" because he was allegedly struck by a nearly spent musket ball on the forehead in the Mexican-American War and it bounced off. His thunderous voice was the reason he was sometimes called "Bull of the Woods."

The cautious Shannon did not want the federal troops to subdue Pardee and bring Caleb May to justice, he wanted them to prevent a war between the Missouri invaders and Pardee, a war that had already

---

59 Fictionalized from (Robinson C., 1892, p. 215)
60 (Robinson S. T., 1856)

started and Governor Shannon now blamed himself for. Secretary of War Jefferson Davis never sent the orders Shannon requested to Colonel Sumner. Davis may have opposed the presence of federal troops because it was a police matter, or he may have opposed them because they would prevent his friend David Atchison (they were college roommates) from attacking Pardee, and he wanted the attack to occur. The former reason is more likely. To Davis the Army was for defense only and not a political tool or a police force. The Constitution and federal laws supported his opinion in this matter.

The meeting with Atchison and Boone was only days away and Shannon was panicking. He could not postpone it any longer. If he allowed Atchison and Boone to attack Pardee from Missouri, his political career was over, he would never be elected or appointed to national office again. Most of the U.S. population resides in the northern, anti-slavery states and he would be a pariah there.

On the other hand, if he sided with Caleb May and his men, he would be considered an outlaw, like them. He faced a dilemma. Shannon was terrified of making a decision and needed help. He ultimately decided he must meet with Caleb May, but it had to be in secret, since most people in Missouri and Kansas believed what they read in the newspapers and considered Caleb a murderer and a thief. Even so, it seemed impossible to arrest him.

Like most Kansas officials and legislators, Governor Shannon resided in Shawnee Mission, as did John Wakefield, the Free-State elected representative to Congress. Shannon sent for him and asked, "Can you set up a meeting with Caleb May? I will meet with him here or in Pardee, but I need to meet with him in the next few days. It is urgent."

Wakefield protested, "Pardee is 70 miles away, it would take more than a day to get a message there and as long to get a response."

Shannon was new to the area and his sense of distance was poor. Wakefield offered an alternative, "Please accompany me to Easton, where we can stay with my friend Stephen Sparks. From there we can easily get word to Caleb May and set up a meeting."

Shannon was desperate, so he quickly agreed. They immediately set off on horseback, each taking two horses. It was early morning and they were able to cover the 55 miles to Easton by just after nightfall, a brutal 14 hour ride with only three rest stops.

They met with Stephen Sparks at his cabin and wrote a message to Caleb May asking for a meeting. Stephen gave the message to his son, Greene, who said, "I can go, but I cannot return until tomorrow morning."

Shannon then asked, "Can you try and bring Caleb back to Easton, so we can meet face to face?"

Both Greene and Stephen gasped. Stephen said, "There is no way we can recommend that; it is far too dangerous for Caleb in Easton to ask him to come here."

Shannon visibly deflated. He was worn out from his ride but determined. He asked, "Stephen can I have a fresh horse? I will ride with Greene to Pardee."

They set off for Pardee, it was slow going in the dark, but they made it safely. Their first encounter was with guards posted on the road just outside town. Greene and Shannon explained who they were, and that Governor Shannon needed to meet with Caleb May. One of the guards escorted them to the May cabin. It was late, but they successfully roused Caleb, who came outside to meet with the Governor. Fortunately, while it was cool outside, it was not bitterly cold as it had been a few days earlier.

Shannon explained his dilemma to Caleb and asked what Caleb recommended he do. Caleb considered the problem for a moment and then said, "Firstly, I murdered no one, they fired on my men and me first. I'm not even sure it was my bullet that killed Cook, we all had Sharps. In Easton, we were protecting Stephen and Greene Sparks, Greene is sitting right next to you. Following that, I was taken from the road peaceably returning home, beaten, struck with a hatchet, and nearly killed.

Secondly, the goods we stole from Stringfellow, were originally stolen from a Russell, Majors & Waddell freighter just outside Pardee, and the thieves killed the teamster driving the wagon to Pardee. Sheriff Dunn was observed participating in the robbery and was present when the teamster was murdered. They were our goods, we simply recovered them.

Recovering stolen property is a legal police action and I am the legally elected Town Marshall."

Shannon turned to Greene, "Is that what happened in Easton? Will you testify to that?"

Greene replied, "Yes sir. That is exactly what happened in Easton. I was there for all of it. You can also get the same story from U.S. Army Captain Martin, who shot Gibson, the man who tried to put his hatchet into Captain May's head."

Governor Shannon then said, "But the wagon and the goods on it were not all you took from Stringfellow, you also took his wife's silverware, their gold, some of their food, their cattle and horses, another wagon, and all their guns."

Caleb replied, "Yes sir, we did that. But he was a clear participant in the blockade and in a conspiracy to starve our town. We deserved some compensation for our suffering. Further, four of the horses we took from Stringfellow's corral had Russell, Majors & Waddell brands on them. They were part of the wagon's team.

We had to defend ourselves and consider the goods we stole from Stringfellow to be just compensation for the damage we suffered during the Missouri blockade. We can prove that Stringfellow had stolen goods in his possession."

Caleb then added, "I have two witnesses, beside myself, that the wagon in Stringfellow's barn was a Russell, Majors & Waddell freighter and I have one witness to the theft of it and the murder of the teamster who was driving it. His name is Elijah Smith. Both he and Pardee Butler identified the wagon in Stringfellow's barn as the freighter, which still had some of the stolen goods in it. Smith is our store owner and most of the goods on the wagon were addressed to him. The labels, with his name on them, were still on the freight boxes.

Elijah Smith will also swear that Sheriff Charley Dunn was present during the robbery of the Russell, Majors & Waddell freighter and during the murder of the teamster.

One more thing, we did report the theft of the wagon to Russell, Majors & Waddell, and they did nothing about it, this left the recovery of the wagon and goods to me as Town Marshal.

You asked me what you should do. First, I think you should acknowledge the truth and take sworn affidavits from all the witnesses. We will not return the stolen goods, and I certainly should not stand trial for murder. The evidence points to self-defense, and in any case, there was a lot of shooting, and they have no evidence or witnesses that the bullet that killed Cook came from my gun. I don't even know if I shot him.

As for Mrs. Stringfellow's silverware and gold, if there is a general agreement that I am innocent of these charges, in writing, we will return it and the other personal property we took from Stringfellow's house, including their guns."

Shannon replied, "OK, let me draw up an agreement to that effect and I can present it to Stringfellow, Atchison, Dunn, and Justice Lecompte in a few days. If they agree maybe we can settle this peacefully. While I'm here I want to talk to the other witnesses and get their statements. My only goal is to stop the violence and prevent a war."

Not a very good sleeper, Blue Tail was out preparing her moon garden. She was reasonably certain that they had just seen the last freeze of the season and wanted to plant hers soon. While working she heard voices over at the May cabin and went over to see what was going on.

As she approached, she said, "Mr. May are you ok?"

Caleb knew her voice and called out, "Yes Blue Tail, I am fine, please come on over."

Blue Tail came out of the night and saw the tall distinguished looking man with Caleb and said, "Hello sir."

Caleb then said, "You are up late Blue Tail, are *you* ok?"

Blue Tail responded, "Yes, sir, just preparing my moon garden for spring."

Caleb considered himself to be an expert on farming and gardening but had never heard of a "moon garden." He asked her, "What is a moon garden?"

Blue Tail answered, "It is good magic. We plant it at night and on nights with a moon it glows and brings good luck and butterflies. I will plant lavender, jasmine, sage, silver queen corn, lamb's ear, dandelions, onions, and thyme." You watch, I teach. You need good luck."

Caleb, the Governor, and Greene all laughed, Caleb said, "Yes, Ma'am I do. Thank you, Blue Tail."

The Governor stood and bowed slightly and said, "So nice to meet you Blue Tail, I am Governor Wilson Shannon."

Greene also stood and added, "I am Greene Sparks, pleased to meet you ma'am."

Blue Tail answered, "Nice to meet you, I am Blue Tail, wife of White Bear, of Kickapoo. Although White Bear recently passed on to the Great Spirit."

The Governor said, "How very sad, I'm sorry to hear he is gone."

Caleb said, "Blue Tail is a wonderful healer, she has helped us since we have no doctor."

Blue Tail said, "White doctors no good. They have no skill or knowledge. Our medicine more powerful."

Caleb laughed and said, "I know that Sam Walker believes that!"

The Governor asked, "Who is Sam Walker?"

Caleb told him the story, and the Governor was both shocked and impressed. He said, "Well, let's see if we can avoid any more of that."

Then he asked, "Is there a place where Greene and I can bed down for the night? We have bed rolls, and we are very tired."

Caleb said, "Our house is full, but we have room in the barn."

Blue Tail said, "We have space and blankets in our cabin, would you please stay with us?"

The Governor and Greene enthusiastically agreed, and everyone went to bed, or in Caleb's case, back to bed. The Governor and Greene were up early, and Blue Tail gave them some bread and bacon. Then they held brief meetings with Milo Carlton, Sam Moore, Andy Elliott, Bill Wakefield, and Elijah Smith. The Governor was satisfied he knew what had happened and drafted up a summary of the testimony and asked all of them and Caleb to sign it. Then he and Greene left to return to Easton.

Later when talking to Caleb, Blue Tail said, "I don't think your friend, the Governor, is a steady man. He is like a leaf and turns with every wind."

Caleb was thoughtful for a moment, and replied, "I agree. My, your English is much improved."

"My English is normal. I was well educated in the Kickapoo school by a teacher who graduated from Yale College. When I relax, I speak good English, when I'm uncomfortable, which is normal around white men, I speak broken English. It is partially nerves, partially because I know that is what they expect. Strange, but true. I have two voices."

Caleb replied, "I'm glad you are relaxed with me, it is a good sign."

An impasse

Governor Shannon made it back to Shawnee Mission in time to prepare for his meeting with Albert Boone and David Atchison. He hoped that when he presented his evidence they would agree to a settlement. He sent word that he wanted John Stringfellow, Justice Lecompte, and Sheriff Dunn to join the meeting, if they were available.

He then drafted an agreement using his notes and the affidavits he had collected in Pardee. In short, the agreement stated what Caleb had suggested.

He knew there was no evidence that May had shot anyone in the Easton battle, and if he did the opposing group fired the first shot and many guns were fired on both sides, it was a general gunfight, and any actions May took were in self-defense. Further, May had been viciously attacked by a Mr. Gibson after his capture, and Gibson was later killed by U.S. Army Captain John Martin in self-defense.

As for the Stringfellow robbery, Shannon knew May was willing to return all the goods except those that were stolen from the Russell, Majors & Waddell freighter. Finally, a search for the killer of the teamster driving the wagon should be initiated immediately, there was a witness to the murder, and he has never been formally deposed.

As Governor, Shannon agreed that that he would not call upon any residents of another state to execute the laws within Kansas. He planned to emphasize this to Sheriff Dunn, this rule will prevent him from raising a large posse and reduce the chance of a larger war.

Finally, the day of the meeting arrived. It was held in the Governor's spacious office in Shawnee Mission and everyone the Governor invited came. Even Chief Justice Samuel Lecompte of the Territorial Supreme Court rode from his house in Leavenworth to attend the meeting.

The Governor's visitors were in a somber mood but all exchanged greetings and wished each other well. The Governor opened the meeting by reading his prepared statement and his proposed agreement and then asked the others for their comments and if they would agree to it.

Governor Shannon was greeted with stony silence for more than a minute. Then finally David Atchison spoke, "This abolitionist, Caleb May, murdered a good man and stole Mrs. Stringfellow's silver and gold, he cannot be set free!"

Then Justice Lecompte spoke up, "David is correct, Caleb May must be tried in a court of law for murder and armed robbery."

Governor Shannon said, "To charge him with murder you must have some evidence."

Justice Lecompte, "I have evidence, sworn testimony from witnesses. That is enough to hold him for trial."

John Stringfellow said, "Simply returning my wife's silver and gold is not enough. They invaded my home, tied up our housekeeper and farm hands, Caleb May and his men must be punished."

Dunn said, "May or one of his men shot me last week, probably for the second time. He must pay for this."

Shannon then reminded them, "You were blockading his town and had plans to burn it to the ground. You held one of his men prisoner, whipped him, and tied him to a tree where he probably should have died from exposure to the cold. May had good reason to shoot you. Besides we have a witness that you participated in a robbery and murder on the road to Pardee."

Dunn replied, "I can prove I was nowhere near Pardee on the day the robbery took place, your witness is lying."

Shannon failed to convince them, so he said, "I was hoping to settle this without more bloodshed, it seems I have failed. I must confer with the President and the Secretary of War. They will not look kindly on an invasion of this Territory from Missouri, and neither will I. Is there anything more? Are your positions hardened?"

Justice Lecompte said, "I stand firm."

The Governor turned his attention to Sheriff Dunn, "Sheriff, you are hereby forbidden to recruit and hire deputies that reside outside the Territory. I have evidence that many of the deputies that blockaded Pardee were residents of Missouri, this cannot happen again."

Dunn simply relied, "Yes sir."

The others agreed and the meeting adjourned.

After the visitors left the meeting, they reconvened in a nearby saloon and restaurant, and Atchison said, "He is weak, it will be up to us to do something."

Dunn said, "I will need to raise another army of deputies and this time there will be no blockade, this time we simply invade the town and burn it down. I will need cannons. Are we all in agreement?"

Lecompte said, "This invasion will be illegal and the President or the Secretary of War may send Federal troops to stop it. You dare not stand up to Federal troops. Further, the northern press will have a field day over this. This is an election year, and the President will not take your side."

Atchison said, "I will write to the President and Jefferson Davis and present our dilemma. Justice Lecompte, will you write arrest warrants for Caleb May for murder and armed robbery? I will need those."

Lecompte said, "Yes, I will need Sheriff Dunn's help in gathering affidavits, but with those I can issue an arrest warrant."

Dunn said, "No problem, I will immediately go to Easton and gather as many as I can."

Stringfellow said, "I will write an affidavit and sign it immediately." Then to Justice Lecompte, "I can ride with you to your home and write it in your presence."

Atchison said, "Very well, let us prepare the case, then I need to write my letters. As the Governor said, the President and Davis are not going to be pleased with this. If they order Colonel Bull Sumner to stop us, he will. I think that damned Sumner is a secret abolitionist."

Atchison continued, "Do not do anything now, it is the wrong time, and we need to prepare. We must wait until we can justify our actions. If you attack Pardee now you attack it as an illegal mob, and what would be the result? You would cause the election of an abolition President and the ruin of the Democratic Party."

Shannon acts

After the men left, Shannon knew they were going to attack Pardee, but there was little he could do by himself. Under the law the Territorial Guard was not under his command, but the President's. This was also true of the soldiers in Fort Leavenworth. So, his first action was to write to May. The letter said:

"To Caleb May:"

You are hereby authorized and directed to take such measures and use the enrolled militia under your command in such manner, for the preservation of the peace and the protection of the persons and property of the people of Pardee and vicinity, as in your judgment shall best secure that end.

(Signed)
"Wilson Shannon."
"Shawnee Mission, May 1, 1856"[61]

Then Shannon wrote three letters, one to the president, one to Colonel Sumner, and a third to Secretary of War Jefferson Davis. He carefully laid out his meetings with Caleb May and with Atchison and his group. He also stated his fears about what Atchison might do. He told them that he still thought his written agreement was the best course of action, but that Justice Lecompte's point that Caleb May should stand trial had some validity.

The Governor requested that the Territorial militia be put under his command and that he be allowed to call upon the federal troops in Fort Leavenworth. He was not optimistic that the President and Secretary of War would grant this request, but felt he needed that authority. Things were rapidly spiraling out of control, and he was worried.

Jefferson Davis

Both President Franklin Pierce and Secretary of War Jefferson Davis received letters from David Atchison and Governor Shannon. Atchison wanted to invade Kansas Territory and destroy Pardee and Shannon wanted to avoid the invasion and wanted control of the Kansas militia and to be able to call up the troops at Fort Leavenworth.

They decided they needed to meet and discuss what to do. The President spoke first, "Why can't that idiot Dunn simply arrest this Caleb May and haul him up before Justice Lecompte?"

Davis replied, "This Caleb May is very capable, he has dozens, if not hundreds, of good well-trained and well-armed men on call. He will not be defeated easily."

---

61 Modified from a letter to Charles Robinson and James Lane. (Robinson C., 1892, p. 206)

The President, "We don't need this problem, the election is in just six months. All the northern states are voting against slavery in any form and most of the southern states are for slavery at all costs. There is no common ground. How can we end this Kansas problem or push it off until next year? The Democratic Party is the party of peace, we say we are the party that can hold the country together and make the free states and slave states coexist peacefully. That is our promise! The Republicans are the radicals that want to eliminate slavery and cause a civil war, which is why they will and should lose."

Davis replied, "Well, good luck with that. Anyway, we cannot use federal troops to arrest someone, regardless of what they may have done. That is a police matter. A governor can ask for help from federal troops if he is being invaded, and an invasion from Missouri might qualify, but if there is a war between Sheriff Dunn and his lawfully raised posse and Caleb May and his militia, that does not qualify. That is a police matter."

"What about the Territorial Guard?"

"The territorial guard is under your control, unlike the state militias in the states. You do have the authority to put it or part of it under the Governor's command in emergencies.

However, I advise against this. Kansas is a powder keg; an increasing number of the settlers there are from the northern states and against slavery. Shannon is trying to thread the needle and is likely to only accomplish stabbing himself with it. He needs to choose a side. I do not see the Governor or the Democratic Party surviving without picking a side in this issue, straddling both sides of this issue is not possible.

I recommend that Sheriff Dunn, the legally appointed police officer of that part of the Territory, raise a posse, swear in all his deputies, and record all their names so there is no confusion about who is a legal deputy and who isn't. Then they should arrest Caleb May as soon as possible and make every attempt not to harm him and treat him well. Do not use federal troops or the Territorial Guard. This *must* be strictly a police operation."

The President responded, "Sounds like good advice, it makes sense, it is legal, I like it. I will notify Governor Shannon immediately of our decision. As for straddling the slavery/no slavery issue, I have no choice. This is my mandate; this is the position of my party. Possible or not possible, we must do it."

When Shannon got the President's letter, he was angry. He immediately told his secretary, Daniel Woodson, "Dunn is an incompetent drunk, there is no way he can take Caleb May and his militia in a fair fight, but Atchison and Stringfellow will do all they can to make the fight unfair. Then there will be hell to pay. The President does not know what he is doing.

I must speak to Colonel Sumner, the Colonel will do nothing without orders from the Secretary of War, but he must be warned. Please send for the Colonel. Then send a letter to David Atchison telling him what the President said and advising Atchison to stay out of the fight, let Dunn handle it."

Woodson replied, "Yes, sir."

Atchison also received a letter from the President, it said the same thing, "Stay out of it."

Atchison had no intention of following these orders.

Atchison met with Stringfellow and Dunn, he said, "The President will not allow a Missouri army to invade Kansas. He will not allow the Kansas Guard or federal troops to help arrest Caleb May and he will not relinquish command of the Guard or the troops to the Governor."

He paused, then continued, "The President says this is a police matter and must be dealt with by Sheriff Dunn. Dunn, you must arrest May, do not harm him, bring him before Justice Lecompte. You can gather your deputies from wherever you want, but formally deputize each one and write down their names, list all of them as residents of Kansas Territory. Keep track so they are official deputies and pay them by the day. I will provide the funds, if necessary, this must all be legal and correct.

It is important to capture May alive and unharmed, if at all possible. The President is afraid of an all-out war in the Kansas Territory and the impact such a war will have on the election."

He then turned to Stringfellow, "John, please help Dunn gather his posse and help with the arrest of May. Also, you are a Kansas resident, I will give you any funds needed, and you will donate them to the Sheriff's office or to the Governor, just do whatever is necessary to make my help legal and anonymous.

OK, are we clear on what must happen?"

Both Stringfellow and Dunn said, "Yes sir."

Colonel Sumner

Colonel Sumner was a bit piqued by the Governor's summons but put his feelings aside as any good soldier does. He immediately got on his horse and began the twenty-mile ride to Shawnee Mission. He arrived in the afternoon and went directly to the Governor's office.

Once the greetings were over, Governor Shannon shared the President's letter with Sumner, and said, "So you see Colonel, aside from an invasion by an organized army or militia from Missouri, you are out of the fight."

Sumner simply responded, "Yes, sir. If it is a police action, I am not allowed to interfere."

Shannon said, "I wanted this meeting to make sure we are on the same page and to let you know I will share what I learn about upcoming coming events with you. I do not know what will happen, but I want you to be informed. I do not think that David Atchison will follow the President's instructions and stay out of it, but he is smart enough to cover his tracks. I also do not think Dunn is smart enough to take Pardee without a lot of help. Caleb May is an impressive person, Dunn is an idiot, but an idiot with a lot of resources."

Sumner was surprised by Shannon's bluntness, and impressed, he replied, "I thank you for the information, you can be assured that I will help keep the peace within the limits of the law and my orders. Certainly, it is not against either of these obligations for me to pay a friendly visit to Mr. Caleb May, introduce myself, and inspect his town's defenses. I will do so sir; if you do not object."

Now it was the Governor who was impressed, "By all means Colonel! I think Mr. May will be honored by a visit from such a notable military expert."

After the meeting, the Governor sent Caleb May a message telling him to expect a friendly visit from Colonel Sumner and assured Caleb that the visit was friendly and meant to be helpful. He also included a summary of his meetings with Atchison, Dunn, and Stringfellow and a warning that Pardee may be attacked in the near future, and that he should prepare.

He did not share his correspondence with the President, he felt that was inappropriate and that the letters were private. He did point out that Justice Lecompte had decided that sufficient evidence existed that Caleb had murdered John Cook to issue an arrest warrant.

Chapter 8
Spring, 1856

Spring was finally here, it arrived late in 1856, and that was after a dry 1855. But by early May rain arrived, and it was perfect timing for planting his crops. Their days were long, from before the Sun was up until after the Sun went down, they worked plowing the fields and planting their seeds. So, when Governor Shannon's letter arrived it was a worn-out Caleb that sat down heavily in his chair at the kitchen table and opened the letter.

Mary May had received the letter and told the whole family and the Butlers about it, so Caleb opened it in front of both very excited families and read it aloud. Caleb had only 6 months of school but he read well.

After reading the letter, Pardee was the first to speak, "Caleb, we are in for trouble, they will gather an army, call it a posse, and attack. There will be no blockade this time, they will come with as little warning as possible."

Mary was still star-struck, "Pa, first the Governor rode all the way here to meet with you in the middle of night and now he writes to you personally. He sent a special messenger all the way here to deliver just that one letter to you! You must be very important."

Pardee said, "Mary, Caleb is very important, an important man."

Mary and her siblings beamed with pride in their father. Jim looked at his adopted family and smiled, thinking to himself, "I am a lucky man."

Maggie said, "Cale don't get a swelled head, you are important, but you still put your pants on one leg at a time like everyone else."

Everyone laughed at that, and Blue Tail said, "Mr. May, you can move forward, or you can move backward. Forward is full of rewards, happiness, joy, comfort, knowledge, wisdom, and maybe blood. Backward is only full of misery, and despair. Walk forward, even if it leads to blood. That is what my people say."

Caleb looked at her for a long moment, and said, "Call me Caleb please. And thank you for your sage advice. You are a wise woman."

Maggie said, "How beautiful Blue Tail. Cale, what will you do?"

Caleb's reply was, "Right now, I'm going to sleep. Tomorrow, I will meet with Pardee, Milo, Sam, Andy, Bill, and Elijah, and we will decide. I'm not so important that I can make a decision like this alone. Maggie and Blue Tail, will you join us? We may need your advice as well."

Maggie and Blue Tail both said, "Yes sir, we will."

Blue Tail added, "In any great undertaking, it is not enough for a man to depend only upon himself. He will always need others, as they will need him."

Caleb looked right at her, admiring her understanding and wisdom.

Pardee said, "Well said Blue Tail, I will quote your wise sayings on Sunday if I have your permission."

Blue Tail answered, "Yes sir, but emphasize these are Kickapoo sayings. Both are ancient, they do not come from me, but from my people."

Pardee nodded and said, "Yes Ma'am."

He then turned to William, "William, tomorrow I need you to take a message to Sam Walker and James Abbott."

William left before the Sun came up. He wasn't sure where Walker and Abbott were, but they were either in Holton or headed toward Topeka, so he headed for Holton, he took two horses so he could move fast.

Early the next morning, the leaders of the local militia met. Caleb read them the Governor's letter and said, "We are in for a fight, men and we must prepare. I know it is planting season and we need to prepare the fields and plant our crops, but we also need to fortify Pardee and prepare our defense plan. William is taking a letter to Sam Walker and James Abbott asking for their help, and for more supplies. As you heard from the Governor's letter, Colonel Sumner is also coming to help us plan our defense, although as I understand it, he cannot fight in our defense."

Milo asked, "What do you think would happen if you simply gave yourself up to Sheriff Dunn and stood trial in Justice Lecompte's court?"

Caleb replied, "I don't know, but I intend to ask. It does seem I am the focus of all this, if all they want is me, then why not give myself up? I have a good case, I can get a good lawyer, post bail, and fight it out in court. I will send a letter to Governor Shannon and ask him. In the meantime, we need to prepare for another invasion. It seems imminent."

They discussed defenses, and decided they needed two more defensive double-walled block houses in addition to the four they already had. All the foxholes needed to be inspected and enlarged, if necessary, each should hold two men. As they were discussing these preparations, Colonel Sumner and two U.S. Army Majors arrived at Caleb's door and asked to speak with him.

Introductions were made all around, and Sumner asked if they could be given a tour of the town's defenses. Caleb and his men happily obliged and took the three Army officers around the town showing them their blockhouses and showed them the nearby foxholes, they also displayed their armory and their Sharps rifles. The three officers were silent, except for asking for clarifying details.

After the brief tour, the three officers walked away from the group and conferred privately, then came back to Caleb and his team. Sumner then said, "Your defenses are rudimentary and will be easily breached by a determined enemy. However, I doubt Sheriff Dunn's deputies will have the necessary skills, equipment, or discipline. Either way, avoiding conflict will be best, if possible."

Caleb replied, "Thank you for coming. Can you make any recommendations for improving our situation?"

Sumner replied, "I'm not sure how practical it is, but a cannon or howitzer on each road would help a lot, and you need elevated positions, towers, or perhaps positions in trees on each road as well. Your blockhouses are fine, but as you say, you need two more. Unfortunately, your enemy is likely to have cannon, and none of the blockhouses can withstand them. The foxholes are a good idea, but they will only be effective in the first few minutes of the fight, after that the enemy will know where they are and will attack them. The men in them must fire at the invaders from the rear, and then retreat into the woods quickly, they must stay mobile."

Caleb answered, "Thank you. One more thing, I am considering offering to surrender myself to stand trial for the crimes I'm accused of. I've done nothing wrong, and certainly have not murdered anyone. I did not shoot Dunn either time, as he well knows. I did recover the stolen property from Stringfellow's barn and took his silver and gold, but we are willing to give the silver and gold back. What do you think will happen?"

Sumner said, "If you can make a deal like that and save your town from attack, that is the best solution. Frankly, I do not think you will be able to hold off Dunn and his men. They will overwhelm your force and cause much destruction. But that is all I can say. This is a police and legal matter, and has become very political, I'm not allowed to be involved."

Caleb invited Sumner and his men to an early dinner, then they left to return to Leavenworth.

Sam Wood, Esq.

Early the next day, William returned with General James Abbott, Captain Sam Walker, and Sam Wood, a Free-State lawyer. William said to Caleb, "Hi Pa! I found them still in Holton, they hadn't left yet."

Caleb said, "Hello! Thank you so much for coming, I need your help."

Abbott said, "Glad to come, we were waiting in Holton just in case you needed us. What can we do?"

Caleb told them about Sumner's visit and that he was considering giving himself up to Sheriff Dunn to stand trial. He said, "I don't want to fight a battle that we are likely to lose."

Sam Wood then said, "I'm Sam Wood, a lawyer from Lawrence, and a Captain in Jim Abbott's militia, I'm very happy to meet you, Caleb."

"Nice to meet you as well, I may be needing a lawyer soon."

"I came because I thought you might be thinking along these lines. I know Justice Lecompte well, and you realize there will be problems if you give yourself up. Lecompte is proslavery and very corrupt. You may want to be arrested, expecting to be released after posting bail to return home and prepare for the trial whenever it comes up. But Lecompte is in charge of when the arraignment and bail hearing will be, and for Free-State defendants, he never seems to have these hearings. For proslavery defendants he has an arraignment and bail hearing the same day."

Wood paused, then continued, "I cannot make your decision for you, this is hard, but if you give yourself up, they may imprison you in Leavenworth or Lecompton indefinitely and never have an arraignment to inform you of the charges against you and set bail. This is a violation of the Constitution and your 6th Amendment right to a speedy trial but seems to happen frequently for Free-State citizens."

Caleb replied, "But if I do not give myself up, my town will be destroyed. They have an excuse to do so, if I give myself up, their excuse is gone."

"This is true, but as a lawyer I just want you to know the potential consequences of your decision. We are not dealing with an impartial legal system; it is stacked against you."

"Mr. Wood, will you act as my lawyer? I can give you a dollar to retain you now. If you are my lawyer, can you try and make the best deal possible with the Governor and Justice Lecompte? Tell them that if I give myself up, I expect a bail hearing immediately and reasonable bail to be set. After all, I have considerable evidence that I did not commit any crime other than to take Mrs. Stringfellow's silver and gold, which I have promised to return."

"Yes sir Mr. May. I will. I need a list of witnesses to the battle in Easton, the robbery of the Russell, Majors & Waddell freighter, and your raid on the Stringfellows. I also need affidavits from the witnesses that will testify that you did not shoot Sheriff Dunn."

"Other than a few people in Easton, like Stephen Sparks, they are all here and available."

"OK, I need to get busy. If we are to cut off this war, we need to get these arrangements made right away. I will send an urgent message to the Governor and to Justice Lecompte that you want to give yourself up for trial, and that I am gathering affidavits and preparing some conditions. That should hold off a war for the time being, but I must gather all the evidence before you give yourself up. This is so everyone knows you have lots of evidence you are innocent, it will, hopefully, handcuff the court. However, that said, Justice Lecompte holds all the cards once you are arrested. This will not be easy."

Sam Walker said, "Give me the messages to Lecompte and the Governor. I will deliver them immediately; I just need two fresh horses."

Wood replied, "Thank you so much Sam, you are the best horseman I know. Not to mention you weigh almost nothing, no wonder horses like you."

That made everyone laugh, even Sam Walker. Sam Wood continued, "I will write the letters immediately. Can I get two people to make duplicates please as I write? One copy for me and one for Captain May?"

Pardee and William agreed to make the copies. With that Wood began composing the messages on paper that was provided by Maggie. He spoke everything he wrote out loud as he wrote it to help Pardee and William as they made copies. To the Governor he wrote, in part:

"Mr. Caleb May has agreed to give himself up to be tried for the crimes he is accused of to avert a battle over Pardee and to ensure the safety of the Pardee residents. This surrender has the following preliminary conditions:

1. An arraignment and bail hearing must take place within one day of his surrender and a reasonable bail set.
2. There will be no attack on Pardee by Sheriff Dunn or his men or any army from Missouri or Kansas.
3. The trial date shall be soon and set firmly during the arraignment and bail hearing.
4. These conditions must be made public.

Once the trial is concluded, Caleb May will return the silver and gold he took from Mrs. Stringfellow."

Once the letter to Shannon was completed and two copies made, he wrote a similar letter to Lecompte. The closing of each letter stated that Wood would gather the necessary affidavits over the next few days and would present the official and final conditions for the surrender personally and as expeditiously as possible.

Once the letters were written, Caleb gave Sam Walker his best two horses, and Walker took off. Walker was a skilled horseman and made it to Justice Lecompte's home in Leavenworth in three hours and delivered the message to him personally. It was just about dark, so he spent the night in Leavenworth and left at dawn for Shawnee Mission, he arrived at the Governor's house in time for breakfast, so the Governor invited him to dine with him. They discussed the events of the past few days.

Once Walker had described the events and breakfast was over, Shannon said, "This is unexpected, but welcome news. The President and Secretary of War will be delighted. I will send them both letters. This must be made public as you say for Mr. May's protection. I cannot be seen talking to the press about this, but you can make a copy of Sam Wood's letter, and I recommend you give it to Bill Phillips, a *New York Tribune* reporter that I think is in Leavenworth today, he is probably staying in the new Planter's Hotel."

Sam took the letter and immediately began copying it onto paper that the Governor gave him.

The Governor then said, "I will call a meeting with Justice Lecompte and Sheriff Dunn immediately and we will discuss this proposal. I doubt they will be able to come up with any excuse to continue with their plans to attack Pardee. And an article containing May's offer in the *New York Tribune* will insulate May from retribution."

"Governor, Sam Wood thinks that Justice Lecompte will do all he can to keep May in jail. He doesn't believe that the Justice will set a date for an arraignment and bail hearing."

The Governor replied, "He had better, his job may very well depend upon it."

The legal case

Once his meeting with the Governor was over, Walker took a copy of Wood's letter to Bill Phillips at the Planter's Hotel in Leavenworth. Phillips was grateful for the letter and quickly interviewed Walker and then collected enough information for a lengthy article on the whole affair. He promised Walker he would write the article that same day and send it to the paper. He told him it might not appear in print for one to two weeks, just getting his draft to New York would take four days.

By the time the interview was over, it was getting late, so Sam got his own room in the Planter's Hotel, had a late dinner with Phillips, and spent the night. The next morning, Walker set out for Pardee to give everyone a full report and return Caleb's horses. The horses were hardy, well built, and well trained. He was thinking about asking Caleb if he would sell them.

It was still early in the day, and Walker's brain was racing as he rode, so much had happened. He had a lot to think about. Although he had over 25 miles to go, he thought he might make the full trip by early afternoon. He hoped Sam Wood was still in Pardee, he needed to tell him about the meeting. Walker was worried about what might happen to Caleb and wondered if he would get out of jail once Lecompte put him in. He well knew that Free-State men, once in jail, were rarely released, hell, they were rarely formally told what they were charged with in an arraignment.

Sam Wood had spent two days taking sworn affidavits in Pardee. He was happy with all of them, but especially impressed with Elijah Smith's detailed description of the robbery of the freighter and the murder of the teamster. Smith was able to describe many of the thieves in some detail, he also provided a good description of the shooter.

Wood took the affidavits at Pardee Butler's dinner table with Pardee and Sybil Butler in attendance and had them witness all of them. Pardee was not a notary, but he was the local minister and a public official. He was as close to a proper witness as the town of Pardee offered. Sybil and Pardee also helped by copying many of the affidavits, since Wood needed two copies of each.

Once done, Wood planned to spend one last night in Pardee and then go to Easton. Early in the afternoon a worn-out Sam Walker arrived, and everyone gathered around to hear the news. Walker filled them in on his extended meeting with the Governor. He also cautioned Caleb, "Do not surrender before Phillips' article is published in the *New York Tribune*. The article might not make the newspaper for another week, but it is your best insurance."

Caleb simply said, "I will be cautious and patient. It seems there is nothing to do now but wait. We shall tend our fields, be vigilant, on guard, and wait."

Early the next morning, Wood left for Easton. He had been assured that both the Sparks and the Minards would welcome him and provide sworn affidavits. When he arrived, he looked over Dawson's Store and the area that had been described so well by his previous witnesses. As they described, the broad Fort Riley Road divided the town in two, half was north of the road and included Dawson's Store, and half was south of the road and included Minard's house. The road appeared to fork in the western part of the town, but the north fork was the true Fort Riley Road and the south fork was simply a lesser road that went to Minard's house and a few other houses on the southern end of the town.

After his exploration he made his way to Minard's cabin. Minard was out in his fields, but his son went to fetch him. Once he was back, Wood asked him to work through his memory of the election day and the battle. It fit well with the other eyewitness accounts he had heard. Then he asked Minard, "Who else should I talk to here before I ride to Sparks' farm?"

Minard said, "Why not interview Dr. Motter? He is in the office next to Dawson's store and was witness to nearly all the events. He also cared for John Cook, the man who was shot and died, he can tell you the details of his wounds."

"Excellent idea, but I think Dr. Motter is strongly proslavery, isn't he? Will he talk to me?"

"He is proslavery, but he is fair, reasonable, and even-tempered. I should think he will talk to you."

So, Wood crossed the road and went into Dawson's store and asked for Dr. Motter. He was led to the door to his office and announced. Dr. Motter stood and said, "How may I help you Mr. Wood."

"Dr. Motter, I'm an attorney investigating the alleged murder of John Cook, I'd like to interview you about the events that night, if it is OK with you. I will take notes and show them to you for your approval and signature before I leave. Is that OK?"

"Yes, that is fine. What are your questions?"[62]

"There were two groups of men, the Free-State men were in and near Mr. Minard's cabin and the proslavery men were here. Can you describe the men and how they were armed?"

"There were about 65-70 men at Minard's, I think nearly all were armed with Sharps rifles or carbines and many of them had revolvers.

---

62 This interview is a fictionalized account of Dr. Motter's testimony before the Congressional committee (Howard & Oliver, 1856, p. 1007)

The legal case

Here at the store, there were about 40 or fifty men, and I think all were armed, but only a few had Sharps rifles, some had revolvers, single-shot pistols, and muskets."

"When did the gun battle begin, and how did it go?"

"It was after midnight and most of the men here at the store were very drunk. The moon was up and there were several lanterns, so there was some light. Stephen Sparks, his boy, and his nephew walked past the store on Fort Riley Road, causing a big commotion and a lot of yelling. About ten men ran after them making threats and jeering them. Sparks got upset and started yelling back.

Mr. Kookogey and I ran to the argument and tried to calm everyone down. I told the men to let Sparks be on his way and gave my opinion that everyone needed to calm down. The men were on a small lane that travels north from Fort Riley Road, and it is lined with fences, I was standing on a stone pillar of one fence trying to keep the men from yelling at each other.

About that time Mr. May came to where we were with about 30 men and called for Sparks to come to him, which Sparks and his son did, Spark's nephew was already with May. May told the rest of us to go home.

At that point, each side retreated, we retreated westward north of the road, toward the store and May and his men retreated to Minard's house, moving westward south of the road. Both Minard's house and the store were west of where we were, but the store was closer. Fort Riley road forks before the store is reached and the main fork goes to the store and minor fork toward Minard's house.

Keeping a watchful eye on each other the retreat continued until the two groups were about eighty yards apart and then one of May's men fired a pistol at us."

Wood then interrupted and asked, "Are you sure it was one of May's men? Did you see someone fire?"

Dr. Motter replied, "Well, no, I didn't see who fired or the flame. It was the sound, and it sounded like it came from that direction."

Wood asked, "OK, where were you standing relative to the other men?'

"I was at the far eastern end of the line of men from Dawson's Store, so I was farthest from the store and north of the road. The pistol, I'm sure it was a pistol, was south and west of me."

Wood said, "Pardon me, I just want to understand. You said the two groups of men were about 80 yards apart, they were each in an east-west line, and both groups were near Fort Riley Road, but on opposite sides and east of both Minard's cabin and the store. The Dawson men were north of Fort Riley Road and the Minard men were south of the road. Is that correct?"

Dr. Motter, "Yes sir, that is correct."

"You realize a pistol or revolver is useless at that distance. I don't think anyone could hit anything with a pistol or revolver at that range, especially at night."

"Ah yes, that is correct. Look, I did not see who shot the pistol, but I have good hearing, and it sounded like a revolver to me. I also did not see a flame or any smoke. One more thing though, I got to Cook right after he was shot and began to care for him immediately. He was in front of the store when he was shot, and he thought he was shot by someone near the store. I discounted what he said at the time, because the Minard men were across the road, in the opposite direction."

"You were facing across the road at the other men, and if it was one of them shouldn't you have seen a flame? How could the Minard men have shot him?"

"I don't know, I'm beginning to have some doubts about my initial thought."

"OK, let's move on, can you remember what John Cook's wound looked like?"

"Yes sir, the shot entered his groin, cut his colon, and likely bounced off the hip bone, probably winding up close to spine. I thought I knew where the ball was, but didn't see it, it was in a dangerous location, I did not try to remove it. I knew the wound was probably fatal, and surgery on a wound like that would only kill him. Judging from the entry wound, it appeared to be a ball, about 70-80 per pound."

Wood thought for a moment and did a rough calculation, "So probably about a .36 caliber ball. Was it a ball? Or a cylindrical Minié bullet? Could you tell?"

"I could not, and like I said I never saw it, but .36 caliber sounds right."

"Is it possible it was a .52 caliber ball or Minié bullet?"

"No, I've seen .50 caliber wounds before, they are much larger."

The legal case

"OK, let's say it was a .36 caliber revolver ball. That would fit all eyewitness accounts of the weapons the men had. Cook thought he was shot from around the store somewhere, he was in front of the eastern side of the store, facing away from the store toward the men on the other side of the road. He was right-handed and firing a heavy musket, so he was probably standing left foot forward and slightly southeast of the store.

He was at the far western end of the line, and you were on the far eastern side and north of the road, which runs east-west, he was in front of you, and farther south. The man who shot him must have been farther west and slightly north. He would have been shooting southeast, if he were a Dawson man, because the Minard men were east and south of him. OK, Cook was facing south with his left foot forward, so, the ball would have entered the right part of his abdomen and traveled across his body to his left hip. Does that sound like his wound?"

"Yes, that is exactly his wound. You're saying a Dawson man probably shot Cook, oh good Lord! I got that exactly wrong."

"Not necessarily, I'm just exploring all the possibilities that fit the facts as you've given them to me. I don't think any of May's men fired their revolvers that night, the distance was too far. They all had Sharps rifles which are accurate at 80 yards, and all their Sharps were bored for .52 caliber cylindrical Minié style bullets. Those are inconsistent with the wound you describe. A Sharps .52 caliber Minié bullet would have gone clear through Cook and killed him instantly.

The only .36 caliber balls that could have been fired that night, that I know of, would have been fired from Colt revolvers. Cook thought that the shot that hit him came from the north side of the road, near the store, you heard revolver fire, and the ball that hit Cook was a .36 caliber ball. I think there is a distinct possibility that one of the Dawson men fired the shot that hit Cook. None of May's men were on that side of the road, they were all south of the road, 80-yards away, heading toward Minard's house."

"Oh dear, I may have gotten it all wrong. Mr. May is innocent. You know I treated Mr. May's wounds later that day, but the whole time I thought he had murdered Cook. Cook wasn't dead yet, but I knew he soon would be."

The interview continued a bit longer, then Dr. Motter approved and signed his affidavit, with Mr. Dawson as a witness. Afterward Dr.

Motter and Wood made two copies of the affidavit, one for Wood and one for Caleb. A saddened Dr. Motter signed them as well. He asked Wood, "Will I have to testify in court?"

"Yes sir, but only to verify that this affidavit is true and accurate."

"OK then, let me know when."

Justice Lecompte

Just as Wood made his startling discovery that the bullet that killed Cook likely did not come from Caleb or his men, Lecompte, Dunn, and Atchison were meeting in Leavenworth. Justice Samuel Lecompte had called the meeting, so he spoke first, "Men, I've just received word that Caleb May is going to give himself up to stand trial for murder. My understanding is that his lawyer, Sam Wood, will be submitting May's conditions and affidavits supporting his innocence to me in a few days. This means that any actions you might take to arrest him must be paused, at least for now. I know Sam Wood, he will have notified the northern press and this means we will be in a lot of trouble if we move against May now."

Dunn said, "That devil! He has outmaneuvered us again. Can we do nothing?"

Atchison said, "Nothing, for now. We do not have cause to attack Pardee unless May is being kept there. Will you keep him in jail?"

Lecompte replied, "I will endeavor to postpone the arraignment and bail hearing as long as possible, but I cannot delay the hearing indefinitely. Wood says he has strong evidence that May did not shoot Cook or you, Dunn. He also has evidence that the freighter he stole from Stringfellow's barn was stolen and the teamster was murdered. He has a witness that will swear that Charles Dunn was a party to the robbery of the Russell, Majors & Waddell freighter and the murder of the teamster. I believe him, and if this comes up for trial, May will be acquitted, if for no other reason than he has the presumption of innocence. Our only hope is to keep May in jail as long as possible by delaying the trial and bail hearing."

Atchison looked at Dunn, but Dunn remained silent and would not meet Atchison's gaze.

The next day, Samuel Wood visited Lecompte at his home in Leavenworth and presented his affidavits and the conditions for May's surrender to him. He laid out the whole case and showed that May and his men could not have shot Cook, and that May could not have shot Dunn, either time. Lecompte responded, "Very good work Sam, but we still must have a trial, Dunn has evidence that says otherwise and only a jury can decide which evidence is more compelling."

Wood replied, "Yes, your honor, I agree, but given this evidence, there must be a prompt arraignment and bail hearing, and a reasonable bail set so that May can tend to his farm and support his large family."

Lecompte replied, "I can agree to have an arraignment and bail hearing as soon as possible. Obviously, I cannot agree to a set bail or even to grant bail without the hearing. I will listen to the arguments offered by both parties and decide at the hearing. Once May is in custody, I will announce the date of the bail hearing, but that is all I can say at this time."

Lecompte paused, then continued, "As for your other conditions, I have spoken with David Atchison and Sheriff Dunn and warned them that any attack on Pardee, once Mr. May has given himself up, is not justified, and will be dealt with harshly. A trial date will be set at the arraignment and bail hearing, and I assume you have already announced May's plan to surrender to the press."

Wood replied, "Thank you your honor, yes, I have notified Bill Phillips of the *New York Tribune* of May's offer to surrender himself."

"That abolitionist rag? Oh, very well. The record of the bail hearing will be part of the public record and will be available the day after it is held, the same will be true of the trial transcript. All the court proceedings will be held in the Territorial capital in Lecompton and Mr. May will be jailed there in the new Territorial jail. Is there anything else to discuss at this time?"

Wood replied, "No, your honor, that is all. Let me give your answer to Mr. May. He will prepare his farm and his affairs and then turn himself in to Sheriff Dunn in Lecompton. We will send word of the day and time, so you and the Sheriff can be prepared."

"Very well, we will await your message."

Jail

When Wood made it back to Pardee, he found that Abbot and Walker were still there. So, they gathered Caleb and his lieutenants and held a meeting to discuss the deal made with Justice Lecompte. After Wood presented the deal Caleb said, "Sounds like it will work, I'm glad he told Atchison and Dunn not to attack Pardee."

Wood spoke up, "Yes, he was very firm about not attacking Pardee, we seem to be safe there. I'm still worried about the bail hearing, he does not have to hold one or allow bail, he can jail you indefinitely, with little or no reason other than you are accused of capital murder. The trial date is totally up to him."

Caleb replies, "Well, that is so, I suppose. But, what choice do I have, other than going to war?"

Walker then says, "Well, Lecompton is close to my farm. My wife and I can keep a close eye on you. The jail will not feed you well, but we will bring you food. We can visit every day. I think you should plan on being gone for a while. If it becomes a problem, Abbott and I will get you out one way or another."

Abbott adds, "Yes, we will. Don't worry. I am usually in Lawrence, and I can visit often also."

Caleb says, "Thank you both. I will need a few days to get the farm in shape so William and Jim can handle it. I will have Milo and Elijah gather the Stringfellow silver and gold and put it somewhere so it can be returned once I'm out of jail. Mr. Wood, please make sure you tell Lecompte we will return it, but only after the trial is concluded and I am free. I think we can say it that way since we have conclusive proof that I am innocent, not that we need anything more than reasonable doubt."

"I will, that is a good idea. He will take offense at that, but he will have the proof right in front of him. One more important thing I discovered recently. Dr. Motter testified in his affidavit that the ball that killed Cook was a .36 caliber ball. He does not have it, he couldn't remove it, but he is sure it was not a .52 caliber. Did any of your men fire a pistol, or a rifle with a .36 caliber ball?"

Caleb looked at his men, they all shook their heads. He said, "No, why shoot a pistol or revolver at 80 yards at night? You can't hit anything. All our men have identical .52 caliber 1852 Sharps' slant breech rifles or carbines, they all shoot modern Minié style bullets. None of them could have fired a .36 caliber ball."

Abbott confirmed it, "I bought all those Sharps in Hartford, Connecticut directly from the factory, they were all identical and all were .52 caliber."

Wood added, "Cook himself, before he died, said that the ball was fired from near the store, that would have been on the north side of Fort Riley Road. Were any of your men north of the road?"

Caleb said, "No. It is not possible, I had all my men south of the main road, we were headed to Minard's house, there is no way any of the men would have crossed the road, too dangerous and, in any case, we would have seen such a move."

"OK, good. I have an affidavit from Dr. Motter and that combined with testimony from all of you shows none of you shot Cook. We don't know who did, but it was a revolver or pistol and from the north side of the road, that takes care of the Cook murder charge. The testimony about where Caleb was when Dunn was shot the first time shows he was nowhere near Dunn's tent. And we have a lot of testimony from the men in the battle showing that Caleb did not shoot him the second time. We are in good shape for the trial. The Russell, Majors & Waddell freighter robbery and murder are well established by Elijah's testimony. It is undisputed that the wagon itself was found in Stringfellow's barn."

"Caleb, can you give me a date when you will turn yourself in, in Lecompton?"

Caleb replied, "Tell them one week from today, on May 20th, I will be there."

Abbott said, "We will be here that day to escort you to Lecompton. These are dangerous times and given that everyone will know where you are going that day, you will need an escort."

Sam Moore, Milo Carlton, Andy Elliot, Bill Wakefield, and Elijah Smith all said they would go as well. Abbott said, "Excellent, there will be no trouble."

The following week was a busy one for Caleb. He worked from sunup to sundown with William, Jim, and Enoch and made sure they knew what needed to be done. Once the week was over, he was exhausted and worried about his family, but knew he had to go. He told William and Maggie not to visit him in jail, he said, "The roads are not safe, I would worry about you all the time. Besides, I know Sam Walker and Jim Abbott will visit."

Maggie and William reluctantly agreed.

He was joined early in the morning by his lieutenants, Jim Abbot, Sam Wood, and Sam Walker. They set out on the 30-mile trip to Lecompton determined, but with heavy hearts.

The trip was uneventful, as expected. No one would molest such a large group of well-armed men. They reached Lecompton by midafternoon and went immediately to the new courthouse.

Lecompton,[63] named in honor of Justice Lecompte, was built on land sold by Sheriff Dunn and David Atchison to the Territory, and the construction company that Dunn and Atchison owned built the courthouse as well as most of the new government buildings in the town.

Upon entering the courthouse, they found Sheriff Dunn and Justice Lecompte waiting for them. Caleb said, "I'm here to give myself up and stand trial for the crimes of which I'm accused—although I'm innocent of all of them."

Just a few seconds after they entered, Bill Phillips of the *New York Tribune* slipped in behind them anxiously scribbling in his notebook. Lecompte glared at Phillips but couldn't say anything because it was a public building, and Phillips was a member of the press.

Dunn walked up to Caleb and said, "You are under arrest, please come with me."

Sam Wood said, "Your honor, when can we expect the arraignment and bail hearing?"

Lecompte answered, "I'll let you know, I need to check my calendar and the prosecutor's calendar. I will set some dates and then ask you to choose one that fits in with your schedule. In the meantime, I'm ordering the Sheriff to keep May in jail because he is accused of a capital crime. Due to the troubles in this area, especially in Lawrence and Topeka, Caleb May will be incarcerated in the Leavenworth jail. This also

---

63 Lecompton was the capital of Kansas from 1855-1861. It was originally named Bald Eagle due to the numerous eagles that nested there.

moves him closer to my residence where I hold most of my meetings with counsels and the accused."[64]

Caleb was then transported to Leavenworth and put in an eight-foot boiler plate-lined iron cell. It had no opening but an iron grate door. His cell door opened to a hallway, other prisoners were to his left, down the hallway, and to the immediate right of his cell door was a heavy oak door, with strong iron straps reinforcing it. It was the cell block door, and it had a small rectangular opening at eye level. The door separated the large jailhouse entryway and meeting room from the cell block. It was normally open during the day.

There was no view of the outdoors directly from the cell block or Caleb's cell. But when the large cell block door was open, light and air from the front windows and front door (also normally open) made its way into the cell block. When the cell block door was closed there was little light. There were other prisoners in the jailhouse, but Caleb could not see them, only hear them.

The cell had a bed with a mattress and a horsehair rug with an old, worn, and frayed cotton blanket for a cover. The door had a small opening for passing food through. He also had a smelly bucket for his waste.[65]

Sheriff Dunn took all his remaining possessions, except for his clothes. He gave Caleb's possessions to Jake De Bard, the jailer.

The lack of light bothered Caleb; it was like being in a tomb. Escaped slaves, and sometimes captured or kidnapped free black men and women were kept in the hallway in front of his cell.

There were dozens of men outside the jail, all armed, and although Caleb could not see them well, he could tell they had muskets, rifles, and revolvers. They yelled about Yankees and abolitionists constantly. They were there to drive back any attempt by the Kansas Legion to free Caleb.

Caleb thought, "They moved me here because of troubles in Topeka and Lawrence? What about the troubles here?"

---

[64] The official Territorial Supreme Court building was in Lecompton, but Lecompte was rarely there, preferring to work from his home in Leavenworth.

[65] Much of the description of the jail is from (Doy, 1860, p. 45)

Slaves in jail

During May's second day in jail, three black men were brought to the jail and put in the jail hallway, outside his cell. The man, named Jack, who brought them told them they had better choose masters, like others had done, and not get into any more trouble. The men answered that they were free men and had never been slaves and that they would rather remain in jail until their friends proved they were free men.

Jack sneered, and said, "Men! Men! You're nothing but damned slaves."

The kidnapper then left, and the three men, named Smith, Hayes, and Riley, came up to May's cell and graciously expressed their sympathy for his plight. They said they had all heard what had happened to him. Caleb replied, "Why thank you. Why are you here? I heard you say you were free men, what happened?"

Hayes replied, "We were on our way to Nebraska City to get away from the kidnappings in Kansas. There, we have been told, free black men are safe. We were with our wives and some other men, when we were captured on the road north of Leavenworth and asked to choose masters, which we would not do. Our wives were taken to Kansas City, probably to be sold down south. We miss them, and do not expect to ever see them again."

Caleb sighed and felt badly for them and said, "I'm so sorry, such an injustice. It makes no sense, you are such young and handsome men, you should be happily settled and starting your families, and now you face a fate worse than death."[66]

Caleb said, "You should ask to see a judge or magistrate and make an affidavit, that should prevent anyone from taking you away before you have a chance to establish your freedom with proof."

The men gave this message to the jailer, but nothing came of it.

The next day, a man came to the jail and told Smith, Hayes, and Riley to get ready to go with him. They refused to go and insisted on being kept in jail. The man's name was John, and he yelled, "I'm your master now, you damned slaves, and by God, I'll make you mind me!"

He told them to put on their coats, handcuffed them, chained them together, and whipped them severely. He tried to make them confess

---

[66] Fictionalize from (Doy, 1860, p. 51)

they were slaves, but they insisted they were free men, even after being beaten.

Caleb witnessed all this through the grated door and said to his jailer, "Jake you must stop this!"

Jake De Bard replied, "I can't. I have no power to prevent this, no law allows me to do anything."

John, the slave master heard this exchange and yelled, "Curse you Caleb May, you are a damned slave-thief."

He then shook his whip at Caleb and told him, "If I had you outside, I would cut your head off."

He then took the men out of the jail and Caleb never saw them again.

Later, Caleb asked De Bard, "What happened to the young men that slave master took away?"

De Bard said, "He took them to Independence, Missouri and sold them for $1,000 apiece."

Thus, three free-born citizens of Ohio and Pennsylvania, were dragged off and sold into slavery, without being given the opportunity to show they were free men. This was done, even though proof they were free men was readily available in the Kansas Territorial public record.

In another sad case, he saw a very dark woman brought in with a light-colored baby. One of the slave traders asked the slave owner what he was going to do with the baby. He answered, "Damned if I know, I'm bothered to know what to do with it."

Just then another resident came in with a young boy for sale. So, the slave owner asked him "Here, don't you want this thing? You may have it for twenty-five dollars." He then snatched the baby from the mother's arms and said, "It weighs twenty-five pounds! Will you take it?"

The man said, "Yes." And the slave owner said, "Take it now."

The child was carried off as the woman sobbed and cried and pleaded for her baby. The woman was later sold for $700 and taken into Missouri, her baby was taken to Platte City and raised by a slave family there. Many similar incidents of families separated in that hallway occurred, and the scenes were heart-wrenching.[67]

At some point, during his second day in the jail, a public meeting was held and they passed a resolution to "Hang and burn the damned

---

67 Fictionalized from (Doy, 1860, p. 63)

abolitionist." De Bard told Caleb this and he waited up all that night for the men to come and hang him, but they never came.

When the jailer's son, named Bobby, brought Caleb his breakfast the next morning, he told him, "Justice Lecompte and Sheriff Dunn prevented the crowd from taking you by telling them they had guns and the only way they were going to get the prisoner was over their dead bodies."

The night before, Lecompte had said to the crowd, "Caleb May is in the hands of the law, and justice will only be meted out to him by the law."[68] Unfortunately, some newspapers, including the Atchison *Squatter Sovereign*, reported that the crowd had hung Caleb, and his family saw the newspaper reports. Maggie and the children were devastated by the news, until they found that the reports were false, and he was still alive.

Justice Lecompte and Sheriff Dunn's brave actions dispelled the mob outside of the jail and it never regrouped.

Jim Abbott and Sam Walker were able to see Caleb on the third day after his arrest. Although Abbott and Walker lived about the same distance from Leavenworth as Pardee, it was an easier and safer trip for them than it was for anyone from Pardee, which was deep in proslavery territory. Besides telling William and Maggie not to come to see him in jail, he let it be known he didn't want anyone from Pardee to come for their safety. He relied on Abbott, Walker, and Sam Wood to help him while he was in jail.

Jake De Bard, came to his cell and escorted Caleb to the spacious front room of the house that was serving as one of the territorial jails. He sat Caleb at a table with Jim and Sam, and then stepped back to the doorway and into the hallway in front of Caleb's cell and waited.

Jim handed Caleb a basket of food and said, "How are you doing? Are they feeding you well enough, are you comfortable? It was hell last night; the town nearly broke into the jail to hang you!"

Caleb responded, "I stayed up all night and could hear them out there, but they never broke in, I understand Lecompte and Dunn stopped them."

Jim said, "That is what we heard as well. I think both Lecompte and Dunn have been told they are in serious trouble if you are hurt in any

---

68 This is like a story in (Doy, 1860, p. 49).

way. They should have known that you would be much safer in Lecompton than here. Moving you here was not to protect you; it was to make it harder for you to escape."

"I think that is so. I guess they think if anything happens to me, they will lose the election. Thank you so much for this food, it looks wonderful! I'm mostly comfortable enough here and they do feed me. It isn't as good as Maggie's food, but OK. I wish they would empty my bucket more often and my cell is dirty, but I'll live."

Jim continued, "We have not heard anything about a bail hearing yet, Wood is meeting with Lecompte today, otherwise he would be here. He will press for a bail hearing soon."

After this initial meeting, Jim Abbott, Sam Walker, or Sam Wood visited Caleb about twice a week. They always brought food and news. Unfortunately, they never knew anything about when Caleb's arraignment would happen or when bail would be set.

After each meeting, De Bard stepped over and didn't say anything, but looked through the food baskets, as well as any new clothes, then always said, "OK, you can keep all this."

After that, he would step back again and watch everything going on. The visits were not allowed to last long. Then De Bard took Caleb back to his cell where he always immediately started in on the food baskets. On the days they visited, Mrs. De Bard always brought him lemonade and ordered Bobby to empty Caleb's bucket. Caleb figured his visitors must always say something to the De Bard's before leaving.

Lecompte's Plan

After Caleb had been in jail for over a month, Lecompte and the Governor met in the Governor's office in Shawnee Mission, and among the subjects they discussed was Caleb May. The Governor said, "We promised Caleb May a prompt bail hearing and yet he has been in jail for over a month, and there has not been one. He hasn't even been formally charged with any crimes!"

Lecompte said, "I have reviewed all the affidavits and they seriously conflict with one another, even affidavits from witnesses at the same event. This is a capital crime, and a person who allegedly shot a peace officer twice. I don't think I can set him free; I have asked Sheriff Dunn to continue his investigation and try and determine the truth of the matter."[69]

The Governor said, "The affidavit from Dr. Motter appears to exonerate both May and all his men in the shooting of Cook, he was shot from the wrong direction and the ball that killed him was a .36 caliber. May and his men were firing .52 caliber Minié balls. It also appears that May could not have shot Dunn the first time and did not the second time, although Dunn was armed and had blockaded Pardee at the time."

Lecompte replied, "Other witnesses saw the events differently, and I must be cautious in capital crimes."

The Governor said, "I will remind you that evidence exists that Dunn participated in a murder of a teamster outside of Pardee, how can he continue to be Sheriff in this area?"

"I have requested that the U.S. Marshall for Missouri investigate that murder, but I have not yet received his report. We will not deal with that issue until I receive his report."

The Governor then changed subjects, "The *New York Tribune* has also interviewed many of the witnesses and reached the same conclusion I have, that May is innocent, and Dunn is guilty. This is an election year, and the public wants peace in Kansas Territory. The President must show that slave-states and free states can coexist peacefully, this is a central tenet of the Democratic platform in this election. May and the Kansas Territory are at the center of this issue right now. You must arraign him, hold a bail hearing, then release him on bail. This delay endangers all Democrats, even the President."

Lecompte replied, "I cannot right now. It is a capital case. Let Dunn gather more evidence and then we will see."

Once Lecompte left, Governor Shannon wrote a letter to President Pierce warning him, "Events have moved out of my control. May is being held without bail or arraignment, the situation here is dire and will affect the election if not dealt with quickly."

Sam Wood met with Lecompte a week after his meeting with Shannon and was also told, "No arraignment or bail hearing at this time."

---

[69] The sorry state of legal justice in the Kansas Territory during this period and the corruption of Justice Lecompte is well documented (Gihon, 1857, pp. 158-164).

Wood knew the outcome of the meeting between Lecompte and Shannon, so he came away from his own meeting convinced that Lecompte would never release May. He met with the Governor and told him the same thing. Shannon replied, with a dour expression, "I agree, and I have written to the President to warn him, this will cause serious trouble, both in the Territory and across the nation. It will have serious repercussions in the election."

Wood said, "Damned the election! Justice was promised and now it is denied, how can he hold May indefinitely without a bail hearing or even an arraignment? My God man, May hasn't even been officially told what he is charged with!"

Shannon said, "Let me investigate my options. Lecompte is the Chief Justice of the Territorial Supreme Court, and he now has complete control over the fate of Mr. May. I'm uncertain of my pardon powers, but certainly the President can pardon Mr. May, let me investigate this. This injustice is extremely dangerous."

Wood replied tensely, "Damn right! Sorry, I don't mean to be disrespectful Governor."

"That is OK, I understand, this is very incendiary, which is the problem."

Immediately after Wood left, Governor Wilson Shannon, rode to Leavenworth and visited Caleb in the jail. Jake De Bard was impressed that the Governor himself came to the jail and escorted him to the table in the great room where visitors could meet with the prisoners. Then he immediately went to get Caleb and asked his wife to bring them coffee and snacks.

The Governor told Caleb, "I am horrified at how you have been treated. All this time and no arraignment or bail hearing yet, it is unconscionable. This injustice means that the Territory will pay Sam Wood's legal fees for your defense, as long as you want Wood to represent you."

Caleb replied, "Yes, sir. I do want Sam Wood as my lawyer."

The Governor said, "Good. I think he is a good choice, but you understand that Lecompte has great discretion in how you are treated."

The Governor then turned to De Bard and his wife who had just brought them coffee and snacks, and said, "I want this man well treated."

Mr. and Mrs. De Bard both replied, "Yes sir, Governor, your excellency sir."

About a week later, in early July, Sam Walker visited Caleb and brought him some food. Walker noticed that Caleb moved stiffly and seemed a little unsteady.

Walker asked, "Caleb are you OK? You seem a little unsteady."

"It is my confinement Sam, I get no exercise, my cell is barely big enough to turn around in. I'm getting weak from inactivity. I do no work and get no exercise."

"I'm sorry to hear that Caleb, we need to fix that."

As Walker moved the food basket over the table and Caleb grabbed the basket with his left hand, Walker gripped Caleb's other hand. Caleb could feel him press a folded piece of paper into his palm. He moved his hand under Walker's so the paper would fall into his palm, then smiled and let go of Walker's hand. He tried to make everything look normal and innocent.

Caleb, then said, "I can't thank you enough Sam."

Then Walker said, "The food is straight from my wife Caleb, and safe to eat, I swear I didn't touch it."

Caleb laughed and thanked him again. Sam then told him the news and told him there was still no word on his arraignment.

After Walker left, De Bard took him back to his cell, and with no one in sight, Caleb was able to read Walker's note. It read, "Lecompte is not going to let you go. Be ready to escape. We will signal you on the day it will happen. The escape will be at midnight that same day."

***

Sheriff Dunn and John Stringfellow were pleased with themselves, they had coached all the proslavery witnesses in what to say and write in their affidavits. They had managed to concoct a somewhat credible and consistent alternative story for all the events. They knew that Lecompte would not free May on bail. Their story would never survive a serious cross examination in court, but they didn't think May would ever make it to trial.

Just to make sure, Stringfellow wrote an article for the *Squatter Sovereign* that summarized their alternative story in very convincing language.

***

It was clear to James Abbott, Sam Wood, and Sam Walker that Caleb May was doomed to spend the rest of his life in prison and there was no legal way to free him. The legal system was solidly stacked against him.

Wood and Walker met with General James Abbott in mid-July. It had been almost two months since Caleb was put in jail, there was no hope for a bail hearing, and they needed a plan to break Caleb out of jail or to get a pardon.

Just to be certain that a jailbreak was necessary, Wood met with the Governor once more a couple of days later and asked him if a pardon for Caleb was possible. The Governor replied, "It is not looking good. The President told me I cannot pardon him, and he does not want to right now. Although we have clear 6th Amendment and 8th Amendment violations in May's case, the President is afraid to pardon him in an election year. I would pardon him if I had the authority, but I do not."

Wood responded, "Caleb gave himself up voluntarily in order to have a fair and speedy trial as dictated by the Constitution. This makes his incarceration both illegal and unconstitutional. If he were to somehow free himself, it seems it would be difficult to re-arrest him. How would that be justified?"

The Governor answered, "Escaping from jail is a crime, he would only add to the charges against him."

"Could he sue Justice Lecompte and Sheriff Dunn in federal court for violating his constitutional rights?"

"He could try, but he is charged with a capital crime, and there is precedent for withholding bail in capital crimes."

"OK, not much to be done then."

"I will contact the President again and ask him to fire both Dunn and Lecompte for the violation of Caleb's constitution rights, but I'm not optimistic."

"OK, thank you Governor for your attention to this matter."

Sam Wood reported the results of the meeting to Abbott, and they began planning Caleb's escape. The team would be the two of them, Walker, two other members of the Lawrence Kansas Legion militia, and Caleb's five lieutenants. The Kansas Legion would fund the operation. All the men would be armed with sporting rifles, revolvers, and bowie knives. No Sharps rifles would be taken, they would cause suspicion, because they were the badge of a Kansas abolitionist.

The men met in Lansing on July 19, just south of Leavenworth. There they met with the editor of the only Free-State newspaper in the area,

Dr. Edwin H. Grant who, it turned out, was a great supporter of Caleb May's cause. Dr. Grant seemed reliable to Abbott, so he told him about their plans to free Caleb. Grant immediately offered to join them and help in any way he could. James Abbott thanked him for the offer but told him he could not ask him to be actively involved, it would be too dangerous. However, Abbott needed information and thought that Grant was in a good position to get it.[70]

Escape!

On July 23rd, Caleb was looking out of the front of his cell through the small visible opening through the combination home and jailhouse's front door. It was open, as usual, for ventilation and light. He saw a man he did not recognize and Elijah Smith walk by the door. Elijah caught his eye and slowly brushed his left eyelid with his left pinky, which was a secret signal only known to members of the Kansas Legion. Caleb's heart leapt! Today is the day.

He remembered that the escape would be at midnight, he didn't know how it would happen, but it would happen that night. Caleb began to gather up his clothes and sent a message to the jailer's wife, Mrs. De Bard, asking for the shirts she was washing for him.

Abbott's initial plan a few days earlier was to bring a false captured prisoner to the jail late at night and use him to get the jailer to open the door and let them in. Once in, they would force the jailer to let May go at gunpoint. However, Dr. Grant told Abbott that prisoners brought in in the middle of the night were not taken to that jail but to another. So, Abbott abandoned that plan and looked for other ways to free Caleb.

Abbott needed more information on the jail, so he sent Sam Moore into the jail to reconnoiter. Sam had not been in the jail before, and he was unknown to the jailer. Sam told the De Bard he had just arrived from Pardee and had a message for Caleb May from his wife.

It was nearly dark when Sam surveyed the jail, and he told Caleb that he had recently seen his wife and kids and they were well and hoped to see him soon. He looked about the jail a lot and brushed his left eyelid

---

70 This account is fictional but based on a real jail break described in (Abbott, 1889).

with his left pinky, just as Elijah had done. He distracted the jailer by criticizing the poor ventilation and suggested improvements. He told the jailer he was a blacksmith and could make all the improvements for him for only $25.

De Bard took his name and told Sam he would ask for the money and be in contact. Sam made a show of thanking De Bard and put him at ease.

Sam Moore left the jail and reported what details he had seen to Abbott and the others. He believed that even with the best tools, it would take two hours to get into the room where May was being held and breaking in like that would be noisy. This was discouraging; two hours was far too long; they were sure to be discovered in less time than that. They needed a new plan, and right away.

However, while they were still meeting and trying to come up with a new plan, Dr. Grant arrived and in a worried voice said, "Men, I was mistaken. It turns out all criminals taken outside the city limits, at night, are taken to De Bard's jail to be held until the next day."

Abbott and Moore were relieved; Abbott exclaimed, "Oh, thank God, that makes it so much easier, we can use the original plan."

The city theatres and saloons closed at 11:30PM, so they moved the time from midnight to 11:00PM, that way the streets would be full of people as they left the jail, and they would be less noticeable. It was raining hard that night; the streets were muddy and moving around the town was difficult, but the rain was also good cover.

The jail was located near the middle of the town and the courthouse was about 200 feet southwest of it. There was a night watchman always stationed at the courthouse, so Bill Wakefield was posted where he could watch the night watchman without being seen.

The rain finally stopped, but the clouds remained, there was some fog and no moon, so it was very dark. It was so dark the men had to hold each other's hands to keep together. When they reached the jail, they stopped, and Wakefield came up to them and reported that the watchman had just visited the jail and returned to the south side of the courthouse and was sitting there. Wakefield took up a position at the street corner to watch the guard and look out for approaching trouble.

Then Abbott assigned the men to their roles. Milo Carleton was to be the leading spokesman, Elijah Smith was to be the horse thief, and

Andy Elliot was to be the second captor. Elijah's hands would appear to be tied, but the cord around his wrists would be attached to a lead ball, concealed in his fist. This is a 19th century weapon, called a sling shot or slung shot, and can be used to send a man into unconsciousness.

Abbott, Walker, Moore, and Wood were well known in the jail, so they stayed away from the jailhouse door. They positioned themselves carefully up and down the street, but out of sight of the jail windows, and stayed in the shadows. It was a dark night, but there were a few natural gas streetlights.[71]

The hidden men were to help Wakefield watch for trouble. When all was quiet, they nodded to the three men who then approached the jail just after 11PM, the 23rd of July. They knocked loudly at the door and in a few seconds a window was opened above them and De Bard, asked "Who's there? What do you want?"

Milo replied, "We have a horse thief we would like put in the jail for safe keeping until morning."

The jailer replied, "Wait a minute and I will be down."

At that moment, Abbott, listening from a nearby alleyway, smiled and pumped his fist. He was now certain they would succeed. De Bard came to the door and let them in and asked, "Do you have a warrant for the prisoner's arrest, are either of you a proper law officer?"

Milo replied, "No sir, we are only private citizens; but the facts in the case are these, this man was in the employ of one of our neighbors down in the southeast portion of this county, and last night, while he and his employer were trying to make a settlement on his pay, they disagreed as to the amount he was due, and came to hard words, and this man left the house. In the morning one of our neighbors' horses and this man were missing. It was generally believed he was the thief, and several parties started out in different directions in search of the horse and thief. It so happened we struck his trail and followed it until nearly night, when we overtook and found him with the stolen horse hiding in a steep creek bank about six or eight miles from the city."[72]

---

71 Coal was mined in the Fort Leavenworth area as early as 1827, natural gas from the mine was used in streetlights, it was called "coal gas" and piped to the central part of the city in wooden pipes. They copied a technology used in Chicago.

72 Fictionalized, more on the actual escape here: (Abbott, 1889).

De Bard, "I cannot jail him without the proper papers. If he isn't guilty, I and my bondsman will be held for heavy damages."

Carlton and Elliot assured him there could not possibly be any mistake about his guilt. De Bard turned to Elijah and said, "Are you willing to acknowledge that you stole the horse?"

Elijah, in a rough and insolent manner replied, "Do you suppose that I am a damned fool? No, sir! I won't admit anything of the kind. I expect to have a fair trial."

Elijah's manner irritated De Bard, and he replied, "I believe you *are* a thief, and I will take a chance and put you in my jail." The prisoner was then taken to the heavy iron-strapped door that led to Caleb's cell. De Bard got the keys and unlocked it, and told Elijah to walk in, but when Elijah saw a drawing of a human skeleton on the wall, he got a startled look on his face, and said, "I will not go into such a place!"

Just then, Milo, taking advantage of the distraction, said, "De Bard, what has become of that old slave-stealer, Caleb May, or some such name?"

De Bard turned from Elijah and replied, "Caleb May is still here." Then Caleb immediately came to the door of his cell with his bundle of clothing.

Andy Elliot saw Caleb and now was sure that he was there, so he said, "This is a mere ruse, De Bard, we have you. We have not come to put a man in prison, but to take the good Caleb May back to his family."

Elijah quickly freed his wrists from his bonds and released the heavy lead ball concealed in his fist. He jumped forward to block the cell block door as De Bard was trying to close it. Then Elliot quickly shoved a large Colt Navy revolver into his chest.

Elliot, a dangerous looking man, said, "It's too late De Bard. If you resist or raise an alarm, you are a dead man. The front door is guarded, the jail is surrounded by armed men. We've come to take Caleb May home to Pardee, and we mean to do it; so please be quiet. We came here to release our friend and have the power to do it."

De Bard said, "Gentlemen, I am in your power and must submit. I will leave my fate and my future to Caleb." The jailer then addressed Caleb, "Caleb, don't you think you had better stay and be legally acquitted by the Supreme Court, instead of getting off in this way, and running the risk of being recaptured, with even more charges?"

Caleb replied, "De Bard, I gave myself up under the promise of a rapid arraignment, where I could post bail, and be freed to go home to my family. My lawyer has gathered overwhelming evidence that I'm innocent of all charges, but none of it has been heard in court. I haven't even been charged with anything officially. I have the right to hear the charges, a speedy trial, *and* a bail hearing.

I am perfectly justified in taking my liberty in any way I can. I have lost all confidence in the Territorial Supreme Court; I do not trust it or Justice Lecompte. My evidence will never be heard there. Therefore, I shall go with my friends and take the risk."

Caleb then shook the hand of the jailer and said to the others, "Boys, De Bard and his family have treated me as well as possible. He has been kind to me."

Abbott, Walker, Moore, and Wood had moved from their hiding places and taken new positions just outside the jail door but kept out of sight from the inside since the jailer knew them. Andy Elliot moved to the doorway, turned and spoke using his most dangerous sounding voice and expression, "De Bard, as I said there is a heavy guard all around the jail, they will shoot anyone who raises an alarm or tries to leave the jailhouse before morning. Every window is being watched."

To emphasize the point, Abbot and Walker shuffled their feet just outside the open door. Then the other prisoners tried to leave with Caleb, but De Bard pleaded, "Gentlemen! Please, my reputation is already harmed, don't let all the other prisoners out, it will ruin me."

The Kansas men at once warned the others back with their pistols, saying, "If you have violated the laws, you must suffer the penalty. We did not come here to interfere with justice, but to set right that which we know to be wrong."

The jailer then locked the heavy door, locking in the other prisoners. Then Elliot reminded De Bard to turn out the lights and remain perfectly quiet until daylight. Any attempt to raise an alarm or to leave or to send a signal will result in them being shot.

De Bard then said, "Gentlemen, this thing will injure my character."

Bill Wakefield, still unknown to De Bard, moved into the room, and replied, "I will publish an accurate account of the rescue of Caleb May that will exonerate you. We will have it published in the Lawrence *Daily Kansas Tribune*."

With that promise, Andy Elliot thanked De Bard for his kind treatment of Caleb but told him he really needed to improve his cell, keep it cleaner, and improve the ventilation. Then the men left.

They closed the front door and waited for all the lights to be extinguished. After a few minutes of waiting, they felt comfortable that De Bard was not going to raise an alarm. Then all the men left their positions and gathered at the corner, out of sight of the jail windows.

They had been carefully watching every window and door to the jailhouse. Abbott did not leave any men behind, as they said they would, and expected De Bard to be restrained by his fear.

As they moved down the street, Caleb nearly collapsed from weakness due to his long confinement with almost no exercise and very little room to move. Wood and Moore had to help him walk. For Caleb, a man used to being fit and strong, it was humiliating, he said, "I can't believe how weak I am after only two months!"

It was cloudy, but the moon had risen, and the rain had stopped, so there was enough light to see. They made their way south, along the main road, which was occasionally lit by streetlights, and they mixed with the people returning home from the theatre. In the crowd they made their way about three miles to the south edge of town, which bordered Lansing.

They split into two groups, the three Lawrence-bound men, led by Abbot, and the Pardee-bound group led by Sam Moore. Walker, who lived in Bloomington near Lawrence, and Sam Wood, who lived in Lawrence, decided to go with the Pardee group. The Pardee group were followed all the way to their stable by two policemen with lanterns. The policemen held their lanterns high in the stable while the men looked for their horses. The policemen waited until Caleb and the men had saddled their horses and rode out of the stable and headed west out of Lansing. As they rode out, they thanked the policemen for their kindness.

The nearest safe town was Easton, which was 13 miles away, too far for so late at night, so they rode a few miles west of Lansing and set up a camp. They had some biscuits, hard tack, and beef jerky to eat for a late meal.

Caleb was delighted, he said, "This is perfect, two months without seeing the stars and the moon, now I see the sky in all its glory. It's like God is blessing me by removing the clouds and showing me this wonderful view as a gift for my escape."

Caleb was still weak and needed help setting up his bedroll near the fire, but once done, and a drink of fresh water with a biscuit, and some beef jerky he felt whole again. He fell into a deep sleep and didn't stir until Sam Moore shook him awake a few hours later at dawn.

They held a little council over coffee and the last of their biscuits around the campfire the next morning. They were far enough off the road so that normally they would not be seen by passersby. Sam spoke first, "I'm sure that the police in Leavenworth now know what happened last night and are looking for us. We headed south when we left the jailhouse, so they will think 'Lansing' first thing and we are only a few miles west of Lansing."

Milo said, "We can make our way northwest, staying off the roads, and come out on Fort Riley Road, and then work our way to Stephen Spark's place and see what he has heard about us. Depending upon what he says we can decide how and when to make our way to Pardee."

There seemed to be some agreement on this, but Walker noted, "Easton is one of the first places they will look for us, so we need to be careful."

With that settled, the group set off across country, avoiding all roads. When they reached Fort Riley Road, they saw they were east of town and traveled parallel to the road toward Easton and Sparks' claim. In less than an hour they reached the Sparks house, which was just southeast of town. Luckily, Sparks was home.

Sparks welcomed all of them and was pleased that Caleb was free, he gave Caleb a big handshake, and his wife, Esseneth, gave Caleb a big hug. They quickly caught Stephen up-to-date and told him they were interested in what was being said in Easton about the escape, if anything. Stephen said, "I'll go to town and see, I've heard nothing yet, but it isn't even noon."

Then Stephen started talking about the gun battle in January in Easton. He said, "Did you know that Charley Dunn was in Easton during the January gun battle?"

A tired Sam Wood was instantly wide awake and completely taken aback, he said, "What? I thought he arrived later, the next afternoon. Where was he? Why have I not heard this before?"

Stephen said, "It's because he didn't tell anyone, I only know because Sam Kookogey mentioned he saw him that night. He was in the store and very drunk just before the battle started. He said it offhand, as if it didn't mean anything."

Wood said, "Didn't mean anything? Everyone told me he didn't arrive until the next day, even Dr. Motter. Where was he when Caleb was being attacked and was nearly killed?"

Stephen said, "I don't know, I'll ask Kookogey, maybe he knows."

Wood said, "Please do that, it may matter. I have no idea what is going on, but as a lawyer, I'm always suspicious when stories conflict and important information is hidden. Something is going on, and I will get to the bottom of it."

A feast in Easton

The men conferred at Sparks' farm and decided to stay there for a day or two and keep out-of-sight. They asked Esseneth and Stephen if they could stay and they agreed. The men set up a temporary camp near the Sparks barn and prepared to stay a while. Sam Moore and Milo Carleton decided that since they brought their hunting rifles they should go hunting to help feed themselves and the Sparks family.

Stephen Sparks left for town to find out what he could about Sheriff Dunn and the escape. Once in town he sought out Sam Kookogey and found him at Dawson's Store. It was now July; and the January battle was not forgotten but everyone had decided that it was in the past, so Sparks had no problem going there. He was on guard but reasonably comfortable in the store.

He found Kookogey and asked him, "How is everything going? Heard any interesting news lately?"

Kookogey replied, "Not much, seems quiet just now."

Sparks then asked, "You mentioned a few days ago that you saw Sheriff Dunn here the night of the battle, do you know when he arrived?"

"I didn't see him until fairly late, I think just an hour or so before the gunfight, he was already drunk. He was hanging around with Mr. Dawson a bit, then I didn't see him again until the next day."

Sparks then found Dawson and asked him what Sheriff Dunn did the night of the battle, and Dawson replied, "I did talk to him that night for a while, but he was drunk and not making much sense. Eventually, I invited him to spend the night and took him to our spare bed upstairs. He went up and laid down, I assume he passed out or went to sleep, I didn't see him again that night."

Sparks asked, "So as far as you know he stayed upstairs here in the store through the whole battle, and even through the fight the next morning?"

"Yes, that is what I remember."

"Wow, he must have really been drunk!"

"Oh, he was. Plus, he had not been drinking much for a long time, I think he had been trying to quit. But that night he really fell off the wagon in a big way."

With that done, Sparks bought a few things at the store to help feed his guests and walked home. Once there, he filled Wood in on the conversations he had in town. Wood said, "So no news of the escape has reached here yet? And Dunn was in the store all that night, and drunk. OK, thanks Stephen, that helps me a lot."

Sam Moore and Milo bagged a deer and strung it up in a tree. They immediately got busy cleaning it and preparing the meat for Esseneth to cook. That put everyone in a good mood, plus Sparks had returned from the store with some spices and their garden had some nice sweet potatoes, peas, cabbages, onions and cucumbers. There would be a great feast that night, everyone felt good.

The men decided to stay that night, and they posted guards. No one in town knew about the escape, or that they were on Sparks' farm, and Dunn had not arrived. At least not yet.

Caleb spoke to Sparks, "Stephen, can your boy Greene ride to Pardee tomorrow and tell my wife I'm here and OK, and ask her how things are going with my kids? Also, pass on the message that we may need help here soon and see if William and some of the boys can ride down here? They should be ready for a fight."

Stephen replied, "He will leave at first light."

The men all feasted and got some needed rest that night, everyone went to sleep early except the guards. Early the next morning Greene took off for Pardee, a two- to three-hour ride.

Dunn's posse

Early on the morning after the jail break, De Bard rode to Sheriff Dunn's house in Leavenworth and reported the jailbreak. De Bard said, "Sheriff, about 12 men [it was actually 10] came and broke Caleb May out of jail last night." Then he related the whole story and admitted he did not know who any of them were. Dunn was furious and said, "How did you allow this? Why did it take you so long to get over here to report it?"

De Bard said, "I couldn't leave until daylight, I left as soon as I could. They posted men to watch the jail and said they would shoot anyone who left the house before dawn. I had to leave the lights off."

Dunn said, "And you believed this! They left as quickly as they could."

De Bard said, "I couldn't take a chance, I have a family."

Dunn dropped it, he said, "Look I have to tell everyone what is going on and raise a posse, I can't stay here talking."

Dunn immediately went to Lecompte's house and told him what was going on. He said, "Caleb May escaped from jail last night. We need to decide what to do."

Lecompte said, "Oh no. This is a problem. The President and Governor will want to do nothing, they can't afford any trouble. The damned *New York Tribune* runs the country, and it is running articles every day on the heroic Free-State Caleb May. Whatever we do has to be done quietly."

Dunn said, "OK, but he did escape from jail, and I'm the sheriff, I must go after him."

"Very well, gather up a posse, I'm sure that Atchison will fund it, but whatever you do, do it quietly, and don't kill May or harm the town, that would make him a martyr and we would have even more problems. Give me a few minutes, because he broke out of jail, I can issue you an arrest warrant and a search warrant for May and his house today."

With the warrants in hand Dunn went straight to David Atchison in Platte City and got some money, then he spent the rest of the day gathering deputies to go after Caleb. When he finally got to bed that night, he was apprehensive, he knew Caleb was dangerous, and now he couldn't even shoot him, but had to capture him. He thought Caleb must have headed straight for Pardee and his family. He would go there first. They would leave first thing in the morning.

***

Just as Sam and Milo were killing and field dressing the deer, Dunn was gathering men in Leavenworth and Platte City to take to Pardee. It took Sheriff Dunn all day and into the evening just to gather his men in Leavenworth and they had a five-hour ride ahead of them. He also needed their names and addresses, and he needed to make sure the addresses were valid Kansas Territory addresses. The time required meant they must wait for morning.

The next morning, the morning of July 25th, Greene Sparks headed out early to Pardee. He was young, only weighed 140 pounds and was on a strong horse, so he covered the 13 miles to Pardee in a little over two hours and was at Caleb's cabin by breakfast.

Later the same morning Sam Moore and Elijah Smith spoke to Caleb, "Captain, we need to get back to our businesses in Pardee, is it OK if we leave now to tend to them?"

Caleb replied, "Of course, we will probably only stay here one more day anyway. I'll see you tomorrow."

Sam and Elijah left immediately for Pardee, but it was a nice day, and they didn't hurry.

Greene gratefully accepted Maggie's invitation to breakfast, and feasted on eggs, bacon, and biscuits. As he ate, he caught the family up on how Caleb was doing, He said, "Caleb expects Dunn and his men to go to Easton soon and he prefers to have the battle there, rather than in Pardee. But we have seen no sign of Dunn yet and the people in Easton don't even know about the jailbreak. Caleb is asking for William and some of his men to come down to Easton as soon as they can."

William said, "OK, but we need to leave some men to guard Pardee, we can't be sure Dunn will go to Easton, or even through Easton. I'll gather ten men this morning and take them to Easton and warn the others to watch the roads from the east and south carefully. We'll need to man the foxholes and blockhouses today."

William left immediately to take care of all that. In an hour he and the other members of the Kansas Legion had positioned themselves. William and ten of the men took extra Sharps rifles since Caleb and the men in Easton only had old flintlocks with them.

By 11:00 everyone was in position. William, Greene, and ten of the local Kansas Legion left to go to Easton.

Dunn had gathered all the deputies he could in Leavenworth but felt he did not have enough. Dunn's reputation had preceded him, and only twenty men would go with him, even at one dollar a day. So instead of riding directly to Pardee, he went to Kickapoo first to try and find more. Kickapoo was a reliably proslavery community, and he thought he could recruit some of the Kickapoo Rangers there. It was a short 30-minute ride, but it took a while to gather more men. By 9AM he had 20 more men, for a total of 40 and, felt ready. They set out for Pardee, expecting to be there in a few hours.

Blue Tail's oldest son, Muscotah, saw Dunn gathering men in the town square and listened to his speech, which was all about capturing that "damned abolitionist Caleb May."

He immediately headed out, well ahead of Dunn, on his strongest horse to warn his mother. He covered the 17 miles in less than two hours. He was stopped on the road before he got to Pardee by the town guards and when challenged he said, "I am Muscotah, son of Blue Tail, and I saw Sheriff Dunn recruiting deputies in Kickapoo to come here to arrest Caleb May. I want to warn my mother."

The guards ask him, "When did he leave Kickapoo? Are you sure he is coming here?"

Muscotah replied, "They said they were coming here, and they said they were going to invade Pardee. I don't know when they left, I left before they did and rode fast, I made it here in two hours or so. They are probably more than two hours behind me."

The guards said, "OK, follow us, we need to warn everyone. Your mother is staying with Pardee Butler."

The guards and Muscotah got to Pardee just after William and his men had left for Easton and spread the word that Dunn was coming and might arrive in less than two hours. They sent a messenger on a fast horse to bring William and the men back.

The messenger caught up with William in just a few minutes, "William! Dunn is headed to Pardee and will be there in two hours, maybe less, you need to go back."

William told him, "Oh good God! We got it wrong, thank you for riding down here and telling me."

Then, "Greene, please go to Easton and tell my Pa. We will go back to town. My Pa should probably come as well. Take my horse, you will get there faster with two horses."

Then William jumped behind one of his men and rode double back to Pardee.

As Greene was headed back to Easton, he saw Sam Moore and Elijah Smith heading north to Pardee, so he told them what was happening. Sam and Elijah were travelling slowly and enjoying the day, but once they got the news, they picked up the pace and got to Pardee as fast as they could.

In the meantime, William and his men had returned to Pardee and helped man the defenses. Their Captain, and all the Kansas Legion lieutenants were in Easton, but the men were well trained and knew what they had to do. All the blockhouses were manned and supplied, men in pairs, went to all the foxholes along all the roads, with plenty of supplies, and the women and children gathered in designated cabins and filled canteens and water bladders. They also made food packages and cartridges. They would need their leaders during the battle, but they knew what to do for now.

Muscotah told them, "Dunn only has 40 men, more or less, and Pardee has more than that."

Muscotah added, "Dunn will take the same route I did, it is the fastest way here from Kickapoo. He will enter Pardee on the east road."

William said, "That sounds right to me. Muscotah, will you come out on that road with me? I need eight others to join us. If he comes down that road, I will meet him and try to turn him around. I need men concealed on both sides of the road as backup in case they decide to fight it out."

Eight men volunteered without hesitation, even though William was only 16, the others treated him as their leader partially because he was Caleb's son, and partially because William was confident, a natural leader of men, and commanded respect.

William then said, "We will meet them, if all goes according to plan, about two miles east, the rest of you, who are not needed to guard the other roads, man the two east blockhouses and both sides of the east road. Remember, if you are on the road, let the men pass you, wait for the blockhouses to fire, then fire on Dunn and his men from behind

Dunn's posse **243**

them, like Pa taught us. We will be in the trees coming up behind them also, don't fire at us, Dunn's men will probably stay in the road."

With that, they took their places. They knew that Dunn could not be far away. William concealed himself just off the road and in front of one of the southern east road foxholes. Muscotah joined another man in his foxhole and the man looked startled, so Muscotah said, "What's the matter, never shared a foxhole with an Indian before?"

The man laughed, and said, "Well not lately. Don't hit me with your tomahawk!"

Muscotah had to laugh at that, and the tension was broken.

The man then asked, "Are you Blue Tail's boy?"

"Yes, sir, I am."

"We really like Blue Tail around here; she is a treasure."

"She is indeed."

Perhaps thirty minutes later, they see Dunn and his men riding toward Pardee. William waited until Dunn was only about 30 yards away and then stepped out onto the road. He held up his hand and told Dunn, "Halt! Why are you here and what do you want?"

Dunn reigned up, and said, "Aren't you William, Caleb May's boy?"

William replied, "Yes, I am, and I still have no taste for whiskey. You've taken quite a beating since we last saw each other. I hope you are feeling a little better."

William paused and then asked, "Why are you here?"

"Sorry about the whiskey in Missouri son. I'm sore and don't move as well as I once did, but I'm doing OK. Thank you for asking. We are here to look for your Pa, he escaped from the jail in Leavenworth. Is he here?"

"No, he is not in town. If you are here peacefully, and mean no harm, you are welcome. If you mean anyone any harm, you must turn around now and leave. We are well armed and well prepared; we will defend ourselves."

Dunn hesitated, he knew if there was any trouble, he would catch hell from Justice Lecompte. He said, "Young William, I mean no one any harm, not even your Pa, but he did escape from our jail, and I have a warrant for his arrest. I must search for him."

William thought about that for a minute, then said, "You may enter the town, but if there is any sign of trouble there will be a fight. Move slowly, and keep all weapons holstered, make no threatening moves."

All the men but Muscotah, came out of the woods on both sides of the road behind Dunn and his men, all with their Sharps prominently displayed. William led the way on foot. Muscotah, a very fit and accomplished runner, ran quickly to Pardee to tell everyone that Dunn was riding into town.

Muscotah reached town quickly and told the men in the blockhouse, "Dunn is coming; and they want to arrest Caleb. If they are quiet and leave their weapons holstered leave them alone; just watch them."

Caleb and his lieutenants had already met with Greene and were on their way back to Pardee. Caleb told his men, "I want to avoid trouble if possible and will stay out of town while Dunn is there."

So, about a mile from Pardee, he left the south road, and made his way through the woods on the south end of his property, leading his horse. He headed to a creek on the south end of his property where he had built a small shed for his farming equipment and hid there. It was surrounded on three sides with woods, with an opening to the north. He was armed with an old flintlock and his revolvers, he felt safe there.

Before he left, he told his men, "I appoint Sam Moore to take my place as captain. Follow him as you would me. He should already be in town."

In the meantime, Blue Tail told Maggie that Dunn was coming, and they were both concerned about Jim. They found him in the barn working on some furniture and told him that he should keep out of sight. It didn't matter if he was a runaway or not, as a black man he could always be kidnapped and sold. Maggie, told him, "I'm sure they will search the barn when they come, you can't be here then."

She gave Jim a revolver, one of the Sharps rifles they had in the house, some prepared cartridges, and a bladder of water and told him to go to the south end of the property and hide. Then she said, "If those men try and arrest or kidnap you, shoot them!"

Jim just replied, "Yes, ma'am. I will surely shoot them."

***

The men who came north with Caleb, went straight to Moore's blacksmith shop and told him he was in charge. Moore led the men to the town center. Dunn and his deputies were already there. As Moore and his men approached Dunn, they noticed Dunn's men had no drawn weapons and they were already surrounded by other members of the Legion.

Dunn had about 40 deputies with him, but when Moore and his men arrived, Dunn was surrounded by 60 well-armed residents of Pardee.

Everyone became quiet as they approached. Sam Moore spoke first, "Dunn, what are you doing here?"

The Sheriff responded, "Caleb May has broken out of jail, I'm here to take him into custody and back to jail. I have a warrant."

Moore said, "Sam Wood is a lawyer, he says that Caleb was denied arraignment and a bail hearing, which is a violation of the 6th amendment of the Constitution. Caleb had every right, under the law, to escape."

Dunn replied, "This argument is misplaced, I am not a judge, and this is not a court. I am a law officer serving an arrest warrant. Now, if Caleb May is here, send him out so I can arrest him, if he is not, I will move on and find him wherever he is."

"He is not here."

"May I see his house? I have a warrant to search for him there."

"Yes, I will take you."

Dunn dismounted and they walked the short distance to the May cabin and Sam Moore knocked on the door, which was opened by Maggie holding a Colt revolver. This was the stern Maggie, not the fun Maggie. She looked straight at Sam Moore and then straight at Dunn with anger flashing in her eyes. Then in her hard "Ma" voice she asked, "What do *you* want?"

The gun in her hand moved to Dunn and did not shake, it was steady as a rock.

Moore said, "Hello Mrs. Maggie, this is Sheriff Dunn. He wants to come in and make sure that Caleb isn't here."

Maggie said, with barely concealed anger, "I know who he is."

After a short pause, and without looking away, she lowered her revolver, stepped aside and said, "He may come in and look, but Caleb isn't here, and I do not expect him. If the Sheriff breaks anything he *will* pay for it."

She didn't say that last part as a question, so Moore wisely did not reply, but a small grin appeared briefly on his face. Moore turned to Dunn, regained his composure, and said, "You may search the house, but do not disturb anything. Mrs. Maggie will not tolerate it."

Maggie added, "We have no whiskey here Dunn, so don't look."

An intimidated Dunn sheepishly replied, "No ma'am."

Dunn walked in slowly and looked around the small cabin for a short time, then went to the barn and found no one there. He found no sign of Caleb.

Dunn left the farm, remounted his horse, and told his men, "He's not here men, we need to look elsewhere."

With that they all left and took the south road toward Easton.

Caleb had left the shed and climbed a tall tree, that was on his property, with a good view of his house. He saw Jim leave and was relieved at that. It looked like Jim was headed for the same shed that Caleb had gone to.

From where he was, he could not see any details, but he did see Dunn go into his house and barn and come out. He also saw Maggie, Mary, his other children, and Sam Moore outside. They all looked OK, which was a relief. He stayed in the tree until nightfall. He had not seen Dunn or any of his men all afternoon and assumed they had left for good.

He went to the tool shed and found Jim. As he approached the shed, he was careful and called out, so Jim knew it was him. Once they connected, they shook hands, and Jim said, "Welcome back Mr. Caleb! I'm really happy to see you!"

Caleb told Jim, "My God Jim, I'm glad to be back and to see you! I think we can go home now."

They returned to the house and Maggie and the kids. Caleb greeted everyone, kissed Maggie, and said, "How good to be home! My God, I'm glad to see you all, you look so good to me."

Maggie said, "Cale you don't look well. Are you OK?"

"I was in a small cell and got no exercise, I'm weak, but I think with activity and work I'll get better soon. I did manage to bathe in Easton, so at least I'm clean. The cell was filthy."

None of them were quite sure what they should do. Maggie told Caleb, "I insist you contact Sam Wood as soon as possible. We need to know what we can and cannot do."

Dunn had already left Pardee, he felt he had no choice. His main deputy, Samuel Salters, asked him, "Why are we leaving so soon? Why not stay and look around more."

Dunn replied, "I am sure Caleb is nearby but cannot risk doing anything to bring him out into the open. It will inflame the town, and probably cause a gunfight that we will clearly lose. The Governor and Justice Lecompte were clear, they do not want a war or any sort of conflict that will inevitably appear in the *New York Tribune* and all northern newspapers. My hands are tied."

Bill Phillips

Bill Phillips interviewed Sam Wood in Lawrence about the escape. Separately he also interviewed Caleb and Maggie about the imprisonment and escape. His series of articles in the *New York Tribune* about Caleb May and his imprisonment in Leavenworth had been a huge success and were reprinted in almost every paper in the country.

Sam Wood summarized the situation after the escape, "Caleb is assured of a speedy trial in the sixth amendment to the Constitution. The eighth amendment guarantees Caleb a reasonable bail. He has neither been arraigned nor had a bail hearing, and no grand jury has convened or considered the case. No man can be held in a jail for two months without being arraigned and formally informed of the charges against him. Caleb must have an opportunity to defend himself and face his accusers. In my view Caleb May had good reason to leave the jail, even though escaping jail is illegal."

Phillips replied, "But, what happens now? Caleb May is free, but he is still a wanted man."

"He is wanted by the bogus legislature, which does not represent most of the people of the territory, the legislature expelled all Free-State legislators, disenfranchising Caleb May, the town of Pardee, and thousands of other settlers. In our view, this invalidates Caleb May's arrest warrant. It isn't legal, it's political.

Further, as you know, and have reported, I've compiled considerable evidence that shows May could not have shot John Cook or Sheriff Dunn, and most of the goods stolen from John Stringfellow's barn were themselves stolen goods that were returned to their rightful owners by Caleb May, as the elected Town Marshall of Pardee, and his men. This includes the Russell, Majors & Waddell freighter wagon that was clearly marked. Why has none of this critical evidence been presented in court? It is because the Territorial Supreme Court and Justice Lecompte have illegally and unconstitutionally denied my client his day in court."

Phillips then said, "But, the legislature is the legal legislative body for the Territory."

Wood responds, "Not to me, and I would venture to say, not to the majority of the legitimate settlers in the Territory. Sheriff Dunn and Justice Lecompte can pursue this illegal and unconstitutional persecution of Caleb May if they want to, but they do so at their peril. Their best move would be to schedule a trial by jury of Caleb May for all the charges against him, and if the jury is allowed to have both Free-State and proslavery jurors, Mr. May and I will appear before the court. The current rule, based on the black laws passed by the bogus legislature, is that all jurors must be proslavery.[73] This rule must be waived for this trial, it must be fair and not political."

When Phillips interviewed Maggie, she said, "But, for now, my Caleb still has a warrant out for his arrest and the warrant is signed by Justice Lecompte of the Kansas Territorial Supreme Court."

Wood responded, "Yes, Ma'am."

All of Wood's comments were included in Phillips' dispatches to the *New York Tribune* and subsequently published. The anti-slavery citizens of the northern states were horrified at the injustice and the lack of due process. The proslavery citizens were equally horrified that Caleb May was free and that the town of Pardee was protecting him from what they considered an appropriate punishment for serious crimes.

***

David Atchison learned of the failure to recapture Caleb May and summoned Sheriff Dunn to his office. Dunn was worried about the meeting but had to go. Atchison had financed his construction business, loaned him money to buy land in Kansas, and arranged for him to be appointed Sheriff of the northern part of Kansas Territory. He literally owed Atchison for everything he had.

---

73 The so-called "black laws" had severe penalties for persons that interfered with slave "property," encouraged slaves to rebel, or spoke, wrote, or printed materials opposed to slavery. For any trial on these matters, jurors who were opposed to slavery were disqualified. In practice, all Free-State citizens were disqualified from serving on a jury in any trial of a fellow Free-State citizen. (Blackmar, 1912, p. 189)

Once he was seated in front of Atchison's spacious desk, Atchison wasted no time. He said, "This disgrace must end. I sent one of my agents to Pardee and he saw Caleb May walking around completely free, in the open, in broad daylight! He escaped from your jail, and you must find and arrest him and bring him to justice. Every day he is free is another insult to you, law and order, and Justice Lecompte."

"But Justice Lecompte does not want me to be overt or aggressive, he won't even let me shoot May. Governor Shannon is in complete agreement with him. There are daily articles on May in the *New York Tribune*! They consider him a hero and so do most of the country.

They also say they have proof he is innocent of shooting John Cook and me. I can assure you in confidence that in the battle at Pardee, he did not shoot me, I know the bullet that hit me did not come from his gun, I was looking right at him when I was hit. The bullet came from another direction. It also seems likely that he did not shoot me through the tent. As for John Cook, it is quite possible he did not shoot him. What I'm getting at is they have a case and Lecompte dare not bring it to trial. Lecompte is even afraid to have an arraignment, he believes that he would be forced to dismiss the case for lack of evidence by the prosecutor."

"I'm well aware of the views that Lecompte, Shannon, and the President have on the matter. They think they will lose the election in November if there is an all-out war in Kansas. They are not thinking this through or thinking long-term. If Kansas becomes a free state, thus surrounding Missouri on three sides, our slaves will not be worth a nickel apiece. We simply cannot afford to let Caleb May go unpunished under the laws the Kansas Territorial legislature passed last year. Those laws make helping slaves run away or writing about freeing slaves illegal. We need those laws. If Caleb May is free, we are admitting that those laws and the legal Kansas Legislature are illegitimate in the eyes of everyone in Kansas, hell, everyone in the country."

Atchison pulled out a large satchel and handed it to Dunn, "Here is five thousand dollars, go out and raise the largest posse you can. We will march on Pardee by the end of the week. I am going with you. We will capture Caleb May and burn the town to the ground. If you need more money, I will get it for you, but we must do this and do it decisively.

"What about the Governor? Lecompte? What about Colonel Sumner?"

"I will make sure that Sumner receives orders not to intervene in this political matter. As for the Governor and Lecompte, the less they know about this the better."

"Yes sir, I will gather a posse."

Once Dunn was gone, Atchison wrote a carefully worded letter to Secretary of War Jefferson Davis. He wrote: "A police action against Pardee is imminent, it will be strictly a police action and the involvement of the federal troops in Leavenworth is not warranted. The action is only to bring a fugitive to justice."

Chapter 9
War

Dunn recruited men, at a dollar a day in Leavenworth, Kickapoo, Platte City, and Weston. When done he had recruited 500 men but suspected only 200 or 300 would show up at his planned muster. The men had to supply their own horse or walk, and their own weapons. But they would be paid one dollar each day, at the end of each day. He planned to muster them in Kickapoo since it was closer to Pardee it had the Rively Trading Post which had everything they needed for the trip and the fight.

It was now Monday, July 28. He planned the muster for Friday, August 1. The attack would be on Saturday August 2.

Word of the plans and the impending attack reached Pardee immediately on Monday July 28th. Dunn's recruiting efforts had been anything but quiet, so word reached the Kickapoo Indians, and since nearly all of them were sympathetic with the Free-State Party and Caleb May, they sent a messenger to Blue Tail to tell her what was happening, and she told both Maggie and Sybil immediately. Once they told Caleb, he sent word to General Abbott and gave his opinion that the attack would be in less than a week, probably on Saturday. Then he met with his lieutenants and asked them if they thought the fight was worth it.

They all said the same thing. "You gave yourself up for trial, and got no trial, this time we fight."

Then he asked them what they needed for themselves and their men. The discussion that followed generated a lot of ideas, but they all required more men and weapons than they had. They expected to face at least 200 men, and they only had sixty. Caleb sent another message to General Abbott requesting 100 armed men.

General Abbott immediately called up his militia, he and Walker set out for Pardee with 70 men, two wagons of supplies, and a small cannon called "Old Sacramento"[74] on Wednesday morning. Bill Phillips, the reporter for the *New York Tribune* asked to accompany them and Abbott said, "Bill, there will be fighting, you might get hurt or killed, do you accept that risk?"

Phillips replied, "Yes sir."

"OK then you can come at your own risk. Will you at least accept a pocket Colt for protection?"

"OK, as long as I can conceal it. I'm a member of the press and should not be armed or fighting for either side."

Abbott, Phillips, and most of the men arrived Thursday afternoon, but the cannon was delayed. It was heavy and hard to move on the rough roads.

Once General Abbott arrived in Pardee, he was in charge, but it was Captain May's town, so he generally deferred to Caleb, who gave Abbott and Walker a tour of his preparations and his plan of defense. Caleb's idea was to have concealed men extending out more than two miles on either side of the road from Kickapoo. These men would not fire on the incoming posse until they heard firing from the blockhouses at the edge of town. Then they would launch a coordinated attack from the posse's rear and right and left flanks, essentially encircling the enemy. With any luck the battle would be over quickly. If the cannon arrived in time, it would be placed between the eastern blockhouses and fired first, straight down the center of the road.

Abbott said, "But what if Dunn doesn't concentrate all his forces on the one road, what if he attacks from multiple directions? That is what I would do. Besides, if Dunn's force is large, they will simply overrun the men in the foxholes and they become sitting ducks to be slaughtered. Your idea works against a small force, but not a large force."

Caleb responded, "He hasn't done that before, but if he does, we need to have some men on all the roads, we need an early warning. We have

---

74 Old Sacramento was a cannon captured from Mexico in the Mexican-American War. In early 1856 it was stolen by proslavery ruffians from the federal arsenal in Liberty, Missouri. Later it was stolen from the proslavery men by the Kansas Legion militia.

foxholes prepared on the other roads, but we will ask them to monitor all activities and report anything significant to us, but ask them not to fire or reveal themselves, except in self-defense. That way we get an advance warning from all roads. I think we should prepare for the primary attack on the main east road but have scouts on all roads. We will need to be ready to move quickly depending upon what Dunn does. Fortunately, Dunn is not known to have much imagination.

Plus, Dunn has always remained on the roads, he has never gone into the woods, except with scouts."

Abbott and Walker agreed, and the three of them quickly divided the duties and set out to position the men and weapons. Abbott and Walker had brought two wagons loaded with weapons, powder, and lead. These were unloaded and distributed. The women and older children knew immediately what to do and set about making bullets and cartridges for all the Sharps rifles and placing them in custom-made leather and cloth over-the-shoulder pouches for the men who would be fighting.

Abbott insisted on each man having a lot of cartridges. He personally inspected every pouch and every weapon to make sure the men were properly prepared. Abbott was very much a detail guy. He even thoroughly inspected Caleb's pouch and rifle.

Sam Moore and his men took up the same forward locations they had in the previous battle, near Dunn's last camp, a little less than two miles east of Pardee. Bill Phillips recorded all that was going on in his notebooks and made many sketches of the town, the people, and the preparations.

Dunn and Atchison Plan

It was Friday and Sheriff Dunn was riding toward Pardee with David Atchison and they discussed tactics and how to capture May. Dunn told Atchison about his last attempt. Dunn said, "My first mistake was to set up camp close to the Pardee Road ford over Stranger Creek. The idea was to have quick access to water and the road but in so doing, I wound up with a camp that was on low ground and nearly surrounded by thick woods. May's men took full advantage of these weaknesses, and their surprise attack led to my quick defeat. I have no intention of repeating that mistake.

The second problem was when I spread my men very thin by surrounding Pardee and forming a blockade. The men on blockade duty had no leader to form a counterattack after I was defeated in the main camp, so they just went home. This is another mistake I do not plan to repeat."

Atchison thought about this for a while, as they rode along quietly, then asked, "How should we attack them this time?"

Dunn said, "There are only three main roads to Pardee, one from the west and Monrovia, one from the south and Easton, and the one we are on, which comes from Kickapoo and Atchison. We need to attack Pardee from all three roads simultaneously. All the roads have blockhouses on them near the town, and we have no cannon, so I'm not sure how we get around the blockhouses. My spies also think there are foxholes along all the roads, which will allow them to attack our flanks and rear as we move on the town, another danger we must avoid."

Atchison noted, "Also, May's men are disciplined and well led. Ours are just collected off the streets, undisciplined and rough. I can lead one group; you will lead the attack along the east road. Who will lead the other attack?"

"Dawson is coming up from Easton on the south road and will meet us at the muster point later today. He will lead the attack on the south road. You will have the attack on the west road."

"Very well, once we are all together and ready to attack in the morning, I will address the men."

By 4PM, Dunn's men began to approach the muster point, which was a hilltop about a half mile south of his earlier camp on Stranger Creek. It was an open meadow, and easily defended. He would not be attacked from the surrounding woods this time.

***

When the men began to arrive and assemble on the hilltop, Sam Moore saw them and sent one of his men back to Pardee with the news. Sam planned to count the men and send hourly reports to Abbott and May. He asked his top man, "How many do you count? I only see 50."

"I see 50 also, but more must be on the way."

"I agree."

Caleb and Jim Abbott were gathered with some of their lieutenants and Captain Sam Walker outside of Caleb's cabin when Moore's first runner approached and told them that the first men had arrived and had started setting up a campsite. They expected more men soon and a runner would be sent out every hour with updates. They immediately sent out runners to all the lieutenants on guard duty that the men had started to arrive, and they predicted an attack or attacks in the morning.

In the early evening, Old Sacramento, the only Free-State cannon arrived in Pardee and was set up between the two eastern blockhouses, facing east.

***

In the growing proslavery camp, Dunn and Atchison pitched their tent and began planning their attack. They also sent men out to scout the western, southern, and eastern roads to Pardee. Dunn had learned a lot in his earlier battle, he did not intend to fail this time. Atchison was a former major general in Missouri's Mormon War. The Mormon War was in 1838, and it was brutal.[75]

When their scouts reported back to Dunn and Atchison, they told them about the cannon and the blockhouses. They also suspected concealed men were along all the roads, but they didn't know how many. In total, they thought Pardee had at least 100 men in arms. They had seen General Abbott, so Dunn and Atchison knew the Kansas Legion from Lawrence were involved.

After some thought Atchison said, "The cannon and the blockhouses preclude a direct assault down the east road, they would slaughter us. We need another way in."

He turned to the spies, "Do the block houses have gun ports on all sides? Or only in the front facing down the roads?"

---

[75] In 1836 continuous fighting between the Mormons in Missouri and the other settlers convinced the government that the Mormons and the other Missourians could not live side-by-side. Much of the conflict was caused because the Mormons always voted as a block as they were ordered to by their leader. In the eyes of the other settlers this distorted the Missouri democracy and gave the Mormon leadership too much power over everyone.

The state government created a new county, called Caldwell, and ordered all the Mormons to move into it. Rapid immigration of more Mormons quickly overflowed the county, and the problems resumed. So, in 1838 and 1839 Atchison drove all the Mormons out of Missouri.

The spies said, "They have ports on three sides, no ports directly face the town, only the doors."

Atchison asked them, "Are there two blockhouses for every road?"

The spies answered, "There are two on the west and east roads, only one at the head of the north and south roads. The north road is not much of a road and is not used often."

Atchison then said, mostly to himself, "And only one cannon, and that cannon is facing the east road. I need to think about this and look at the roads myself."

Atchison then left and looked at the east road blockhouses, then went north to the north road blockhouse. The north road had a creek with steep banks and a lot of cover all along its west side. The road was rough, as the spies reported, but serviceable. He said to himself "This is the perfect place for my main attack."

He returned to camp after sunset and told Dunn about his decision. After discussing the situation, Dunn said, "I will check this out, the west road is too well defended to be an option, and Dawson will attack along the south road."

***

Nearly all the men they expected arrived at the muster location by sunset, including Dawson and his men from Easton. In addition, John Stringfellow brought about twenty men from Atchison. In all they had just over 200 men, many were indifferently armed, but they were all armed.

The men "found" three cows. They had no idea who they belonged to, but they slaughtered them and the cooks that Dunn had hired in Kickapoo made a nice beef stew and everyone was fed. Then Dunn brought out some whiskey and they began drinking and singing, it went on late into the night until everyone fell asleep.

***

Sam Moore and his men watched the activities in Dunn and Atchison's camp with interest, in shifts while reporting back to Abbott, Walker, and May hourly. Their count of the men came to 215, not counting the cooks and camp followers. Abbott and May decided they did not know how Dunn would attack, but they were pretty sure it would come tomorrow, they turned in and got some sleep.

The next morning everyone was up early, they ate, drank their coffee, and took their stations. Caleb told Maggie that he needed to take William to the fight. He left her with her pocket Colt, a Colt Navy revolver, and the shotgun, and asked, "Will that be enough? We are set back from the south road and the blockhouse is between here and the road."

Maggie noticed Caleb's worried expression and said, "Yes, Caleb, we will be fine. Mary and I shoot well, and Enoch is coming along. Sybil, Blue Tail, and Muscotah are close. Jim is here, he also has a pocket Colt and a Sharps. Don't worry about us, just drive those ruffians off."

Caleb was still worried but uplifted a little by Maggie's bravery. Maggie was concerned for her family and wanted Caleb to stay home but knew he could not. Her immediate concern was to alleviate his fear and worry about them. She wanted him to go with a clear head and clear conscience.

Sam Moore and his men monitored all the activity at the proslavery camp carefully. The men there did not get up and jump out of their bed rolls quite as quickly as the men in Pardee.

***

Dunn and Atchison got all the men up and assembled, Atchison stood before them and spoke.

"Gentlemen, Officers & Soldiers! - This is the most glorious day of my life! This is the day I am a border ruffian! The Sheriff has just given you his orders and has kindly invited me to address you. ... You have endured many hardships, have suffered many privations on your trips, but for this you will be more than compensated by the work laid out by the Sheriff, - and what you know is to be done as the programme of the day. Now boys, let your work be well done! Faint not as you approach the city of Pardee, but remembering your mission, act with true Southern heroism. At the word, spring like your bloodhounds at home upon that damned accursed abolition hole; break through everything that may oppose your never flinching courage! Yes, ruffians, draw your revolvers & bowie knives, & cool them in the heart's blood of all those damned dogs, that dare defend that damned breathing hole of hell. Tear down their blockhouses. Mr. Dunn is not only Sheriff, but deputy Marshal, so that whatever he commands will be right, and under the authority of the administration of the U. S.! - and for it you will be amply paid, besides having an opportunity of benefiting your wardrobes from the private dwellings of these infernal slave-stealers. Courage for a few hours & the victory is ours, falter & all is lost! - Are you determined? Will every one of you swear to bathe your steel in the black blood of some of those black sons of bitches."[76]

That morning, before breakfast, Dunn and Atchison had ridden to survey the east, south, and north roads out of Pardee and carefully examined all the maps that Atchison's spies had made. They decided Atchison's idea that the main attack should be down the north road was best. It was the least defended.

In order for the plan to work optimally, an attack down the east road was needed as a diversion. Both attacks would be mainly from off the road where cover was available. Atchison would lead the main attack down the north road, well after Dunn had attacked down the east road. Dawson would attack up the south road with a small force, just to make sure that defenders would remain in the south road blockhouse and not available to help defend the north road.

There would be no attack along the well-defended west road. They decided that May and Abbott would post men there anyway, just in case.

Atchison had a plan to take out the blockhouses. They had their men prepare some wagons loaded with hay that they stole from the farms around their camp. These were driven as close to the blockhouses as they could get safely and prepared to be pushed to the blockhouses and set afire. Dunn and Atchison had learned that the Kansas Legion militia would normally not fire unless the target was less than 200 yards away, so they would remain beyond that as long as possible. Atchison did not have to contend with a cannon on the north road and he only had one blockhouse to deal with.

The movement of proslavery men toward the east and south roads was reported accurately by the Legion scouts in the foxholes, but they missed Atchison and his men heading toward the north road because the men took a long route, first going very far north to Camp Creek, then west to the north road before turning south toward Pardee. In this way they didn't pass any of the men in the eastern foxholes until the attack was under way. This was important for Atchison because he want-

---

[76] Fictionalized from a speech given by Atchison, as recorded by (Root, 1856).

ed the attacks from the east and from the south to be well underway before he advanced. His plan was to simultaneously advance in two parallel attacks, one straight down the north road to the blockhouse and the second down the creek bed to the west of the road.

The diversionary attack on the east road, led by Dunn, was first, then 15 minutes later Dawson's men attacked from the south. Dunn placed his men both on the road and off both sides of the road in the woods and tall grass and they advanced carefully under cover but did not fire. Dunn's first overt action was carried out by twelve men, pushing two wagons loaded with hay down the road as fast as they could go toward the blockhouses. Once they were in range of the guns from the blockhouses, the concealed men on both sides of the road and those in the road opened fire on the blockhouse to cover for them.

Old Sacramento

This was all seen by Caleb, who was in the blockhouse south of the east road, and his men. He yelled out to the cannoneer, Ottawa Jones, and told him to fire on the wagons.

Jones was an educated Chippewa Indian with a British father, who had been adopted into the Ottawa tribe, which was the origin of his nickname "Ottawa." John Tecumseh Jones, or "Tauy" Jones, was married to Jane Kelly, a woman from New England, and ran a successful trading post on the Marais des Cygnes River in eastern Kansas. He was respected throughout the territory, active in Free-State politics, and a member of the Kansas Legion.

Jones lined up the cannon, which was already loaded with a six-pound (3.5 inch) cannonball. Jones had an eye for range and was an experienced cannoneer. He touched off the shot, which landed just in front of one of the wagons, bounced once, and put a large hole in it. Jones and his men quickly reloaded the cannon, but by the time they were ready the second wagon had already been pushed up against the northern blockhouse and the men were setting the hay on fire.

The men in the foxholes remained hidden until all of Dunn's men passed their foxholes, then they popped up and fired at the advancing men they could see, they hit many and caused a lot of confusion and panic at the rear. Each time a pair of men from the foxholes fired, the proslavery invaders panicked and ran away from them.

As they had been trained to do, after firing a few shots and panicking the enemy, they retreated into the woods. Remaining in the foxholes would just make them easy targets. Once in the woods they kept on the move and made their way back to the town. The proslavery invaders eventually regrouped and came back to attack the foxholes but found them empty.

Caleb was in the southern blockhouse and firing at the men setting fire to the hay in the wagon pushed up against the northern blockhouse, he hit one who went down, but the others kept at it and set the hay burning, then they dropped to the ground and hid in the tall grass at the edge of the road, several of them drew revolvers and fired at both blockhouses. More proslavery men rushed up both sides of the road to help them. Fortunately, many of the proslavery raiders in the back of the columns were busy with the foxholes and there were fewer men attacking the blockhouses than Dunn had planned on.

Caleb quickly noticed there were not nearly the number of attackers they expected. He had been afraid for the men in the foxholes, they could have easily been overwhelmed by the invaders and become sitting ducks, but in this case, they were effective, they panicked the proslavery rear and severely blunted their attack

The first wagon, the one that took the cannonball, was not entirely out of commission and men were still pushing it down the road. While it had a large hole in it and it had lost a lot of hay, it was still moving, at least it was until Ottawa Jones put another cannon ball right through it, which effectively split it into two pieces, breaking the back axle. The cannonball also took out one of the men pushing the wagon.

By then the northern blockhouse was fully on fire and the men in it had to run. Some ran back toward the town and others tried to run to the southern blockhouse where Caleb was. Two were shot by the proslavery forces that were trying to group around the burning blockhouse. Abbott had been in the northern blockhouse but was forced to abandon it with the others when it caught fire. He ran out and took cover behind a large tree with bullets crashing all around him. He turned his Sharps on the invaders and shot one clean through his chest, quickly reloaded and shot another. Abbott's accurate fire, the fire from several other Free-State fighters as they abandoned the burning blockhouse, and Caleb killing another invader, stopped the proslavery advance on the north side of the east road. Abbott quit firing and began to look around to see what was going on, he needed the big picture. "Why so few men on the east road?" he asked himself out loud.

Runners had arrived from the foxholes and reported fighting on the south and north roads, he asked, "Where is the main attack? Does anyone know? It isn't here."

He quickly ran over to the south blockhouse, there was a lull in the fighting due to the casualties and time required to reload. He found both Walker and Caleb, and said, "Caleb, can you check the north road and Walker the south road? I have no reports of fighting on the west road. This is clearly not the major advance, one of the other roads must be the main attack, we need to get the cannon to wherever it is."

Caleb and Walker immediately set out to check. Fortunately, none of the proslavery advances made it into the town interior and they could move freely. Walker made a quick detour to the May cabin to make sure they were OK. He knocked on the door and Maggie opened it holding her pocket Colt, both Mary and Jim were behind her, both holding full-sized Navy Colts. Walker smiled and said, "I'm sure glad I'm not a proslavery invader!"

Both Maggie, Jim, and Mary laughed, and Maggie said, "You are fortunate indeed! Welcome Mr. Walker."

Walker looked around and didn't see any danger, but he could hear the fighting down the south road and behind him, both north and east. He said, "I'm just here to check on you for Caleb and William, are you all OK? Do you need anything?"

Maggie caught him up to date, "We are fine, no attacks here or at Pardee's house. Mary, Jim, Enoch, and I are armed and watching all directions to the house. Over at Pardee's, Sybil, Rosetta, Blue Tail, and Blue Tail's son, Muscotah are watching all four directions also. They are fine. Pardee has gone with William to help at the south road blockhouse. Last I heard that attack was not a big deal. Pardee and William think it is only diversion"

"Good, that is what General Abbott wants me to find out. We are holding them off on the East Road and they are taking heavy casualties, we have a few wounded, but no serious wounds yet. We need to know where the big attack is coming from, if it isn't here on the south road or on the east road, it must be down the north road. Our scouts have seen no activity on the west road. Glad you are OK, I need to go to the blockhouse and check on things there, and report back."

After he left Maggie told Mary, "He is a good-hearted man."

Mary replied, "He is indeed, but he looks no older than William!" Then she giggled. Maggie just smiled.

Walker left the May cabin and headed south to the blockhouse on the south road. Mary ran over to the Butler cabin to tell them the news.

Walker was spotted well before he got to the blockhouse by the Kansas Legion soldiers who quickly opened the back door to let him in. Some of the men were at the south wall firing occasionally through the gun ports, but William and Pardee were only observing and looking out their gun ports. William explained, "We were attacked about an hour ago, but only by a small force, perhaps 25 men, indifferently armed and not very aggressive. They aren't hitting anything, sometimes not even the blockhouse. They appear to be a diversion and seem to know their only job is to keep us pinned down here.

We have no injuries, and we have hit at least two of their men. I don't think we killed or seriously injured either of them, our men are only shooting when good opportunities arise. If you need more men up north, we can easily spare four and still defend this position."

Walker replied, "Good. I checked on your Ma, and she is fine. Pardee, she said your house was fine, Blue Tail and her son are there helping. William, Jim, Enoch, Mary, and your Ma are guarding your house."

William responded, "I pity any proslavery invader that tries to attack those houses!"

Walker and Pardee both laughed, Walker said, "I'd rather face Caleb in a fight!"

Everyone laughed at that. Then Walker said, "Pardee, if you can help hold this blockhouse, can William and three others come with me?"

Pardee said, "Sure, this attack isn't bad, I'll stay here. We can keep them busy. We'll come north if they withdraw."

With that, William, Walker and three others carefully made their way north, as Pardee and the men left in the blockhouse stepped up their firing to keep the proslavery attackers busy. They quickly made their way to the southern blockhouse on the east road, the northern blockhouse was a smoldering ruin and unusable. The cannon had been moved to the center of town.

The attack

General Abbott was waiting for them at the rear door to the blockhouse. He said, "The main attack is from the north along the north road, Caleb is there already, we need to move all the men we can spare up there and get the cannon up there. There seems to be no activity on the west road, but we are keeping a small guard force there just in case. Can both of you come with me to the north road blockhouse? Caleb, Elijah, Sam Moore, Milo, and Bill Wakefield are already there, we need to plan a counterattack as soon as possible."

William grabbed his new Sharps rifle and said, "OK, let's go."

They immediately walked back into town and helped push the heavy cannon and its supply wagon up the north road. William had inherited his father's sharp eyes and spotted some activity to the west of the north road, across from the blockhouse. He knew these invaders had not been spotted from the blockhouse because the only firing from it was from the north side, none from the west side. He stepped away from the cannon, estimated the range to be about 250 yards, and took careful aim at the man he saw, and fired. A red mist appeared around his head, and he fell. Almost immediately, a flame arose where the man fell. This was followed by furious firing from the area where the man fell toward the blockhouse, which was quickly returned.

Abbott yelled, "Wow! Outstanding shot William. I don't know how you did that from here, but we can move the cannon up there ourselves. You can run ahead; they need you more than we do. It looks like the proslavery attackers are trying to set fire to the blockhouse with something."

Abbott quickly looked around and found two horses. He quickly hitched one to the cannon and the other to the supply wagon to help them pull them faster. He shouted, "They really need this cannon men!"

William looked around carefully and then picked his way north to the blockhouse. There was a lot more fighting going on up there than he had seen anywhere else. He heard a shot from his right, and dove for the ground. His sharp eyes spotted movement to the east of the blockhouse, which was an open meadow with a few trees. He saw a man climbing a tree with a satchel, not 50 yards from the blockhouse. He's up to no good, William thought. He took careful aim, this shot was less than 200 yards, and fired. The man and his satchel fell out of the tree.

William looked around. He was lying on the ground, and hard to hit, but he was in the open on the east side of the road and felt vulnerable. He spotted several more men near the same tree, they were gathered over the fallen man. No fire from that side of the blockhouse yet, so they had not been spotted. William rolled to his side, put another cartridge from his pouch into the breach of his Sharps rifle, took careful aim at the closest man and fired. The man screamed and fell, and his companions began firing at the blockhouse. The proslavery attackers hadn't seen William yet, so he quickly reloaded and fired again, another man fell. Then there was furious firing from the blockhouse on that side and all went quiet. Firing continued on the west side as well, so William saw his opportunity, rose off the ground quickly, and ran to the blockhouse. With a father's intuition, Caleb saw him and opened the door so William was able to run straight in without slowing down.

Caleb hugged his son and asked, "Are you hit? Are you OK?"

William said, "No, I'm fine, but we must cover for Walker and Abbott. They are bringing up the cannon and cannon balls with some other men."

Caleb asked, "William, did you just shoot four men on the way here? Because we sure didn't shoot them."

William just said, "Yes sir."

Sam Moore yelled, "Way to go son! I think you saved us from being burned out." The other men in the blockhouse cheered William, and he turned red in the face, which caused more cheering. Then everyone quickly got back to work.

Caleb smiled at his son and swelled up a little with pride, then he looked down the road and saw Abbott, Walker and the others struggling with the cannon and the wagon of powder and cannonballs behind it. Then he said, "Men! Fire at anything that moves on either side of the blockhouse, we must get that cannon and wagon of supplies up here."

They had no gunports on the back of the blockhouse, so he opened the door and he and William posted themselves on either side of it and looked for targets. It only took William a few seconds to see men sneaking past the blockhouse on the west side of the road, he immediately took aim and shot the lead man, who screamed and fell. The west side of the north road was thickly wooded and contained a stream with steep banks on both sides. The gully was deep enough to hide a full-grown man. The east side of the road was more open, and the nearest woods offering concealment were one hundred yards from the road. William knew all this from his teenage explorations. He pointed this out to Caleb and said, "There could be 50 men in that ditch, and we couldn't see them. Their logical attack is down that streambank."

Caleb said, "Yes, and our counterattack will need to be up that stream, but we need to watch both sides. I've pulled all the men from the foxholes, so we have no spies to tell us what is going on."

Caleb, announced to the men in the blockhouse, "Men, double up on the west wall, but we need men on the north and east as well. Keep sharp."

William and Caleb kept up the fire on both sides of the road to the south as Abbott, Walker, and the men helping them, brought up the cannon. Abbott and his men were moving quicker with the horses helping them.

**

By the time Atchison assembled his 130 men on the north road, south of Stranger Creek, and about 1,000 yards north of Pardee, the attacks from the east and south had already started. He told his second in command, "I like attacking from this direction because there is only one blockhouse, it has thick woods, and that deep gully. Perfect protection for my troops as they advance into Pardee."

He sent some men down the side of the road to fire at the front of the blockhouse, as well as a wagon loaded with hay. They kept the men in the blockhouse busy, while he sent his main force down the streambank to enter the town under cover. He told them to advance slowly and not to fire from the streambank, if there was need to fire, leave the stream and move closer to the road. Atchison told them, "Don't help the enemy find you. We must surprise them."

**

With the horse's help, the cannon was nearly at the blockhouse when the wagon loaded with hay approached it. The men in the blockhouse

The attack

kept firing at the wagon, but the men pushing it were well concealed and it was hard to pick out a target. Abbott and Ottawa Jones quickly unhitched the horse, rotated the cannon so they could aim it at the wagon, and fired. The cannonball went right through the wagon about chest high and hit one of the men, killing him instantly and spreading hay in every direction. The other men pushing the wagon scattered in all directions, Bill Wakefield and Sam Moore each hit one of the scattering men. The wagon sat in the middle of the road unattended.

Abbott and Walker came into the blockhouse and asked Caleb for the status. Caleb answered, "We have a big fight on our hands, but only two casualties that I know of yet. We've probably killed or wounded at least twelve of their men. The real threat is from the streambed to the west, we've seen a lot of men coming from the streambed or maybe firing from there. I think the main advance will be along that bank, as William said fifty men could come up that streambed and we wouldn't see them. We need to attack them in it."

Abbott looked to the west and saw what Caleb meant. He said, "OK I will organize a force. Sam Moore and Elijah Smith, you live up here, take your men and set up a defense along that creek in the woods. Keep them from entering the town through it. Bill Wakefield and Andy Elliott, take some men and go back in town and check on the west road, especially near where this creek crosses it. They might go all the way down the creek and come out on the west road."

Everyone said, "Yes sir." And took off to accomplish their duties.

Sam Moore's cabin sat between the creek and the north road, so he and Elijah, positioned their men along the eastern side of the creek between the north road blockhouse and Sam's cabin, which was between Pardee and the blockhouse. Then they headed to the cabin, where Sam spoke to his wife, "Honey, we think the proslavery men are coming up the creek bed, you should take the kids and go into town, you will be safer."

His wife had a revolver strapped to her waist and was carrying a double-barreled shotgun. She started to protest, but then listened to the gunfire from the north, and realized Sam was right. She composed herself, then said, "I don't like leaving Sam, but I need to for Caroline and Michael."

Sam said, "I love you and I love Caroline and Michael, thank you for doing this, I couldn't live if anything happened to the three of you."

She said nothing in response, just kissed Sam briefly and then silently gathered a few things and their savings to load into their buggy and then she, Caroline and Michael boarded it and left for town. He and Elijah watched them go, then Elijah said, "She was not happy about that."

Sam said, "No she was not, but she and the kids need to stay safe, they are my whole life. OK, we need to work our way north, along the creek bed. If it is clear, fine, if not we clear it."

Elijah merely said, "Yes sir."

Sam and Elijah walked to the creekbank and then began working their way north along it. As they met their men, they ask them to come with them. Once they had all four men, Elijah took two of them and crossed the creek, so they covered both sides. They were near the blockhouse when they heard movement and took cover, rifles at the ready. The noise was getting louder, so they knew the men they were hearing were moving toward them.

Suddenly, proslavery men rounded a bend in the creek, with their identities certain, Sam, Elijah and their men opened fire and killed or wounded several of them, the survivors retreated around the bend, took cover, and began firing back. Sam sent one of his men to the blockhouse to get more men and began firing at anyone that moved. But there were too many and they had to fall back. They moved back quickly, stopping to reload and fire when they could.

Sam told his runner, "Tell Abbott and Caleb that we have engaged a large force in the creek bed. We need that damned cannon!"

The runner made it to the blockhouse quickly since it was only about 100 yards from their position. By the time they got there, the sound of the shooting had alerted Abbott, he immediately sent Caleb with most of his men to the fight. But they only had ten extra men, and it was not enough. The proslavery force was large, and very soon Caleb, Sam and their men were retreating down the creek bed toward Pardee.

They were close enough that Abbott could see what was happening, but he needed men in the blockhouse. He sent runners to the other blockhouses requesting men. Elijah and a few others were wounded, Elijah was shot in the upper right arm, but the bullet just passed through the flesh of his arm, without breaking the bone, and he was able to bandage it and continue fighting, but two of the men shot had more serious injuries.

The attack

The proslavery attackers had much heavier casualties, Abbott didn't know how many, but then he wasn't sure how many there were to start with, he had estimated 215, but was that right? His only advantage was that the proslavery attackers were concentrated in a long line in the creek bed.

Dunn and Atchison were able to focus nearly all their men into one attack, but they could not maneuver. Abbott still had to split his smaller force to cover at least three entrances to town, if not four. He just didn't have the resources he needed.

Sam Moore, Elijah Smith, and Caleb continued to retreat southward toward town, but did it in an orderly fashion and inflicted heavy casualties on the invaders. Caleb tried to estimate their numbers, but other than counting over 50 he really didn't know. He tried to position his men along the streambed, on both sides so each man had a clear line of fire, he told them, "Mind your hind sights men, too many shots are going over their heads!"

Every time they thought they had the proslavery advance stopped; more men appeared and drove them back farther. In the meantime, a new assault was forming at the blockhouse, and Abbott was pinned down there. Eventually, a new wagon of hay started down the road toward them. Ottawa Jones and two of his men left the blockhouse to fire on the wagon, but Ottawa was shot in the left chest and had to crawl back to the blockhouse. His men successfully loaded the cannon but did not aim well and fired the cannonball clear over the wagon and it bounced harmlessly down the road. The wagon kept coming until it was pushed against the blockhouse, then the invaders successfully set the hay on fire with a match and gunpowder. Almost immediately the blockhouse caught fire and Abbott, and his men had to abandon it.

They fled down the western side of the road where there was more cover and received fire from the north of the blockhouse and from the creek bed to the west. But they managed to take cover and return fire. They were over five-hundred yards north of the other Free-State fighters, but behind many of the proslavery men. The blockhouse burned furiously, but they managed to find concealed positions and harassed the proslavery men in the creek from an elevated position. Abbott divided his force into two units, one to harass and follow the men in the streambed to the south of them and one to hold off the men coming from behind the blockhouse to the north. Fortunately, they had good cover in the thick woods surrounding the creek bed and remembered to bring all their ammunition with them.

The men in the creek bed had to climb the gully walls to get cover, as they did that it turned into a very bloody shooting gallery. The proslavery attack along the creek bed depended completely upon surprise to be successful. When they were discovered, their position became a liability.

Abbott, Walker, and their men mercilessly shot everyone they could see, killing over a dozen men in the creek. Simultaneously they were able to keep the men to the north at a distance. Once the massacre was over, they began to follow the proslavery men as they headed south and harassed them mercilessly from the rear. The proslavery men that did make it out of the creek, started shooting across the creek at Abbott and his men. The battle was furious, both to the north and to the west, but miraculously, except for Ottawa Jones, no other Free-State men were hit.

Jones' wound did not appear to be serious or critical, although it was painful. The ball or bullet bounced off a rib and went on through and then out of the skin. Abbott got him to a secure and well protected location in the woods, and said, "Tauy, I need to take care of that, or you'll never make it out of here."

Jones, said, "Yes, sir, I'm ready."

Abbott got his shirt off and cleaned the wound using water from his canteen and a towel he had in his pack, then he sprinkled some gunpowder on the wound, and lit it with a match. Tauy Jones, grimaced, but did not yell out. Then Abbott wrapped a towel around Jones chest tightly and secured it with a belt. Finally, he put Tauy's shirt back on him and asked him how he felt.

Ottawa Jones was in a lot of pain, but said, "I feel better, the belt keeps my rib steady. I think it was cracked by the bullet. I can walk, I think."

With that he stood and hobbled after Abbott.

Even though Abbott, Walker, and their men were north of most of the proslavery invaders and the other Free-State men were in front defending the town, the proslavery men continued to advance. The forward group was less than 200 yards from the edge of the town and near Sam Moore's now abandoned cabin.

A group of them left the creek bed and using gunpowder and hay from Moore's barn they set the cabin on fire along with his neighbor's cabin, which had also been abandoned. The closer the proslavery invaders got to the town, the more Free-State men joined the defense, as Bill Wakefield, Andy Elliott and their men moved to defend the town from the north road attack, which was mostly in the creek bed.

Abbott noticed that the shooting from the far north died to nothing, but he was too busy to think about it. His rear-guard men came up to join him in harassing the rear of the proslavery forces in the creek and along the north road.

While Abbott's forces effectively surrounded the proslavery invaders and were causing high casualties, the proslavery fighters had the advantage of a lot of cover and superior numbers.

***

Atchison and Dunn met well north of the now destroyed north road blockhouse, and Dunn said, "Our primary job is to get Caleb May, and his cabin is south of the town. This battle is likely lost. Dawson still has men south of town, but isn't doing much, I think we need to move south, relieve Dawson, and launch a separate attack from there straight to May's cabin."

Atchison agreed, and immediately turned over the north attack to a lieutenant, as he and Dunn gathered up 25 mounted men and rode two miles east to Pardee Road, then south past Pardee and back west to the south road where Dawson and his men were. Dawson's men had stopped firing at the blockhouse and were just watching it. At this point the blockhouse only contained Pardee Butler and three other men, everyone else had gone north to fight and drive out the invaders.

The south blockhouse was a little over a quarter mile south of Caleb's cabin and located near the western edge of his farm. The area was open, with little cover. Atchison and Dunn's men had brought a wagon of hay with them. They unhitched the horses, turned it around and began to push it north toward the blockhouse. Pardee saw this, and said, "They mean to burn us out men, be sharp, try to hit them as they show themselves."

Every time one of the men behind the wagon stuck his head up or around the hay, they fired but hit no one. The invaders quickly pushed the wagon right up to the block house, scattered some gunpowder on the hay and lit it. The dry hay caught quickly and soon the whole blockhouse was in flames and Pardee and his men had to abandon it. They ran to the north, toward Caleb's cabin, turning to fire on their attackers as they could. One of Pardee's men was shot in the back and fell, Pardee stopped to check him briefly and was sure he was dead. He said a quick prayer for him and then ran for the May cabin.

He and his two remaining men made it to Caleb's cabin and Maggie let Pardee in. Maggie had her pocket Colt, Mary still had her heavy Navy Colt, and little 10-year Enoch had the shotgun. Jim had his small Pocket Colt revolver and a Sharps (a gift from Caleb) with him. He left the house and joined the three men behind the house.

Pardee stayed inside, but the other men took defensive positions around the cabin. Dunn, Atchison, and their men were mounted and rode up to the front of the house with their arms in hand, but not firing them, and demanded that everyone come outside.

Maggie and Pardee looked at each other. Maggie asked, "Should we fight?"

Pardee said, "I don't think we can, there are too many."

Dunn and Atchison had 25 mounted and armed men; the situation was hopeless. Pardee's men and Jim had their weapons ready but did not fire. Dunn and Atchison's men moved to surround the house and just stood at the ready, they knew they controlled the situation. Atchison spotted Jim and shouted "What is that black man doing here? Did you run away boy?"

Jim replied, "I am a free man, I work for Mr. Caleb."

Both Maggie and Pardee confirmed this. Maggie said, "He has worked on this farm for 50 cents a day, plus room and three meals for a long time. He is a skilled carpenter and a free man."

Atchison replied, "Well we'll see about that. We'll take him back to Missouri and find out who he ran away from. Won't take long."

Then he told Maggie, Pardee, Jim and everyone to put their guns on the ground, which they did. Jim had a Pocket Colt in his pocket and left it there, miraculously no one noticed it or searched him, he laid his Sharps on the ground.

Muscotah and Blue Tail heard the activity over at the May cabin and Muscotah immediately ran to the center of town to look for help. They didn't have enough guns to take on Atchison and Dunn themselves.

***

The attack

Fighting was still going on in Pardee, but the attackers never got closer than the edge of the town. At this point, every available man, woman, and child over 15 years old were actively defending the town. The residents had all taken cover and were firing with precision. Enough had joined the fight and now they outnumbered the remaining proslavery attackers north of town, the attackers could make no progress. They stalled at first and then began to retreat.

Everyone in town was either shooting, making bullets, or preparing cartridges. Ottawa Jones had regained some mobility, and with help and a strong horse, he positioned his cannon so it would shoot cannonballs down the creek bed. These deadly shots bounced their way down the steep-sided gully like a giant pinball, dismembering or killing all men it hit. The cannonballs were terrifying and drove every one of the invaders out of the creek. Once out of the creek and the dense surrounding wood they were easy targets for the Kansas Legion.

The creek was now owned by Ottawa Jones and his Old Sacramento cannon. Besides directly killing several of the invader's, the cannonballs removed all the cover initially enjoyed by the attackers. The casualties on the proslavery side were devastating and the invaders, who survived, began to desert. That battle appeared to be won, and the town was saved. The wounded Ottawa Jones was in pain but enjoyed being hailed as a hero. He pumped his fist in the air and gave an Indian war whoop with every cannon shot. He was gratified that he still had cannonballs and powder in his supply wagon.

Just as the battle was being won, Muscotah found Caleb and told him what was happening at his cabin. Caleb's expression turned hard and fierce as he asked, "How many?"

"About 25. They are mounted and have surrounded your house."

Caleb set about gathering some men.

Maggie

Atchison gathered everyone in front of the house and sent a man to search the house to make sure no one was left inside. He put the family and Pardee's men under guard and took all the weapons from the ground.

Maggie and all her children, Mary, Enoch, Priscila, Sam, Catherine, and baby Isaac, plus Jim, Pardee and his three men, were kept together in a small circle about 10 yards west of the house, Atchison assigned two men to guard them.

Dunn approached the group and asked, "Mrs. May, where is your husband, Caleb? I have an arrest warrant for him."

She replied, "He isn't here and I'm not sure where he is."

Dunn returned to the house and conferred with Atchison briefly, then turned to his men and ordered, "Fire the house!"

Two men dismounted and went to the barn to get some hay, stacked it against the house, sprinkled gunpowder on it and lit a match, then looked up at Dunn."

Maggie yelled, "Wait, wait! Can I go in and get a few things before you burn the house down? Please?"

Dunn hesitated briefly, then said, "OK, you have two minutes, go in and get what you need to save."

Dunn's man dropped his match and stepped on it. Maggie went into the cabin and retrieved the box with their money, their records, and important letters, her hat pin, and a small gold locket and chain that had a picture of her and Caleb in it, then came back out of the house, well within the two-minute limit.

Dunn watched her rejoin her family and said, "Go ahead, torch it."

The man lit a new match and threw it into the hay, and it began burning quickly. Very soon after that, the log walls on the cabin caught fire. Maggie and her children began crying at their loss. Pardee, Jim, and the Free-State men stared at the fire helplessly.

***

Caleb was able to gather thirty mounted men, including William, Muscotah, and his best lieutenant Sam Moore, to accompany him to the cabin. They were available because the fighting in the north had died down to next to nothing as the proslavery invaders deserted or were shot. At least fifty, maybe more of the proslavery forces were dead or seriously injured. It was too early to say the fight was over, but the northern battle nearly was. Caleb led the men to his cabin as the remaining men began mopping up the northern battle and taking prisoners.

Once they got close enough to see what was going on, Caleb saw his cabin was aflame and his family were in front of the cabin and maybe

10 to 15 yards west of the house. His beautiful wife and all his younger children were sobbing.

Except for the two men guarding his family and his friends, the other proslavery invaders were gathered in front of house and watching it burn. Dunn and Atchison were watching the fire and smiling, some of their men were laughing and cheering the flames. Dunn yelled, "This is the happiest day of my life!"

Caleb and his men were about 100 yards north of the house and behind the celebrating raiders. They were at the edge of a wooded area and partially concealed. They had not been seen yet, so Caleb quietly asked his men to dismount, they all had Sharps that were accurate at 100 yards, but they needed to dismount to fire with the greatest accuracy. They were too far away to hear what Dunn yelled over the flames, but he could see Maggie hang her head, she was clearly devastated, and he was furious.

His sharp eyes noticed that Jim and Pardee had spotted them and were looking straight at him, but no one else was. The others were all entranced by the flames. Jim looked straight at Caleb, he smiled slightly and put his hand in his pocket, then moved back a few steps. He turned to the two guards who were watching the fire and paying no attention to their captives. Jim was clearly moving away from the family and simultaneously moving slightly closer to the guards and more behind them. The guards were foolishly standing right next to one another and watching the fire, Dunn, and Atchison. Jim carefully stayed behind the guards and out of view, he waved Pardee away. Pardee carefully touched Maggie and led her quietly away from Jim, she quietly nudged her kids along with her.

Caleb was enraged, but under control, he saw Jim and the others move and said, "Quietly now, spread out into a semicircle with the open side facing south, toward the cabin, don't fire unless you must. Sam, William, and Muscotah, beside me now. Everyone must watch Jim carefully; he is going to make a move. When he does shoot. Don't hit Jim or my family. Jim may be able to take those two guards, focus on the men at the house."

Then he said to Sam, "You take out Atchison, I'll take out Dunn. William and Muscotah be ready to shoot. After Sam and I shoot, some the men at the house might try and fire, Muscotah far right, William far left, don't shoot the same man. The rest of you hold your fire unless more of them raise their guns."

Atchison was closest to Maggie and the family, but still at least 10 yards east of them. The guards were too close to the family, they couldn't shoot at them. Jim knew this, and once he saw Caleb's men dismounting and moving into position for an attack, rifles at the ready, he quickly pulled out his Colt and shot the nearest guard in the center of his back.

Almost simultaneously, just as he saw Jim move, Caleb shot Dunn, a half second later Sam shot Atchison. At the same time as Sam's shot, Muscotah and William fired and brought down the farthest left and right men of the group at the house.

The noise of the fire did not cover the shots. Jim had dropped the nearest guard, but the second guard turned to Jim, just as Jim was moving his pistol toward him. The guard was very fast, he drew his gun and moved left at the same time. Jim's first shot missed, so he dove to the ground and rolled as the guard fired two shots from his revolver, they both missed and just threw up dirt when they hit the ground in front of Jim. Jim stopped rolling, and from the ground aimed as carefully as possible and shot the second guard in the chest. At just that instant, the guard got off a shot that hit Jim in his left armpit. Jim rolled away from the family and watched the other men who were about 10 yards away. None of them were looking at him or the family, all were focused on Caleb and his men walking toward them from the north. His chest hurt like hell, but he was mobile and still had his revolver. He was now south of the family, so he crawled closer to the men. Dunn and Atchison's men were in total disarray and panicking. Jim could see that Atchison, Dunn, and two others were down.

At that instant Caleb and his men were firing relentlessly. They aimed at every man that had a gun in his hands. Most of the men didn't know where all the bullets were coming from and wildly looked around, all they could see were men falling off their horses.

The men finally turned and looked north and saw Caleb and his men for the first time, and one of them said, "Oh shit!"

In their panic they ignored Jim and the family, so Jim, lying on the ground, raised his revolver and shot the two closest men. This reminded the men that he was there and one of them turned to shoot Jim, just as a bullet from one of the Free-State men hit him in the head and nearly decapitated him.

Jim reached the first guard he had shot and took his revolver and fired into the men, hitting two of them as the others ran the only way they could, to the east.

The kids were all screaming, Isaac was screaming as only a baby can. Maggie was carrying Isaac and trying to hustle all the children west, away from the fighting. She got all of them to lay down.

Pardee recovered from his initial shock and dove to the ground next to the second guard and grabbed his gun. He rolled over and shot at one of the raiders twice but missed. That was the last chamber in the gun.

Pardee's men all ran to the fallen raiders and grabbed their guns and started shooting at the retreating and panicked raiders.

A few of the remaining panicking and leaderless raiders realized they were outgunned and nearly surrounded and dropped their weapons and held their hands up, hoping no one would shoot them.

Caleb and Sam reloaded quickly, they told Muscotah and William to take some men and lock up those that had surrendered in the barn. Then they rode after the retreating raiders who had decided to run. Caleb yelled at Sam, "We will capture or kill all of them."

They fired into the fleeing men mercilessly, until they all stopped, turned, and dropped their guns. They all raised their hands in surrender.

Maggie quickly went to Jim and told him to be still, she needed to tend to his wound. Jim said it was nothing, Maggie said, "I'll be the judge of that, be still."

Blue Tail arrived, as if from nowhere, with her medicine bag and she and Maggie cleaned and dressed Jim's wound, over his protests. Blue Tail and Maggie looked at the wound and it appeared the bullet had gone through the flesh on the left side of his chest and exited out of Jim's side, it was a bloody mess, but didn't look like it had hit a bone. When it exited, it also took a bit of Jim's left arm.

Maggie shouted to Mary to get some water from the creek, then she brought the water to a boil on a part of the still burning house and cleaned the wound, which was very painful for Jim. Then Blue Tail used a needle and thread to sew both wounds closed. Finally, Blue Tail and Maggie wrapped the wounds in some clean fabric that Sybil provided.

Jim was still in agony but hid it well. He was relieved when Blue Tail said, "It look worse than it is, I think you recover."

Maggie said, "Jim I want to thank you for saving us, you are the hero today."

Blue Tail agreed, "Jim you *are* hero, bless you. You are as brave as a Kickapoo man! I did the best I could, I think you will heal."

Jim smiled and was pleased to be recognized by them. All he could think of to say was, "Thank you ladies, I was happy to do it."

Shortly afterward, Caleb and Pardee came up and they also proclaimed him the hero of the battle, Caleb said, "Jim, I owe you a debt I cannot pay, you saved my family."

Pardee said, "Our congregation owes you Jim. I plan to say as much on Sunday. We are forever grateful to have you here. God bless you son."

Jim was moved and could think of nothing more to say, but a tear appeared in one eye. He just smiled and shook Pardee and Caleb's offered hands.

Maggie and Blue Tail watched the whole scene with approval and big smiles. They moved on to tend to other wounded of both sides. Several of the wounded were seriously injured and Blue Tail could do little to help them but did what she could with Maggie's help.

There were lots of scrapes and bruises, but miraculously Jim was the only Free-State man shot in the fight at the May cabin. Elsewhere, though, there were many Free-State men wounded in other parts of the town. Maggie, Blue Tail, Sybil, and several others with the skills needed worked on them, as well as the wounded proslavery raiders well into the night.

Caleb and his men collected all the guns and weapons from the surviving raiders and ordered the captured men to his barn with the other captives. They locked the barn, and he assigned several men to guard them.

In the meantime, Maggie and Blue Tail checked on Dunn, he was conscious but wounded in the chest. Blue Tail examined the wound and shook her head. Dunn looked at her, and gasp, "Will I die?"

Blue Tail, in her now blood-stained dress, and with a compassionate expression, just nodded her head.

Dunn turned to Maggie, who was covered in dirt and blood, and said, "I shot Cook in Easton. I was drunk, didn't know who he was, saw he was loading a musket and shot him. I'm sorry."

Maggie

Blue Tail was trying to stop the bleeding from his chest with a bandage, but to no avail, Dunn closed his eyes in great agony and died.

Maggie just stared at him a moment, then turned to Blue Tail, who simply said, "He's gone."

Maggie, got up, and went to Caleb, "Cale, Dunn just died, but in his last words he admitted that he shot Cook. He was drunk, saw him reloading his musket and shot him."

Caleb, also covered in blood and dirt, said, "Good Lord! Sam Wood said he was in Easton that night, but he thought Dunn was passed out drunk in the store. I need to find Wood and tell him this."

Atchison was wounded, but it looked like Atchison would survive. Of the 25 men that Dunn and Atchison had led to Caleb and Maggie's house, ten were dead and nine wounded.

Maggie, Sybil, and Pardee gave the wounded and the survivors in the barn some water and cloth and told them they should take care of themselves for now, then they attended to the local wounded.

After that, everyone was quiet, nothing was said, and everybody started searching for wounded survivors and helping them. As they searched, they also tried to clean up the war-torn town as much as possible. Everyone was filthy, but no one had time to clean themselves.

All the captured weapons and supplies were stored in Caleb's weapons shed that served as his militia's armory. The invader's supplies were distributed to those Pardee residents that needed them most.

The May house was still burning furiously and was nearly down to its limestone block foundation. Caleb looked at his wife and William looked at his mother. Maggie said, "We are all right, they didn't hurt us. Caleb, do what you think is right, but we are OK. I managed to save our money and the letter establishing our claims."

The men rounded up all the raider's horses and put them in Caleb's corral and they put all the saddles, blankets, and supplies in Pardee's barn for storage.

Sam Moore went to what was left of his home and led the cleanup effort there. Mary and Caroline were crying, but still working hard to clean up the mess the fire had made. Sam told them, "The battle is over, and we won. William was brave and a hero of the battle. He did well Caroline, you should be proud of him. He probably saved my life and his father's life."

Caroline stopped crying and smiled, she said, "Was he Pa? he was brave? Oh, how wonderful, I can't wait to see him and hear him tell his story. It is so sad our houses were burned. I hate Sheriff Dunn and all his men!"

Then she burst out crying again at their loss. Sam, Mary, and Michael came to her, and Sam hugged her close, and said, "My sweet Caroline, my love, we will rebuild. We will fix all this, look, the foundation is solid thanks to Caleb's high-quality cement. The barn is OK and so is my shop, we will be fine honey."

Mary also reassured her, but added, "Sheriff Dunn is dead honey, he was a bad man, but he is gone now."

Caroline started to speak, then stopped herself, then started crying harder. It was all too much for her. Then she said, "I'm so proud of you Pa, and William too, you saved us all."

Mary turned to her husband, kissed him, and said, "I could ask for no better husband, I love you and you are my hero Sam"

Michael added, "Pa you are my hero, I love you."

Sam didn't cry, but he felt like crying, all he could say was "Thank you, thank you all." He smiled at Michael, tousled his hair and then began storing all the captured goods from the northern invading army in his barn.

***

William asked his father if he could go see how Caroline was and if he could help them. Caleb said, "Yes, by all means. We are fine here, go and try to help them, we have lots of help here."

"Thanks Pa!"

William grabbed his horse and rode straight to the Moore's farm. As he approached their smoldering cabin, he saw the family hugging each other in front of the burnt wreck of their former home. William felt a lump in his throat and pain for his friends. He slowed his horse and walked it respectfully onto their property and said, "I'm so sorry this happened to you, let me help you clean up and get ready to rebuild."

Caroline beamed at William, through a face streaked with tears mixed with dust and ash, and said, "Pa says you are a hero! He says you were brave and fought well! He says you saved him! I'm so proud of you."

William was taken aback, "I don't understand, everyone fought, some were shot like Jim was, I'm not a hero I just did what I was told to do."

Sam said, "I saw you attack the men coming for the north blockhouse! You saved us all. Everyone in that blockhouse, you *are* a hero my boy."

A crowd had gathered to help the Moore family, and everyone nodded in agreement with what Sam had said. Some of the men came up and gave William an encouraging slap on the back and shook his hand.

William looked at the ground embarrassed by the praise, then he gained his composure and said, "Thank you sir. Thank you everyone."

Sam smiled uncharacteristically and said, "That shows good manners boy, you do your Ma and Pa proud."

Caroline was quiet but studied William carefully. She had not really taken him seriously before, but that was changing.

***

Everyone in town watered and fed all the horses and other stock. None of the animals had received any care all day. Both the May and Moore cabins were essentially gone, no need to waste any water on them. After examining the raider's horses, several townspeople reported to Caleb that most of the proslavery horses had local brands and were probably stolen.

Caleb was furious and said, "We hang horse thieves here. We will have a trial. No one is going to get away with anything."

Pardee said, "Caleb, we killed the Sheriff and wounded former Senator Atchison. There will be hell to pay for this."

Word that Dunn had been killed and Atchison was wounded circulated quickly on both sides. The proslavery raiders who were not already locked up, fled immediately, but the destruction they had brought to Pardee remained.

People quietly went about cleaning up and preparing to build new cabins for the May and Moore families. The invaders had stolen cattle, wagons and horses from most of the area families, and they all told Caleb what they had lost. Caleb did his best to restore their losses from the stock and goods captured in the battle.

Bill Phillips was running all over town interviewing anyone he could get to stop for a few minutes. He sent off a quick dispatch with just the essentials of the battle nearly as soon as the battle was over. In his dispatch he promised his editors daily reports for the foreseeable future.

It took four days for his dispatches to reach the *New York Tribune* office, but once there, they were published immediately. His articles were read across the country because the *Tribune* was the newspaper of record. The battle pushed the election off the front pages and gained the attention of everyone.

Phillips' initial dispatch emphasized that the proslavery invasion was a real invasion and not just a police action. After sending his first dispatch, he managed to collect Caleb, Jim Abbott, and Sam Wood for a joint interview on the battle. It was then Caleb was finally able to tell all three of them for the first time about Charley Dunn's last words. Wood exclaimed. "Damn, when I heard that he was in Easton that night, I wondered. Now we know, he admitted it with his last breath, he shot Cook while he was drunk! Caleb, you went to jail for nothing."

Bill Phillips immediately started writing, "I must get all this down on paper now, this is an emergency dispatch, the whole country must know this. I must talk to Maggie and Blue Tail and get their firsthand stories tonight!"

His second dispatch went out that very night. Then he interviewed the proslavery captives and found that nearly all of them were from Missouri, not from Kansas, and were paid by David Atchison. He took down the names and home addresses of everyone who would give them to him.

Atchison was still locked up in Caleb's barn and refused to be interviewed, but Phillips sketched him in obvious captivity. The sketch was later published to the humiliation of Atchison. Blue Tail did a good job on his wound, and he eventually fully recovered, a small consolation.

Some of the townspeople gathered the dead into wagons and took them north of Pardee to the town cemetery and laid them out side-by-side. In all they eventually counted 60 proslavery dead and seven Free-State dead. The reason for the discrepancy was mostly poor tactics, but the difference in weapons was a factor also. Blue Tail noticed the difference in the wounds, the .52 caliber bullets from the Free State Sharps rifles made a devastating wound.

Bill Phillips drew pencil sketches of the dead lined up in the town cemetery and the burned down cabins and blockhouses. Phillips was old-school and illustrated his own articles.

Anyone with some experience in medicine helped care for the wounded, but the most critical patients were treated by Blue Tail or a doctor who rode down from nearby Camp Creek. The schoolhouse and post office were made into temporary hospitals.

William and Muscotah let the healthy captives out of the barns where they were imprisoned and gave them picks and shovels to bury their dead. The captives were afraid they would be hanged for stealing horses, and asked what would happen. William and Muscotah said they didn't know, but there would be a trial. Some of the men said they would help rebuild the town, if that would help their cases. William said he would pass that on.

Caleb, Sam Wood, and Abbott wrote a full account of the battle and the aftermath and signed it. They made three copies of the original and signed all of them. Pardee Butler witnessed the affidavits, and Sam Wood left to hand-deliver the copies to Justice Lecompte and Governor Shannon. One signed copy went to Bill Phillips to be published.

In the affidavit closing, they asked that the fighting stop. They attested that they had no confidence in the current justice system, the Territorial Supreme Court, or in the Territorial Legislature. They pointed out that this left no alternative to fighting, but fighting was not a proper solution. When the affidavit was published in the *New York Tribune,* it caused a national uproar.

Afterword

The war between the proslavery and Free-State settlers continued for nine more years and did not end until the Civil War was over. During these nine long years, proslavery settlers continued to kidnap both runaway slaves and free black men to sell, or to collect a reward for returning them to their "owners" in Missouri or the Indian Territory.

The Free-State settlers had an active underground railroad that transported runaway slaves, mostly from Missouri, Arkansas, and the Cherokee Nation (part of the Indian Territory), to Lawrence, then to Pardee or Holton, and then north to Nebraska City, Iowa, and finally to Canada.

Hundreds died in the battles that were fought over slavery and many houses and farms were burned to the ground. Atrocities occurred in both Kansas and Missouri and to both proslavery settlers and Free-State settlers.

William and Caroline were married in 1857, and their daughter Jannel was born about a year later. With some help from Caleb and Maggie, they bought their own farm near Pardee.

When the formal Civil War started in 1861, William joined Company F of the 13th Kansas Regiment of the 2nd Brigade of the 1st Division of the Union Army of the Frontier. He quickly rose to the rank of second lieutenant and led Company F in the Battle of Prairie Grove, due to the absence of his captain and first lieutenant. He was wounded in the leg on January 7, 1863, in that vicious battle. The battle was the bloodiest in the Civil War west of the Mississippi River. He was promoted to Captain by the end of the war.

Pardee Butler ran a freighting service from Kansas City to Pike's Peak from 1861-1864, he was in debt at the time and debts had to be paid. Pardee passed away peacefully in 1888 in Farmington Kansas. His daughter, Rosetta Hastings, was to become a popular writer and speaker. She wrote a book about her father and Caleb May that became one of the principal sources used to write this novel.[77]

Caleb May was made a colonel in the Union army and his unit of 100 men were assigned to defend Atchison County from a possible invasion from Missouri. Caleb was the only Kansan to participate in all three Free-State constitutional conventions and he was a signatory to the final Kansas Constitution.

Caleb and Maggie remained in Atchison County until about 1870 when they moved to a new farm near Coffeyville, Kansas. Both farms contained very successful orchards where he grew apples, peaches, and other fruits. He and Maggie sold their farm and moved to Eustis, Florida to live with William and his family in 1884, when Caleb was 68 and Maggie was 61. Maggie died a few months after they arrived in Eustis, on October 24, 1884, and Caleb followed Maggie four years later, passing on August 27, 1888, at the age of 72 years. Caleb passed away only two months before Pardee Butler. William and Caroline took good care of them in their final months and years.

Senator David Atchison and Dr. John Stringfellow were leaders of the proslavery movement in Kansas and Missouri and acted pretty much as they are portrayed in this book. Their behavior during this period is well documented. One good source is Senator Charles Sumner's speech to the Senate.[78] It was this speech that led to Sumner being viciously caned on the Senate floor by Preston Brooks, a proslavery Democrat from South Carolina.

Atchison lived until 1886.[79] He was twice elected Senator from Missouri and presided over the Senate for most of both terms. He was born in Kentucky. During the Civil War he was Major General of the Missouri State Guard. He lived out his days as a lawyer and lobbyist. Atchison never married.

---

77 (Butler, 1889)

78 (Sumner, 1856)

79 *St. Joseph Weekly Gazette*, Feb. 4, 1886, page 12 and *The Shelbina Democrat*, Feb 17, 1886

Charley Dunn, as portrayed in this book, is a composite of the real Charley Dunn and Sheriff Samuel J. Jones. Jones moved to New Mexico in 1858, where he died in 1883 in La Mesilla.[80] The real Charley Dunn stabbed Isaac Cody and did became a captain in Atchison's militia. It is unclear what happened to him after the Kansas troubles.

Dr. John Stringfellow was born in Virginia in 1819.[81] He graduated from the University of Pennsylvania medical school in 1845 and moved to Carrollton, Missouri where he married Ophelia Simmons, the niece of Governor John E. Edwards. He founded Atchison and the Squatter Sovereign with his good friend Robert Kelly in 1854. He was speaker for the first "bogus" legislature of the Kansas Territory. He served in the Confederate Army as a captain. In 1871 he returned to Atchison for a few years after the war and later moved to St. Joseph, Missouri where he lived until his death in 1905.

Justice Samuel D. Lecompte was born in Maryland in 1814. He graduated from Jefferson College in Pennsylvania with honors in 1834. He was later admitted to the bar in Maryland and practiced law in Carroll County. After being elected to the Maryland state legislature he was appointed to be the Chief Justice of the Kansas Territorial Supreme Court by President Pierce in 1854. With help from David Atchison and Dr. John Stringfellow he became president of the Lecompton Town Company, and he succeeded in making it the Territorial capital. He was a partner in several Kansas railroads and became quite wealthy. After the Civil War ended, he changed his political party to Republican, was a probate judge in Leavenworth, followed by serving in the state legislature from 1867-68. He died in Kansas City in 1888, the same year as Pardee and Caleb. He and his wife, Camilla, had 13 children.[82]

Samuel B. Walker was elected Sheriff of Douglas County four times and in 1872 was elected as a Kansas State Senator. He was born in Pennsylvania in 1822. He was a skilled cabinet maker and settled in Kansas in 1854. He was a Major in the First Kansas Volunteer Infantry

---

80 *Las Cruces Sun-News*, Jan. 5, 1884.
81 *St. Joseph News-Press*, July 24, 1905
82 *The Effingham Times*, April 28, 1888, page 2.

Afterword

by the end of the Civil War. He married his wife, Marion, in 1842. He passed away in Lawrence, February 6, 1893.[83]

James B. Abbott was born in Hampton, Connecticut in 1818.[84] He came to Kansas in 1854. He smuggled Sharps rifles from New England to Kansas as described in this novel. Abbott worked very hard later in life to provide for the education of the feeble minded. In real life, he led the team that broke John Doy[85] out of prison, this story is the basis for Caleb May's escape from jail in this book.

Samuel N. Wood was born in 1825, in Ohio to Quaker parents. He married Margaret Walker Lyon in 1850 and went to law school in Ohio. He passed the Ohio bar in 1854. That same year he moved to Kansas and was immediately active in the Kansas underground railroad. He and Margaret had four children. In 1890 he became involved in a local feud over which city would be the county seat of Stevens County Kansas, southwest of Dodge City. While the fight was raging, he was assassinated by James Brennan. Brennen shot him four times and Wood died immediately on June 23, 1891.[86]

The Rev. John Tecumseh Jones or "Tauy" Jones or Ottawa Jones was an excellent cannoneer in real life and fought for the Free-State people. He was a good friend of John Brown and James Abbott. He was born in Canada in 1808 to a Chippewa mother and an English father. He had a difficult childhood and was raised by his older sister and her husband in Michigan and later by the Connor family where he learned English and French.

Tauy Jones was able to attend a Baptist school in Indiana and learned several Indian languages there. After graduating from the Baptist school, he enrolled at Madison University in New York as a theology student. He eventually made his way to Kansas in 1833 with the Ottawa Indian tribe where he acted as their interpreter.

In 1844 he was adopted into the Ottawa tribe and married Jane Kelly, a missionary from Maine. The couple bought a farm just north of present-day Ottawa, Kansas. He also built a popular hotel and trading post

---

83 *Fort Scott Daily Tribune*, Feb. 7, 1893, and the *Lawrence Gazette*, Feb. 9, 1893
84 *Lawrence Weekly World*, March 4, 1897, page 4.
85 (Doy, 1860) and (Abbott, 1889)
86 *The Weekly Republican*, July 3, 1891, page 2.

on the military road connecting Fort Leavenworth and Fort Scott. The Jones house was burned to the ground twice during the Kansas troubles by proslavery border ruffians. Tauy Jones was a co-founder and supporter of Ottawa University. He passed away in 1873. You can still see his final home in Ottawa, Kansas. It is listed in the National Register of Historic Places.[87]

William Addison Phillips, often referred to as Bill Phillips, was a notable journalist for the *New York Tribune* in the mid-19th century. Born in Scotland in 1824, he moved to the United States and became a significant national figure in the anti-slavery movement. In 1855, when he first came to Kansas he was also appointed by Horace Greeley to the editorial staff of the *New York Tribune*.

Phillips traveled extensively in Kansas to report on the political situation, and his passionate dispatches to the *Tribune* helped garner support for the Free-State cause. In 1856, he published *The Conquest of Kansas*, which further solidified his reputation as a key figure in the struggle against slavery.[88]

Most of the other characters, except for Milo Carlton, Pardee Butler's brother-in-law, are fictional. People like Blue Tail, Muscotah, Sam and Mary Moore, and Elliot Smith existed at the time, but I had no specific people in mind when I created their characters.

Pardee (now extinct) was the first town created in Center Township, and it was established by Caleb May in October 1854. The first town officers in Pardee were Pardee Butler, Milo Carlton, William May, S. G. Moore, A. Elliot, and Bill Wakefield. You can see where some of the names used in the book came from. Milo Carlton was born in Massachusetts in 1814, he passed away in 1894 and is buried in the Pardee Cemetery. He was very well thought of in Pardee.

---

[87] Wikipedia and https://legendsofkansas.com/john-tecumseh-jones/
[88] https://legendsofkansas.com/william-phillips/

Pardee Butler's Obituary

ATCHISON DAILY CHAMPION, October 23, 1888, page 5:

REV. PARDEE BUTLER.

One of the Pioneers of Atchison County.
An Early Victim of Pro-Slavery Lawlessness.
Sent Down the Missouri River on a Raft.
And Tarred and Feathered in Atchison.

Rev. Pardee Butler, who died, at his home near Farmington, on Saturday last, had been, for thirty-three years, a prominent figure in this State. He came to Kansas early in 1855, and located on Stranger Creek, in this county. He was an ardent and fearless Free State man, and came to Kansas, as did thousands of our early settlers, to oppose the aggressiveness of slavery.

We present below some extracts from the *Squatter Sovereign*, then the pro-slavery organ of the Territory, detailing some interesting incidents of his life. They show how fearlessly and consistently he fought the fight and kept the faith.

The *Squatter Sovereign* (*The Champion's* predecessor) of August 21st, 1855, contains the following account of the mobbing and rafting of Mr. Butler:

"On Thursday evening last, 16th inst., one Pardee Butler arrived in town, with a view of starting for the East, probably for the purpose of importing a fresh supply of Free Soilers from penitentiaries and pest holes of the Northern States. Finding it inconvenient to depart before morning, he took lodging at the hotel, and proceeded to visit portions of our town, everywhere avowing himself a Free Soiler, and preaching the foulest of abolition heresies.

He declared the recent action of our citizens in regard to J. W. B. Kelley, the infamous and unlawful proceedings of a mob. At the same time stating that many persons in Atchison, who were Free Soilers at heart, had been intimidated thereby, and feared to avow their true sentiments; but that he, Butler, would express his views in defiance of the whole community.

On the ensuing morning our townsmen assembled *en masse*, and deeming the presence of such persons highly detrimental to the safety of our slave property, appointed a committee of two to wait on Mr. Butler, and request his signature to the resolutions passed at the late pro-slavery meeting in Atchison. After perusing the said resolutions, Mr. B. positively declined signing them and was instantly arrested by the committee.

After various plans for his disposal had been considered, it was decided to place him on a raft composed of two logs, firmly lashed together; that his baggage and a loaf of bread be given him; and having attached a flag to his primitive bark, emblazoned with mottoes indicative of our contempt for such characters, Mr. B. was set adrift on the great Missouri, with the letter R legibly painted on his forehead. He was escorted some distance down the river by several of our citizens, who, seeing him pass several rock-heaps in quite a skillful manner, bade him adieu, and returned to Atchison.

Such treatment may be expected by all scoundrels visiting our town for the purpose of interfering with our time-honored institutions, and the same punishment we will be happy to award all Free Soilers, abolitionists, and their emissaries. If this should prove insufficient to deter them from their dastardly and infamous propensity for negro stealing, we will draw largely on the hemp crops of our Missouri neighbors, for a supply of the article, sufficient to afford every jail-bird in the North a necklace twelve feet in length."

The article continued in this strain for about a half column, denouncing the Free State men in the most violent language; warning all the Free Soilers that Atchison County was no place for them; and declaring that all such characters must be driven out.

In the same issue of the paper appears the following:

"A Mr. Finney, a noisy and troublesome Free Soiler, was badly beaten, on Saturday last, in this city, by a pro-slavery man whom he had insulted. Two other persons entertaining free soil views were knocked over and silenced, on the same day. Abolitionists in this vicinity are in hot water."

In the *Squatter* of September 4th the following additional account of the rafting of Mr. Butler is published:

"THE FLAG HE SAILED UNDER.

The Rev. Pardee Butler, who was recently shipped from this place on a raft, left our town in grand style. On a high pole, securely fastened to his bark, floated an extensive flag, on one side of which was painted a 2:40 horse [a 2:40 horse is slang for a fast horse running at full speed] doing his best, with Mr. Butler on his back; immediately beneath him carrying one of his sable brethren. He was represented exclaiming:

'To the rescue, Greeley; I have got a negro.' Over the painting, in large, legible letters, were printed: 'Eastern Abolition Aid Express.' The other side of the flag bore the following inscription: From Atchison, Kansas Territory. The way they are served in Kansas. For Boston. Cargo insured; unavoidable dangers of the Missourians, and Missouri river, excepted.'

Let future emissaries from the North beware. Our hemp crop is sufficient to reward all such scoundrels."

Mr. Butler was warned by the mob, not to return to Atchison, but he firmly replied that he would come to the place whenever his business called him here; that no threats, nor fear of consequences, would deter him from going wherever his business called him, nor from expressing his opinions on any subject. His raft landed about four miles south of the city, near, if not at, the site afterward selected for the now extinct town of Sumner. From thence he made his way to his home, near Pardee.

He went east, a short time afterwards, and contributed enormously, by speeches and personal influence, in sending to Kansas many Free State men, and in arousing the public sentiment of the North to realizing sense of the purposes and methods of the proslavery oligarchy. The brutal, inhuman and cowardly action of the proslavery mob at Atchison gave him National prominence, and secured for him, wherever he went, large and attentive audiences.

On the 30th of April, 1856, Mr. Butler again visited Atchison, for the purpose of buying some supplies. His presence soon became known and excited the passions of the pro-slavery men to fever heat. A mob soon gathered and seized him. The more violent demanded, as they had on the previous occasion, that he be hanged, but the cooler and more cautious among them prevented his murder. It was finally resolved to give him a coat of tar and feathers, and escort him out of the town. The Squatter Sovereign of May 6th contains the following account of the affair:

"Pardee Butler. This contemptible tool of Abolitionists, who, a short time ago, was shipped from this place on a raft, had the audacity to again visit this town. As our citizens were not willing to allow an Abolition spy to visit them with impunity, they politely treated him to a coat tar and cotton, and escorted him out of town, promising him, in the event of another visit, a hemp rope.

The time is past when such cowardly and contemptible Abolition rascals and can hold up their heads in Atchison, and we promise all of like stamp who may visit this place a severer punishment than was meted out to Rev. P. Butler. A word to the wise is sufficient."

But the end of the pro-slavery reign of terror in Kansas was drawing near. Such men as Col. Caleb May, Capt. A. S. Speck, Archibald Elliot, Milo Carlton, and others, had settled in the country, along the Stranger Creek, and were fearlessly advocating Free State sentiments. Col. May was, in fact, as bold and determined as Mr. Butler. He had been warned not to come to Atchison, and word had been sent him to leave the Territory. He replied in a characteristic letter, the lofty courage of which atoned for its crude orthography, saying that he went where he pleased when he pleased; that he had a rifle and revolver, and knew how to use them; that whenever he came to Atchison he intended to bring them with him; and that any persons who came fooling about him there, or around his house, would get hurt. The sturdy old Kentuckian came to the town whenever he pleased, without molestation.

Mr. Butler was a minister of the Gospel; Col. May was a fighter. They were equally brave, but the pro-slavery mob, while attacking the man of peace, never attempted to disturb the Kansas "Leatherstockings,"[89] who, they knew, never went an inch out of his way to avoid a fight.

At that very time, too, notwithstanding the threats and vaporings of the Squatter Sovereign, the Free State men were gathering in the

---

89 "Leatherstockings refers to the main character in James Fenimore Cooper's *Last of the Mohicans* series of books published between 1823 and 1841.

town as well as in the country. A dozen or fifteen located in Atchison as early as 1856, but they maintained a discreet silence concerning their opinions on the Slavery question. In the winter of 1856-'57, several others, holding like opinions, located in Atchison, and early in June, 1857, the pro-Slavery owners of the town, recognizing the inevitable, issued a card inviting immigration from any quarter, and pledging protection to all comers, no matter what their political opinions might be. This invitation brought many Free State settlers to Atchison. That same month, the Squatter Sovereign was purchased by a company of Free State men, including Ex-Senator Samuel C. Pomeroy, Judge F. G. Adams and the late Robert McBratney. These gentlemen made it a Free State paper, and, after publishing it a few months, sold it to O. F. Short, who continued its publication until February, 1858, when it was purchased by the present proprietor [John A. Martin], who changed its name to *Freedom's Champion*, and has ever since been its publisher.

From that day on, Mr. Butler was a frequent contributor to the columns of the paper, and prepared for it, some years ago, a very interesting series of letters on Pioneer Days in Atchison County.

A Testimonial to Caleb May

From the *Atchison Daily Champion*, Jan. 24, 1874, page 2.

> Letter from Col. May
> Our old friend Col. Caleb May, formerly of Atchison County, now living in Montgomery County, sends us the following letter:

> Coffeyville, Jan. 12, 1874.
> "John A. Martin: Dear Sir:
> Enclosed please find postal order for $6.00, which please place to my credit on subscription to *The Champion*. Keep on sending till ordered stopped. I can't well get along without it. I have read it ever since it was published, and expect to as long as I live. Wishing you continued prosperity, I remain, Your old time friend,

> Caleb May."

Col. May was one of the first settlers in Atchison County, and one of the bravest of the "Old Guard of Freedom," when to be a Free State man required nerve and resolution of the highest order.

He was a member of the old Topeka Constitutional Convention, and of the Wyandotte Convention, which framed the present Constitution of the State. He is as brave and true a man as we ever knew, and we are glad to know that he is prospering in his present location.

All the old citizens of Northern Kansas know Col. May and respect him. He never enjoyed the advantages of a thorough education, but his mind is strong and clear, and his heart is honest and true. Locating in the midst of pro-slavery men, and often in deadly peril because of his Free State convictions, he never wavered or hesitated in expressing his opinions. Tall, angular, endowed with great physical strength, and a dead shot with the rifle, he was a man of mark and influence among the Free State settlers of Northern Kansas in the days of 'Border-ruffian' rule.

The old 'Free State Guard' of Atchison county were all men of rare courage and strong convictions, Pardee Butler, Col. May, S. J. H. Snyder, A. S. Speck, the Connellys, C. A. Woodworth, Dandridge Holliday, the Eilers, W. J. Oliphant, Archibald Elliott, Milo Carlton, and many others living in the country around Atchison, then the head-quarters of the pro-slavery men, and of such ruffians as made up Bufford's South Carolina gang, maintained their principles at the hazard of their lives, and fought the good fight until the end. They deserve the respect of the people of Kansas. They and their associates held the fair heritage of this beautiful land for Freedom. They were pioneers in that great struggle which only a few years later shook the continent and broke the fetters of the slave.

We wish someone would write a history of those early days in Atchison County, and of the trials and vicissitudes through which these men passed. It would be full of interest, not only to all old settlers, but to the later comers, and would preserve the memory of a band of noble men who were true to Freedom when it cost something to hold steadfast in the faith. Rev. Pardee Butler is amply competent to undertake this task, and we hope he may do so. We would take great pleasure in publishing in *The Champion* such historical reminiscences of the early days in Atchison County.

Bibliography

Abbott, J. (1889, January 15). *The Immortal Ten and the Rescue of John Doy.* Kansas State Historical Society Collections, IV. Retrieved from https://jeffersonjayhawkers.com/the-immortal-ten-and-the-rescue-of-john-doy/

Alexander, K. (2022, June). *Border Troubles in Leavenworth, Kansas.* Retrieved from Legends of Kansas: https://legendsofkansas.com/leavenworth-border-troubles/

Bisel, D. G. (2012). *The Civil War in Kansas, Ten years of turmoil.* Charleston: History Press.

Blackmar, F. W. (1912). *Kansas: a cyclopedia of state history, embracing events, institutions, industries, counties, cities, towns, prominent persons, etc.* (Vol. 1). Chicago: Standard Publishing Company.

Bondi, A. (1910). *Autobiography of August Bondi 1833-1907.* Galesburg: Wagoner. Retrieved from https://books.google.com/books?id=gw-ioAEACAAJ&printsec=frontcover&source=gbs_ge_summary_r&cad=0#v=onepage&q=Benjamin&f=false

Brown, G. W. (1880). *Reminiscences of Old John Brown.* Rockford, Illinois: Abraham E. Smith. Retrieved from https://www.amazon.com/dp/B01F-NBKUAA/ref=dp-kindle-redirect?_encoding=UTF8&btkr=1

Butler, P. (1889). *Personal Recollections of Pardee Butler with Reminiscences by his Daughter, Mrs. Rosetta B. Hastings and chapters by John Boggs and J.B. McCleery.* Cincinnati: Standard Publishing Company.

Clark, C. (2019). *Caleb May.* Retrieved from Kansas Bogus Legislature: http://kansasboguslegislature.org/free/may_c.html

Cody, W. F. (1879). *The Life of Hon. William F. Cody, known as Buffalo Bill.* Retrieved from http://www.gutenberg.org/ebooks/10030

Collins, D. E. (1994, November 21). *The Samuel Collins - Patrick Laughlin Incident.* Retrieved from Kansas family History: http://www.kansasheritage.org/research/families/collins.html

Connelley, W. E. (1918). *A Standard History of Kansas and Kansans*. Chicago, USA: Lewis Publishing Company. doi:http://www.ksgenweb.org/archives/1918ks/toc.html

Cova, A. R. (2012). Samuel J. Kookogey in Bleeding Kansas: A "Fearless vindicator of the rights of the South". *Kansas History: A Journal of the Central Plains, 35*, 146-163. Retrieved from https://www.kshs.org/publicat/history/2012autumn_de_la_cova.pdf

Doy, J. (1860). *The Kansas Narrative of John Doy*. New York: Thomas Holman. Retrieved from https://play.google.com/books/reader?id=wPypAqnFwLsC&hl=en&pg=GBS.PA1

Emmett, D. (1853). *Jordan is a hard road to travel*. Retrieved from Remembering the old songs and wikipedia: http://www.lizlyle.lofgrens.org/RmOlSngs/RTOS-Jordan.html

Etcheson, N. (2004). *Bleeding Kansas, Contested Liberty in the Civil War Era*. Lawrence, Kansas, USA: University Press of Kansas. Retrieved from https://www.amazon.com/gp/product/0700614923/ref=dbs_a_def_rwt_bibl_vppi_i0

Frohman, C. E. (2019). *John Brown Junior*. Retrieved from Rutherford B. Hayes Presidential Library and Museums: https://www.rbhayes.org/collection-items/charles-e.-frohman-collections/brown-john-jr/

Gihon, J. (1857). *Governor Geary's Administration in Kansas*. Philadelphia: King & Baird, Printers. Retrieved from https://quod.lib.umich.edu/cgi/t/text/text-idx?c=moa;idno=ABA0699

Gold Rush Stories. (2019). *Gold Rush Stories*. Retrieved from Gold Rush Stories: https://camcca.wordpress.com/dr-charles-robinson-governor-of-kansas/

Historic Lecompton. (2019). *Constitution Hall*. Retrieved from Historic Lecompton: www.lecomptonkansas.com/learn/constitution-hall-state-historic-site/

Howard, & Oliver, M. (1856). *Full Congressional Report on the Kansas Troubles, with the views of the minority*. Washington: Cornelius Wendell. Retrieved from https://play.google.com/store/books/details?id=CoLE1Wl0GJ0C&rdid=book-CoLE1Wl0GJ0C&rdot=1

Howard, W., & Sherman, J. (1856). *Troubles in the Territory of Kansas*. Congressional Report, House of Representatives, Washington DC. Retrieved from https://babel.hathitrust.org/cgi/pt?id=hvd.32044105355069;view=1up;seq=5

Iowa History Project. (2019). *Iowa and Slavery*. Retrieved from Iowa History Project: http://iagenweb.org/history/moi/moi30.htm

Johnson, D. T. (1962). *Pardee Butler: Kansas Abolitionist*. Kansas State University, History. Manhattan: Kansas State University. Retrieved from https://archive.org/stream/pardeebutlerkans00john/pardeebutlerkans00john_djvu.txt

Kansas Historical Society. (1855, November 12). *Kansas Memory*. Retrieved from https://www.kansasmemory.org/item/221061

Kansas Historical Society. (2019). *Kansapedia*. Retrieved from kshs.org: https://www.kshs.org/kansapedia/andrew-horatio-reeder/12181

Kansas Historical Society. (2019b). *Kansapedia*. Retrieved from https://www.kshs.org/kansapedia/john-calhoun/15131

Krauthamer, B. (2019). *Slavery*. Retrieved from Oklahoma Historical Society: https://www.okhistory.org/publications/enc/entry.php?entry=SL003

Lawrence Republican. (1859, April 7). Trial of John and Charles Doy. *The Republican*. Retrieved from https://www.newspapers.com/image/ 366783903/?terms= John%2BDoy

Leonhardt, C. F. (1870). *The Last Train That Passed Over the Underground Railroad From Kansas Territory*. Retrieved from Kansas Memory: https://www.kansasmemory.org/item/221986

May, A. (2019). *Blood & Honor: The People of Bleeding Kansas*. American Freedom Publications LLC.

Mildfelt, T. (2011). *The Underground Railroad in Kansas*. Symphony in the Flint Hills Journal. Retrieved from https://newprairiepress.org/cgi/viewcontent.cgi?referer=&httpsredir=1&article=1038&context=sfh

Missouri Democrat. (1859, August 2). Statement of the Rescuers of Dr. Doy. *Chicago Tribune*. Retrieved from https://www.newspapers.com/image/466318679/?terms=John%2BDoy

Phillips, W. (1856). *The Conquest of Kansas, by Missouri and her Allies*. Boston: Phillips, Sampson and Company.

Rives, J. C. (1856). *The Congressional Globe: Containing the Debates, Proceedings, Laws, Etc. of the first and Second sessions, 34th Congress, Volume 4* (Vol. 4). Washington DC, USA: John C. Rives. Retrieved from https://play.google.com/books/reader?id=UPBfAAAAcAAJ&hl=en&pg=GBS.PR1

Robinson, C. (1892). *The Kansas Conflict*. New York: Harper & Brothers, Franklin Square. Retrieved from https://www.amazon.com/dp/B06XR75QXQ/ref=dp-kindle-redirect?_encoding=UTF8&btkr=1

Robinson, S. T. (1856). *Kansas; Its Interior and Exterior Life*. Retrieved from http://www.kancoll.org/books/robinson/r_intro.htm

Root, J. P. (1856). *Copy of David R. Atchison's Speech to pro-slavery forces*. Kansas Historical Society. Retrieved from https://www.kansasmemory.org/item/90822

Starr, F. (1854, September 19). *Starr, Frederick, Jr. (1826-1867), Papers, 1850-1863*. Retrieved from The State of Historical Society of Missouri: https://digital.shsmo.org/digital/collection/frontier/id/302

Sumner, C. (1856, May 19). *Senate of the United States*. Retrieved from www.senate.gov: https://www.senate.gov/artandhistory/history/resources/pdf/CrimeAgainstKSSpeech.pdf

The Holmes County Republican. (1859, July 21). Case of John Doy - Letter from Prison. *The Holmes County Republican*. Retrieved from https://www.newspapers.com/image/186725762/?terms=John%2BDoy

Topeka Constitutional Convention. (1855, December 15). *Topeka Constitution*. Retrieved from Kansas State Historical Society: https://web.archive.org/

web/20080705182848/http://www.kshs.org/research/collections/documents/online/topekaconstitution.htm#article1

Walker, L. (1896). Reminiscences of Early Times in Kansas. *Kansas Historical Society Transactions,* 5, 74-76. Retrieved from https://archive.org/details/collections05kansuoft/page/74

About the Author

Andy May is a writer, blogger and author living in The Woodlands, Texas. He was born in Lawrence, Kansas, but never really appreciated how interesting Kansas history was until he researched his second book. He enjoys golf and traveling in his spare time. He is also an editor for the climate blog Wattsupwiththat.com, where he has published numerous posts and is the author or co-author of eight peer-reviewed papers on climate change and various geological, engineering and petrophysical topics. He has also written about computers and computer software. His personal blog is andymaypetrophysicist.com.

He retired from a 42-year career in petrophysics in 2016. Most of his petrophysical work was for several oil and gas companies worldwide. He has worked in exploring, appraising, and developing oil and gas fields in the U.S., Argentina, Brazil, Indonesia, Thailand, China, the U.K. North Sea, Canada, Mexico, Venezuela, and Russia. He helped discover and appraise several large oil and gas fields.

Caleb May is the younger brother of Andy's great-great grandfather, Isaac May.